Merry Christmas My Carm, Enjoy this Novel I Love you very much! Pam

MURDER *at the* FRENCH COUNTRY INN

A Novel by

Clyde Deighton

Clyde Deighton

Penny Loafer Press, L.L.C.

This book, with the exception of the people and places noted on the acknowledgements page, is a work of fiction. To the best of the author's knowledge, the gangsters' stories and other historical details outlined in the Appendix to this book are true. All other characters, names, places, and businesses are fiction and the result of the author's imagination. Any resemblance to actual events or persons, living or dead, is purely coincidental.

Published in the United States by Penny Loafer Press, L.L.C.
Lake Geneva, Wisconsin.

www.pennyloaferpress.com

Book design and layout by Jennifer L. Wambach for
Peterson Marketing Group, Inc., www.petersonmktg.com

ISBN 978-0-615-42172-8

Printed in the United States.

No animals were harmed during the writing of this book.

This book is dedicated to my Huckleberry Friend;

together, as young boys, we shared the most wonderful summers.

AUTHOR'S NOTE

The French Country Inn really exists. Physical descriptions in this book are based on the actual inn, with one major exception: its underground features, while rumored, do not remain. The inn's true history during the gangster era is detailed further in the appendix to this book.

Kirsch's award-winning restaurant also exists, and it offers fine fare. The chefs and all culinary mischief portrayed in this novel are entirely fictional.

Chapter One

I am a quiet man. I don't mean to say that I'm a man of few words — in fact, on more than one occasion, I've been accused of employing more words than necessary to make a point. I'm a quiet man in the sense that I've come to prefer a peaceful existence to the hassled maze of the contemporary rat race. Recently that desire led me to return to Geneva, Wisconsin, a backwater rural township where I'd spent seven perfect summers during my youth.

I grew up in a Chicago working-class neighborhood. It wasn't heaven, but it had its good points. Summer entertainment consisted of playing stickball in the streets and ring-a-levio in the alleys between the rows of modest brick bungalows. Our house was near Bryant Park, where my friends and I clambered up trees and hiked among the scruffy bushes like bold explorers. Bryant also had a peach of a swimming pool where we wiled away long afternoons as we swam, held informal diving contests, and splashed and bothered all the neighborhood girls who dared to invade our sacred territory or call us morons.

When I reached the tender age of ten, my life changed dramatically. That was the year my father stretched the family budget to buy a vacation home in Wisconsin. It came with an acre of land, thirty-some oak trees, a wood-sided shed, ivy-covered trellis, and an old stone birdbath. Most importantly, it came with lake rights. Our small white cottage was only a short hike from Geneva Lake, the biggest jewel in a necklace of lakes that stretches across southeast Wisconsin. An even shorter hike took me down a wooded hill to Lake Como, a smaller and much quieter body of water. Geneva Township spans the ridge between the two lakes, then wraps around Lake Como and extends north and east into the countryside. Encompassing about thirty square miles, it's a realm of farms, cottages, and country homes, along with a handful of resorts and quite a few taverns. Recent developments include a posh golf club and an urgent care center for victims of stray golf balls.

I only spent seven summers in Geneva Township as a boy, but I considered it my home. The first Friday after the school year ended, Dad packed my mom, my little brother, and me into the Ford Fairlane and we started our two-hour trek to Wisconsin. My dad would head back to the city and work during the week, but the rest of us stayed put. Unless there was a wedding or a funeral, I didn't cross the state line again until Labor Day. I made some new pals in Wisconsin—a few locals, but mostly other refugees from Chicago. Our city versions of hiking, swimming, and diving gave way to their country counterparts. My father even bought me a BB gun, and I went hunting in the expansive woods along the abandoned railroad tracks down by Lake Como. Those BB-gun safaris led to the demise of enough gophers to outnumber all the buffalo ever slaughtered by Bill Cody. Had there been a Carl Spackler trophy honoring the decimation of gophers, I would've been the lifetime recipient.

I fell in love with those halcyon days of summer and wanted them to last forever. They didn't, of course. As August rolled in, I felt a tinge of fear because I knew Labor Day was swiftly approaching. When I spotted the first "back to school sale" sign in the local five-and-dime store, I suffered cold sweats. The last two weeks of summer, I seldom slept at all, but the nightmare always happened anyway: before I knew it, I was back to my old Chicago stomping grounds, attending the purgatory known as Catholic school—more specifically, Saint Isaac Jogues Grammar School. The moment I slid into my wooden desk to face those implacable nuns, I'd begin to count the days until the following summer.

Although I hated my grammar school, I was fascinated by the life of the eponymous saint. Isaac Jogues was a Jesuit priest who was martyred while spreading the word of Jesus Christ. His tongue was cut out by heathens, and his fingers were chewed to the bone by hungry dogs; then he was scalped, tortured, and ultimately decapitated. I often wondered whether some of the same nuns who taught at my grammar school could've been among the tribe that tortured and murdered the hapless Father Jogues. Even if the nuns weren't supernaturally old, they were, at the very least, fully capable of such atrocities. Once after I sassed Sister Beatrice, she gave me a look that left no doubt she would like to rip out my tongue and chew my fingers to the bone. Instead she gave me the usual rap on the knuckles with a heavy yardstick.

Each school year felt like a repeat of the previous one. My graduation from Saint Isaac Jogues Grammar School led to my enrollment at Saint Malachy Academy High School. Different school, different location, similar torture. Only instead of nuns, my tormentors at Saint Malachy were Christian Brothers.

In algebra class, I neglected equations and focused on a special calendar I created to track the days until summer. I thought of myself as a prisoner marking the time left in his sentence. "Only ninety-seven days until June Seventh," I would say to myself softly. A month later, which always felt like a decade, I'd quietly announce, "Only sixty-nine days to freedom."

It's been more than twenty years since those adolescent school days, and my hatred of confinement in old classrooms still lingers like the chalk particles that hung in that stale, uncirculated air. I don't dwell on those experiences, relegating my worst recollections of the nuns and brothers to a dark corner of my distant past. Instead, I prefer to reminisce warmly about those blissful days of summer in Wisconsin.

A former friend of mine once told me that my recent return to the Town of Geneva was a feeble attempt to recapture my youth — no different from the actions of a forty-year-old man who buys a red

Porsche in a vain attempt to forgo the aging process. I've never had a midlife crisis; my wife had it for me. She ran off with a friend — the same guy who later informed me why I'd chosen to move back to Wisconsin. But that, too, was something I tried not to ruminate about.

All thoughts of bygone days dissipated as I pulled the township's Jeep into the snow-crusted parking lot of my destination and opened the door to face the January cold. The wind slapped the side of my head, and my late father's bellicose voice echoed in my ears: "Keep your mind on your work, son, and quit your daydreaming." It was nighttime, so technically I hadn't been daydreaming. Besides, "daydreaming" helped pass the dreary days of winter and relieved the boredom of my routine.

As my feet crunched across the snow, I became far more attentive to the matter at hand. I like things quiet and easy as a rule, but in my line of work, being lax is an open invitation to trouble. I was standing in front of a seedy bar named The Rustic Cove. Located on the outskirts of the township, it was frequented by a hodgepodge of characters, from farm boys to bikers to flatlanders. "Flatlanders" is a term Wisconsinites use for Illinois tourists. There weren't many tourists around in January, though—too cold and not enough action. I knew precisely what I would see when I entered the tavern: a lot of green-and-gold jackets, mullet hairstyles, considerably more tattoos than teeth, and plenty of facial hair, especially on the women.

Earlier in the evening, the stationhouse had received a telephone call from the bartender, saying the O'Malley brothers had started another ruckus. I'd taken my time driving to "The Cove," as everyone called the bar, following back roads instead of a more direct route. I didn't have to hurry because I understood the situation inside. The O'Malleys were twenty-something construction workers and the only two Irishmen in town who couldn't hold their liquor. I knew exactly what had happened, because it had happened before, and always in the same sequence: After only one beer, they had lost their Gaelic amiability. By the time a second beer had passed their respective gullets, they had become obnoxious, first arguing between themselves, then with some other drunk or two. A third brew had led to still more insults and abuse, then a minor fracas had occurred, after which the bartender had threatened to call the police.

Unfortunately for the Irish brothers, they could handle a fight about as well as they could tolerate liquor. They always seemed to lose, but that never stopped them from fighting—or ignoring the bartender's warning. A couple of bar stools would be thrown after that once in a while, a window might be broken—then the bartender would finally call the police.

Invariably, everyone would be settled down before I even reached the parking lot. That's how it always went, so I seldom hurried anymore.

I faced a haze of smoke as I walked through the door. The Clean Air Act hadn't spread to rural Wisconsin yet.

"Evenin', Chief. Buya a beer?" asked the bartender—the same one who'd made the telephone call to the stationhouse regarding the drunk-and-disorderly conduct.

"No thanks, Scottie, I'm on duty. Besides, I haven't had a tetanus shot in over ten years." The place was a sty. A 5,000psi pressure washer couldn't have removed the scum from the walls and the floor, not to mention the grime under the fingernails of the clientele. I made a motion with my index finger. "Okay, you two—O'Dooley, O'Riley, or whatever your names are—come here."

"It's O'Malley, Chief," one of the brothers said, slurring slightly. "And everything's fine now—it was all a misunderstandin'. Right, Scottie?"

He gave the bartender a silly grin and a pleading look, but when Scottie ignored him, he obsequiously begged me to "ask Scottie" — as if the bartender were the arbiter of all things legal and proper in Walworth County. I said nothing, but motioned again with my finger.

Dutifully, they both shambled over and asked almost simultaneously, "What's the big deal, Chief?"

I told them to pay their bar tab and immediately walk home. I also informed them that I would drive past The Cove every half-hour, and I had better find their car still parked in front, but they were not to be inside or anywhere nearby for the rest of the night. "If I come back and find either of you turkey birds within a thousand yards of this place, I'm going to run you in," I said.

"On what grounds?" the younger one protested.

"What are you, a lawyer?" I asked in my don't-mess-with-me voice. "How about aggravated stupidity?"

"But, Chief, you know we live three miles away, and it's cold outside. Aw, shit, it's really cold outside."

"Tough," I said. Then I walked out to the Jeep, a blue late-model version with marked sides and lights on top. I climbed inside and turned on the engine and sat there, pretending to write something important on a notepad until the O'Malley brothers had left the bar and were well on their way up the road.

Chapter Two

I radioed headquarters from the parking lot of The Cove. No calls had come in while I was inside the bar; no complaints, no disturbances of any sort—not even a fender bender on the icy roads. Except for the minor O'Malley ruckus I'd just dealt with, it was a quiet night, as it usually was in the off-season.

I waited about five minutes, jotting some notes, then slowly drove up the road. Thirty yards ahead, the beam of my headlights revealed the silhouettes of the two O'Malley boys. One was blowing into his cupped hands and dancing from one foot to the other to keep warm. His brother was peeing on a dead bush on the side of the road. I pulled alongside them.

"Get in," I said.

"Ah, geez, you're not gonna pinch me for whizzing in the road, are ya?" said the younger, hastily zipping his fly before he turned around.

"Nope, I'm just going to drive you two home. I wouldn't want you to catch pneumonia—afraid I might lose my job."

The younger one reached for the back door of the Jeep, grinning. "Yeah, that's right. If we freeze, I could sue you then, right?"

"Sure. Right after you thaw out, sober up, and get that law degree."

The two drunks climbed in the back, behind the cage. I dropped them at their home, an old cottage that could've used a little of their carpentry work. It wasn't the first time I'd been their free taxi.

I decided to make my usual rounds before I headed back to the stationhouse, which was little more than a collection of offices and a holding cell in the Town Hall. I looked at my watch. It was 12:45 a.m. I drove east on Highway 50, then north down Como Road to the lake. The descent was steep and icy, and I was glad for the Jeep's four-wheel-drive. Heavy woods hugged the ditches on both sides. Only a few security lights were visible in the isolated houses among the trees.

A few hundred yards from the shoreline, the road leveled out and led me to Mars, otherwise known as Mars Resort. A couple of cars were still parked in front. Most likely the staff, I thought. Mars wasn't actually a resort; it was a rustic bar and grill known for its ribs. The place had been around since I was a kid, but my Dad didn't take us out for dinner much back then.

I turned left on West End Road and followed the shore. The houses there were close-set on both sides—a mix of old summer cottages and newer, slightly grander homes. Nearly all were dark and completely sealed up against the winter cold. Two deer stepped into the road from the side nearest the lake, then paused in the glow of my headlights. They looked a lot like the O'Malley brothers. Their breath steamed through their nostrils as they stared at me, alert but unafraid; then they bounded into the woods up the hill. For a moment, I considered giving pursuit so I could give them a Breathalyzer test. I decided it was too much work.

One of my favorite late-night coffee stops was just ahead along the shore. A collection of wood-sided buildings painted dove gray, the French Country Inn was a small, historic resort. The most recent owner had completely refurbished it, but when I was a kid, it was an old, abandoned hotel with weeds sprouting three feet high all around it. One of my pals thought the place was haunted, so of course he dared me to sneak out with him after dark and spend the night camped there. We never did, and the place didn't look haunted to me now. Quiet? Sure. And very secluded. But not haunted.

I pulled off the road across from the inn and reached for my Thermos. The small east parking lot was completely empty, as I'd expected. In the west lot, however, I counted eleven parked cars.

"What's this all about?" I muttered. I set my Thermos back on the seat, unopened.

On nearly any weekday night in January there might be one, maybe two cars parked at the inn, at least after the restaurant had closed. The Christmas and New Year's guests were gone. A nice snow could bring a few hearty tourists up from Chicago on winter weekends, but this was Sunday night—Monday a.m., actually—and after a one-day warm-up last week, most of the snow was packed hard and crusted with ice.

I moved the car toward the two-story house that held the lobby and a restaurant, then got out quietly, trying not to disturb any guests. Most of the license plates appeared to be from Illinois, which was not unusual. I climbed the wood steps onto the front porch and checked the lobby door. It was locked. I peeked inside—empty and silent, with one small lamp glowing softly. I walked past the white wood columns and around the side of the building, toward the lake, and peered through the window of the small restaurant bar. It was also quiet and dim. No Roy, no Rick, no Amber—the three bartenders had all gone home. I thought I saw something overhead, and I glanced up. I knew this building had one private suite upstairs, which was used by the inn's owner, but the windows were pitch black.

I left the porch and walked over to the guesthouse. Long and narrow, the shake-sided building was two stories tall but only one room deep, so every room overlooked the lake. It was about a dozen strides away from the lobby, and in the gap, a wind pushed in from the lakefront. I continued past the long row of doors, then around the two smaller buildings beyond. Everything seemed copacetic, nice and calm. Just the way I liked it.

I returned to my vehicle and continued a slow tour of the

lakeshore drive, just to make sure there were no miscreants running around, looking for trouble. By the time I circled back for my coffee break, it was just after 1:30 a.m. I backed my Jeep onto a high spot of ground across from the inn so I could see the full expanse of the property, then poured a cup from the Thermos and slumped in my seat to get comfortable.

There were other resorts in the township, but I had an odd affection for the French Country Inn, and I liked to keep an eye on it. I supposed it might've resembled something from the French countryside, but I hadn't been to France and my name wasn't Pierre. Tonight it looked more like a Currier and Ives print without all the people. Christmas lights dangled like icicles from the eaves of the long guesthouse, and an amber-colored spotlight illuminated a wreath hung below the peak of the roof. On the lawn, a balsam tree and a Scotch pine were bedecked with tiny lights. I chuckled, recalling a joke: "Why do they call those little lights Italian lights?" goes the setup. "Because they're not too bright."

The inn's current owner is an Italian guy from Chicago named Anthony Navilio—the same one who renovated the property in the Eighties. I'd spoken with him only once, rather briefly, as he passed through the restaurant bar. I didn't get enough of a read to judge his personality or his intelligence, but he'd done a good job renovating the property. If I had money and a girlfriend, or a girlfriend with money, I'd probably bring her here.

I sipped my coffee and looked at my watch. It was 1:37 a.m., another gray-black night in southeastern Wisconsin. Dead quiet, just the way I liked it.

When I was a kid, I liked to watch reruns of *The Untouchables*, the TV show about agent Eliot Ness and his bloody battle with Capone and other gangsters from the Prohibition era. If I had known how closely the inn's history was tied to those gangsters, I would've snooped around a lot more often back then. After I moved back to Geneva as an adult, I began to stop at the inn during my off hours, trekking through the lobby to get to the bar. I made acquaintances with the innkeeper, Mary Haggermaker, and she told me a little bit about the inn's history. It had been a lakeside resort for more than a hundred years. Early on, it was more like a family camp. During Prohibition, it was also a speakeasy serving bootlegged liquor. Supposedly the owner was on good terms with big-name thugs like Dillinger, Baby Face Nelson, and Bugs Moran—at least, a lot of gangsters and their molls had stayed at the inn, sometimes even using it to hide out from the Feds. It was certainly secluded enough for that, I realized.

The inn dates back a lot further than the gangster era, though. According to Mary, one of the early owners was Danish. Along with about twenty-seven million other people, he'd attended the 1893 Chicago World's Fair, officially known as the "World's Columbian Exposition." Afterward he bought a building or two from the Danish exhibit, which the Danes had built to show off their fine craftsmanship. The buildings were disassembled and shipped by rail to Lake Como, then reconstructed along the shore as part of a rustic resort that included a dining hall and the owner's residence. The train tracks from Chicago and Milwaukee ran right past the place, dropping off guests and their suitcases, along with their fishing poles and trapshooting guns.

Those tracks were long gone by the time I moved back here, but the inn's lobby still looked like the foyer of a gracious old house, which it essentially was, with its original woodwork intact. I was admiring the oak staircase and the inlaid floor when Mary Haggermaker and I struck up our first conversation. I pointed at the fine workmanship in the railing and said I wished I could be that good with my hands. Come to think of it, my ex-wife used to say the same thing.

I finished the coffee and checked my watch again. It was 1:45 a.m. I was about to put the Jeep into gear when I noticed something moving down by the shore, between the inn's lobby and the adjacent guesthouse. Or at least, I thought I did.

With flashlight in hand, I left the car and walked toward the lake. The wind picked up a small dune of crystallized snow, and it swirled about me like a whirling dervish. I stopped to listen. I swore I heard voices then—maybe a woman's soft laugh. I heard a clank and walked toward the wood deck outside the bar, where a fallen icicle lay in pieces. Then I heard the voices again, which were more like a murmuring, seemingly from the other direction.

I stand six-foot-two in thick-soled shoes, and I have a stocky build, with thick arms and a broad chest. I hate disruption, but I take pride in my readiness for action. All of which generally makes me impervious to fear. I also have a keen sense of alertness, honed by years of experience with the Chicago Police Department. Yet I couldn't help but notice that this night had an unfamiliar and unsettling quality.

I made another complete tour of the inn on foot. Nothing.

I decided my mind was playing tricks on me. Or maybe it was just the wind.

Feeling the cold crawl up my spine, I returned to my car and drove back to the stationhouse to await my relief officer, who would arrive at precisely 3:00 a.m. The radio started playing an old Pasty Cline song that I liked, "Walking After Midnight." Even with the song, I was unable to shake the uneasy feeling that had come over me.

Chapter Three

The law-enforcement budget of Geneva Township is even smaller than its population, so its police chief does not have the luxury of sitting behind a desk all day, pushing paperwork and barking orders. I work a patrol shift here, just like the officers under my command, three of whom are technically part-timers. I could excuse myself from night detail at any time, but truth be told, I enjoy working a few graveyard shifts every month. I find it relaxing, good for the psyche.

Besides, it wasn't as if I had anything better to do with my winter nights.

It was dead quiet in the stationhouse. At that time of night, all our calls rolled over to the county sheriff's office, and we used their dispatcher. I leaned back in my chair and stared at the big clock on the wall. Time seemed to pass in slow motion. The minute hand clicked, and it was 2:27 a.m. The clock took me back to Saint Isaac Jogues Grammar School, when I had stared at a virtually identical clock face, counting the minutes as I waited for the end-of-day bell to ring. Of course, now I wouldn't race outside like a kid with bees in his pants. At exactly 3:00 a.m., I'd be greeting Officer Bert Burr, a guy who was never early, and never late. Bert had probably come out of his mother's womb right on schedule, too.

I reached for my coffee cup—by this time, I'd switched to decaf—and misjudged the distance, sloshing a little brew onto the desk. As I swiped at the mess with my sleeve, I picked up a photo to keep it dry. It was the only picture on my desk, a shot of me and Dave

Tedeski, bass fishing on Lake Como almost fifteen years ago. It'd been a great day—no fish, just plenty of sun, beer, and bologna sandwiches. An old girlfriend of Dave's had happened by the dock and snapped the photo. Dave was grinning and holding up his hands, boasting about the one that got away.

My huckleberry friend, I thought, recalling a lyric by Johnny Mercer. My mother had always liked Frank Sinatra's version of "Moon River," which Mercer wrote with Henry Mancini for the movie *Breakfast at Tiffany's*. Later I became a fan of Mercer myself. I read somewhere that when the lyricist was asked to explain what he had meant by a "huckleberry friend," he'd responded, "If you have to ask, you'll never know."

I didn't have to ask because Dave Tedeski was my own huckleberry friend. We were both Chicago kids, but we'd met at Lake Geneva that first summer, when we were both ten. A bunch of free-roaming kids had gathered in the neighborhood park near our cottages, and we were choosing sides for a softball game.

"I'll take the kid in the blue shirt," I'd said.

He was tall and lean, and he held the bat in a fashion reminiscent of Duke Snider, the great Dodger centerfielder. From then on, Tedeski was known as "The Duke"—that is, when he wasn't called by one of his many other nicknames, such as Ski, Davie, Tedski, or Teddy. Once in a while, I even called him Dave. But no one ever called him by his baptismal name, David, except his mother, who always used it when she was angry with him.

The Duke had actually lived pretty close to me in Chicago when we were growing up, but he went to public school, so our paths didn't cross very often in the city. But we spent the next few summers becoming best friends. We hiked through the woods, hunted gophers, and shot at cans to perfect our aim. We also learned to water-ski together, tested our limits with alcohol, and stumbled over the facts of life.

Tedeski was the reason I became a cop after I tried college and failed. The Duke and I had also tried our hands as bartenders, electricians' apprentices, and property managers. We'd even made an ill-fated attempt to purchase a gas station together. At age twenty-two, at Tedeski's urging, we both filled out applications in hopes of joining the Chicago Police Department.

Ski's father had some political clout. He helped me pass the entrance exam, and he got the Duke past the physical exams. Tedeski had a little eyesight problem. He could shoot straight even while half-drunk, but he still needed glasses to read. We entered the training program at the police academy at Twelfth and State, and thirteen weeks later, we were two of Chicago's finest men in blue.

We moved up the ranks pretty fast because we were good at what we did. Tedeski worked gangs and homicide. I was on traffic, next vice, back to traffic, then the tactical squad. During those nine hectic years with the Chicago Police Department, I steadily became aware that I needed something else in my life—something I knew I would never find in the precinct halls of Chicago. By the time I hit thirty, I was spotting gray hairs, my belly was getting thick, and I was usually depressed or argumentative. I wanted a change for change's sake.

I could name a hundred reasons and tell a hundred stories to stress the point which led to my leaving the Chicago Police Department, but one story stands out among the rest. It was not the most horrific, egregious, or most violent act I had ever witnessed while I was on the force down in the city. It was just the psychological straw that broke this camel's back. During an interrogation of a burglary suspect, Officer John Morley punched the alleged perp to the floor, then stood on a chair and jumped squarely on the man's head.

It wasn't the beating that riled me—I'd seen that kind of thing before. It was the fact that Morley, and not some animal, had done it. I couldn't comprehend what kind of rage had taken hold of this normally decent man, what had caused him to suddenly jump upon another human being's head. I feared that I was just a year or three away from being overtaken by a similar depravity, so I resigned, despite Tedeski's appeal not to do so.

After a short break from police work, I took a position with a much smaller suburban department, hoping it would offer some quiet. Over the years, I had formed a professional bond with the chief of police up in Noringtown, Illinois. Noringtown was a fast-growing Chicago suburb whose police department was growing exponentially. I was only unemployed for two weeks before I became one of Noringtown's men in blue. A few short years later, the local population had grown to nearly a hundred thousand, and the same kind of violence and corruption I'd seen in the city were lying right at my doorstep again. I saw the lifestyle I'd sought slipping farther and farther away, so I resigned once more—this time, I thought, for good.

Police work and quietude are polar opposites, like music and rap, ethics and politicians. I lamented how I should have pursued a different line of work at age twenty-two—maybe as a mortuary assistant or lighthouse attendant. A couple years ago, I'd found myself edging toward forty, recently divorced, newly unemployed, with no real dream to follow. Both my parents were dead. Without giving it sufficient thought, I decided to relocate to Wisconsin and move into the house I had inherited, the one my father had purchased all those years ago.

I heard a door creak, and Bert Burr entered the stationhouse, jolting me out of my reverie. It was time for me to go home.

I looked up at the wall clock. It was exactly 3:00 a.m. How does he do that? I wondered. It's unnatural.

Chapter Four

Morning came quickly. I had instructed Officer Burr to give me a wake-up call and a rundown of last night's events, asking him to call sometime after 9:30 a.m., but no later than 10:30. He called at precisely 10:30 a.m.

Bert informed me that he'd stopped at the French Country Inn that morning because he too was curious about the eleven cars in the parking lot on a cold Sunday night in January. One car belonged to a Florida couple, who'd be checking out soon. The rest were from Illinois. The innkeeper, Mary Haggermaker, explained that she had booked a writer's workshop for the entire week. Eight fledgling wordsmiths were camped out at the inn and using the meeting room in one of the new buildings. Pretty nice digs for a week, I thought. Maybe they'd negotiated a good rate.

Bert paused as he checked his notes. "It's being led by the well-known short-story writer Professor Solomon Feri," he said. "That's F-E-R-I, not like, um, a fairy with wings or anything. His female assistant is there, too, so that makes ten of them. I don't think this group will be giving us any trouble unless they're big drinkers, Chief."

"Not unless they think they're Hemingway with a gun or something."

"What, Chief?"

"Never mind," I said. "So, this Feri is well known? Ever heard of him?"

"No, that's just how Mary described him."

I'd never heard of Feri either, but then, they don't make a lot of movies or TV miniseries from short stories. I pictured the workshop: a bunch of Stephen King and Anne Rice wannabes, sitting around the fireplace, discussing plot lines and dialogue with some snooty professor who'd never published a novel but probably had tenure at a small liberal arts college somewhere out in the cornfields. But who was I to judge? I could barely write my own police reports.

I told Officer Burr I would head to the station after I'd consumed a hearty breakfast and a gallon of coffee. I hung up the phone and wondered why Bert's parents had named their only child Albert. Hadn't they considered what it sounded like? Albert Burr could've been the name of a serial killer. Al Burr and Bert Burr both sounded ridiculous. Bert once confided he'd been called "Bertber the Elephant" as a kid, but he was anything but tubby now. These days most people—except for yours truly—call him Bert Burr as if the two names were inseparable. "Where's Bert Burr?" "Is Officer Bert Burr available?" "May I speak to Bert Burr, please?"

I grinned and made myself some fried bologna, four scrambled eggs, and a large pot of coffee. I had no cream, so I dropped a medium-size scoop of vanilla ice cream into the cup. Then I sipped my java and smacked my lips in enjoyment.

"Seems like another wonderful, peaceful day in paradise," I said out loud to my four-legged deputy and best friend. Naturally I'd named him Dawg. He padded over, his toenails clacking on the old linoleum, and I gave his big, floppy ear a rub.

It was a sunny day, cold and crisp, just the way I liked it. I read the morning paper while I finished my breakfast and my pot of coffee, then I let Dawg out for the second time. "Looks like a snowstorm might be brewing, don't ya think?" I said to him as he padded past. He ignored me. No doubt he had other things on his mind.

The phone rang. It was Dorothy, my right hand at the stationhouse.

"G'mornin', Chief. I just got a call from Judge Goggin. He wants you to stop by this morning and pick up some court orders that need to be served."

"Have Bert do it," I said.

"Sorry, Chief. Bert Burr just left—his shift is over. Geary's here now."

"Have him do it, then."

"The judge asked for you to come over personally, Chief. He wants to talk with you about something."

"Any idea what that 'something' is?" I asked. Dorothy had a knack for knowing things. People liked to talk to her, but she was not a big gossip herself, and that made her indispensable to me. She had also grown up in the township. Compared to Dorothy, I was a newcomer in town.

"Sorry, Chief. Don't have any details. What should I say when I call him back?"

I let out a sigh. "Okay, tell Judge Goggin I'll be there within the hour. Can't be anything too urgent. How are things going otherwise?"

"All quiet on the western front. Also on the eastern, southern, and northern." She laughed. Dorothy always got a real kick out of her own jokes. But she was the glue that held the stationhouse together, much more so than I. She was also quick of mind, a good decision-maker, and she was the only member of the staff who could brew a decent cup of coffee—besides me, of course.

I readied myself, then drove into Lake Geneva proper, a picturesque burg with just over seven thousand inhabitants. Geneva Township wrapped its northwest boundaries, but they were not alike—Lake Geneva was filled with shops, restaurants, and hotels, and though it was small, it was the biggest community on the lake, drawing hordes of tourists every summer.

Seeing as how I'd only consumed sixteen cups of coffee this morning, I stopped for a "venti" latte—twenty ounces of pure caffeine with a dash of cholesterol. For years, the only chain in downtown Lake Geneva had been a Radio Shack, but the city was growing fast, and it now had a Starbucks alongside the gift shops. A Wal-Mart loomed at the east edge of town. Could a Chipotle Grill be far behind?

By the time I arrived at Judge Goggin's chambers, it was almost noon. I had consumed so much coffee that I was as jumpy as a duck in a Chinese restaurant. I took a deep breath, then entered Goggin's office.

"Mornin', Judge, nice to see you," I said.

The judge did not bother to look up from his desk for several moments. Instead he shuffled through a stack of documents as if he were ready to file them in the wastepaper basket. Finally he nodded, picked up a manila folder, and handed it to me.

"I've got six court orders in there for you, Chief. Five are minor—the usual peace bonds, subpoenas for depositions, that kind of thing. It's the one eviction notice that worries me. That's what I need to talk with you about." He paused and looked at me pointedly, just to make sure I was paying attention.

"It's an eviction notice for the Zubeck property," he continued. "To put it bluntly, Ben Zubeck and his wife are both crazy. I want you to serve that notice yourself—don't send any of your officers in your place. You can bring one along if you insist, but tell them to stay in the car. Approach Zubeck alone and stay on your toes."

"What's this all about, Judge?" I asked, annoyed to be told every inch of my job without hearing any worthwhile facts. "Get to the point."

Goggin gave me a look that said he would've liked to sentence me to a year on an Alabama chain gang. I regretted my tone at once—I didn't have energy to waste on a pissing match with this judge, or any other.

Eyes glaring, he continued. "The point being, Zubeck is a bad apple. I've had him in my court a number of times in the past, charged with assault, domestic violence, threats, you name it. You ever heard of him, Chief?"

"Can't say that I have," I admitted.

"Well, every one of those cases was dropped. I suspect some type of intimidation took place, against either a witness or a plaintiff, but we could never prove anything one way or another."

The judge took a sip from a glass of water and carefully patted his lips dry with a handkerchief before he went on. My time is your time, I thought.

"Zubeck has been pretty quiet lately, but at the end of last year, the Saint James Bank foreclosed on his house and his land. He has a small farm, which runs about seventy acres. Or, he used to. That Navilio guy bought the entire property at the county sheriff's sale." The judge raised an eyebrow. "Do you know him?"

I nodded. "Not well, but I've seen him around."

That Navilio guy, as the judge called him, is Anthony Navilio, the owner of the French Country Inn. He supposedly owned a few other local properties, too, all commercial, but he had a reputation for not being very shrewd, because he'd overpaid for the ones he coveted. I wondered why Navilio would take an interest in Zubeck's farm, but I didn't interrupt the judge.

"Ever since the start of the foreclosure proceedings, Zubeck has been making wild threats. The bank president, John Nash, was in my courtroom several times with his lawyer, Dick Howarth. Nash was getting threatening telephone calls late at night. It unnerved the whole family."

"When was that?"

"A couple of months ago. We had no evidence that it was Zubeck who'd made the calls, but I issued a restraining order anyway. A lot of good that'll do when you're up against a nut like Zubeck, though."

"Do you think Nash is in any real danger?" I asked.

"Possibly," the judge said, "but I suspect Zubeck's real rage is vented at that Navilio guy. And since both the Zubeck and Navilio properties are in Geneva Township, the problem is on your turf."

It was at least the second time the judge had referred to the owner of the French Country Inn as "that Navilio guy." I wondered what kind of a relationship they had.

"You know Ron Frankel?" the judge continued.

"Everybody knows Frankel, Judge." Ron Frankel was likable guy who made such regular appearances at his favorite bars and cafes that he already had a sandwich and a martini named after him. He handled real estate, so maybe that was his connection here.

Goggin nodded. "Well, yesterday Ronnie told me that he'd run into Zubeck at Herb's gas station. Zubeck started ranting about how that Navilio guy was going to pay, because no one could take Zubeck's property and live to enjoy it. Zubeck's exact words, according to Ronnie, were "You go tell that dago FIB that his days are numbered." Frankel complied—he told Navilio. But since I'm the one telling you, apparently that Navilio guy didn't do anything official about it. This is all second- and third-hand, but you can check it out and draw your own conclusions."

"Where's that Navilio guy now?" I asked. "Anthony Navilio, I mean."

"Ronnie said he was staying at the French Country Inn for a few days. He has an office there above the lobby. But I don't know if he's still around."

I assured Judge Goggin that I'd serve the eviction notice to Zubeck myself, and the judge reiterated his concerns. "No offense to your staff," he said, "but I wouldn't want some fresh-faced rookie to overreact and start a war if Zubeck gets aggressive. Zubeck hunts everything legal and probably more, and he's old-school. I wouldn't be surprised if he answers his door with a shotgun."

"Point taken, Judge."

I decided to serve the notice as soon as possible, but I didn't plan to go alone. I'd let Geary continue his usual shift and ask Officer Madden to join me. Besides being my best officer, Annie Madden was unflappable, and she had a whole lot of common sense. You can teach a cop many things, but common sense is innate, I've found—you either have it, or you don't. Basketball coaches like to say you can't teach height—you're either tall or you're not. The same thing is true with common sense.

Chapter Five

Officer Madden and I made two unsuccessful trips out to Zubeck's property. As we drove there again, I hoped the third time would be the charm. Of course Zubeck himself would not be charming. Even under the best of circumstances, no one is ever happy to be served an eviction notice.

I was legally bound to serve the notice in person, not simply peg it to the door, which would give Zubeck leeway to claim later that he'd never received it. I also wanted to size up this guy firsthand. I'd telephoned before the first visit, but the line had been disconnected, and if Zubeck had another phone, I didn't know the number. I doubted he was hiding from us—he sounded like the kind of individual who'd actually welcome a confrontation. From the looks of things, Ben Zubeck and his wife were simply not at home that day.

By now I owed Annie Madden a favor. She hadn't originally been on duty for the day, so I'd offered to take her next nightshift in return.

I walked around the old farmhouse. Its white paint had peeled to bare wood on more than half the siding. Then I checked on the decrepit outbuildings again. The Zubecks didn't appear to keep any animals, and the fields hadn't been farmed in years. A rusty pickup truck was mired in the mud and ice.

"Any sign of him?" Annie asked when I returned to the car.

"Struck out again. Not even a fresh tire track."

Annie looked around. "This place gives me the creeps, Chief."

"I'm sure the value is in the land. It's not a bad spot, after all."

Zubeck's acreage was at the edge of the township. A long gravel drive led to the house, which sat on a small rise among towering old oaks with broken limbs. The rear windows looked west past an old orchard to a broad stretch of open fields.

It was just past 4:30 p.m. The wind had picked up, and there were some light flurries in the air. It was quickly becoming colder and darker. I was just about to turn the ignition in the Jeep again when we heard a car approaching fast on the drive. It had one headlight, no bumper, no license plates. The car skidded to a stop about fifty feet from our vehicle, and a barrel-chested man leaped from the driver's side.

"What the hell are you son-of-a-bitches doin' on my property?" he yelled, trundling forward into the beam of my headlights. The man was in his sixties, but he was almost my height and still looked pretty tough. His face was leathery and covered with sharp gray stubble, and he was wearing a cap with fleece lined earflaps, but I still recognized Ben Zubeck from his driver's license photo and an old arrest file I'd seen.

Annie and I had stepped out of the Jeep as soon as we saw his car. I gently motioned for her to stay put near her door, so the Jeep would give her a little cover in a worst-case scenario. Not that I expected to get shot at or anything—it just paid to be ready. Judge Goggin had warned me that both Zubeck and his wife were crazy. I eyed Zubeck's old Ford sedan, but I saw no sign of anyone still sitting inside it. Either his wife wasn't with him, or she was hiding behind the dash.

"I asked you a question," Zubeck continued. "Waddaya doin' on my property? Unless you got a damned warrant, you're trespassing. Hell, you're trespassing anyway."

"Mr. Zubeck, I am a duly sworn officer of the law," I said calmly, holding out my badge at arm's length for him to see. "I'm here at the behest of the court. It's my job to serve you these eviction papers, and to advise you that you have ten days to vacate the premises. You take these papers now, and we'll be on our way. It's as simple as that." I held the eviction papers out toward him, but he waved me away and headed toward the house.

"I don't have to listen to your bullshit. Get off my property."

"Is your full name Benjamin Vernon Zubeck?" I asked. "And do you currently reside at W2122 Styvan Road, in Geneva Township?"

Zubeck stopped. "What kind of idiot question is that? You know damned well who I am and where I live. You're here, aren't you?"

Of course I did know the answer to both inquiries, but during a tense confrontation, I always ask a couple of easy questions. They often help to diffuse a potentially combative situation.

"We're sorry about your troubles, Mr. Zubeck," Annie added.

Zubeck said nothing. I held out the papers again, and this time he grabbed them from my hand and inspected them. It was probably too dark for him to read, even with the beams of the Jeep's headlights shining upon his house.

Zubeck spat on the snow, then pointed a finger at me. "You tell that fuckin' dago carpetbagger—"

"Mr. Zubeck," I interrupted, "it wouldn't be a good idea for you to make threats in front of me or any other police officer."

Zubeck stared at me hard, his eyes watery and gray in the cold. Then he spoke slowly and deliberately, through gritted teeth. "You just tell that Navilio guy that him and me will be chatting real soon. Tell him, 'Delenda est Carthago.' "

"Mr. Zubeck—" I began.

"What, are ya some kinda Polack, so I gotta spell it out for you? Day-len-dahestCar-thay-go, you moron. That dago will know what it means." With that, he went inside and slammed the door.

Chapter Six

As we left Zubeck's driveway and pulled onto the main road, Annie Madden finally turned in her seat and took her eyes off the house behind us. "What the heck was that all about? Why is some psycho hillbilly speaking Greek to us?"

"I think it's Latin, not Greek," I answered. "It's some kind of saying, but I'm not sure what it means. Let's see if we can remember the exact words and have Dorothy look it up on the Internet."

We both tried to repeat the phrase. As it turns out, it's not easy to parrot a string of Latin, especially if you can't see it written. After a few minutes, Annie had Dorothy on the radio. "Okay, so it's either duh-linda ess or dar-len-duh est, then something that sounds like cargo or escargot . . . Right. Thanks, Dorothy."

We made a couple routine stops on our way back to the station, and along the way, we discussed our perceptions regarding Zubeck and his current state of mind. There were three words we agreed on: desperate, hostile, and irrational.

Neither Annie nor I knew the exact circumstances under which Zubeck had lost his property, but I didn't have much sympathy for the guy. I suspected he was the kind who took zero responsibility for his own problems and viewed everything as someone else's fault. If he'd quit paying his mortgage, it was the bank's fault. If the county had foreclosed because he didn't pay his taxes, it was the government's fault.

"Whatever happened to personal accountability?" I asked. "These days, you break the law, it's because your mother was overbearing and she made you eat too many Twinkies. So, let's all sue the Hostess baking company."

"Hey, I happen to like my mother. I blame the lawyers," Annie joked.

I smiled. "Well, in this case, Zubeck is clearly blaming Navilio, even though Anthony Navilio probably had nothing to do with the foreclosure. He was just the highest bidder after the fact."

"Yeah, but that's not how Zubeck sees it."

"The question is, is Zubeck all bluster, or is he likely to get violent? And if so, how far will he take it? He has a history of making serious threats, and he's been involved in assaults, but he has no convictions yet."

"Well," said Annie thoughtfully, "we know that most violent assaults are perpetrated on people who have a more personal history—family against family. That's been true locally, too. We've had some bar fights that got nasty, and a lot of drunk-driving incidents. But the only murders we've had here in the last ten years involved a wife who stabbed her husband, and a son who was shot by his own mother."

"Good thing Zubeck isn't a woman then."

Annie laughed. That was one of the things I liked about Annie—she usually got my sense of humor.

There was a brief pause, then she continued. "I do think something is likely to happen. But if you want me to guess, I'd say Zubeck will take out his frustrations on Navilio's car or one of his buildings. Guys like Zubeck need someone to be mad at. They need someone to hate. They're so filled with anger that if they don't have an outlet, they just explode."

That was another thing I liked about Annie—she had a whole lot of common sense. She had great legs, too, but as her boss, I tried very hard not to notice.

"Officer Madden, I think you've hit the nail on the head. I'll drop you off at the station so you can finally get home. Then I think I'll go have a chat with Mr. Navilio and tell him the facts of life regarding the mental state of Benjamin Vernon Zubeck."

We were within a few hundred yards of the stationhouse when Dorothy finally radioed back. "Tell Chief I've got it," she said to Annie. "It's a Latin phrase. Delenda est Carthago. Or, more accurately, Carthago delenda est, depending on who you ask. It's attributed to Cato the Elder in the ancient Roman senate."

Dorothy paused. I knew she was stalling for effect—or waiting for us to admit we still had no idea what it meant.

"Okay, Dorothy," I said impatiently. "What's the translation?"

"Well . . . the best translation is 'Carthage must be destroyed.' But what it really means is, if you have an enemy, don't leave him or his city standing to rise another day. The ancient city of Carthage wasn't just destroyed. First, everyone was either killed or driven out. Then the city was set on fire and completely plowed under."

Annie and I looked at each other but said nothing. That bad feeling I'd had earlier was back—and it was getting stronger.

Chapter Seven

It was time for me to pay a visit to Anthony Navilio, owner of the French Country Inn. I decided I'd go home first so I could let Dawg out, take a quick shower, and jump into casual clothing. I wanted my visit to be informal. Like many Italians, Navilio had a reputation for being mercurial, and I didn't want to get him all riled up. Zubeck already had cornered the market on "rash and stupid." Besides, if I didn't happen to see Navilio, I could have a talk with Jim Kirchschlager and Ron Frankel, who were certain to be at the inn's restaurant—or more accurately, the restaurant bar. I intended to join them for a friendly drink and find out what they knew about Zubeck and Navilio, and it never looked good to consume alcohol while wearing my uniform.

The restaurant had it own entrance at the side of the main building, where a blue awning identified it as "Kirsch's." I parked in the west lot and entered through the inn's lobby instead. I always took that route. I loved the old-world charm of the foyer, and I liked to give a wave to the innkeeper on duty. Apparently, Mary had stepped away for a moment, because the desk was unmanned. The fireplace beside it wasn't burning tonight. I glanced up the long honey-oak stairway and eyed the gallery that wrapped the upper level of the lobby. It was quiet upstairs, where Navilio had an office and a deluxe suite, but that didn't mean he wasn't around.

I headed toward the restaurant, crossing through a tea lounge with another fireplace. Most of the restaurant occupied a rambling addition behind the main house. The area with the lobby was the oldest part of the structure, but much of the building dated to the Roaring Twenties. The restaurant had so many little "back rooms" for private parties that it was hard to keep track of them all.

Just as I'd expected, Ron Frankel and Jim Kirchschlager were sitting at the restaurant bar, which had the flavor of a back room, too. Navilio's suite was overhead, but as far as I knew, there was no direct route between that and the restaurant. I made a mental note to ask Jim Kirchschlager if there were any back stairs—it couldn't hurt to know the layout of the place in case Zubeck came calling.

Kirchschlager went by the nickname "Kirsch." He had a decanter of red wine in front of him, which told me he was drinking a bottle from his private collection. He'd showed the wine cellar to me once—hundreds of bottles of fine wines, ports, and cognacs, all stashed in the basement like a pirate's trove. For many connoisseurs, the consumption of an extra-fine bottle of wine might be a rare indulgence, but for Kirsch, it was a way of life. He'd uncork a four-hundred-dollar Châteauneuf-du-Pape or a six-hundred-dollar Mouton Cadet Reserve almost as easily as other people uncapped a nice beer.

Next to Kirsch sat Ronnie Frankel, who was pontificating on some arcane topic. I could always tell when Frankel was in his oratory mode, because he swirled his finger upward into the air as he talked. His signature drinks—a Grey Goose vodka with a touch of Chambord and a sidecar of diet Coke—were standing on the bar directly in front of him, like toy soldiers awaiting their orders.

"Gentlemen, gentlemen," I said as I approached, "what a rare sight this is, finding you two at Kirsch's bar, consuming some type of alcoholic beverage."

Kirsch raised his glass. "Hey, look what the cat dragged in."

Frankel exhaled from his cigarette and grinned. "Evening, Chief—and what a rare sight it is seeing you here. My eyes must be deceiving me."

"It's probably just the vodka and smoke," I said.

Kirsch offered to buy me a cocktail, and Frankel, beaten to the punch, immediately said he'd sponsor the next one. They were like peas in a pod, sixty-something and a little crusty on the outside, perpetually young on the inside.

"You know," I said, "some people might consider a free drink to be a bribe. After all, you two might be attempting to ingratiate yourselves with an officer of law, thinking I might look the other way, should there be some legal infraction in the future."

"I don't know what other people think, but I certainly do consider it a bribe," said Kirsch, waving me toward the empty stool beside him.

"Me too," added Frankel. "Why else would anyone spend money on a mope like you?"

"Gee, thanks," I responded. "You two really know how to humble a guy. And officially, I'm off duty, by the way."

"Are you ever really off duty?" Kirsch remarked.

"Good point," I said.

"Maybe a better question would be, are you ever really on duty?" Frankel quipped. "I'd hate to think we won't get our money's worth tonight."

I ignored him and ordered a domestic beer, a brand I knew they didn't stock. It was a little game I played with the bartenders at the French Country Inn. Roy, this evening's bartender, opened a bottle of Heineken and poured it into a pilsner glass.

I took a sip and turned back to my friends. "Have you seen Navilio here tonight?" I asked.

"Nope," Frankel said. "He went back down to Chicago already. Probably because I told him all about the Zubeck situation. You know about that, right?"

I nodded. "It's why I'm here."

"Yeah, I thought Judge Goggin might fill you in. This morning I came here and told Navilio about my encounter with Zubeck at the gas station, and I emphasized what a nutcase Zubeck is. The 'zoo' part of his name really fits. That guy should be in a zoo, or at least a cage. Anyway, you missed Navilio by five hours. When I came back tonight, Mary told me he'd already gone home to Chicago this morning. Looks like he'll stay down there the rest of the week."

"Good," I said. "That's one less thing I have to worry about. I served Mr. Zubeck his eviction notice this afternoon—and you're right, he's not the calm-and-collected type. He and his wife now have ten days to vacate the property. With Navilio out of town, maybe the threats won't escalate to bodily harm."

"Well, Navilio might be a greaseball," Kirsch said, "but he isn't a stupid greaseball." Anthony Navilio was essentially Jim Kirchschlager's landlord. Kirsch owned the restaurant, but he leased the space from Navilio. "I talked to Tony around eleven this morning, just before he left here. He told me he had business back in the city, but I could tell he was just getting the heck out of Dodge, because it was right after Ronnie told him about Zubeck's threats."

"Yeah, that's right," Frankel added. "I bet Navilio figured the threats must be serious because I got up at the crack of ten a.m. just to come over here and tell him about it. Navilio has never seen me out before five o'clock."

"Come to think of it, neither have I," I said, "unless a Bloody Mary is involved."

"Always the comedian," Frankel retorted. "Don't quit your day job, Chief—whatever that is."

While we were talking, five people entered the lounge and sat down at the far end of the bar, where it turned at a ninety-degree angle to form an L. Most of them looked like literary types right out of Hollywood central casting—wire-rimmed glasses, wild hair, unkempt beards, tweed sport coats with suede elbow patches. One guy was even smoking a Benson & Hedges through a slim cigarette holder. There was one woman in the group, a dishwater blonde, petite but stacked, mid-thirties. She cozied up to the oldest looking guy in the group—a gray-haired man with wire rims and a tidy goatee.

I ordered another beer, this one at Frankel's expense, then returned the favor and bought him a cocktail. I didn't offer to buy one for Kirsch. I was sure the bottle of wine he was drinking cost more than I made in a week.

For a while the three of us remained drinking at the bar; then we ordered some hors d'oeuvres. I confirmed that Navilio usually came up here on a Monday or Tuesday morning, worked from his office upstairs a few days, then headed back to Chicago before the weekend to spend time with family. Since today was a Monday, he probably wouldn't be back for a week at best—maybe longer, under the circumstances. I made a note to get his Chicago number from the innkeeper, Mary Haggermaker.

Two more women entered the bar, a pale blonde and a brunette. They gave a quick nod and a hello to the group at the end of the bar, then sat down a few stools away, so they could talk privately. I switched to a vodka martini while my two compadres continued with their usual cocktails and conversation.

Frankel was positing some theory about the Zen of ice fishing when a laugh from one of the two women a few seats beyond him caught my attention. The blonde was seated with her back to me and I could not see her face, but she had short, curly hair and a good figure. The other, the brunette, was listening more than she was talking, then she nodded and laughed again. Even through the haze created by Frankel's cigarette, I could tell she was an extraordinary beauty—dark eyes, pale skin, full red lips, and thick, dark hair falling to her shoulders. She was the kind of dame a film-noir gumshoe might be tempted to pick up, even when he knew he shouldn't.

The innkeeper, Mary, came in, a serious look on her face, and headed toward the two women. She addressed the blonde, and after a brief exchange, which I could not make out, the blonde woman turned and followed Mary back toward the lobby, frowning with her heavily lacquered lips as she bustled past. Two seconds later, Kirsch and Frankel swigged down the last vestiges of their beverages and called it a night themselves, making a few smart remarks about going dancing. I waved them off without paying much attention—I was much more interested in the brunette.

The four barstools between the dark-haired beauty and me were now empty. We smiled at each other.

"It appears our friends have abandoned us," I said.

"My friend will be back," she said.

"Luckily, my friends won't."

She laughed. "They do seem like quite a pair. The fellow with the beard—that was Jim Kirchschlager, the owner of the restaurant, right?"

I cupped a hand to my ear. "Pardon me?" I'd heard her just fine, but I wanted an excuse to move two seats closer, which I did. She smelled of perfume and white wine and was even more beautiful at close range. She had a sophisticated look about her, and I wondered if I was reaching too high. I was definitely out of practice.

She repeated her question about Kirsch.

"That's the guy," I said. "Do you know him?"

"He and I have spoken a few times, but he doesn't seem to remember me very well. I always have to reintroduce myself."

"I don't think I would ever have that problem—not remembering you, I mean." I'd said it as glibly as I could.

"You're very kind." She extended her hand. "I'm Greta."

I shook her hand, momentarily struck dumb.

She looked at me expectantly, then offered, "Wait—let me see if I can guess who you are. Since you and Kirsch are friends, or seem to be, and . . . since this is the off-season, then you must be one of the locals, too."

"Actually, I'm an immigrant. I vacationed here every summer

when I was growing up, but I've only been a full-time resident for a few years, so I still don't qualify. Kirsch is a local, though."

"Are you from Chicago, then?"

"Born and raised," I said. "How about you—where do you call home?"

"Chicago now, but Toronto originally. I consider both cities my home." She sipped her wine. "You aren't going to make me guess your name, are you?"

Before I could answer, our attention was diverted by a large, coatless man who blustered into the bar through a French door that opened onto the lakeside deck. His chest and neck were as thick as a linebacker's. I estimated that he hadn't shaved in two days; there was almost as much salt-and-pepper stubble on his face as on the top of his head, which had a receding hairline and a buzz-cut. He appeared to have gotten a head start on drinking. He didn't bother to close the door behind him, and a swirl of light snow and cold air followed him into the room. The bearded man with the cigarette holder in his mouth arose from his stool and closed the door. Meanwhile, the large man sat down at the bar, two spots beyond Greta. He demanded a "Jack and Coke" and mumbled something unintelligible to himself.

When Greta turned back to me, her smile was gone.

"A friend of yours?" I asked quietly.

"Hardly," she said. "He's just part of our group."

"The writers' workshop?"

She looked at me curiously. "That's right. Everyone at that end of the bar is part of our group, though a few are missing. We're attending a workshop here for the entire week. How did you know that?"

"Small town," I said. "So you say you've been here at the inn before. Is that how you know Kirsch?"

"Actually, I only said that I'd spoken with Kirsch several times, but yes, I've been here before. Did you know that you ask questions like a cop?"

"Guilty as charged," I said. "I'm the local police chief."

She laughed. "You're not serious, are you?"

"Actually, I am." I tried to gauge her reaction. Some women think the badge is interesting, even appealing, but for others, it's a turnoff. It didn't seem to faze her.

"Let's try this again," she said, extending her hand. "I'm Greta, a legal alien with no prior convictions. And your name would be?"

"Chief."

"As in chief of police?"

"Yes, but I've had the nickname all my life. The job is just a coincidence."

"That's quite a coincidence," she said. She gave me a seductive little smile. "Are you sure you're not pulling my leg, officer?"

"No, ma'am. That might be considered harassment."

She smiled and sipped her wine again. I glanced at the burly drunk just down the bar from her. For the moment, he seemed to be immersed in his own thoughts and his drink. He was a little overweight, but he had the vestiges of a military bearing—ex-military, I guessed. I turned back to the brunette.

"So, Greta . . . what is it that you're writing? If you don't mind my asking another question, that is."

"I don't mind at all. As a matter of fact, I'm writing a book about this inn. It has a fascinating history. I found out about it the first time I stayed here, about three years ago, and then I started doing some research."

"Are you writing fiction or nonfiction?"

"Nonfiction, but it's not dry by any means. I might do a historical novel later, I don't know . . . that's not really my arena. Do you know anything about the inn's past?"

"I know the oldest part of the house was originally part of the

Danish pavilion at the Chicago World's Fair in the late 1800s. Does that count?"

"That's just the beginning of the story. I'm looking at the next century, focusing mainly on the Twenties and Thirties, especially the Prohibition era—that's when things really get interesting. Did you know this was a speakeasy and a gangster hideout?"

"I'd heard rumors, but nothing too specific. I'd love to hear about your research, though."

My interest was genuine, but at the same time, I kept looking at the man behind her. He'd downed his first Jack and Coke like water, and he had just asked Roy for another. As a drunk, he was potentially more trouble than the O'Malley brothers.

"Originally, this was the Lake Como Hotel," Greta was saying. "During the Twenties, it was owned by Christian Hermansen and his son Hobart—'Hobe' Hermansen, as his friends called him. When Prohibition rolled around, Hobart ran an illegal gambling and drinking operation here, did some bootlegging as well. Later on, he had some help from his wife, Lucille. They both had some very intriguing Chicago connections . . . especially Lucille. I assume you've heard of Bugs Moran, Capone's arch rival?"

I nodded. To a Chicago kid who'd grown up watching reruns of *The Untouchables*, the name "Bugs" Moran was as familiar as Al Capone. The two thugs had controlled nearly all the illegal activities in Chicago and the surrounding area. But they were bitter rivals, and their gangs were literally at war, with tommy guns blazing and blood running in the streets. The most infamous battle was the Saint Valentine's Day Massacre—which was a hit on Bugs's gang. Capone's henchmen murdered a number of Moran's men, but Bugs himself escaped harm.

"Hobart ran the hotel from 1921 to 1971," Greta continued. "He met Lucille through his good friend Bugs. In fact, Lucille was married to Bugs first, and she had a son with him. They all stayed here together. But then at one point, she left Bugs and took up with Hobe."

"You're kidding," I said. "And Bugs was okay with this?" I couldn't think of an "ex-husband" who might be less forgiving than Bugs Moran—a man who had earned his nickname for his crazy, if not psychopathic, outbursts.

"Now, that's the question, isn't it? I'm still working on the research, but it all seemed strangely amicable," Greta said. "In a way, even businesslike."

She went on to explain that Moran and his gang members had used the Lake Como Hotel as a safe house. It was a comfortable, out-of-the-way place where they could drink, eat, gamble, and escape the pressures from Capone and his gang. They also stayed here while they were running from treasury agent Eliot Ness and his famous G-men, a.k.a. The Untouchables—the same men who eventually took down Al Capone.

"Moran and Lucille would come here with Moran's bodyguards," Greta continued, "and Hobart Hermansen always made them feel at home."

"Evidently Lucille felt even more at home here than Bugs."

Greta smiled again. "You can see why I'm fascinated. This story is filled with personal drama, but it's more than that, of course. It's a window to those times—the misguided politics, the crime, the corruption, the economic struggles of the Depression. And all of those threads lead here, to the edge of Lake Como. Have you ever been inside that little cottage down by the shore—the one just behind the newer two-story building, L'Auberge, where our writing group is staying?"

I nodded. "I haven't been inside, but I know the one you're talking about. I think the innkeeper calls that little house 'the Cottage.' "

"That's it. Originally it was known as the Doll House, because the gangsters' molls liked to stay there. It wasn't just Moran who visited, either. But I'll save the tales about Tommy Carroll and Baby Face Nelson for later."

"Later" sounded good—it meant there might be a "later." I

could have listened to Greta talk for hours. Her voice was subtle and a bit low, her expressions passionate. She had a mystique that reminded me of the movie stars of the 1930s and '40s, like Greta Garbo and Gene Tierney, with a body to match.

"Can I buy you another glass of wine?" I asked.

Before Greta could answer, her friend—the one who had left with the innkeeper—blew back into the lounge like a blonde witch on a whirlwind. The woman literally inserted herself into our conversation, standing in between us, without any pleasantries or apologies.

"You'll never believe it, Greta. I am so annoyed. Traumatized, really."

"Chandra," said Greta, in a voice that gently indicated her dissatisfaction with her friend's rude manner, "I'd like you to meet Chief. Chief, this is Chandra Harper, a friend of mine, and a fellow writer in the group."

The woman nodded quickly at me and then continued to speak to Greta as if I weren't present, unleashing a diatribe that reminded me of a tape on fast forward, or maybe a socialite on amphetamines.

"I cannot believe I had to pack up all my things, just like that, and change rooms—not just once, mind you, but twice. Something to do with that electrical problem in my room in L'Auberge. Apparently, it was only my room that had the problem, of course. Do you know, I'm not even in the same building as you are now? First they tried to put me into one of their standard rooms. It looked pretty nice, but it wasn't as nice as my original suite, so I told that Mary woman absolutely not. After all, if I am going to be inconvenienced by not staying with my friends and fellow writers—and if I have to go trekking outside in January just to meet with you in the gathering room every morning—then I should really get an upgrade, don't you agree?"

In the brief pause, Greta nodded. "Absolutely. So—"

"So," Chandra continued, "I just demanded the best suite at the inn. I explained to that Mary woman that I simply cannot deal with these traumatic situations. And then she showed me the king suite upstairs in this building—which is even farther away, of course, but the suite is absolutely marvelous, so I don't think I'll mind too much." She glanced over at the burly drunk, who glowered back at her, then lowered her voice to a whisper. "Thank God I'm not staying close to him anymore—now that would be doubly traumatic. He's acting like a complete fool."

I did a rough mental tally: Chandra Harper had used some form of the word trauma at least three times in a five-second span. If she thought changing rooms in a luxury hotel constituted a "traumatic" experience, I wondered how she'd describe an actual trauma, such as, in her case, a hangnail.

Still ignoring me, Chandra Harper suggested to Greta that they move to a small table by the wall to be more comfortable. To my dismay, Greta got up to follow her, giving me a little smile and a "nice-to-meet-you" that made it clear our conversation had ended. I sat alone and nursed the rest of my drink, hoping that Kirsch and Frankel might return.

Chapter Eight

Still several seats away from me at the bar, the large man who had blustered in from the lakeside deck continued brooding and drinking alone. By my count, he was now working on his third Jack Daniels and Coke, on top of whatever else he might have guzzled back in his own room. He had become more agitated after Chandra and Greta moved to the small table against the wall. I noticed that Chandra had arranged herself with her back to him.

The drunk banged his almost-empty glass on the copper-topped bar and turned toward the two women. "Come on, Chandra. Get over here," he demanded. "Quit playing games."

Chandra did not turn to look, but I was sure she'd heard him. I saw Greta glance up at the man over Chandra's shoulder, then return her attention to her friend, whispering something across the table.

"Damn it, Chandra," the man growled. "Get over here, please. See? I've asked you nicely. So get your ass over here."

Chandra did not obey and continued to speak with Greta in low tones. Although I strained my ears, I couldn't make out their conversation.

The man raised his voice another level. "Chandra, come over here right now, goddammit."

Chandra responded with a light wave that seemed to indicate "in a moment" or "go away," but then she got up. "Well then," she said sweetly, and loudly enough for the drunk and anyone else nearby to overhear. "I'd better go settle things with the macho-man before he creates a scene." She walked over to the drunk, and the two immediately became engaged in a conversation. Chandra's words weren't fully audible, but her voice had a calm, soft quality. Evidently she was trying to quiet the man down, and it seemed to be working.

Greta moved to the stool next to me and put her empty wine glass on the bar. I motioned to the bartender. "My treat, Roy," I said.

Greta thanked me, then leaned her head closer, as if confiding a secret. "Chandra should never have taken up with that man," she said in a low voice. "But, of course, that's exactly why she did it."

I asked how long the two star-crossed lovers had known each other. Greta explained that they had met at one of Professor Feri's previous workshops, and that Chandra had only been "dating" the Jack-and-Coke man—a Gulf War veteran named John Ratz—for the past month or so. "I didn't even know exactly how much they'd been seeing each other until we got here," Greta whispered. "Chandra told me she had only wanted a short fling, but now John has other ideas."

"I'll bet," I said. "He doesn't look the literary type. Aren't writers supposed to be more sensitive and intellectual, short on muscle but filled with angst?"

"Not necessarily," she said. "What about Ernest Hemingway? Or Norman Mailer? They weren't exactly sissies."

"Yeah, but that palooka over there doesn't look like much of a thinker. He looks more like a Teamster or a professional wrestler."

Greta smiled. "You know what they say, you can't judge a book by its cover. But in John Ratz's case, you might be right. I'm sure he only came here to be with Chandra. He wasn't even signed up for this session until a week ago."

Ratz's voice began to grow louder. As his demeanor became angrier, Chandra appeared to grow smaller.

"Ain't gonna happen that way, Chandra," I heard Ratz say. "It just ain't gonna be that easy." He turned back toward the bar and demanded another drink. "Jack on the rocks, no Coke."

Roy's reply was diplomatic and professional. "I'm sorry, sir, but it appears you've had enough for tonight. How about a club soda or a cup of coffee? It's on the house."

I began to maneuver myself out of my seat. I had a pretty good idea where this was heading.

At the same time, Chandra Harper seemed to find her backbone and her voice, because she straightened up and started to yell at her suitor. "Oh, for Pete's sake, John. Just go back to your room. You're making a complete ass of yourself!"

Ratz fixed his gaze on the bartender, but at the same time, he reached out and grabbed Chandra's wrist. "I said gimme a fucking drink, asshole!" He punctuated his sentence by giving Chandra's small arm a sharp twist.

Chandra screamed. I was already within arm's length when Ratz turned his head and looked down at the wilting Chandra Harper. I seized the wrist of the man's right hand—the one holding Chandra—and he let go of her, sliding off his seat and lurching aggressively in my direction. He was larger than I was, and probably stronger, but he was also drunk, surprised, and rising from a seated position. I twisted his wrist and arm, employing a kansetsu-waza judo move that I'd learned from a martial arts instructor on the Chicago police force. As Chandra stumbled backward in shock, Ratz immediately dropped to his knees, striking his forehead on the bar rail on his way down. I now had his arm extended backward and upward, so that he was unable to struggle without subjecting himself to severe pain and the risk of a torn rotator cuff.

Ratz grimaced. "Let go of me, asshole, or—"

I responded by giving him a hard punch on the back of his head with my free hand, just to let him know I was serious.

"Oh, my God," Chandra cried out. "Will someone please call the police?"

"He is the police," Roy responded.

Keeping the joint-lock on Ratz's wrist, I slowly guided him to his feet, until he was leaning forward against the bar.

"Would you like to spend the evening down at the jailhouse?" I asked. "Or would you like to leave this bar quietly, return to your room, and stay there for the rest of the night? Those are your only two choices—jail or your room, comprende? Now, as your new best friend I urge you to pick door number two, so we can all get on with our nice, quiet evening." I twisted his arm a little to emphasize the word quiet.

Ratz agreed to go back to his room. His bravado seemed to be gone.

I slowly released his arm, and he stood, rubbing his shoulder. I didn't think he'd make another move, but I was ready for it.

"Can I have that cup of coffee first?" he asked. "I could really use some coffee."

I told him no. The last thing I wanted was a wide-awake drunk. Instead I asked Roy to bring a bottle of water.

Roy uncapped a bottle of La Croix and set it on the bar. I gave it to Ratz. His eyes were watery and bloodshot, but he already appeared to be less intoxicated. An adrenaline rush often has a sobering effect.

"Drink this," I ordered. "Then you're going to your room to sleep it off. And you'll stay in your room for the rest of the night, because if I find you anywhere else before tomorrow morning, I'll charge you with assault and drunk-and-disorderly, and you'll be staying at my jail instead of this inn. And trust me, you won't like the view at the jail. Are we straight?"

He nodded his understanding. I asked him what vehicle he was driving; he told me—a late-model black Ford Explorer. I explained that I or another officer would be checking the parking lot every half hour to insure he wasn't driving tonight. I'd given the same speech to other drunks at least a hundred times before. Sometimes it seemed all I ever did around the township was deal with drunks who liked to start bar fights.

As Greta consoled Chandra back at their table, I escorted Ratz outside and around to the front of the building. "What's your room number?" I asked. He told me it was 222 "over there" and pointed to L'Auberge, where most of the writers were staying. Navilio had added this building to the inn a few years ago, and I knew it had maybe four deluxe suites up above, plus another four downstairs, along with a meeting room. Ratz's suite was upstairs, but I figured he could get there by himself all right. I watched him meander over and use his key to let himself in through the building's outer door.

The door closed behind him, but I stood outside for a few minutes to make sure he was in for the night. I spotted his Explorer and jotted down the license plate number. The thought of a drunk like him careening around our country roads on a wintry night scared the hell out of me. Then I went back inside to the bar—not because I was convinced Ratz was in for the evening, but because my fingers and toes were getting as cold as the frozen waters of Lake Como.

My huckleberry friend, Dave Tedeski, once told me a little a story. It was something he'd co-opted from a Czech humorist, changing the storyline to fit a barroom. According to the Duke, every bar has three kinds of denizens. First, there are those who see a cocktail and want to drink it. Then there are those who see a cocktail and want to throw it in someone's face, except they never do. And finally, there are those who actually throw the cocktail. Mr. John Ratz, I was certain, belonged in the third group.

Chapter Nine

When I returned to the bar, Roy had a snifter of brandy waiting for me. "Thought you might need this, Chief," he said.

I took a sip. It was top shelf, and I lifted the glass toward Roy to show my appreciation. He nodded and went back to polishing some glassware.

Chandra and Greta were at their old places at the bar. Neither looked up, so I didn't speak to them as I took a seat a few spots away—near enough to overhear them if I tried, but not so close that I was right on top of them. Their heads were inclined together, and Greta was rubbing her friend's shoulder in a consoling gesture. A member of the restaurant's wait staff appeared and set an array of hors d'oeuvres in front of them. Comfort food, I thought.

Chandra stabbed a piece of flatbread into a dip and said something about how shocked and embarrassed she'd been that Ratz could act like "such a creep" in public. Evidently, he'd only been a creep in private before. She used the word traumatic another half a dozen times, then Greta told Chandra not to blame herself, because you can't be responsible for the actions of other people. "Sometimes," Greta added, "you just have to get out of the way before they self-destruct."

So true, I thought. As a cop, however, I seldom had that option.

I glanced toward the far end of the bar. The three literary types who remained had also ordered some appetizers, and they were continuing their conversation as if nothing had happened.

Eventually Chandra got up from her barstool and gave Greta

a quick kiss on the cheek. They hugged, then Chandra came over to me and thanked me for "saving" her, and announced she was going to turn in early. She had tears in her eyes as she left Kirsch's bar, slipping out the door that led toward the inn's lobby. A more chivalrous person might've asked if she needed someone to walk her to her room upstairs. I did not. She didn't have that far to go anyway.

Besides, Greta was alone again, and looking more enticing than ever. I moved to the barstool next to her. I hoped the commotion with Ratz hadn't killed my entire evening.

"Howdy, sheriff," Greta said, employing a touch of western drawl. "I guess you really are the law in these-here parts. Is your white horse tethered out front?"

"Just my Jeep, ma'am. But like I said, I'm the chief of police, not the sheriff. The sheriff has a bigger badge and he works for the county. I work for the township."

"Oh, that's right," she said, losing the drawl. "Chief. The nickname thing. What is your real name, anyway?"

"Seriously, everyone just calls me Chief."

"I see. Well, seriously, Chief, it's a good thing you were here tonight. It might have become very ugly if you weren't here to handle John Ratz."

"Oh, I don't know. I think my good friend Roy might've been capable of roping and hog-tying a man in my absence."

The two busboys standing in the restaurant doorway burst out in laughter at the obvious overstatement. Roy, the bartender, was much smaller than John Ratz, and he was known for his amiable temperament.

I eyed Greta's glass. "More wine?" I asked.

She hesitated, then said yes. "Thanks, I guess I am a little wired."

At the end of the bar, the three other members of her group were still engrossed in their conversation. The handsome dark-haired man in the turtleneck gave a hearty laugh, responding to the professorial man in the tweed jacket. Meanwhile, the dishwater blonde sipped a cocktail and appeared to be mesmerized by the professor. The two other men who'd been here earlier had already left the bar.

"The man in the jacket. Is that your leader, Professor Feri?"

Greta followed my gaze. "That's right," she said. "I don't think he was pleased with John Ratz's behavior."

"How can you tell?" I asked.

She laughed. "By his disdainful gaze. He did ask Chandra if she was all right while you were gone. But I don't think he cares to get in the middle. This is pretty awkward for everyone. I hope Professor Feri just asks John Ratz to leave."

I asked Greta to tell me more about Feri and the workshop. It was Ratz who interested me most, but I didn't want to focus on him too obviously.

Greta said most of the group had met three years ago, in a weekend writing class that Feri had conducted as a personal experiment. The workshop at the inn was like the classes, only more intensive. Participants would exchange drafts and give critiques in group sessions, and do a few writing exercises. Feri would also meet with each writer individually. The rest of the time each participant was free to focus on his or her own project, making the week a kind of writer's retreat. "None of us writes for a living, but we're all very serious about our work," Greta said.

Suddenly I was thirsty again. I ordered a "vodka rocks,"slightly dirty with two blue-cheese olives. Then I asked what Ratz was working on.

"As far as I know, it's a memoir," Greta said.

"You haven't read it?"

She shook her head. "Ratz is the only one here who is secretive about his work. He only shares his writing with Professor Feri. All I know is that he's supposedly writing about his years in the military, especially during the Gulf War. Maybe the writing is a kind of therapy. He obviously has a few unresolved issues."

Great, I thought. First Zubeck, now Ratz. All I needed was an unhinged postal worker to complete the set. I started dreading the week ahead. Then I reminded myself that while a lot of people have unresolved issues, they don't usually surface all at once. And in any case, those issues didn't have to ruin the rest of my evening.

"What about the trinity over there at the end of the bar?" I asked. "What are they working on?"

"Well, the man in the tweed jacket is Professor Feri, as you know. He's here to lead the workshop. We aren't reviewing his writing, of course, but for the past several years, he has been working on a massive historical novel about two brothers who are soldiers during the Hundred Years War. Feri is meticulous about the historical research. The brothers, however, are fictional."

"The Hundred Years War? Gee," I said sarcastically, "now that sounds like a bestseller."

"Don't be mean. Professor Feri might not ever finish his novel, much less publish it. But he is an excellent teacher. He has great insight, and I find our sessions extremely helpful."

I looked at Feri. His tweed coat was rumpled and his gray hair was thinning, but he still managed to exude an air of superiority as he peered over his wire-rim glasses. I hadn't even spoken to the man yet, and already I disliked him. I've always wondered why a guy like him has the ability to hold a woman under his spell.

Greta continued. "The woman next to the professor is his research assistant, Evelyn Durst. Evelyn isn't writing anything—at least, not at the moment. Her position here is simply to assist Feri."

I'll bet she assists him, I thought, and in several positions. Fortunately I didn't say it out loud.

"The other fellow," Greta continued, "the one in the black turtleneck—that's Emile Tavilion. He's an entrepreneur, a very interesting fellow. Apparently he has made a lot of money through his investments, especially real estate. He pursues writing mostly as a hobby. I've read his first fiction attempt, and I must say it's excellent. I was a little surprised. He doesn't act or speak like someone who would be interested in writing or in literature."

"In other words, you can't judge a book by its cover," I said.

Greta slapped me lightly on the arm and smiled. "Stop that."

I asked her what Tavilion's book was about.

"Cops, detectives, murder, intrigue—the things in your line of work."

"Sorry, ma'am. We don't have too many murders around these-here parts," I said, mimicking Greta's earlier western drawl.

Greta laughed. "I'm glad to hear it. Emile's current project is nonfiction, though. He's working on a how-to book about building investments and power. You won't believe what it's called." She waited for me to ask, but I didn't hazard a guess. She continued anyway.

"Emile is a huge Godfather fan—especially the novel, which of course goes into much more depth and detail about the Corleone family and their business arrangements than the movies do. The title of Emile's book is *How to Build Wealth and Power Using the Business Principles of Don Vito Corleone, the Godfather.*"

"It's a little long for a title," I said, "but it's a good one. I'm a Godfather fan myself. I'd probably buy a book like that—and I'd definitely pick it up off the shelf."

"Emile has been working very hard, and he thinks he can have the book finished by late spring. I've read several passages, and if you're a Godfather fan, you'll love it."

"What is Chandra Harper working on? I hope it's not one of those self-help books on dating and relationships." As soon as said it, I knew it was in bad taste. When it came to sarcasm and liquor and generally putting my foot in my mouth, I almost never knew when to quit. Luckily, Greta didn't seem too bothered by the remark; she just wrinkled her nose at me.

"Chandra's book is a cross between a memoir and a journal. She considers it a work of passion, or, in her own words, an obsession."

"Sounds interesting," I lied. I was pretty sure the word traumatic appeared a lot.

"Actually, it is—or at least, her reason for writing is interesting. Very interesting, in fact. Several years ago, her sister, Cassandra, died from botulism poisoning. Chandra believes it was a murder, not an accident, even though the police say there's no evidence of foul play. Chandra's book delves into her own investigation and how obsessed she has become with her sister's death." Greta sighed. "It's sad, really. She just can't let it rest."

"Not exactly light reading. Who does Chandra think murdered her sister?"

"Her sister's fiancé, a man named Torrence. He and Cassandra were living together in Minneapolis at the time of the murder—the alleged murder, anyway."

I considered making a joke about how bad relationships seemed to run in Chandra's family, but I kept it to myself. I didn't want to see Greta wrinkle her nose at me again.

"Chandra's suspicions are not completely groundless," Greta continued. "The fiancé did have the means to poison someone. I don't know where he is now, but then, he was a master chef and an instructor at a culinary institute. Chandra believes that he cultivated the botulism spores at his school, and then placed them in Cassandra's ahi tuna at a sushi bar where they often ate together."

"That's why I never eat raw fish," I said. "It's much too dangerous."

"You're terrible," Greta chided. "Chandra takes this all very seriously. Her theory is a little 'out there,' I admit, but it isn't impossible."

"Not impossible," I agreed. "But also not likely. Most famous poisoners were women. And I've never heard of a murder by sushi."

Greta acknowledged the joke with a little smile. "Chandra's book is not just about her sister's murder, though, or even about her efforts to solve it. She and Cassandra were twins. Most of the book describes how the death has affected Chandra's own life—her depression, her many infidelities, her inability to move forward in any kind of positive direction."

"You said infidelities. She's married?" It didn't surprise me, but it did put a slightly different spin on the Ratz affair.

Greta nodded. "That's another piece of the story, I guess. It's not exactly a marriage of convenience. More like a marriage of friendship."

"So, what you're suggesting is, either her husband looks the other way, or he tolerates the infidelities." For all I knew, Chandra was just getting back at her husband for his infidelities. Or maybe he was gay. I'd seen it all in this small town.

"I've probably said too much already," Greta answered. "It's their private business. Suffice it to say that Chandra's book is very sad. In a way, it reminds me of the writings by Virginia Woolf and Sylvia Plath."

I thought Virginia Woolf was a movie about a bad marriage, and the Christian Brothers hadn't put Sylvia Plath on my high school reading list, but I nodded sagely—I didn't want Greta to think I was uncouth or uneducated. Then I switched the subject.

"So, you're working on a book about the French Country Inn and its gangster history. Would you mind if I read some of it?"

"No, that would be fine," she said. "Maybe we can make arrangements later. I'll pick out a chapter for you."

The conversation was going pretty well, I thought, but I realized I had to shift the focus away from death and Chandra Harper. My dirty martini had begun to give me dirty thoughts. I was quite enamored with Greta, the way she spoke and carried herself, not to mention the suppleness of her body, which was obvious to me even beneath her winter clothes. She wore slim, dark jeans tucked in black boots, and a red sweater that hugged her curves and matched her full red lips. I noticed the way her eyelashes brushed her skin when she lowered them, and I saw that the pupils in her brown eyes were a little dilated, confirming her interest in me. But maybe it was just wishful thinking. Or the dim light.

I often told myself the reason I never dated was because I didn't want to be the subject of small-town gossip. The fact was, I just wasn't very good at dates, or hookups, or whatever the term-du-jour was. Also I hadn't felt any strong romantic yearnings in a long time. Sure, there were those rare occasions when I spotted Officer Madden out of uniform—meaning, she was wearing her civvies at the grocery store. Annie Madden was the one female who could still arouse me just by standing next to me and talking about nothing but broccoli and cantaloupe.

But now there was Greta. And unlike Officer Madden, Greta was not off-limits.

I decided to coax Greta away from the bar to an intimate corner where I could whisper sweet nothings into her ear. So, I lied and said the cigarette smoke was bothering me, and asked if we could move to a table near the fireplace. We carried our cocktails the several yards to the inglenook. It was cozy enough for me to make advances toward Greta, yet far enough away from the prying ears of the bartender.

All systems go, I thought.

Then Chandra Harper came back into the room. I would not have been more disappointed if the duo of Kirsch and Frankel had returned to show off their new dance moves.

Chapter Ten

While she was back at her room, Chandra Harper had changed into wedge-heeled slippers and a pink velour lounge suit that looked like a cross between pajamas and expensive exercise gear. As soon as she spotted Greta, Ms. Harper made a beeline for our fireside table and helped herself to the seat between us.

To my surprise, Chandra was comfortable appearing in public without makeup. Her face was scrubbed clean, with no trace of the heavy foundation she'd worn earlier. Her blue eyes were still red from crying, but she had nice skin; I only saw one little blemish on her lower cheek, which was covered by a dab of Clearasil. Her loose blonde curls were still damp around the edges. She was much more attractive this way, kind of like a farm-fresh version of Marilyn Monroe. Tedeski called it the "granola look": no makeup, pink cheeks, an outdoorsy feel. Of course, the pink velour and Chandra's personality didn't fit the "outdoorsy" part, and a camping or fishing trip with Chandra Harper would be completely out of the question. It'd be too "traumatic," especially for the guy.

"I just couldn't sleep, not a wink," Chandra was saying, as if whatever Greta and I were talking about was completely unimportant. Everything always revolved around Chandra, even in the best of times. She lived in her own Chandra Universe.

"I took a hot bath in the whirlpool," she continued. "Then I made some notes for tomorrow's session, and I started reading a new book. I even made some chamomile tea. Nothing, absolutely nothing worked."

"What are you reading?" I inquired. I hoped her answer would not be "a little something" by Sylvia Plath. I was surprised when she said *The Ox-Bow Incident* by Walter Van Tilburg Clark.

As it happened, I knew the title because I'd seen the movie. "I didn't have you pegged as a reader of Westerns," I said. "It seems a little lowbrow for your taste."

She frowned at me. "Have you read it, then?"

"No, but I do know—"

"I didn't think so," Chandra interrupted, "because it isn't lowbrow at all. It is a complex morality tale." She proceeded to explain that the book was recommended by none other than Richard M. Daley, the mayor of Chicago. It seems "Da Mayor" has a reading program in which he recommends books to high school students and the hoi polloi in order to promote literacy. It was like Oprah's book club, but with a smaller audience. Coincidentally, last month "Hiz Honor" chose *To Kill a Mockingbird*, one of Oprah's all-time favorites.

I hadn't read that book either, although I'd seen the movie with Gregory Peck. I didn't say so, however. Even if I'd wanted to, I could not have interrupted Chandra.

"You really should check out the mayor's list and do some reading yourself," she concluded. "You might actually enjoy it."

Greta asked me what I had meant to say about *The Ox-Bow Incident*.

"Nothing important," I said. "Only that I know the story because I've seen the movie several times. It's a classic. And I didn't mean to imply the novel itself was lowbrow, Chandra. I just assumed you might consider it lowbrow."

"Then perhaps you shouldn't make assumptions," Chandra said.

"Professional hazard," I countered. "We cops get paid to make assumptions. And not to bring up a sore point, but my assumptions about your friend John Ratz and his propensities while drinking were right on the money, honey."

I regretted the remark immediately. I was getting defensive, and I realized that I would score no points with Greta by sparring with Chandra Harper.

"Well," said Chandra haughtily, "whatever assumptions you might have made about me, I can assure you that I have a very broad spectrum of interests, and not only in reading."

"I'm sure you do." I sipped my vodka and took a bite from the blue-cheese-stuffed olive as if it were a cyanide pill. I had a feeling I was not going to enjoy the rest of the evening. I strongly dislike pretentious people, and so far, everyone currently in the bar except Greta and the bartender, Roy, had an air of pretension about them. It was thicker than the halo of smoke that usually surrounded Ron Frankel.

Chandra began to prattle on about *The Ox-Bow Incident*. Something about her cadence reminded me of a waiter who had once worked at Kirsch's restaurant. He'd adopted a manner of speaking that suggested he had spent years in Buckingham Palace teaching the King's English to royal offspring. The waiter was from Ottumwa, Iowa.

"Do you read anything?" Chandra asked. "Or do you just watch movies?"

I took a bigger sip of the vodka, then answered, "I read some, but yes, I do prefer movies. You might say movies are my preferred source of entertainment and knowledge."

"Oh, my God," Chandra said in a stunned manner, pressing her palm to her pink velour bosom. "Not another person who doesn't read. You know, Mark Twain said a person who knows how to read, and who chooses not to, is just as ignorant as a person who is illiterate."

I thought about Tedeski's list of barflies. At this point, I was type two—the person who wanted to throw his drink in someone's face, but would not. It'd be a waste of good vodka.

Greta sat silently, suppressing a smile. To my annoyance, she seemed to be enjoying her friend's attempts to make a jackass out of me. No doubt she also wanted to see how I would extricate myself from the situation. Part of me wished John Ratz would just return and slap Chandra Harper senseless.

"I didn't say I don't read at all," I answered. "I'm just not an avid reader. I don't know about you, but frankly, I don't have a lot of free time. As for movies being a source of knowledge, I do think I've gleaned a lot of knowledge from films as an adult."

"So, you watch adult films?" Chandra said coyly.

"Very funny. No, I don't mean porn or trashy B-grade movies—I mean the great movies, such as *Patton*, *Schindler's List*, and *To Kill a Mockingbird*, or even your morality play, *The Ox-Bow Incident*. I also enjoy documentaries. I guess I'm just the type of person who learns more by watching and hearing than by staring at words on a page."

I thought I had made my point quite articulately.

"Oh, don't get your boxers in a twist," Chandra said. "I didn't mean to assault your male ego. It's obviously fragile."

I felt my face growing red, but before I could retort, Greta decided to rescue me. "I love a good movie myself," she interjected. "But Chandra really is one of the best-read people I know. And she has an amazing ability to remember details like names and dates and places—she has almost total recall. Go ahead, Chief, try to stump her."

"No, thanks," I said quickly. "I concede her superiority. I've already admitted that I don't read a lot of books."

"Oh, come on," Greta said. "You watch movies that are based on books. Name any character from any book turned into a movie. I'll bet Chandra can tell you the book's title—and the author, too." When I hesitated, she urged, "Come on, Chief, we could use a bit of fun."

This was not the sort of fun I had in mind, but I saw that I had little choice in the matter, other than to quit the game and leave the field entirely. "Are old movies okay?" I asked.

"Of course," Chandra said with smug confidence. "Old or new, it doesn't matter."

I thought for a moment. "Tom Joad," I said.

Chandra scoffed. "My good sir, I will not even dignify that with an answer. You simply must make it more difficult. And make sure the next character's name is not Holden Caulfield."

"Actually, they never made a movie from *Catcher in the Rye*," I countered. "J.D. Salinger never sold the movie rights. He said Holden wouldn't like it."

Greta laughed. "You may have met your match after all, Chandra."

Even Chandra smiled. "We'll see about that. Okay, next name," she prompted.

"Wolf Larsen."

"*The Sea-Wolf* by Jack London," Chandra answered quickly. "Great book, great movie. You see? I watch movies, too, and I still find time to read."

"Chauncey Gardiner."

"*Being There* by Jerzy Kosinski."

I thought for a moment. "Colonel Cathcart."

"*Catch-22*, Joseph Heller. Come on now, give me a challenge."

I paused, searching for another good character. "Tom Wingo."

"*The Prince of Tides*, author Pat Conroy."

"Carmen Sternwood."

"Sternwood, hmm, Sternwood . . .," she murmured.

I thought I finally had her beat, but then she answered, "Oh yes, Carmen Sternwood. She was the daughter of General Guy Sternwood in *The Big Sleep* by Raymond Chandler."

"Very good, Chandra," I said, genuinely impressed. I hadn't expected her to know Raymond Chandler. "Okay, this is my last challenge. Walter Neff."

Chandra raised her brows. "You know, that one is difficult.

But . . . because I have read the book, and I have also seen the movie, I have the correct answer. It's *Double Indemnity* by James M. Cain. In the movie, the character's name is Walter Neff, but in the book, it's Walter Huff. Did you know that Raymond Chandler wrote the screenplay, too? And that the movie *Body Heat* with Kathleen Turner and William Hurt was essentially a remake?"

"I did not," I answered truthfully. I was warming a bit toward Chandra, but only just a little bit. "Greta was right—your recall for details is very impressive."

"Thank you," Chandra replied, "but it's really not much of a talent. I'm just wired right when it comes to recalling names and other trivia."

"She can also do the opposite," Greta said. "If you name a book's title, she can rattle off the cast of characters." She turned to Chandra. "Didn't you tell me once that my name is a character in something? Greta Olsen?"

"*Murder on the Orient Express*," Chandra responded. "The character's name has a different spelling, though."

For a moment, it seemed we'd hit an awkward lull in the conversation, but then Greta broke the silence. "Judging by your choices, Chief, you prefer old movies to new ones. Is that right?"

"It is. I think old movies are like old houses," I said. "They have better details and a lot more character. There are exceptions, but it seems movies are all action these days. Or they're filled with screaming teenagers and toilet jokes. They just don't have the same level of plot or dialogue or inventiveness as the old classics," I said.

Greta nodded in agreement.

Chandra remained silent, which was unusual for her. She was looking off into space and had become lost in thought. She sighed heavily, then asked, "So, Chief, what type of drink do you think I should have if I really need a good, deep sleep?"

"Have you considered hemlock?" I asked.

We all laughed, even Chandra. "Actually," I continued, "sambuca is the drink that knocks me out—that should work, as long as you don't have more than two. Have you ever tried it?"

Both ladies said no, but they'd like to.

I called over to Roy and told him to fix us up with three sambucas and three decaf cappuccinos. When he brought the elixirs to the table, I warned him that two each would be our limit.

"Okay, Chief," he said with a wink. Then he returned to the back of the bar.

Chandra eyed her drink. "What's floating in here?" she asked.

"Finally, a subject I am comfortable with," I said. "Those are toasted coffee beans—exactly three beans, if it's done right. Some people say they represent the Father, the Son, and the Holy Ghost. Or, they just enhance the flavor. The Italians call them tre mosca, which means 'three flies.' They're supposed to bring good luck."

"Hmm," Greta said. "I can't say that flies sound very appetizing, but we could all use some good luck."

"I think it's charming," Chandra said. She took a sip and considered it. "It's quite strong, but it's very good. What is the flavor, licorice?"

I nodded. "Pretty close. It's anise."

Greta sampled a coffee bean and smiled.

Chandra took several more dainty sips, then asked me a question that made me wish I knew more about sambuca. "I don't suppose you do any writing, do you, Chief?"

"Why, yes, I am a prolific writer," I stated proudly. Both women had a look of disbelief, which quickly changed to intrigue. "Last summer," I continued, "within a thirty-day period, I wrote fifty-five parking tickets and twenty-seven speeding tickets."

Both women groaned in unison, and then the moment I had been waiting for arrived. Chandra said she was tired and left abruptly.

Unfortunately, Greta said that she too was now falling asleep. She rose and asked Roy for her bar tab.

I told her tonight was my treat, but Roy said he thought Kirsch would want to pick up all my cocktails for the evening, considering the trouble with John Ratz. I felt a bit like Captain Renault in the movie *Casablanca*, easily bought and short on scruples, but I did not refuse the offer.

I thought about asking Greta if I could walk her to her room. I was worried it might be too forward. Luckily for me, Greta suggested it herself while I laboriously pondered the issue. "I hope you won't mind," she said, "but I'm afraid that our Mr. Ratz could still be lurking around."

"I don't mind at all," I answered.

We headed toward the lobby together. When we reached the front desk, I glanced up the stairs toward the gallery, fearing Chandra Harper might come flying out of her room to tell me her hors d'oeuvres had been tainted with botulism, or maybe challenge me to another word game. All was quiet.

Greta hadn't worn a coat, so I put mine around her shoulders as we headed outside. A heavy snow had begun to fall, and the wind was biting. Ratz's car was still parked among the others, frosted white. L'Auberge wasn't far, but we scurried to the door of the building.

"Oh, God, it's bitter out there!" Greta exclaimed, shaking the snow off my coat in the hallway. She handed it back to me. "Now I'm wide awake again."

"Ratz said he was upstairs, in 222. Is that right?" I asked.

"I think so," she answered. "He's upstairs, anyway. Second door on the right."

I asked her to wait for me, because I'd come back and check her room, which was on the ground floor at the far end of the hall. Then I climbed the staircase, leaping two steps at a time. I approached Ratz's door. It had a blue ceramic plaque with a painted goose and the number 222 on it. As quietly as possible, I pressed my ear to the cream-painted wood next to the goose. I could hear the faint din of a television. I could also hear someone snoring. It seemed Ratz was sleeping off his drunkenness, just as I'd instructed. I was not totally convinced he was in for the entire night, however, so later, I would radio my patrolman and have him make periodic checks on the inn. In light of Zubeck's earlier threats, it was a good idea anyway.

When I returned downstairs, Greta was standing in the open doorway of her suite. Apparently, she hadn't waited for me. The lights in the room were dimmed, and flames jumped in the gas fireplace behind her. I had the sudden urge to take her in my arms and deliver a kiss that would make her knees buckle and her panties moist.

Instead, I heard myself ask if she would like to have dinner with me at Kirsch's tomorrow night. She accepted, and I told her I would pick her up at seven o'clock.

"I'll be ready at eight," she replied. Then she stretched on her toes and gave me an unexpected schoolgirl kiss on the cheek. I thought it was a kiss-off until she said, "Would you mind checking my room after all? To be honest, I am still a little frightened by John Ratz."

I was pretty certain he was upstairs asleep, but I made a quick tour of the suite—it didn't hurt to make sure the French doors facing the lakefront were locked. I was having trouble deciphering the signals Greta was giving me. I asked if she wanted me to keep her company for a while, until she felt more relaxed and sleepy. "Strictly in a professional manner," I said. "After all, I am the chief of police and a trained professional."

She smiled. "Okay," she said, "as long as it is strictly professional. And only until I fall asleep. Then you can let yourself out." She gave me a strong stare that convinced me I would not be helping her get relaxed in the way I'd hoped; instead I was to be her guardian only, watching over her until she slept. And then, I would let myself out. Never mind that it would be safer if I left now, so she could just throw the deadbolt and attach the door chain behind me before she went to sleep.

I was disappointed and a little confused by this turn of events, but I've never been very good at understanding women. I'd been asked to do things in a professional capacity before, some of which even involved handcuffs, but this "watch me until I sleep" situation was completely new. Maybe it was just Greta's way of vetting me. Maybe it just wasn't the right moment. We had, after all, set a date for tomorrow.

I sat in the cushioned wicker chair by the fire and picked up a newspaper while she went into the bathroom and readied herself for bed. It was too dim to read, so I fantasized about what she might be wearing, or not wearing, when she stepped out. The door opened, and I saw that she'd donned a pair of white silk pajamas. On Greta, they looked quite sexy.

She quickly crossed the room, climbed into bed, and turned off the bedside lamp. Then she snuggled deep under the covers and hugged a pillow, turning her back to me. "Good night, Chief," she said. "Thanks for being so thoughtful. I'll see you tomorrow night for dinner."

"Good night, Greta."

It was a little like an episode of *The Waltons*. At least Chandra and Ratz and the rest of the writing group weren't chiming in like all the Walton kids.

I sat watching the dark-haired goddess, hoping for a whispered invitation that never came. Eventually I quit hoping, and her breathing became deep and even. I clicked off the gas fireplace, then quietly slipped out the door, making sure that it locked behind me.

Chapter Eleven

After I slipped out of Greta's suite, I walked down to the frozen shore of Como Lake. The combination of cold, snow, and wind had whipped its ice-covered surface into a work of art that only God and nature could have rendered.

The snowflakes stung as they struck my face, but the cold was a welcome antidote to the heat I'd felt in Greta's room, picturing what was under her silk pajamas. "If God is the sculptor of women," I mused aloud, "then Greta Olsen has the ultimate body of evidence."

It was nearing midnight, but I stood motionless for a few minutes, taking in the scene. Mesmerizing dunes of snow slowly formed and shifted on the ice before me. The twinkling porch lights of the condos and cottages across the lake were barely visible, flitting in and out of view like tiny stars through the veil of falling snow. The real stars were invisible in the gloom above.

Just as I was about to leave, I spied something moving on the lake, maybe a hundred yards from where I stood. I thought it might be a deer—wild animals often crossed the frozen expanse at night. Standing silent and still, I listened to the wind and peered through the shadows until the specter on the lake took a definite shape.

This was no deer. It was a man, alternately crouching and lumbering as he slowly made his way east. He was following the course of the shoreline, walking about sixty feet out from land's edge. The veil of snow made him appear ghostly. Like the lights across the lake, he was in soft focus, coming in and out view. At times I wondered whether I was actually seeing him at all.

He appeared to have no pole, no bucket—nothing to suggest that he was an ice fisherman coming in or heading out for the night. Nor did his lumbering gate suggest to me that he was drunk or confused. I decided that any nutcase who was skulking around the lake in the wee hours of a night like this was up to no good. Except for me, of course, but I wasn't skulking.

Could it be Ratz? I wondered. Maybe he'd awakened and decided to pay a little visit to Chandra, rekindle the romance through charm or force. But why would he walk on the lake? The only reason was to avoid being seen or heard as he passed by the lakeside rooms.

Ben Zubeck seemed the more likely candidate if trouble was afoot. Delenda est Carthago, he'd said. Carthage must be destroyed. Maybe Zubeck's vendetta against Navilio had begun, and the inn was the target. Of course, Zubeck might not know that Navilio had left town, so he might imagine that he could destroy his enemy as well as the inn. I was relieved to see the figure wasn't carrying a can of gasoline or a Molotov cocktail.

The interloper did not see me as I watched him continue to make his way east. Every few steps, he would pause, then look back toward the inn. I followed his gaze. It seemed to lead toward the building called L'Auberge, where the writer's group was staying. If I didn't move soon, I realized, I might lose him in the night.

I took a few steps in his direction. He saw me then and began to run. My hunter's instinct kicked in and I started after him, heart and feet pumping fast. Despite wearing leather-soled dress shoes, I gained on my quarry. I was almost upon him when he suddenly changed directions, like a flanker on a football field avoiding a tackle by a defensive back. I lunged and barely grazed his short, heavy coat with my outstretched hand. Then I fell so fast and so hard that my forehead slammed into the ice before I could break the fall. I landed face down with one arm crumpled beneath my torso and the other still stretched overhead.

The man I was chasing must've stopped and reversed direction, because as soon as I started to rise, I felt a swift stomp in the middle of my back, slamming me back into the ice. Then, just for good measure, I received a hard kick in the head. It came so quickly that I thought maybe there were two attackers instead of one. I saw black and gray, and when my eyes cleared and I lifted my aching head from the ice, I saw my one lone attacker running west, disappearing into the dark and snowy night.

Even if I had wanted to give chase again, there was no way I would possibly catch this guy. I breathed heavily and rested on the lake's surface, pulling my arm out from underneath me. My elbow throbbed almost as badly as my head. Slowly, I rolled to my knees and tried to rise. I immediately felt dizzy and nauseated, so I lay back down for a moment, using a small dune of snow as my pillow.

I tried to remember any pertinent details about the man who'd assaulted me. He'd seemed a little shorter than I was, but not by much. He also wore dark, heavy winter gear from head to toe. I was pretty sure he had been wearing a ski mask. It might have been Zubeck, I reasoned, though the person I'd been chasing was pretty nimble. Maybe I just didn't want to admit that I'd been outrun by a man at least twenty years my senior. No doubt his heavy boots provided far better traction than my dress shoes. Still, I vowed to get in better shape.

After several minutes of rest, I moved to my knees again. I took it very slowly. I still felt dizzy and nauseated, and this was not a good place to puke and black out. I would quickly become a frozen and unsavory Popsicle, or worse yet, get covered with snow and become a speed bump for a passing snowmobile. It would have been nice to see a Saint Bernard with a cask of brandy coming to my rescue right about then. Maybe Dawg would come instead. That reminded me: I had to get home to let him out.

I touched my sore temple and forehead; they were both tender, but there was no blood. I looked around to see if there were any objects left behind atop the ice and snow, any footprints, any clues. There was nothing. The wind and snow had already begun to obscure whatever footprints remained . . . except for one faint impression. The boot that had made it seemed at least two sizes larger than my own. No wonder my head hurt. I'd been kicked by Bigfoot.

I crouched down to pick up a handful of icy snow to apply to my aching temple. As luck would have it, I picked up something else as well: a shard of something hard, about two inches long. It looked like a piece of white plastic. I held the object with my fingertips. I had no idea what it was. It could've been left by the perpetrator. Or it could've just been some fishing detritus that'd been sitting there already. Whatever it was, I tucked it into the pocket of my coat so I could examine it more closely later.

Cold and still dazed, I headed for home, and to the bottle of vodka that would help assuage my bruised ego along with my forehead. New plans for tomorrow were taking shape. First, I'd treat myself to a morning-after breakfast at Muddy's tavern. And then I would pay a visit to Ben Zubeck and John Ratz and see what size shoes each of them wore.

Chapter Twelve

It was a grim morning. I awoke with a headache that I wished I could blame entirely on the large foot that had introduced itself to my temple last night, but I suspected at least half the problem came from the seductress beside me. I wished with all my heart it was Greta sitting there next to my bed. I closed my eyes, picturing her red lips and her dark, shining hair, her lithe body wearing nothing but a smile as she slipped between the sheets on my bed and joined me. Was she truly as perfect and radiant as I'd imagined, or had the liquor played games with my memory?

When I opened my bleary eyes again, they were greeted only by the bottle of pale Polish vodka that stood on my mahogany bedside table. It was the same bottle of vodka that I'd rendezvoused with last night after I got home, feeling sad, lonely, and literally beaten down. The bottle was still staring at me and I stared back. The black bottle cap rested askew atop her long glass neck. The silhouette suggested a Frenchwoman wearing a beret. The top right corner of the label was wet and sweaty, and the label drooped down over itself, exposing the thin opaque veneer of its undergarment. The woman dared me to suck a little more nourishment.

Last night had ended just as many nights had ended recently. I'd used the vodka as a substitute for everything missing in my life, and at the top of that list was an honest relationship, someone to care for again, someone who actually knew and cared for me in return. I might have found quiet in this little corner of Wisconsin, but I hadn't found peace of mind.

The bottle of vodka continued to bait me with its haughty, insolent smirk. It wasn't prancing and strutting like a peacock to draw attention. It didn't have to—it understood the control it had over my life, knew its power to fuel my self-loathing and demented thoughts. I felt like the ventriloquist who trades insults with his wooden alter-ego, long after the show has ended and the audience has left the theater.

I knew I needed a better companion. I hoped it might be Greta. I closed my eyes and pictured her again, and imagined how I might see her tonight. Then I heard a groan and opened my eyes to see Dawg's face, drooling on the edge of the bed. He pawed at my arm, indicating his need to go outside to relieve himself. "At least I have you, boy," I said. "And sometimes, I even like you more than the vodka."

He barked impatiently, unappreciative of the compliment. I got up and opened the door and watched him trot down the steps. Then I shut the door behind him and headed for the shower while the coffee started brewing.

Dawg has simple needs and simple habits, and I knew what would happen next. I had followed him on his favorite morning jaunt so many times that I knew exactly what he would do and where he would go. First, he would lift his hind leg on the frozen red-twig dogwood in the backyard, even though he had been reprimanded time and again not to do so. Then he'd look over his shoulder. If I wasn't standing there to call him back inside, he'd assume it was a "Muddy's day" and head pell-mell down Sylvan Drive. At Grimley Park, he'd linger at the water fountain. Had it been summer, he would have been bedazzled by the clear water that poured from the mouth of the lion statue, and sometimes he might jump into the shallow turquoise pool below. Today he'd lick any icicles that had formed on the lion's paws, and then, after a brief survey of the park, he would move on to the dormant azalea bushes that formed a semicircle around the children's playground. Once there he would take a sniff or two, then pee again, lifting his leg as high as he could to impress the next canine visitor. Then he would chase a rabbit into a thicket of red barberry bushes or send a gray squirrel clambering up one of the towering old oaks. After that, he'd cross the street and mosey downhill toward the lake, where he hoped to harass a few ducks and geese along the shore. The last vestiges of open water were long gone in January, however, so there would be no waterfowl, and he'd hurry on, heading west to the tavern called Muddy's on the Lake.

On busy days, he'd simply sit in front of the tavern door until he could follow a patron inside. If he had to wait more than a few minutes, however, he would bellow for attention. Upon seeing him, the bartender would take a half-pound patty of ground sirloin out of the stainless-steel refrigerator under the back bar, and put the piece of meat into a red plastic lunch basket layered with wax paper. It looked just like the burger-and-fries basket the other patrons got, except for the contents.

The entire adventure, including the inhalation of his red-meat breakfast, would take Dawg about thirty-five minutes, tops. During that time, I'd down one cup of coffee, brush my teeth while taking a cold shower, and dress. Then I'd walk the half-mile or so to the tavern, where I would join my trusted best friend and have my own favorite Muddy's breakfast: a stalk of celery planted in a Bloody Mary with a side of three green olives skewered on a yellow plastic toothpick.

It was the best and bloodiest Mary on the lake, made with tomato juice, Mr. & Mrs. T's mix, freshly ground horseradish root, Worcestershire sauce, lime juice, a dash of angostura bitters, a wedge of lemon, an ounce of Aquavit, and a double shot of Smirnoff's vodka. Sometimes the concoction would be ready and waiting for me. Not this morning. Instead, Gus nodded from behind the bar and presented me with a tab that already showed a $5.95 charge for the dog's sirloin burger.

"Hey, shouldn't I get some sort of a discount?' I asked. "I mean, you didn't include the bun, the fries, or the condiments. Dawg only eats the meat, and it's not even cooked. In fact there's no labor cost to you at all—it's out of the fridge, into the basket, and onto the floor. Try that with any other customer."

"Yeah, yeah," Gus replied. "Haven't we had this conversation before? I'll pass your comments on to the owner the next time he's in. Meanwhile I'll put an extra stalk of celery in your breakfast."

He started making the Bloody Mary. Both Gus and I knew the complaint about the bill wouldn't go any further. Gus Baldwin was the sole proprietor of Muddy's on the Lake.

My friend glanced up from his work. "Does that hurt?" he asked, pointing at my forehead. I'd already seen it in the bathroom mirror, of course. The bluish lump on my temple wasn't bad, but it was hard to miss, even though half of it was hidden in my hairline.

I realized Gus wanted me to say no just so he could use the age-old retort about how it killed him to look at me, so I beat him to the punch line. "Not as much as it hurts to look at your ugly mug."

Gus chuckled. "Well, what happened? Finally work up the nerve to kiss some dame?"

"I cut myself shaving," I said. A bruise on my head wasn't a common occurrence, but I wasn't about to describe last night's events. It was too damned embarrassing.

Gus mumbled under his breath, but he didn't press the issue, as I volunteered no further information. Instead he finished the Bloody Mary, as any good bartender would.

I looked around. So far, Dawg and I were the only customers on this weekday morning. Gus had once boasted that Muddy's was the oldest saloon in the area. Judging from the wear and tear on the furnishings, the worn paint on the window mullions, and the striated grooves on the oak foot rail, caused by the persistent rubbing of patrons' shoes, that claim was probably true. In summer, Muddy's was a busy watering hole—half filled with locals, half filled with well-heeled tourists.

The decor played up the age and history. On the north wall, there was a gallery of portraits, all men and women of literary renown. To the best of my knowledge, none of them had ever actually visited the bar. Gus hadn't labeled the photographs, so his customers viewed it as a game to name them.

I'd learned them all over the last several years. Papa Hemingway posed in a display of macho affectation, next to a portrait of William Faulkner, whose craggy, creviced face reflected his alcoholism. Jack Kerouac, Eugene O'Neill, and Emily Dickinson were on display as well, along with James Joyce and Henry James.

Above the old-style jukebox was a black-and-white photograph of an attractive man and woman. He was standing in a jaunty position, wearing knickers and a cardigan, with wavy, slicked-back hair. She was pregnant and seated with her hands folded on her round belly, with a sweater draped over her shoulder. Her hair was a short wavy bob, in the style of the Jazz Age. The identities of this handsome pair had remained a mystery until a student from Aurora University supplied the names. It was F. Scott Fitzgerald and his wife, Zelda. Later I'd heard that Zelda suffered from either schizophrenia or bipolar disorder, which made her behavior generally erratic. Scott, of course, was well known for his drinking. Both would've fit right in with the cast of characters who frequented this lakeside establishment.

On the south side of the building were photographs of Chicago gangsters from the Roaring Twenties. Like other Chicagoans, they'd come to southeastern Wisconsin to escape the city heat—except their idea of "heat" was a little different. Gus claimed that Muddy's had been a speakeasy during Prohibition. Gangster stories swirled around nearly every old bar in central and southern Wisconsin, so I'd never paid much attention before. Now I wondered whether Greta had stopped in here during her research and whether she knew which stories were true.

Two of the ebony-framed photographs featured Alphonse Capone. The first showed him as the kingpin of the Chicago underworld. The second had been taken after his release from Alcatraz prison, when he was a dispirited, syphilis-ridden ex-gangster. There were also sepia-tone portraits of George "Bugs" Moran and John Dillinger. Baby Face Nelson was pictured with his arm stretched around his favorite moll. The gallery pictured black elongated limousines from an era long past: Hudsons, Packards, and an occasional Duesenberg parked beside buildings which, like the gangsters, were undoubtedly all gone now.

Gus had the sense to put the bloodiest photo at the back of the room, near the walk-in beer cooler and the cigarette machine, so it'd be hidden from any child who wandered in with an adult. It was a two-by three-foot blow-up of the actual death scene of the Saint Valentine's Day Massacre, which had occurred on February 14, 1929. Five crumpled, bullet-ridden bodies—all members of Bugs Moran's gang—lay on the floor in dark puddles of blood. The adjacent wall was peppered with brain matter and viscid material. The men had been standing there before Capone's hit men had opened up with their tommy guns. Happy Valentine's Day, boys.

The décor created a weird personality split. The tradesmen, blue-collar workers, and all the outdoorsmen who were partial to cigarettes and cold beer preferred to inhabit the south side, along with the gangsters. The north side, where the eyes of the literary elite looked on, drew the visiting dilettantes, yuppies, and Gen-X-ers, as well as the conspicuously consumptive baby boomers who owned condos and homes in the area, which often ran to seven figures. Muddy's was also a favorite getaway for Ron Frankel, Jim Kirchschlager, and many others who had real names but were known by some other moniker such as Hump or Clam. Other than a good-mannered hello or goodbye, the two groups rarely interacted. When they did, it usually involved a game of pool or a fistfight, with the latter fueled by the mercurial combination of alcohol and available women, or alcohol and opposing pro football teams.

I looked at the photos of the gangsters again and thought about Greta's research on the French Country Inn. She probably didn't need any help, but I figured it couldn't hurt to lend a hand, maybe ingratiate myself. "Say, Gus. Who do you know around here who might know all about the gangster history of the area?"

Gus wiped a glass. "Let's see. There's Norman over at the Bayside in Williams Bay . . . And there's an old-timer who comes here to the bar who knows a tale or two. Why do you ask?"

"I've got a friend who's working on a book."

"Really? You've got a friend?"

"Very funny."

"I'll give it some thought, see who I come up with . . . You know, there was a lady here a couple summers ago, asking the same kind of questions. Dark hair, tight red sundress. A real looker. I don't remember every good-looking broad who comes in here, but this one was something special, a real femme fatale. Every guy twenty-five and up was staring at her, and some of the younger ones, too."

I didn't respond—I didn't want to discuss Greta with Gus, assuming Greta was actually the woman Gus was referring to. In any case, my love life, such as it was, was off-limits.

"Want another?" asked Gus from behind the bar. Apart from the day cook, Gus was the only man working today.

"Yeah, gimme one more. But add a little extra horse to the equation this time, will you? I still need to wake up." I hoped the horseradish root would work like smelling salts and lift the soporific haze that I still felt from last night's Polish vodka. I didn't think this morning's vodka would make a difference one way or the other.

"Not working today, Chief?" Gus asked. It was an idle question; I doubted that Gus cared either way. He placed the second cocktail on the bar in front of me, and I took a small sip, then downed a quarter of the elixir in one gulp.

"Nope, I don't work Mondays, my man. I keep my schedule clear just in case I've had a bad weekend."

"Today's Tuesday," Gus informed me.

"Damn it," I said. I looked at the wall clock. It was almost ten, time for the weekly staff meeting to begin. "Are you sure?"

"Yeah, I'm sure. It's Tuesday. Maybe you should put the dog in charge of your agenda—he knows we're closed on Mondays." Gus tried to rub the remark under my skin, but I was too distracted, and it beaded off me like water on an unctuous duck.

"Ah, crap. Put the Mary in a plastic cup—I gotta go." I checked my face in the nearest mirror, which was part of a Rolling Rock beer plaque. Directly above it was a portrait of Oscar Wilde, foppishly dressed. I looked bad by comparison. I ran my fingers through my hair and wiped my lips with my sleeve, then fled out the door, drink in hand and dog in tow. I hurried back home as fast as I could so I could let Dawg in the house and retrieve my car.

By the time I'd reached the Jeep, most of the Bloody Mary was spread behind me like a broken trail, with the end of it dribbling up my pants leg. I put the plastic cup between my lips and clamped down with my teeth, holding the cup in place while I fumbled with my keys. I started the car, then steered with one hand and reached behind the seat with the other in order to pull my briefcase to the front. I opened it and spotted my yellow pad, which held the notes from last week's meeting. I breathed a sigh of relief, then tilted my head backward with the cup still clenched in my mouth and sucked the last of the Bloody Mary through my teeth to my throat, the way a whale sieved plankton through its mouth and down its gullet.

Hair of the dog, I thought. Then I realized I was literally drinking and driving. I hoped that particular dog wouldn't come back and bite me in the ass.

"Damn it, damn it," I said over and over again, in unison with the turning of wheels as I drove to the stationhouse. I vowed once again that I would drink far less and become much more organized and punctual. I parked the car, grabbed my briefcase, and deposited the cup into a waste receptacle, then rushed to the second-floor meeting room. My hand searched my pockets for a breath mint as I entered through the open door. I couldn't find a mint.

Bert Burr sat waiting in the room. No one else was there yet.

"Hiya, Chief," Bert said.

"Where is everyone?" I asked, trying not to huff from the race I'd just run. "Did they all leave already?"

"No, Chief. Everyone is still coming. I'm just the first one here. We know you're always late for Tuesday meetings, so the others pushed back the time half an hour."

"Good idea. Guess that makes you early," I said with a grin.

"Guess so," Bert said. Then he frowned, suddenly serious. He hated not being exactly on time.

Chapter Thirteen

When we were both on the Chicago police force, my pal Dave Tedeski liked to say Geneva Township was in a different time zone. It's not, of course—he just meant that time seems to move more slowly after you cross the border, even if it's the one between Illinois and Wisconsin. "Once you move up north," he said, "you'll be on Geneva time."

According to Ski, if you were a tourist, "Geneva time" meant kicking back and relaxing after you'd intentionally lost your watch in the lake. If you lived here, it meant never having to say you were sorry or to offer an explanation when you showed up late for an appointment. It turned out he was right. Unlike Officer Burr, I was habitually tardy. I was always embarrassed by it, but no one else seemed to care at all, including my staff.

I checked my watch. Having realized I was now ten minutes earlier than most of them, I left Bert in the meeting room and scurried back downstairs to the cubbyhole known as my office. I fished a zippered kit with spare toiletries out of my desk and took it to my personal "water closet" to freshen up. It was literally just a closet with a sink and a mirror, but it occasionally came in handy.

I brushed my teeth, then assessed my appearance as I combed my salt-and-pepper hair into submission. I thought about Greta and our upcoming date. Was I really handsome enough for her, educated enough? Frankly, I thought I did okay on the first question. I wasn't the best-looking guy around town, but without being vain, I thought I had a certain rugged appeal. My hair was still thick, with more pepper than salt, and I was in excellent shape for a man my age, although the person who'd outrun me on the ice last night might think otherwise. I combed my hair a little more carefully so it half-hid the bruise on my temple. It would have to do. Then I huffed into my hand. There were no obvious Bloody Mary fumes, but to be on the safe side, I pulled out a bottle of Old Spice to cover the scent. The cologne had been there since I took the job, and I only wore it when I was desperate. Had it been wine, it would have turned to vinegar by now. I poured a dab in my hands and gave my face a couple quick slaps, then headed back upstairs.

I found all five officers assembled for the weekly meeting, including my favorite, Annie Madden. Occasionally I would ask Annie to take charge of the meeting, and this seemed like a good day for it. She did not object. I grabbed a cup of coffee, and as I stepped past her, I sensed her staring at the bruise on my temple. Before she could draw attention to it, I muttered, "Don't ask."

"Don't ask what, Chief?" asked Officer Burr.

"Hey, what happened to your noggin?" piped Jerry Shea, a twenty-something guy who worked part-time and spent most of his off-hours in a gym.

I mustered a smirk. At least my underlings were observant—a good trait for cops, after all. "If you must know, I was conducting an experiment with the laws of physics. Turns out, gravity is more powerful when you're standing on slick ice."

Everyone chuckled but Annie, who raised an eyebrow but didn't probe. I had no wish to explain the details of my late-night encounter with Bigfoot along the frozen shoreline of Lake Como. It wasn't as if anyone here could help me identify my assailant, so the story would just make me look bad. Nor did I wish to describe my prior liaison with Greta, such as it was, or why I was bounding around the lake wearing dress shoes after midnight. The last thing I needed was to have my over-eager staff investigating my so-called love life.

I handed Annie my folder of notes, which she added to her own. She quickly reviewed the minutes of our prior meeting for the group, then summed up the week-long record of business. Number of moving violations issued: nine, including two for reckless snowmobiling. Number of disturbances: one. Burglaries or "B and E's": none. Thefts: one. Arrests: none.

I love the off-season in a small-town resort area—nothing of great consequence ever happens. Instead, it would be another week with no red tape, no state reports to fill out, and no one to reprimand—unless, of course, I wanted to call Bert on the carpet and bawl him out for harassing teenagers.

"What was the one theft?" Officer Geary asked.

"I was just about to get to that," Annie Madden said. "The crèche caper continues. This time, the thief hit Saint Catherine's, right here in Geneva, and they took the entire nativity scene. Father Brady reported it missing from the front of the church last Thursday morning. It was a nice set, and pretty heavy—all hand-painted on carved wood, with figures about four feet high. Most likely it was stolen late Wednesday, or maybe in the early hours of the morning on Thursday."

She looked down at the notes I'd given her.

"That makes a total of seven thefts in Walworth County during the last six weeks, more than half in our jurisdiction. Someone really has a perverted sense of the Christmas spirit."

"Maybe it's some members of the local chapter of the American Civil Liberties Union," Geary said.

Everyone laughed.

"Hey, I'm serious," Geary continued. "It wouldn't surprise me. They might say they have other motives, but the ACLU has been trying to kill Christmas for years. I mean, the schools can't even have a Christmas concert anymore—it's a 'holiday concert' and the kids sing songs you don't even recognize. The schools don't call it Christmas vacation anymore, either—it's winter break."

"Uh . . . okay, Geary, you follow that ACLU angle, see where it leads," Madden said, trying to suppress a smile.

Officer Shea groaned. "Well, if you ask me, people leave their decorations up way too long anyway, including the churches. I just wish the thief would swipe all those icicle lights and plastic Santas that are still up at Easter." Jerry Shea was tall, blond, and handsome, but he did have one imperfection: a larger-than-normal amount of bulbous skin between his nostrils.

Geary retorted that Shea's comment had made him a primary suspect in the burglaries. Shea, in turn, demanded that Geary account for his own whereabouts on Wednesday night and Thursday morning—after all, maybe Geary was just trying to divert suspicion from himself.

Annie looked at me for help. When I shrugged, she warned everyone to stop with the nonsense. "Come on, guys, this is a serious matter. Most of the thefts are landing on our doorstep. And the story caught the attention of a reporter from the Janesville newspaper. He's following it pretty closely, and really milking it. Pretty soon they'll start poking fun at us for not solving it. I don't know about you, but I don't want to be the laughingstock of the county."

Officer Burr raised his hand as if he were a fifth-grade student. "Have we obtained a more complete description of the stolen nativity scene?" he asked.

Annie looked stunned, then suppressed another smile. "Uh, no . . . But I think it's fairly safe to assume that it includes figures of Mary and Joseph and the baby Jesus, as well as three wise men, some farm animals, and a little wooden hut."

Everyone snickered but Bert, who wasn't embarrassed in the least. What Bert lacked in common sense, he made up for with hard work, and of course, none of us could ever forget he was always punctual—he was perhaps the only person in the entire county who fit that description.

"Okay," he persisted, "but don't we have to know which pieces go back to which place when we find them? I mean, the Lutheran church only lost their baby Jesus. What if someone decides to switch the Jesuses? Or maybe tries to alter the pieces and sell them?"

"You mean, you think there's some kind of chop shop for nativity scenes?" Shea asked. "It's probably just teenagers, Bert."

As they discussed the thefts among themselves, I found myself thinking of Christmas past, when I was on the Chicago police force. One day before Christmas, I was sent to the old Saint Patrick Church on Adams Street, on the near west side. The priest, Father O'Donnell, had reported their nativity scene stolen from outside the church. My fellow officers at the Monroe Street Station were outraged, and they went on a mission to find the purloined crèche. Within a short time, one of the officers found the stolen items in the window of a storefront church on west Madison Street. It was hard to believe that a man of God, a fellow reverend, would do such a deed, but it was true.

I interrupted the banter to relate my story to the staff. Then I told them to notify Racine, Kenosha, Burlington, Janesville, and some of the other large towns in adjacent counties of the recent thefts, and confirm whether they had experienced any related activity. "Officer Madden is right. We have to treat this seriously. Unless something more important comes along, consider it your top priority."

Annie continued with the meeting, answering questions, some of them hypothetical or about situations which were highly improbable. She handled herself with the aplomb of a veteran officer on a police force in a major metropolitan area, and I admired her for her composure. She was younger than I was, but I could picture us together. We certainly had a lot in common—our work, outdoor activities, our love of old movies. She also looked darned good in her uniform. It gave her just the right amount of authoritativeness and androgyny—not too feminine, as if she were a china doll, but not too mannish either, suggesting a perfect amount of athleticism for a female officer. Of course, I was pretty sure she looked even better out of uniform.

"Anything else you'd like to undress?" she asked.

I felt my face turning red. "What's that?"

"Anything else you'd like to address?" she repeated. "You've got the name 'Zubeck' jotted here in the margin."

"Uh, right," I said, turning to the others. "Yesterday, Officer Madden and I served an eviction notice on Ben Zubeck, full name Benjamin Vernon Zubeck. He has a farm out near Durnin Road." I explained the particulars and gave a description. "Zubeck has made several threats against the French Country Inn and its owner, Anthony Navilio. Navilio is the one who bought Zubeck's land at the foreclosure sale."

"Are you expecting any kind of serious trouble?" Geary asked.

"Probably not," I answered. "I just want you to be aware of the situation. Maybe take an extra tour past the inn if you're on a night shift, that kind of thing. It never hurts to be vigilant."

"I checked on their parking lot last night the way you asked," said Officer Burr. "That black Ford Explorer stayed put all night, as far as I could tell. And I confirmed it was registered to John Ratz, your drunk and disorderly guest."

"The inn has rats?" Shea joked.

"Ratz, as in R-A-T-Z," Bert continued patiently. He turned back toward me. "I phoned Mary Haggermaker again this morning, Chief. She said Ratz was having breakfast in his room, but everything seemed fine there. She also said some of the other guests were talking about how well you handled Mr. Ratz with your jujitsu moves at Kirsch's bar." Bert made a couple slow-motion air-chops, like a movie ninja. "You're a regular hero, Chief."

Annie glanced at the file. "I don't see an official report on this encounter," she said with a smirk. "But nobody ropes 'em like you do, Chief."

"This sounds like a good story," said Officer Shea. "Is that how you got that bump on your head, Chief? Tangling with Mister Rat?"

"No," I replied sternly, "it is not. The bar thing at Kirsch's was a non-incident. I stopped by the French Country Inn to talk to Anthony Navilio about Zubeck's threats, but Navilio wasn't there. I just happened to be around when this guest, John Ratz, got a little surly. He's a tourist, so let's not ruin his vacation unless he gives us a reason to."

I didn't tell them I still intended to check out the big guy's shoe size the first chance I got. Nor did I mention my plans to return to the inn for a date that same night. Fantasies about Annie Madden aside, I was really looking forward to seeing Greta again. I sincerely hoped I'd be able to come on to Greta the way I would never be able to approach Annie. With Greta, there was no professional obstacle to get in the way—just my own two left feet.

We went back to talking about Ben Zubeck for a while. Geary reminisced about his own teenage years, explaining that some kids he knew had tangled with Zubeck and regretted it. "You sure don't want to take a bat to that guy's mailbox. You'll wind up with buckshot in your behind—or in your head."

"Is that what happened to your head, Geary?" Shea asked. "Explains a lot."

Before they could start the nonsense again, Annie read a notice from the neighboring police department in Lake Geneva. They wanted some help during their annual winter carnival and international snow-sculpting competition, which always took place the second weekend in February. The competition was a big to-do, with helicopter rides over the lake and a lot of tourists in the area. Bert said he planned to assist.

Finally, Annie reviewed the roster of hours for the week ahead—who was on patrol, who was on call, and whether any swaps or changes were requested. She reminded me I was taking a shift for her a week from this Friday, in exchange for her help with the Zubeck warrant. With nothing else to discuss, we adjourned.

Annie and I were the last to leave the room. I poured another cup of coffee and sat down to make a couple notes to myself before I left.

She handed my meeting notes back to me as she passed by. "So, you fell on the ice, is that what you said?"

"Yup, that's what happened."

She looked at me skeptically. "Well, thanks for taking my Friday-night shift next week."

"My pleasure." Without thinking, I added, "Got a hot date?"

"You bet," she said as she walked out. "Very hot. But it'll probably just be me, a glass of wine, and a big tub of steamy bathwater."

I wished she hadn't said that.

Chapter Fourteen

My mother loved Frank Sinatra, Tony Bennett, Dean Martin, Vic Damone, and all the other great Italian crooners. But most of all, she loved Perry Como. It went beyond just loving his music. Although she was happily married, I sincerely believed she would have left my dear old dad and my brother and me standing dumbfounded in the driveway if Perry Como had ever asked her to run away with him.

In fact, I probably owe my existence to Perry Como. One day, years ago, my mother told me exactly that as she twirled around the kitchen, listening to Perry Como. Her smile was so unnerving that I didn't ask her to elaborate. The images in my head were bad enough. No kid ever wants to think about his parents having sex, but from that day on I could picture the night I had been conceived: my mom and dad doing the big dance as Perry Como crooned on the record player. No doubt my mother had imagined she was doing the dance with Perry instead. God forbid she had called out his name in the throes of passion. But as I said, I try not to picture it, partly because I've inherited my mother's old record player and all her old vinyls, and now I like listening to the same old crooners.

After the Tuesday staff meeting, I was back in my kitchen by noon, singing along with Perry while making a bologna omelet for Dawg and me, and wondering what to do with the rest of my so-called day off. Before returning home, I'd driven back to the French Country Inn to check on John Ratz and eyeball his shoe size. His black SUV had been absent from the lot, and no one had answered at his room, but according to Mary, the innkeeper, he hadn't checked out. She proceeded to explain that the other members of the group were all in the gathering room of L'Auberge, having a fireside seminar. I didn't want Greta to think I was stalking her, so I didn't look in. I did briefly consider asking Mary to let me into John Ratz's room so I could examine his spare shoes, but of course I had zero right to make the search. And unless my own blood was actually on his shoe at this moment, it would prove nothing anyway.

Having finished lunch, I decided to rest up for my big date with Greta. A Sinatra album dropped into place on the phonograph as I stretched out on the couch. I thumbed through a *National Geographic* and pondered all the places I might never get to visit. Before long, I was in la-la land, dreaming of my big dance with Greta as Frank sang "Fly Me to the Moon." After a while, Chandra popped into the picture, but Greta and I were somehow in the shower now, and Chandra pulled open the curtain and purred, "You really should've invited us, Chief," . . . and then I saw Ben Zubeck standing right beside her, wearing a farm dress and making a stabbing motion at me with an enormous and bloody butcher knife as a fire alarm began to go off.

I woke up to the phone ringing. It was Officer Shea. I checked my watch and breathed a sigh of relief—it was only a little after five o'clock. At least I wasn't late for my date.

As I rubbed the sleep from my eyes, Shea breathlessly explained that he had just returned to the stationhouse after giving pursuit of a suspect—a "high-speed pursuit," he added. The "alleged perpetrator" had shot out the spotlights on the sign that advertises the turn-off for the French Country Inn, at the top of the ridge along Highway 50.

"Geez, Shea. Did you just say 'high speed'? You didn't hit anything, did you—or anyone?"

"Of course not," Shea replied. "I know how to drive, Chief."

I made a mental note to make sure my staff understood our policy and procedures for embarking on a high-speed chase. It would make a good topic for our next weekly meeting. "Okay, start from the beginning," I said. "Did you actually see who shot out the sign?"

"Well, no . . ." Shea admitted. He explained that he had been driving along the south shore of Lake Como when Dorothy had received a call about some shots fired up near Highway 50 and Red Chimney Road. Shea had sped to the scene to investigate. He'd spotted an old sedan driving away and proceeded to follow the car for several miles. "He was moving fast, and I lost him near Durnin Road," Shea said excitedly. "It was already getting dark, and he was driving without headlights—come to think of it, he must not have used his brakes much either, because I didn't see brake lights. I figure he ducked down some farm road in the woods. I was about a mile past the Zubeck place when I lost him, so I circled back and waited at the end of their driveway. I didn't see any lights on in the house, and I didn't see a car, so if it was him, he was lying low. But it had to be him, Chief. Don't you think? Especially after what you said, about Ben Zubeck making threats about the inn."

I asked a few more questions. Shea described the car as "old, dark, big, and very fast." He'd observed a passenger in the sedan, but he hadn't gotten a good look at either that person or the driver, and he hadn't read the plates because there wasn't a plate on the rear bumper. It wasn't until later that Shea had gone back to the scene of the shooting and confirmed the damage to the lights on the sign.

"Whoever it was, they were a pretty good shot," Shea noted. "I waded through the snow and checked the sign, and I didn't see any misses—just the row of exploded spotlights. Should I go back to Zubeck's place and poke around?"

I told him no. "We have no way of tying him to this other than our own suspicions. And I don't see any sense in poking a stick at Zubeck tonight just to see if he jumps. Officer Madden and I will swing by tomorrow and have a little chat with him. She has a real knack for calming people."

Shea's voice revealed his disappointment, but he agreed.

"Just keep your eyes open and stay vigilant," I added. "I'm having dinner at Kirsch's tonight, and I'll do the same."

An hour later, I found myself showered, dressed, and twiddling my thumbs. My date with Greta wasn't until eight o'clock. I reached for the bottle of vodka, then thought better of it. Instead I decided to ignore my own advice and take a ride out to the Zubeck property. I had a sudden urge to check out the owner's shoe size. Even though I intended to be nonconfrontational, I took my Glock 9mm along.

Fifteen minutes later, the wheels of the Jeep were crunching down the snow-and-ice-covered driveway of the Zubeck farmstead. The place looked even more desolate and decrepit than it had the day before. Shea was right—it appeared no one was home. In fact, when I shined my flashlight into a front window of the house, it looked as if half the interior had already been cleared out. I walked around the property and checked the outbuildings, careful along the way not to step in anything that would have a peculiar odor. I hadn't noticed any animals yesterday, but with Zubeck, you could never be too careful—he might've left a few booby traps for me.

I suddenly thought of a scene in the movie *Last Tango in Paris*—the one in which Marlon Brando reminisces about his teenage years on a farm. His character's entire life was fouled because he stepped into a pile of manure just before he took his date to the big high school dance. I didn't want my future with Greta to be similarly compromised. At dinner I could imagine her asking, "What is that horrible smell?" to which I could only answer, "It must be the escargot—who can say where they've been crawling?"

I often wonder about all the strange little scenes that continually play out in my head. One day, no doubt, they will be my undoing. Assuming the booze doesn't pickle my liver first.

Chapter Fifteen

Contrary to my usual tardiness, I managed to arrive at the inn about twenty minutes early for my date. Greta had stated adamantly that she would be ready for me at eight, so I planned to ring her room precisely two minutes after the hour. I didn't want to seem overeager.

I used the opportunity to head to the lobby and chat with Patti Bartz, who was working the desk that evening. One of her coworkers, Debbie Vanderstappen, had stopped in to keep her company.

"Any luck finding whoever shot up our sign?" Patti asked.

I shook my head. "Not yet, but Officer Shea is looking into that as we speak."

Patti smirked. She recognized a line when she heard one.

"Mary thinks it's that Zubeck guy," Debbie said.

I realized the entire staff of the inn probably knew about Ben Zubeck's threats by now. If Kirsch and Frankel hadn't filled them in, Shea or someone else probably had. The local shrubs might look dead in January, but the grapevine thrived here year-round.

"Don't you think it could've just been some teenagers or something?" Debbie continued. "You know, somebody just looking for a thrill or a cure for cabin fever or an excuse to shoot something? The sign is almost a mile from the inn, and it's all by itself at the turnoff. It might've just looked like a good place for target practice."

"Could be the case," I said, though I doubted it was true. "Do you know if Mary's been in contact with the owner of the inn today?"

I had yet to connect with Anthony Navilio, but I planned to give him another call tomorrow.

"I don't know," Patti said. "I think he's out of the country."

I raised my brow. "He's not in Chicago?"

She shrugged. "You could ask Mary to be sure. But I heard he took his family to Italy to go skiing or something like that. Now if I took a vacation in January, you can bet I'd go someplace warm. Like Hawaii. You ever been there, Chief?"

Before I could answer, I heard a door opening above us, along the gallery that overlooked the lobby. I turned to see Greta stepping out of Chandra's suite.

"Hello, Chief," she called out. She genuinely looked pleased to see me. "I thought that might be you I heard. I couldn't remember if we were going to meet in the lounge, or if you were going to call my room, so I decided to come over and visit with Chandra for a while."

Chandra appeared in the doorway behind her. She had a brandy in her hand and raised the glass. "Good evening, Chief. Good to see you again."

I winced from kicking myself. Why hadn't I suggested that Greta and I go somewhere other than the inn? I could feel Debbie and Patti staring at my back with curious amusement, and I was sure they'd be chattering about my date the moment I left the lobby. Meanwhile, Chandra looked like a she-devil who could spring over the oak railing of the gallery in a single bound. I recalled my crazy dream and her complaint about not being invited into the shower with Greta and me.

As if reading my mind, Chandra said, "Oh, for Pete's sake, Chief. I hope you don't play poker with that face. Don't worry, I wouldn't dream of intruding on your date. Greta is all yours now." She pecked Greta on the cheek and gave me a wink as she closed the door.

Greta floated down the stairs, slow and slinky, watching me watch her. She was a little dressed-up for the circumstances, but I appreciated the effort. She wore a black straight skirt with a tasteful slit that made her legs go on forever. On top of that was a matching cashmere sweater, the kind you might see in the Forties, only it was snug and casually unbuttoned and just short of slutty. I envied the sweater for all the places it went. She looked damned good and I was pretty sure she knew it.

"Why don't we go ahead and have a drink in the bar?" she asked, linking her arm in mine.

I smiled. Greta was definitely my kind of woman.

This evening's bartender was Rick. He was standing at the far end of the bar as we came in, enjoying a conversation with Professor Feri and his assistant, Evelyn Durst, and Emile Tavilion, the *Godfather* fan. Each member of the trio was sitting in exactly the same location as the night before. "Everything changes, yet it always stays the same," I said to myself.

"Pardon me?" Greta answered.

"Sorry, just thinking out loud. Let's take a table by the fire after we get our drinks."

Aside from the trio, we were the only two patrons in the bar. Kirsch and Frankel must have had other plans for a change. Greta ordered a Cosmopolitan and I ordered a Rolling Rock. Rick placed a Heineken in front of me.

Greta leaned toward me after we'd sat down, and I inhaled her perfume, which was subtle and a little bit spicy. "I wanted to thank you again for being so sweet last night," she said in a soft voice.

"It was my pleasure, ma'am," I replied.

"I know it might have seemed strange. But frankly, ever since our group checked in, I've had an uneasy feeling at night. The bitter cold makes the buildings complain. And then, of course, there was that whole episode with John Ratz . . . But with you in my room, I slept like a baby."

"Really, it was no problem. I didn't even file a report."

"I hope not," she said. "A gentleman never tells." She reached out and gently placed her finger on my forehead, touching the bruise. "Ouch. Tough day at the office, Chief?"

I was flattered that she'd noticed. I didn't think the bump looked that bad anymore, except maybe for the edges, which were already turning green.

"It's nothing. I walked into a door last night," I lied.

"I'll bet you were helping another damsel in distress."

I didn't disillusion her. "How was your day?" I asked. "Did you learn anything new in class? I sure hope your friend Ratz was in a better mood this morning."

"You're funny. John Ratz is not my friend, you know. And he never showed up for breakfast or for our workshop today. I asked Professor Feri if he'd left the group, but no such luck—apparently John was just taking the day off. I thought maybe he was out ice fishing with you all day."

I chuckled. "I like to fish, all right, just not through the ice. Most of the natives would disagree, but I think it's too cold to drink beer outside in January. And I only fish when I can drink beer."

"I'm sure the fish like that policy, too. What do you catch here when it's warm?"

"Bass, mainly. The occasional perch. Do you fish?"

"Of course. You're looking at a champion fly-fisher."

"You're kidding."

"Yes, I am," she said, smiling playfully. "But I can sit in a boat and enjoy the sun and hand someone a beer now and then—as long as you don't ask me to bait a hook or clean a fish. I'm not very good with blood and guts."

"I'll keep that in mind," I said. Having exhausted this line of banter, I took another swig of my beer. Show interest, I thought. "So, you're from Toronto, eh?"

She nodded. We briefly swapped histories. I learned that Greta had moved to Chicago as a teenager. Now she was working in a brokerage firm downtown, which she found a little boring. We had something in common: we'd both been married once, and we were now divorced. She didn't offer any details about her marriage, however, and to my relief, she didn't ask for any of mine.

She sipped her Cosmopolitan and looked around the room. "I just love this place," she said. "It really has a hideaway feeling. It must have been a perfect spot for a speakeasy and an intimate little gambling den in the Twenties, don't you think?"

"Well, you know what they say. What happens in Como, stays in Como."

She raised a brow, and I quickly added, "It does have a lot of character."

"And a lot of characters," she said. "You grew up here, right? What was it like when you were a kid? Did you poke around here much?"

"Around the inn, you mean? No, back then it was kind of a dump. The current owner did a restoration in the Eighties. Of course he made a few upgrades, which you probably know. You wouldn't find a hundred-year-old inn with two-story suites or whirlpool lofts with fireplaces. How did your group come to pick this place, anyway?"

"I suppose that was my doing," Greta said. "Indirectly, at least. I used to come up to Lake Geneva in the summer—just for the day or a weekend, not like you. I got tired of the big resorts, and I wanted a quiet place away from downtown. I discovered this inn. Before I knew it, I was learning about gangster lore and researching a book. And then my writing group got interested in the inn, and, long story short, we thought this would be a good choice for a winter retreat. I think Chandra suggested it, actually."

With the mention of Chandra, I drained the last of my beer, which I'd been guzzling as if it were summer. Greta's glass wasn't empty yet, but I asked if she wanted another and then ordered a second round.

What I really wanted was a shot of vodka, but I told Rick to fetch me a Coors. He brought me another Heineken.

"How's the writing coming?" I asked.

"It's not as easy as I'd hoped, but I'm not discouraged," Greta said. "Everything worthwhile takes some effort—and patience. Don't you agree?"

I nodded. "The gangster angle sounds intriguing, though. How do you go about researching a historical book like yours? Without witnesses, I wouldn't know where to start."

"The Internet is a good resource," she said. "And I've spent hours looking through library files, and public records and deeds, old newspaper accounts, magazine articles, files from historical societies, that kind of thing. There are also quite a few books out about the gangsters who rose to power during Prohibition, and the G-Men who hunted them. Most of the authors don't focus on this part of Wisconsin, but a woman named Rose Keefe has published a biography on Bugs Moran, which mentions Lake Como quite a bit. It's called *The Man Who Got Away*."

"How did he get away? Didn't Moran eventually wind up in prison?"

"You're right, he did—he was sent to Leavenworth. But that wasn't until long after Prohibition had ended, and he was leading a burglary ring. The title refers to his escape from Al Capone's hit squad on February 14, 1929. Capone and Moran's gangs had clashed in Chicago for years, and Capone intended to put an end to it. Moran only got away because he was late for a meeting with his top men. They were at a garage on the North Side. Seven of Moran's associates were gunned down execution-style."

"Ah, the infamous Saint Valentine's Day Massacre. I was just looking at a photo of the crime scene this morning."

"That's a strange way to start your day. Any particular reason?"

"Nah. There's a bar and grill near here called Muddy's on the

Lake. The owner has a gallery of old black-and-white gangster photos on the wall. The massacre photo is hanging up between the cigarette machine and the men's room."

"You know, I think I've stopped in there once—the tavern, not the men's room, of course. Do they have a gallery of writer photos, too?"

"That's the place. As a matter of fact, the owner mentioned a regular who might have a few stories you'd be interested in—an old-timer. I could try to set something up for later if you'd like. For another night, I mean."

She smiled. "Another night would definitely be better. I'd much rather spend this evening with you."

"Yeah, and any friend of Gus Baldwin's would probably just pull your leg or spend the night gawking at your gams anyway. Not that I'd blame him."

She smiled again and sipped her drink. Her red lips left a faint kiss-mark on the rim of the glass.

"You know," I said, "I've always wondered about that Valentine's Day scene. A group of well-dressed mobsters are all lying in a bloody heap together, stone cold dead, with their coats on. All shot in the back. Not one of them put up a fight. How did Capone's henchmen pull that off? And if they were that good, how could they let Moran get away?"

"The authorities asked the same questions in 1929—and so did Capone, I'm sure—but the full story didn't come out for years. It was a case of mistaken identity. As I said, Moran was running late, but Capone's lookout mistook another guy who'd already arrived for Bugs. It was midmorning, so darkness wasn't an excuse, but one of Moran's men did look a lot like Bugs, with the same burly build and height. And he was wearing a long black coat and a black fedora, as Moran often did. So, the lookout signaled the assassins. Right after that, two men went in dressed as policemen. Moran's men thought it was a routine roust, so they cooperated by lining up against the wall for a frisking. Only, it wasn't a frisking, obviously. I'm sure Moran's men thought the cops were just looking for a bribe. No offense to current company, of course."

"None taken. Bad cops still exist. They're just not the majority."

"Anyway, as soon as the victims' backs were turned, two more assassins stepped in and sprayed them with machine guns. The only survivor was a German shepherd owned by Moran's mechanic, who was one of the seven men killed. The dog was howling and hiding under a beer truck near the pool of blood when the real police arrived. Of course, conspiracy theorists say that real cops were involved. No one was ever convicted of the murders."

"No wonder Moran needed a getaway up here."

"Doesn't everyone?" Greta said. She took another sip of her drink. "I hope I'm not going on too much—I'm a little obsessed with the gangster lore. I'm probably boring you."

"Not in the least," I answered. In fact, I was listening to Greta with all the interest of a horny freshman who finds himself smitten by the teacher with beautiful legs and a tight-fitting sweater. I could barely contain my impure thoughts. Besides, it was easier to listen than make small talk, and with every sip of her Cosmopolitan, Greta's lips became a little looser and more voluptuous.

"Did Old Scarface ever visit the inn?" I asked.

"Apparently, Capone did come here at least once," Greta replied, "but without any bloodshed. When this was the Lake Como Hotel, the guest list was a veritable who's who of gangsters—including Dillinger, Baby Face Nelson, Tommy Carroll, Jimmy Murray . . . along with their girlfriends and molls, of course. Or wives. Nelson's wife, Helen Gillis, was just a little gun-toting slip of a girl herself. In fact, Helen and Baby Face were both here right before Baby Face had his final shootout with the Feds, down in Illinois. But none of the other gangsters had the same kind of connection with the owner as Bugs Moran and his wife, Lucille."

"Right. You mentioned that little triangle last night. At least, it sounded like a triangle."

"Rose Keefe's book is a good source on that. I managed to speak with a relative of Hobart Hermansen myself—Hobart ran the inn back then. Keefe also located one of Moran's sons. It seems Bugs and Lucille first came to Lake Geneva hoping to find land to build their own summer getaway. Lucille was a French-Turkish immigrant, a mysterious dark-eyed showgirl. She already had a young son, John, when she and Bugs met, but by all accounts, Bugs was a very good father to him."

"A family man? Guess it's possible," I said.

"Of course at one point, Bugs and Lucille discovered this place. They must have enjoyed their stay, because they came here often after that, and they became good friends with Hobart Hermansen. Technically, the inn was still a family business then, and Christ Hermansen may have had a stake."

"Christ?"

"It's short for Christian. He was Hobart's father. I've seen some old ads from the 1930s that say the inn was owned by 'Christ Hermansen and Sons.' But everything else suggests Hobart was fully in charge. He had a house just a few hundred yards down the shore, and sometimes Bugs and Lucille even stayed there. After the massacre, things went downhill for Moran. He'd lost his best men, and he had a host of legal problems, money problems, heat from the Feds . . . The next year, Lucille filed for divorce and came up here with John."

"Moran's stepson," I said.

"Right. For a while, at least, Bugs kept visiting," Greta continued. "He married another woman in 1931. Meanwhile, I'm sure it was much safer and easier for Lucille to live here. The Como Hotel was a good fit for her, too. She was smart, and she had connections through Bugs. She helped Hobe manage the hotel and keep the booze flowing. She also organized poker games and other gambling activities. The inn became a real hot spot, the kind of place where no one asked questions or cared how you made a living, as long as you behaved yourself—and spent your money, of course."

"That much hasn't changed."

"Are you familiar with that bed-and-breakfast just down the shore?"

"The Water's Edge, you mean? I know it, but I've never been inside."

"That was Hobart Hermansen's private home. Hermansen didn't have the kind of reputation for violence that Bugs Moran had, but it appears he didn't mind working outside the law. That house was built with a very strange underground garage, so cars could be loaded and unloaded in secret. It also had a big vault and a money-counting room."

"In other words, Hermansen had a lot of cash—or his friends did."

"The bootlegging and gambling operations were definitely profitable. Hermansen also owned a nice hotel in downtown Lake Geneva, overlooking the lakefront. It had illegal gambling operations, too, which lasted at least until the Forties. Unfortunately, that hotel was razed in the early Seventies, which is a shame, because it was designed by Frank Lloyd Wright. Do you remember it?"

"No, but it's too bad it's gone."

Greta nodded and looked toward the frozen lake. "Have you ever gone fishing just offshore here with a metal detector?" she asked. "Or dragged the lake for some reason?"

"Uh, no," I said. "Why?"

"There's a rumor that Hobe once caught wind of an impending raid, and, as a precaution, he threw all his slot machines off the end of the pier, just before the G-Men arrived."

"I'm pretty sure those machines aren't down there now."

"Probably not," Greta agreed. "But who knows? Still waters run deep. They could hide a lot of secrets."

"You've got a writer's imagination, all right. But the lake is actually pretty shallow off that pier. If there were a body or any buried treasure down there, I'm sure we'd know about it by now."

Both our glasses were empty, and, to my surprise, Greta had stopped talking. I looked around and realized that the trio at the end of the bar had left without my noticing. Rick raised the bottle of vodka inquiringly. I shook my head.

"Shall we head in for dinner?" I said.

"I thought you'd never ask," Greta replied.

Chapter Sixteen

As I'd expected, the dining room at Kirsch's was nearly empty. Apart from Friday and Saturday nights, the restaurant saw little traffic at nine o'clock on a January evening. The usual trio from Greta's writing group had taken a table in the far corner, although there wasn't much to see out there at this hour. They nodded at Greta and me as we walked in. Another couple was seated by the fire—a slim, elderly gentleman and an austere-looking woman, neither of whom seemed to be having a good time. The woman was staring at the fire, and the man was more attentive to his profiteroles and chocolate sauce than to his companion.

A young waitress hurried out to greet us, a ginger-haired girl who always wore a ponytail and a charming smile and whose name I could never seem to remember. "I hope you're surviving the cold," she said cheerfully.

"Say, where has the chef been lately?" I asked. "I haven't seen hide nor hair of him—except in my soup."

Greta pinched my arm, but the waitress looked thoroughly confused. "What did you say about the soup?" she asked. "Um, I could ask Chef Drew about it. He's still in the kitchen."

"Never mind," I said. I've always hated having to explain my own jokes. Few people understand or appreciate my witticisms, and this waitress was not among those few. But I had been wondering whether the chef was in. Like so many in his profession, Andrew Turkley liked to schmooze with guests, flirt with female staff members, and hold court with the bar patrons when Kirsch wasn't there. In fact, I used to wonder if the chef was ever in the kitchen. All the famous TV chefs had nothing on Andrew Turkley, as far as Turkley was concerned. He called himself "Chef Drew." I called him Chef Turkey, but not out loud. I didn't want him to add spit to that imaginary hair in my soup.

The elderly couple was leaving, so we took a table by the fire, away from the other writers. The waitress recommended the hibachi-style Chilean sea bass, a signature dish at the restaurant. Greta concurred. I was craving beef, but I didn't want to seem like a carnivorous alpha male, or get too stuffed and sleepy for later, so I ordered the bass as well. We agreed on a bottle of chardonnay. Before the smiling waitress could hurry off, I asked her to tell Chef Drew that I was dining here tonight.

In the next instant, I was worrying that Greta might think I was putting on an air of self-importance. In truth, I was just hoping the chef might spring for some after-dinner cocktails. I've never seen myself as the proverbial big fish in a small pond. I'm more like an odd duck—one who prefers being unimportant and who enjoys living in a nice, quiet pond with a no-wake zone.

The waitress brought us our wine and some warm bread and announced that Chef Drew had sent the wine with his compliments.

"Are you and the chef here friends?" Greta asked.

"Not exactly," I said. "He's a nice enough guy, but chefs and I don't mix well as a rule."

"Why is that?" she said, giving me a curious look.

"I had some bad experiences when I worked in restaurants down in Chicago. Of course, that was a long time ago, before I became a police officer. And it's not as if anyone tried to murder me with sushi or anything like that."

"I hope you won't make that same wisecrack to Chandra," Greta said. "I told you she's very sensitive about her sister's death."

"Believe me, I won't." I had no intention of talking with Chandra at all. "Seriously, though, don't you think that a lot of chefs are full of themselves? Ever since Emeril and Wolfgang Puck became celebrities, every hash slinger in every greasy spoon in America is suddenly an artist. One time this real blowhard of a chef got his nose all out of joint—just because I said I didn't want my duck too rare. So this chef asks me if I'd tell Picasso which colors to use if I had commissioned a painting. I said I probably would pick the colors, if I was going to eat the painting afterward."

To my relief, Greta laughed. "So, how was the duck?"

"He did it my way. But later I kept wondering if he had spit in it, or something worse. I stayed away from that restaurant a long time after that. Then Kirsch finally fired the chef."

"That was here?"

"Yeah, but Kirsch hired Chef Turkley after that. And I have to admit, the guy annoys me sometimes, but he is pretty talented with his bass."

Right on cue, our fish arrived. As always, the dinner at Kirsch's was excellent. We ate and drank slowly, and chatted about gangsters some more. Greta filled me in on Jimmy Murray—another acquaintance of Hobart Hermansen. Murray ran a club called the Rainbo, on Harlem and North Avenues down in Chicago. Before that, he'd helped finance and mastermind the biggest train robbery in the history of the country, which had taken place in 1924, about thirty miles outside the city, at a remote little railroad crossing called Rondout, Illinois.

"I can't believe you haven't heard of the Rondout Train Robbery," Greta said teasingly. "They made a movie about it and everything."

"What was the movie called?"

"*The Newton Boys* with Matthew McConaughey."

"That explains it," I said. "It's too recent. And I'm not a McConaughey fan. The whole shirtless-hunk-with-a-constant-grin thing doesn't do much for me."

"Funny, it seems to work on me," Greta said.

She explained that the Newton Boys were a band of Texas

brothers who'd robbed a series of banks and trains—without any bloodshed. Then they hooked up with Murray and a corrupt postal inspector, who had worked out a plan for them to hit a mail train outside Chicago. It was carrying roughly three million dollars in Federal Reserve currency, untraceable bonds, and loose diamonds. Some of the Newton gang boarded the train in Chicago, and the rest moved in for the take at Rondout.

"It was total chaos," Greta said. "The Newton Boys tossed formaldehyde bombs into the train to flush out the clerks. Then the train suddenly backed up, and the gang shot one of their own men by mistake. The boys still made off with the loot, but everyone involved was eventually arrested. They handed in some of the loot, but no one knows exactly how much was on the train, so it's likely someone kept part of it."

"Interesting," I said. "What happened to Murray?"

"He only served a few years," Greta said. "After he got out, he opened up his own restaurant, the Rainbo, where he served barbecue and bootlegged liquor. And befriended Dillinger and Baby Face Nelson and Hobart Hermansen. And maybe become a mole for the Feds . . . Murray was an ex-politician, so he knew how to play all the angles. But that's enough gangster talk for one night, I think. I'd much rather talk about you."

Suddenly I felt nervous again. I didn't want the night to end, but I wasn't ready to make my move, so I suggested we order dessert and coffee and after-dinner drinks, and Greta agreed.

"It's been a long time since I've been on a date," I said. "I'm having a great time."

"Oh, is this a date?" Greta said in jest. "I hadn't realized." Then she lowered her voice and ran her forefinger over the top of my hand. She packed a lot of heat in that one little finger. "I'm having a wonderful time, too, Chief."

It felt perfect, which should have been my first clue that it wasn't. The second clue was harder to miss. Moments after our brandy arrived, the blonde she-devil appeared on the radar, at twelve o'clock and moving in fast.

I groaned.

Chandra sat down, then wriggled her rear end into the chair to get more comfortable. She was wearing the same pink velour lounge suit that she'd worn the night before. She flashed her white teeth. "So, you two, how's the date coming along?"

"Chandra," I said. "I thought you weren't going to join us tonight."

"Well, you know us girls," Chandra said. "We do like to change our minds." She took a sip of my brandy without my permission. "Ouch, this is strong stuff. What is it?"

"Turpentine," I answered.

"Oh, you can unclench now, Chief. I'm just getting a coffee to go." She waved at the waitress as if she were hailing a cab.

"I need a decaf espresso with extra cream," she informed the waitress, "and that raw sugar that comes in the little brown packets. Bring the sugar separately, please. Oh, and be sure it's the raw sugar, and put in lots of cream this time, and make extra sure it's decaf, okay? I don't want to be up all night. You can put it on my room tab—I'm in 303 upstairs."

"Yes, ma'am," the smiley young waitress replied sweetly. "Decaf cappuccino, extra cream, raw sugar in the little brown packets. Coming right up."

"God, I hate it when they call me ma'am," Chandra said after the waitress had departed. "I'll bet she forgets the extra cream."

I bit my tongue. Greta smiled apologetically, but the perfect moment was gone. Instead of imagining all the things I might do with Greta, I was thinking of all the things I wanted to do to Chandra. Like pull out my Glock and blast her right through the little brown sugar packets when they arrived.

To my amazement, the fantasy had some very convincing sound effects.

Chapter Seventeen

If it had been the Fourth of July weekend or New Year's Eve, I would have thought I was hearing fireworks. Instead I wondered if maybe someone had hurled a rock through a window. A split second later, when the second window was shattered, I knew for sure that gunshots had caused the eruption of glass.

By now I'd pushed Greta to the floor, and I was pulling the chair out from under Chandra, who seemed too stunned or oblivious to move. The tiramisu which she had commandeered from me fell in her lap, then she too was on the floor, gasping.

"Are you all right?" I asked Greta. Instinctively, I'd drawn my Glock from beneath my sport coat, and I was holding it as I spoke.

She nodded, wide-eyed. I motioned both women to stay down, then crawled army-style toward the French doors that opened toward the shoreline. I glanced around the restaurant as I went. Luckily, it was almost empty—the other writers had gone before the shooting started.

When I reached the doors I peeked outside, but I could see nothing out on the ice except the fishing shacks that dotted the frozen lake. Just then a third bullet pierced the outdoor sconce above my head. "Shit," I whispered. Not wanting a stray bullet to mortally wound any fishermen who might be out on the ice, I opened the door and fired off three quick rounds, aiming high into the air. At this point I had no idea of the gunman's location—or locations, if there was more than one man. Then I saw a light and heard sounds from a single snowmobile heading at full throttle toward the north shore.

My police radio was in the Jeep, and I wished I hadn't left it there. I needed to contact Officer Shea. With any luck, right about now he was on patrol along the opposite side of the lake.

I spotted Rick crouching by the bar and instructed him to call the county sheriff's office immediately. "Tell him three shots fired, suspect fleeing on a snowmobile toward the north side of the lake. I'll be in pursuit in my Jeep."

Rick nodded and moved toward the bar phone.

I looked at Greta, who had crawled over to assist Chandra and keep her from getting up off the floor. Without trying to sound like a bad impression of Arnold Schwarzenegger, I called out, "I'll be back."

My Jeep was parked in the west lot, only yards from a spot on the shoreline where I could drive directly onto the lake. It had been below twenty degrees for weeks, so I didn't worry about plunging through the ice as I headed across. The only dangerous spots were on the edges where a stream flowed into the lake.

While I talked to Shea on the radio, I shifted gears, picking up speed in order to cross the ice as quickly as possible without spinning out of control. I already knew that finding the shooter was probably a lost cause—unless he did something stupid. A snowmobiler could maneuver down trails and unmarked pathways that only another sled or a four-legged animal could follow. But I also knew that I had to make an attempt and hope that luck would be on my side.

Shea and county officer Mike Williams were waiting for me on the north shore, a few yards above the boat launch where I drove off the lake. When I saw their squad cars parked alongside each other, I knew they had no trail to pursue.

"Did either of you get a look at him?" I asked.

Williams shook his head. "No luck, Chief, not even a glimpse. Sorry."

Shea's long face told the same story.

"Okay, Shea. You go ahead and take a drive through the area, see if you spot anything unusual. Stop at the pubs over here and look for a warm snowmobile, ask a few questions. From the sound of it, the shooter had a high-caliber rifle. I'm heading back to the inn to check on things there."

Like a down-on-his-luck poker player who had just lost his table stakes, I drove back across the lake, more slowly this time, wondering what had become of my quiet little town. In the last two days I had been threatened, kicked in the head, and shot at. What could go wrong next?

Two investigators from the Walworth County Sheriff's Office were at the scene when I arrived. We conferred a bit, and they pointed out the bullet holes in the wall—just a few feet from the table where Greta and I had been having dinner. Another officer was looking for shell casings on the lake. I checked on Greta and Chandra, who'd yet to be interviewed, and told them once more, "I'll be back."

Then I headed out to help Jerry Shea. I circled the township twice, and together Shea and I visited the dark-and-empty Zubeck homestead. On my return to the inn, I stopped two snowmobilers who were cruising down Schroeder Road, but they were just a couple of teenagers out for a night ride, an unlikely pair to be taking deadly aim at a group of restaurant patrons.

By the time I returned to Kirsch's an hour later, the county's team had gone. The restaurant was empty except for Rick, who was sweeping up the broken glass, and Santiago, a cook, who was nailing plywood over the broken windowpanes. Nothing can clear out a joint like an old-fashioned shooting. Or put a damper on a date.

I told Rick that I would add a police detail that would cruise the area throughout the night. Then I went outside and walked the grounds, looking for a prowler . . . and perhaps a beautiful woman named Greta. I found neither until I approached L'Auberge and peeked through a French door into the gathering room on the first floor, where, to my delight, I spied Greta. To my dismay, I saw Chandra sitting beside her. Both women appeared to be nursing a nightcap by the gas fireplace.

They weren't alone. The trio of literary types had emigrated here, too, and they were now ensconced in a corner of this new locale. I surmised they were discussing the same topic they had been engrossed in hours earlier.

I knocked quietly on the glass and Chandra came to the door. Looking directly at my face, she asked, "Yes? Who is it?"

Only after I'd asked her to unlock the French door did she allow me to enter. Greta was already pouring a shot of vodka over a glass full of ice, and she handed it to me. "I'm so glad you're back, Chief. Did you catch whoever was shooting at us?"

"No luck," I replied. "The shooter was driving a snowmobile. I'm afraid they slipped into the woods across the lake."

Without wasting a moment's time, Chandra started in on me. "What kind of a town do you have here, anyway? It's a miracle no one was killed. Why didn't you do something to stop this mess? This is supposed to be a first-class establishment!"

"I can assure you, Chandra, this kind of thing does not happen here every day—not even in the third-rate establishments," I answered defensively. "As you are probably aware, shootings are far more common in Chicago, and they're often connected with gang activity. Although I can't say for certain what happened yet, I'm almost positive that isn't the case here."

"Meaning what—you have no idea what happened?"

"You're not being fair, Chandra," Greta intervened. "After all, Chief's first instinct was to make sure we were safe. Thanks for helping us onto the floor, by the way."

Chandra scoffed. "Yes, thanks ever so much. Thanks to you I'll probably need a chiropractor now, too."

I ignored her. Instead, I asked about the status of the rest of the group. Apart from the trio in the corner, the others had turned in for the night, including John Ratz, as far as she knew.

"Look," I said, "I don't think you'll have any more problems here tonight. I'm sure the county officers told you the same thing. But just to be absolutely safe, take the usual precautions when you turn in—draw your drapes, lock the doors. Since you're in the other building, Chandra, I'd be happy to walk you back to your suite."

Greta walked over to Chandra and put her arm around her. "You do look really tired, Chandra," Greta said. "Maybe you should take a hot bath or take one of your sleep aids tonight—something gentle and safe, you know? Just keep your phone by your bed. If you still can't sleep, you can always give me call."

Chandra nodded. As we walked past Greta, I whispered, "I'll be back soon. Will you wait up?"

She nodded.

The lobby was locked tight when we reached it, but luckily Chandra hadn't forgotten her room key, which also opened the main door on the front porch. As we passed through and entered the lobby, Chandra said, "I hope you can keep someone from shooting at me again."

"I'll do my best," I said. "Seriously, Chandra, this was probably a one-time thing. I doubt you'll have any more problems, but as a precaution, I'm having someone keep a close watch on the inn tonight."

When she reached the landing, she turned. "Would you mind checking my room for me, please? I'm sorry I was such a shrew to you earlier. I was just upset."

I hesitated. I knew Greta was waiting for me, but it wasn't such a strange request, all things considered. As if reading my thoughts, Chandra added, "Please, Chief. It'll only take a few minutes."

Against my better judgment, I followed Chandra up the stairs. They creaked softly underfoot. I asked her to wait on the gallery while I checked the suite—not because I thought it was unsafe, but because

I didn't want to encourage any misunderstandings between us. Given her fragile state of mind, and everything Greta had told me about Chandra's infidelities and sexual appetite, I didn't want to be caught in an awkward position.

I saw nothing out of order in the room. It was more masculine than the suites in L'Auberge, with heavy black leather chairs in the seating area. I noticed that Chandra had a bottle of brandy and some pill bottles on the bedside table, but I wanted to get out quickly, so I didn't examine the labels. Besides that, she was standing in the doorway, eyeing me. She walked in and poured some brandy into a glass.

"Can I tempt you?" she said, lifting her brandy. "I think I have another glass somewhere." Her blue eyes were fixed on mine, and I swear I saw a little flicker of flame behind the pupils. She stepped closer and stroked my arm. "I promise you Greta won't mind," she purred.

I wasn't the least bit tempted. "No, thanks. Everything looks fine here. Good night, Chandra."

She followed me to the door. "You know I was just testing you, don't you, Chief? For Greta's sake. A girl likes to know what kind of company her friends are keeping."

"Whatever you say," I muttered, starting down the stairs. At the bottom, I turned. Chandra was still watching me. The light from her room shone through the edges of her curly blonde hair, and for a moment, the she-devil looked almost sweet.

She smiled and swirled her brandy. "There are ghosts in this building. Did you know that, Chief?"

"No. I'm going now, Chandra. Be sure to lock your door. And be careful with the booze and those pills. You might start seeing things."

"I'm completely serious. Ask Greta about the ghost named Jack. She knows—it's all part of her research. And I can vouch for it. There are a lot strange sounds in this building at night. Of course, the dead have never frightened me. It's the living we have to watch out for."

"Well, you're right about that," I said. I remembered the tale of her dead sister, and I almost felt sorry for her—almost. "Good night, Chandra. Sleep tight."

"Good night, Chief," she said, closing the door.

I heard the lock click into place. Before leaving, I ducked my head into the bar and said good night to Rick, who was preparing to close up shop. Then I secured the lobby and headed back into the cold.

Chapter Eighteen

When I returned to L'Auberge, Greta was alone in the gathering room, still nursing what I hoped was the same nightcap. She smiled as I tapped on the French doors again, and rose to let me in.

"There you are, stranger. I was wondering what happened to you."

It was around midnight. The ice had nearly melted into the vodka she'd poured for me earlier, but it was still on the side table.

"You were gone a very long time," Greta continued. "Did you enjoy your little assignation with Chandra?"

Her tone was playful, which was good, because I had no idea what an assignation was, but I was pretty sure it had something to do with my being an ass. Or touching someone else's.

"I did check Chandra's room for her, but I absolutely did not enjoy it."

"So what are you saying, you're a glutton for punishment?"

"You've got me there. Actually, Chandra wanted to tell me a ghost story. She said I must not know Jack, so I should ask you about him. Any idea what the hell she was talking about?"

Greta sat back down by the fire, and I took it as a cue to join her. "There are all sorts of stories about this inn being haunted," she said. "Just ask Mary Haggermaker and Patti Goff."

"Okay, I will. But I still don't know Jack."

Greta smiled at my little joke. "Do you really want to hear this?"

"Sure," I said, picking up the vodka she'd poured earlier. I suddenly realized I was still nervous about seducing Greta. The conversation and drink were a necessary stall tactic.

"Well," Greta continued, "as the story goes, the inn is haunted by John Moran, Bugs's stepson. That's our Jack."

"Did John Moran die here, then?"

"No, but close by. After his mother married Hobart Hermansen, John became Hobart's stepson and eventually started working here. He also worked at Hermansen's other properties, which included the Geneva Hotel downtown and a place in Boca Raton."

"I still don't get why he'd haunt this place—not that I believe in ghosts, of course."

"Well, in the late Fifties, John supposedly complained to friends that his stepfather was hiding assets and cheating him out of his inheritance. John said he was going to search Hobart's office for evidence—here, at this inn. Shortly after that, John Moran was found dead at the Geneva Hotel. The official cause of death was coronary thrombosis. But according to some witnesses, there were copious amounts of blood all over John Moran's face, and on the floor and the bed."

"All right, for the sake of argument, let's assume he was killed there. Why would he haunt the inn?"

"Maybe he was haunting his stepfather. Another theory is that he loved it here so much that he never wanted to leave. It's just a story. But there are others, too—rumors of low-level gangsters who met their end here and refused to stay quiet after death. There was a lot of rough justice in the Twenties and Thirties. Maybe someone did get away with murder here." She swirled her glass. "Pretty scary, huh?" she said teasingly.

"Nah, not for a tough guy like me. But if you're afraid of ghosts, I'd be happy to keep you company. I'm pretty good at that, you know."

She laughed. "That's sounds nice. Why don't we go to my

room? Then you can tell me a bedtime story." She stood and led me by the hand.

As we entered the hallway, I hesitated. "Can you hold that thought for just a few more minutes?" I asked. "I'll be right back."

"You have got to be kidding." She put a hand on her curvy hip. "What now?"

"I promise this will only take a second. I'm just going to check on Mr. Ratz."

It occurred to me that the county investigator might not have talked to him. I didn't believe that Ratz was a likely suspect as our shooter earlier, but the man did have a temper, and as a veteran, he knew his way around guns, so I couldn't leave this stone unturned. I bounded up the stairs to his suite. I could hear the television on in the room, and someone coughed. I rapped on the door.

Ratz greeted me wearing an open robe and boxers, with his face unshaven, feet bare. The room beyond was well lit, and I spied two empty beer cans, an open pizza box, and at least a half-dozen cans of Mr. Pibb. A laptop computer was open on the table. "Yeah?" he asked, scratching his belly hair.

I quickly rattled off an interview. Ratz was grouchy, but he complied. Yes, he had heard the commotion next door. No, he hadn't bothered to investigate—he had been embarrassed by the scene in the bar last night and wanted to stay clear of other people for a while.

I watched his eyes and body language as he spoke. It was possible that he had gone out earlier tonight, but I was inclined to believe his account. I told him that several officers would be watching the inn until morning. He seemed completely disinterested. Then I left—but not before I took a good, hard look at Ratz's bare feet. They were far from pretty. They were also surprisingly small for a man of his size. At least I'd found out one thing of use: he probably wasn't the guy who had kicked me in the head last night. I hoped gaining that knowledge hadn't cost me my chance with Greta.

I headed back downstairs and rapped softly on her door. When she opened it, she was still dressed, but her suite appeared as if it had been prepped for seduction. The shadows from the flames of the fireplace licked and darted across the walls. I stepped inside, and saw that the rose-colored duvet was folded back invitingly. In the corner, two large scented candles were burning, one cranberry, the other lavender, their aromas mingling.

"You do know an open flame can be dangerous," I joked.

She closed the door and stepped past me, brushing my behind with her hand. "A little danger is good sometimes, don't you think?"

With feline grace, Greta moved to the side of the bed and quickly slipped off her skirt and sweater, then her black bra and panties, letting each piece drop to the floor as I watched. Then she slid into the bed and flipped the top sheet off her body, exposing her breasts, her waist, and one long and shapely leg. My eyes were still adjusting to the gloom, but even through the flickering shadows, I could see that her body was more athletic, her breasts firmer than I had imagined. Okay, so I had also imagined the fun I would have undressing her myself, but this was good, too.

There were no catlike movements when I undressed, however. I was more like a bull at a stud farm. Thankfully I remembered to yank off my socks and managed to do so without falling on my face. I slid between the sheets and we kissed like two lovers whose lips hadn't touched other lips in a long, long time, which in my case, at least, was the truth.

She pulled her tongue from my mouth and I reluctantly let it go. She put a finger on my lips. "You can't stay, you know," she said.

My heart sank like a rock in a hot tub. I began to think this woman was the all-time queen of tease. I even began to wish that I'd considered Chandra's offer.

Greta must have realized my confusion because she quickly

added, "I don't mean that you have to go now. I mean afterwards. I don't want anyone in my group to see you leaving here in the morning."

"Oh," I said. "I thought it was bad form to kiss and run. I've always been told that leaving right away and not calling the next day are the two biggest sins a man can commit."

"I don't want everyone to think we slept together like a couple of horny bar tramps. Just stay with me until I fall asleep again, okay?" She hesitated. "I know it sounds cliché, but I'm really not in the habit of doing this kind of thing. I have strong feelings for you, Chief. I hope you feel the same way."

"I do, I really do." It sounded childish and awkward. George Burns once said that if you can fake sincerity, you have it made. He was right—just look at politicians. The irony was that I did have feelings for Greta, but I've always had a problem with any kind of touchy-feely communication. I should probably practice sincerity in my spare time.

"You're right, it's better if I don't stay the night," I said. "I told my patrol officers to keep a close eye on the inn, and my Jeep is parked outside. They'll think something is up—well, you know what I mean."

"Will your officers be here all night long?"

"No, but they'll drive by intermittently. I also told them to keep watch on the house of the man who I suspect fired those shots tonight."

"So, you know who did it?"

"I have my suspicions."

"Oh," she said, pulling up the covers. "How many officers will be on duty tonight, watching the inn after you leave?"

"Two of my men, and maybe one county officer. That's for the whole township, but I'm sure you'll be safe. I really don't believe this guy will be back tonight, Greta. And I'll only be a phone call away. I live close by, and I'm never really off duty."

She smiled. "Well, I certainly hope you're off duty now."

She moved closer to me, pressing skin to skin. Then she kissed me and placed her hand between my legs. I was still fully aroused, despite the protracted conversation. I stroked and caressed her body, which felt warm and silky.

Suddenly she pulled away from me for a second time.

"Wait," she said, pressing her hand against my chest. "I need to hear one thing before I sleep with you."

I thought she was going to ask me if I loved her, or if I would respect her in the morning. Either way, I prepared myself to answer in the affirmative, with the most sincere tone I could muster.

"Before I sleep with you," she continued, "I have to know your name."

"Just call me Chief. Honestly, everyone does." I nuzzled her neck.

"No," she said, pushing me harder. "I won't sleep with a man when I don't even know his name. Now, tell me your real name—first, middle, and last, Mister, just the way it appears on your birth certificate. I promise I won't tell anyone else."

I would have preferred to tell her I loved her. Truth be told, my name isn't all that embarrassing, but I did hate it growing up, and I've become very accustomed to Chief. I pulled her close to my body and whispered my given name into her ear.

She laughed out loud. "I'll take your secret to the grave," she promised.

And then we made love.

Chapter Nineteen

For years, I have spent my Wednesday mornings at home, making a few phone calls and whittling down the endless pile of paperwork that accompanies my job as a small-town police chief. The rule I tell my staff is not to interrupt me unless it's an emergency. If it's before ten, they are not to call unless the emergency involves a flying pig or a dead human body. I always stress human, because it is not unusual to encounter a four-legged carcass in Walworth County. Road kill is far too common, especially during the hunting season, when virtually every woodland creature is on the run. My staff understands that I have zero interest in claiming the fresh meat from a car-struck deer. And naturally I do not want to be bothered whenever a tourist runs over a rabbit unless I have plans to make road-kill hasenpfeffer for dinner, which I almost never do on a Wednesday.

This particular Wednesday was unusual, however. For one thing, I'd awakened with a smile, thinking about the beautiful tourist I'd left behind at the inn. Sex with Greta for the first time had been very good. The second time had been even better. I had slipped out of her room just after three in the morning, leaving her deep asleep and dreaming sweet dreams.

At home I'd awakened again shortly before six. With the coffee brewing, I called Officer Burr to get an update on his drive-by patrols and make sure there had been no further disturbances at the inn. He confirmed that all appeared quiet, so I proceeded to let Dawg out, then called Dawg back in, curtailing his breakfast run to Muddy's on the

Lake. By seven o'clock I was showered, dressed, and sitting down to work at my kitchen table.

I was drinking my sixth cup of joe and filling out a payroll request when my home phone rang shortly after eight. The caller ID showed Dorothy's line at the stationhouse.

Frankly, I considered not answering. I suspected Dorothy was just eager to hear details about last night's "headliner" events. Given the local grapevine and her sleuthing abilities, she probably knew quite a bit about my date and the restaurant shooting, but that wouldn't stop her from wanting to know more. Of course, she would probably open by asking me where Geary had stashed the emergency supply of toilet paper.

I picked up on the third ring.

"Is that you, Chief?" Dorothy started in.

"Yes, Dorothy, it's me. Dawg only answers for Publisher's Clearing House."

"Oh, Chief, this is so unbelievable . . ." Her voice was filled with desperation.

I sat up straight. It was not like Dorothy to panic.

"Calm down, Dorothy," I said sternly. "Tell me what happened."

"Officer Burr just called. He's at the French Country Inn—you better get over there right away. They found a body, Chief. Bert says it's a murder!"

"Are you sure?" I asked. "I just spoke with Bert a couple hours ago."

"Yes, I'm sure!" she shrieked, now sounding annoyed as well as panicked.

"Okay, Dorothy, stay calm. Is Bert or anyone else in any imminent danger? Has there been another shooting?"

"No . . . no, I don't think so."

"I'm three minutes away," I said, reaching for my coat. "Is the victim male or female? Where is the body, and what makes Bert think it's a murder?"

"He didn't say, Chief. He's so shook up he didn't tell me anything! He just said someone is dead, and there is a lot of blood—lots of blood. He wasn't sure if he should call you at home, so he asked me to call you instead."

I shook my head. I love my staff. Despite my "rules," they still call me about every possible bit of minutia—last week it was something about the coffee filters. Yet Bert was still stumped on whether to call me about a dead body.

As I headed out the door, I phoned Bert on my cell. He picked up immediately.

I cut off his excited jabbering. "Tell me where the body is," I said, climbing into my car and starting it.

"Upstairs, above the lobby. Suite 303," Bert said.

Chandra's room, I thought. I breathed a guilty sigh of relief—for a moment, I'd thought maybe it was Greta. Her door had locked behind me when I'd left her sleeping, but just like the night before, it wasn't chained, the dead bolt hadn't been thrown. Maybe I was selfish, but it had briefly crossed my mind how awkward it would be if I had to explain my presence in the victim's room—if Greta had been the one murdered. Of course, I'd been in Chandra's room, too, but at least we hadn't had sex.

"Have you ID'd the victim?" I asked. "Can you tell the cause of death?"

"Not with absolute certainty, Chief—I didn't want to touch anything until you got here. But I have a tentative ID. Debbie saw the body from the doorway, and she said it does look like the guest assigned to 303, a woman named Chandra Harper. She's lying face down. And . . . well, she's very dead, Chief. Very dead."

"Where are you now?" I asked, ignoring his comment. No one

is ever just a little bit dead—you can be dead for a short time or a long time, but dead is dead.

"I'm in the lobby," Bert replied nervously.

"Okay, that's fine. Keep everyone clear of the scene," I ordered. "I'm almost there."

I slowed at an intersection and hit Dorothy's number on speed-dial. I told her to notify the coroner and the county crime lab's investigation team. "Tell them I'll meet them at the inn," I said. Then I instructed Dorothy to tell no one else about the situation. "I mean it, Dorothy. Tell no one. If I need assistance from another officer, I'll call you."

I wished that I had thought to tell Dorothy this earlier. If she had already passed along news of a murder to her husband or anyone else, then by noon all the local hangouts would be abuzz with stories of a serial killer on the loose. Either that, or everyone would be claiming that a bunch of Kool-Aid-guzzling Rastafarians had committed mass suicide at the inn.

I had good reason for my concern. There had been another death at the French Country Inn, before I became chief of police. It was 1986, right after Anthony Navilio had reopened the place. The death was in no way suspicious—an elderly man had suffered a massive heart attack and died in bed. Yet within an hour, a story had circulated through half the county, describing how Navilio's own father had been murdered in a mob-related hit. Some people still believed it. I did not want the same kind of rumor-mongering to happen on my watch, especially with the help of my own staff.

As I approached Lake Shore Drive and sped the last half-mile toward the inn, I looked up at the sky over Como Lake. Another winter storm was brewing. It wasn't the weather that made me wary, however. I was checking for a flock of flying pigs.

* * *

When I arrived at the French Country Inn, Officer Burr was guarding the doors to the lobby. He ushered me inside.

"I haven't let anyone else go up to that room, Chief," Bert said. "I've also cut off access to the lobby and asked all the staff to stay clear. Debbie was working the front desk today. I asked her to wait for you in the bar, in case you have any questions. She had all the inn's calls transferred there."

Bert's face was ashen, but he seemed to have collected himself. I was impressed by his efforts to keep the crime scene secure and untainted. Perhaps all those hours he spent watching TV police dramas had finally paid off.

"Who found the body?" I asked, pulling a pair of booties over my shoes. I had a pair of crime-scene gloves in my pocket. I carried both in my car, but this was the first time I'd be using them in a murder investigation in Geneva Township.

"That'd be Tracy."

"Tracy?" I asked.

"You know—the waitress with the ponytail," Bert said. "Reddish blonde hair? Always smiling?"

I thought of the waitress who had waited on Greta and me the prior night. If that was Tracy, she probably wasn't smiling this morning. I nodded at Bert to continue.

"Tracy was helping with breakfast chores for the writing group. She had an order to take muffins and coffee to the woman upstairs at seven forty-five, and the door to the suite was ajar . . ." He swallowed, no doubt picturing the scene. "Well, she's pretty shook up, but she's waiting for you in the bar with Debbie. There are a couple paramedics from the fire department here, too. Debbie called 911, but there wasn't anything they could do to help her. They said they'd hang around a while, though, in case you want to talk to them, too."

"Did they move the body?"

"No, I made sure they didn't. It was obvious she was too far gone."

I took a deep breath. "Okay. That's good work, Bert. I'll talk to Tracy and the others when I come back downstairs. The county investigators should be on their way. You wait for them here, make sure the lobby stays secure."

Bert nodded. He looked relieved that I hadn't asked him to go upstairs again.

The steps creaked as I went up. I stared at the carpet, saw no footprints, no obvious trail that the killer might've left. The door to Chandra's room was open. I checked the lock and frame. There were no signs of forced entry. A tray with a pot of spilled coffee and some muffins lay on the floor just inside the doorway. I took out my digital camera and began to click away: entrance, ceiling, windows, bathroom, sitting area, bedside table, bed, floor. I wanted a visual inventory of every nook and cranny, everything I could see without actually moving the body. And it was a body. There was no reason to check for a pulse—not with the amount of blood at the scene.

The victim was lying beside the bed, face down on the floor. Her legs were partially covered by a duvet that had been dragged halfway off the mattress. Blood had soaked into the bedding and mattress, and there was a broad red stain across the back of the victim's pale blue nightshirt. I thought I could make out two stab wounds in the fabric. Her left arm was crumpled next to her torso, but her right arm was stretched overhead, as if reaching. Her right hand was resting atop a hardcover copy of the *The Ox-Bow Incident*, the book she'd told me she was reading when we spoke in the bar. A paperback copy of *To Kill a Mockingbird*, the selection from the Mayor's reading club, was also on the floor beside the body, amid assorted pill bottles and other items that appeared to have been knocked off the bedside table.

The victim's blonde curls were in a loose array about her head, and her face was turned sideways. I let the camera zoom in. One blue eye was fixed open, shocked and accusing, and her pouty lips were twisted in complaint. It was Chandra Harper, all right. And this time, she had most definitely suffered a traumatic experience.

Chapter Twenty

I stepped outside for some air. The sky had turned a mean shade of gray, the wind was gusting from the lake, and tiny snowflakes were spinning through the air like confetti thrown against a giant fan. The snow was too light and dry to accumulate, except where the wind had pushed it into sugary drifts in a corner or against an obstacle. In my head, words and ideas were swirling around just like the snow, but I was unable to hold on to any theory or thought. I just felt numb.

It wasn't the first body I'd seen. It wasn't even the bloodiest, given the traffic fatalities that went with my job. But the murder had struck me harder than I would have expected. I had disliked Chandra Harper. I had wished bad things upon her. But I had not wished her dead. The question was, of course, Who had?

After I'd left the murder scene and gone back downstairs, I briefly questioned the staff in Kirsch's bar. Tracy confirmed Bert's account: Shortly before eight, she carried a tray with a continental breakfast to suite 303. Chandra had ordered it the night before. There wasn't usually room service, but Chandra, ever resourceful, had arranged for special treatment. Getting no response and having found the door slightly ajar, Tracy went inside to leave the tray on the table. "When I saw her there, I dropped the tray on the floor and screamed," she said. "I just froze."

The sound brought Debbie running from lobby. Debbie had dutifully called 911, then asked for the police—and the paramedics, just in case. As it happened, Bert was cruising the lakeshore nearby, and he was on the scene in less than a minute.

I asked Debbie who had access to Chandra's suite as well as the building. She confirmed that none of the other guests' keys would even open the lobby after it was locked at night. Apart from the owner, only she and trusted members of the restaurant staff had keys to the building or a master key, and to the best of her knowledge, no key was missing. "I can't imagine how anyone got into the building, let alone her room, unless she opened the door herself," Debbie said, sniffling. "We're careful about security, even though nothing ever happens here. Well, not until this . . ."

As I stood outside afterward, sucking in the cold air, I pondered her statement. What was happening to my quiet little town—and could I have stopped it? I did not blame myself for Chandra's death, but I still had to ask the what if's. What if I had posted an officer in the lobby, or parked a squad outside the inn all night, instead of relying on intermittent drive-by patrols? What if I had personally surveyed the inn and its grounds after I'd left Greta's room, instead of heading straight home? Was it really so important that I leave quickly and head back to my own bed to replay my adventures with Greta in my dreams?

I felt more than a tinge of remorse. A woman was dead on my watch, in my township, and only a short time after I'd personally bade her goodnight. Perhaps the murder had even occurred when I was still on the premises, cavorting in bed with another guest. If that detail became widely known, it would cause me grief for the sheer ridicule factor alone. But I couldn't worry about that now. There were far too many other questions spinning in my head.

Had the killer been watching the inn and waiting for me to leave after last night's shooting? Had he or she been watching Chandra or her room? Had Chandra Harper even been the target—or had it been Anthony Navilio, whose suite she had taken? Could it be that

Chandra Harper had simply been in the wrong place at the wrong time?

Ultimately, it was not my responsibility to answer those questions. From the start, I knew I would turn this investigation over to the Walworth County major crimes force as soon as they arrived. That was the procedure here. When it came to murder, the county took charge, aided by the state of Wisconsin. Technically, I'd be part of the investigative team, but if this were a chess game, I'd be a knight at best, and maybe just a pawn. I accepted that—in this case, I even preferred it. I did plan to assist the county's lead man, Roger Tyrrell, to the extent he desired, however. I might even do a little digging on my own. I generally got along with Tyrrell, and he wasn't threatened by the skills I had acquired during my years with the Chicago Police Department.

The Walworth County team arrived roughly forty-five minutes after I had. We conferred briefly, and I reported what I knew so far, which wasn't much. Then they immediately began crawling over Chandra's room and the adjacent areas. They reminded me of ants on a sugar cube. Bert and I cleared out of their way until they were ready to talk with us again.

And so it was that I found myself still standing outside, pondering the mystery and sucking in cold air, as Greta's car pulled into the far side of the lot. She stepped out and waved at me, then propped a cardboard tray with two cups of coffee on the roof of her black Lexus. After she shut the door, she began walking in my direction with the coffee in hand and a sassy little sway in her gait.

"Hey there, officer," she called with a smile. "Fancy meeting you here." Her smile faded as she noticed the officer stringing yellow tape across the porch in front of the lobby. Then she stopped, squinting at the squad cars at the side of the inn.

I met her halfway and took her elbow. "Let's go to your room," I said.

"What's all the commotion?" she asked. "Please don't tell me someone shot up the restaurant again. You promised that was a one-time thing!"

"Let's go inside," I answered. "It's too cold out here."

As soon as she had opened the door to her suite, I led her to a comfortable chair. I took the coffee from her hands and set it in on the adjacent table.

"Okay, now you're scaring me, Chief," she said. "What's going on?"

I searched for the ideal words but failed. "There's been a murder. It's your friend Chandra. I'm afraid she's dead."

Greta's eyes opened wide, then her face twisted in agony. She buried it in her gloved hands and started to weep. I knelt on one knee next to her chair and awkwardly hugged her, making my shoulder available for her grief.

After steeling herself, she looked at me, eyes red and wet. "How did this happen, Chief? Who did this? Oh, my God—was it John Ratz?"

I shook my head. "I can't tell you that, Greta, because we don't have the answers yet. All I can tell you is that the investigation is underway. I really don't know much more."

For several minutes we remained silent, Greta in the chair and I at her side. Then she rose and walked to the fire and turned it on, and removed her gloves and coat. "Oh, poor Chandra . . ."

She reached for one of the coffees and wrapped her hands around the cup. Then she pointed to the other. "I went into town to get a couple lattes—for a treat, you know? That one's for Chandra, but she won't be needing it now, of course." Her voice cracked, and she sniffled. "You can have it if you'd like."

"When was the last time you spoke with Chandra?" I asked, ignoring the offer.

Greta looked bewildered. "Well, you were there, Chief. It was last night—just before you walked her back to her room. Chandra and I didn't talk again after that." She paused. "My God. Was she—do you think she was killed while you were here with me? While you and I . . . were . . .?"

That was not an image I liked myself. "We don't know anything for sure yet, Greta."

Her lips quivered, and she began to tear up again. "I need to lie down now," she said. "I hope you don't mind, Chief, but I think I'd just like to be by myself for a while."

I nodded. I helped her into bed and placed a glass of water on the end table. Then I kissed her on the forehead and told her I would return as soon as I could. As I walked down the hallway past the gathering room, I saw that Professor Feri and several of the guests had assembled there. I glanced inside.

Professor Feri immediately stood up from his chair and walked toward me. "Please, come in," he pleaded. "Tell us what has happened. Is it true? Has Chandra Harper been murdered?"

"Yes, I'm afraid that's true, but I have no details yet. I'm heading back to the main building to meet with the county's investigative team. After that, I will tell you what I can. In the meantime, your group should remain here in this building until we've had a chance to speak with you. You may not realize it, but you might have heard or seen something that can help us with the investigation."

I looked around the room at each of their faces. They were all long and sad. The professor's assistant was blotting tears from her eyes, and Emile Tavilion was commiserating with two of the other gentlemen. I did a quick head count. Only two people from the group were missing—and I'd just left one of them in her room.

"Professor Feri," I said, lowering my voice. "I wonder if you can tell me the whereabouts of one of your writers, John Ratz . . . the fellow who gave us a little trouble in the bar Monday night."

Feri looked at me incredulously. "He's upstairs," he said. "But surely you could verify that yourself."

"When was last time you spoke with him?" I asked.

"Why, just a short time ago on the phone. He told me he was making some good headway on his book, so he wouldn't be joining our session again this morning. Surely you're not implying—"

"I am not implying anything," I said. "But of course, I'll want to talk to him later, just as I'd like to speak with all of you."

"I see," Feri said. "I can see how John's behavior might lead you to suspect him, but I feel I must speak on his behalf. Admittedly, the man has a temper, but I cannot believe that he is involved in this tragedy in any way whatsoever—nor is anyone else in this group. I can assure you, I am a very keen judge of character."

"Thanks, I'll keep that in mind," I said. "I'm sure your insights will be very helpful when you and I have a chance to sit down and talk more. In the meantime, please ask the members of your group to stay away from the lobby. And try not to tie up the inn's telephone lines unless it is important. I will return as soon as I have some news to share with you."

Before I could escape, the assistant, Evelyn Durst, trotted up and touched my arm. In a low voice, she whispered, "Are we safe here? I mean, first the shooting and now this. It's so horrible. Maybe we should all just check out and leave!"

I assured both her and Feri that their group was indeed safe, and that I saw no reason they should not finish out the week at the inn as planned, although in fact I had no cause to be certain of anything. Then I asked Evelyn to check in on Greta. "She's in her room, lying down. She's pretty broken up over the loss of Chandra."

"Of course," Evelyn replied. "Oh, she must be devastated. I'll go right now . . ." Her words trailed off as she trotted down the hall.

* * *

As usual, the boys from county were slow and methodical. When I returned to Chandra's suite, a crime scene tech was still combing over it as if he were searching for a fragment of a lost contact lens. The lead investigator, Roger Tyrrell, was standing next to the body.

I knocked on the open door. "Find anything pertinent yet?" I asked.

Detective Roger Tyrrell was a stocky man with wide shoulders and a thick neck. With his white mane of hair and his dark, bushy eyebrows, he reminded me of a certain college basketball coach, although I'd never seen Tyrell sweat or lose his cool.

Tyrrell motioned me inside. "Come on in, Chief," he said. "So . . . we have two large wounds. Stabbed twice in the back, probably with a large-bladed knife. The blood trail stops with the body. We found no murder weapon here in the room, the hallway, or the lobby. So far, we haven't found anything directly around this building, either. Do you think you could gather one or two of your guys, help search the grounds, check all the nearby Dumpsters, see if you come up with anything?"

"Sure," I said. "Anything we can do to help." I sensed that my staff and I would be relegated to grunt work. I felt a tinge of resentment, but I didn't let it show. I was just glad the township didn't have garbage pickup today—otherwise Tyrrell might have "my guys" checking every trash can lining the road.

"As I was saying," Tyrrell continued, "the victim was stabbed twice. The first time, she probably was lying down in bed, asleep. That one didn't kill her—it was off to the right side, below the shoulder blade."

He spoke dispassionately, as if the "victim" had not been human, but merely a prop or fixture in the room.

"Judging from the way the covers are pulled from the bed,

the second wound was inflicted as she tried to move away from her attacker. Here, like this." He moved his own body in an attempt to show me how Chandra might have reacted. "But there were no defensive wounds. Only the two stabs, one very deep and lethal. She didn't struggle against her attacker."

He pointed to the wall with the fireplace. "I believe she rose almost to a sitting position, on to the side of the bed, but still facing away from her attacker. She was holding the covers with her left hand when the second blow came."

Tyrrell was animated as he replayed the death scene. "The force of the second blow and her own momentum caused her to go down to the floor. In the process, she knocked over the bed lamp, her face creams, and all the other stuff on the bedside table, including those two books. She might've been grabbing for something, or maybe she was just getting her balance."

Chandra's motionless body lay on the floor where I had first seen it earlier this morning. Next to her body lay a tattered paperback. Tiny droplets of blood lay atop the silhouette of a bird in flight. It was a copy of *To Kill a Mockingbird* by Harper Lee. "The timeless classic of human dignity that unites us all," appeared in white letters at the top of the front cover. There is no human dignity at a crime scene, however, especially when murder is involved.

A container of Aveda face cream and a tube of body lotion were on the floor next to Lee's novel, with several pill bottles scattered beside them. I'd photographed each one. The first was a prescription bottle for Ambien, a powerful sleep drug. Another was a prescription for Percocet, a pain reliever. The third was an OTC antihistamine–pain reliever combination for nighttime use. She also had a bottle of melatonin, No-Doz, and some high-strength ibuprofen.

I looked around again, searching for details that might have changed since I'd last seen Chandra alive. The brandy had been moved to a tray on a table in the sitting area. Two glasses were beside it, both washed and turned face down on the tray.

"I should mention that I spoke with the victim myself last night," I said.

"In the restaurant, after that shooting, right? I read the reports just before I came."

"Yes, but I was also here in her room around midnight. Strictly professional," I added. "She was unnerved by the shooting, and she asked me to walk her upstairs, check things over before she turned in for the night."

"When it rains it pours," Tyrrell said. "Think there's any connection between last night's shooting and this?"

I frowned. "It's a pretty big coincidence to have both things happen in the same place in one night. But right now I don't see it. The shooting in the restaurant felt like the work of a crazy. This feels more calculated."

Tyrrell nodded. "My thoughts exactly. Still, the victim was present at both scenes. Can't rule out a connection just yet." He looked up at me. "So, you got a good look at things in the room before I arrived here, right? Did you notice any significant changes compared to last night?"

"I've been trying to remember, and only one thing comes to mind. Did you find a laptop computer?"

Tyrrell looked up. "No, I don't think that's been inventoried. Where was it?"

"I didn't actually see it, but the victim was here with a writer's group, and there was a black zippered case on that table last night. My guess, it contained her laptop, maybe a few notebooks. She was writing on something, and it wasn't stone tablets."

"Good point. We'll look into that," Tyrrell said.

I took a closer look at the book under Chandra's right hand. It was a hardcover copy of *The Ox-Bow Incident*, the classic Western novel that she and I had discussed not-so-pleasantly during our encounter in the bar.

A disturbing image came to mind: I envisioned Chandra, undead and bloodied, rising to a seated position on the floor and presenting the book to me. "Read this," she said, "you illiterate movie-loving ignoramus. It's a complex morality tale." The image was eerily real.

"What do you make of the book?" I asked Tyrrell, pointing to the novel beneath Chandra's stiff, well-manicured hand. Her painted fingernails were as red as the drops of blood.

"The book?" Tyrrell asked. "Nothing, really. When she fell to the floor, she dragged everything off the bedside table. Her hand came to rest on that book."

"Do you think that she could have been reading the book just before the murder? Or maybe fell asleep with it in her hand?"

Tyrrell had already told me he thought the victim was asleep, and on her stomach, when the attack had occurred. But I liked to ask questions and prod from a new angle just to see if the answers might change. I wondered if Tyrrell had any alternate theories or assumptions he wasn't sharing. Besides, the book looked curious to me.

"No, she didn't fall asleep while reading," he said. "The estimated time of death is somewhere between three and six a.m.—the autopsy should narrow it down a little more. The light on the end table wasn't switched on, only the bathroom light and the desk lamp. The victim was probably afraid of the dark, maybe a little on edge after the shooting. But she didn't have light to read by. And the only people who read in the middle of the night are the ones who can't sleep."

Tyrrell spoke convincingly of his crime scene assumptions, but they were still assumptions, not fact.

"How long do you think she survived?" I asked. "Between the stabbing and the time of death, I mean. Could she have maybe lost consciousness, then regained it after the killer left?"

"Again, we'll have to wait for the autopsy. But I think she bled out pretty fast." Tyrrell seemed definite in his response. "Look at the way these blood streaks are located, the arrangement of the debris. I think she was trying to pull herself forward so she could reach her purse, which is over there in the corner." He pointed to Chandra's oversized designer-label purse, resting a few feet away against the wall. "She probably wanted her cell phone, but she was unable to reach it. The book was just in the way, along with all the other stuff she knocked off the table."

"Might be interesting to check the cell phone records."

"We'll do that, of course. But since the phone was in her purse, she obviously didn't make any dying declarations."

There were two parallel streaks of blood to the left on the carpet, above Chandra's head. With my ballpoint pen, I reached out toward Chandra's hand. "May I?" I asked.

Tyrrell nodded. "The on-scene medical is done. Knock yourself out."

I lifted the victim's hand from its resting place on the book. Her first two fingers lay atop the word Ox in the book's title. Her ring and pinky finger were tucked under her palm, and there was blood on the fingertips.

Imaginary undead Chandra turned her head in my direction and spoke. In my feverish fantasy, she became two Chandras—one ghostly and animated as she rose up on one elbow, the other prone and stiff. "Ox, you idiot," said the animated version. "As in, Read the book, you dumb ox. That is, if you're not too busy bedding my friend."

I ignored her and addressed Tyrrell. "Why do you think the killer only stabbed her twice? Why didn't he stab her more, slit her throat or something, to make sure she was dead?"

"Obviously the two stab wounds did the job, but it's a reasonable question. Three or more stab wounds would usually indicate rage. Of course, that needn't be solely against the victim. Sometimes, it's just a general sense of rage within the killer."

Officer Tyrrell spoke as if he was the veteran cop from Chicago, and I was the relatively inexperienced observer. But I had to give him credit where it was due—he was more adept at his trade than some of the so-called pros I'd encountered in Chicago.

"My sense of it?" Tyrrell continued. "The killer is someone who wanted this woman dead, but there was no great sense of rage toward the victim. This was not an act of uncontrolled anger—it's colder, more calculated. I think our killer is most likely a man, given the force of the blow, but a very strong woman could have done it, too. The killer might have even stood here a while, watching his victim struggle, assessing whether two blows would be adequate. Of course, it could be otherwise. Maybe he—or she—heard something or someone after he'd plunged in the murder weapon, or even had a pang of remorse, and that's why the killer stopped with two strikes. At this point, who knows?"

"Or maybe . . . the killer saw a ghost," I muttered.

Tyrrell ignored my comment. "Okay, so here's what we've got so far. There appeared to be no break-in, no struggle. And if the victim had struggled or made any noise, it probably didn't matter—this room is isolated, it was late, and it's possible nobody would've heard her screams anyway. In addition to the cell phone, her purse contains over three hundred dollars. She also had some expensive jewelry here, including a rock of a wedding ring, which is still on her finger. In short, it doesn't look like robbery was a motive. It's a fairly safe assumption that the victim was asleep, so . . . she didn't open the door for her killer. Unless, of course, she let him in before she fell asleep, which raises the question of a liaison gone bad. The autopsy will confirm whether the victim engaged in sexual activity last night. But I believe either the killer had a key to the room, or the door was left unlocked."

"I think she locked it when I left here around midnight," I said.

"But I suppose she might have slipped downstairs after that, maybe got something from the bar, then forgot to relock it. Booze and pills can make you sloppy, assuming she mixed them."

"Yeah. They can also make you choose some pretty strange bedfellows," Tyrrell said.

I wondered if he was hinting that he knew about me and Greta. I didn't bring it up—that part of my evening didn't seem like pertinent information. Not yet, anyway. But he was looking at Chandra's body as he spoke, so I decided he was just mulling over the possibility of her after-midnight love life.

"The fingerprints and some of the evidence reports may tell us more later on," Tyrrell continued. "But since this is a hotel room, it's bound to be full of prints. We've got a lot of ground to cover. I'm going to need your help on this one, Chief."

"Sure. Whatever you need."

"Our best place to start is the victim herself," Tyrrell said. "Who she knew, who she pissed off, who benefited from her death. The usual suspects."

"I agree," I said. "I'd like to see if I can't get a copy of the book she was working on. It was very personal from what I understand, almost like a diary. We might not find that missing computer, but we can probably get a copy of some files from the professor who's running this workshop. I'd like to see if there's anything there that might point us toward the killer."

"That's a good idea. I was hoping you'd work the whole content issue—confirm what she brought up here, including that laptop, discs, journals, jewelry, other personal items—anything you can discover that would help. To tell you the truth, we're still swamped with the Hauftmann investigation, and I'm real close to solving it. I don't want to pull my best guy off it just yet. Do you have some time?"

"I'll make the time, Roger. I can also do the interviews with everyone here at the inn today, see if they have any suspicions."

Tyrrell paused. "Sure, okay. Do the preliminaries as soon as you can, work the content at the same time. We'll compare notes when you're done. I've already got someone started on the financials, checking her debts and assets, who benefits from her death, all the pertinent details."

"Anybody notify the next of kin yet?" I asked. "I believe she is—was—married."

Tyrrell nodded. "That's right—to a . . ." He checked his notes. "Hector Harper. She listed him as an emergency contact list when she registered for the workshop. We already tracked him down in Chicago, and we're having him come up here. He should arrive this afternoon."

"Well, if that's it, I'll get started," I said.

"Thanks, Chief. Oh—and don't forget about the Dumpsters. It stinks, I know, but someone's gotta do it."

"Roger that, " I said, heading toward the door.

As I descended the oak stairs, I imagined the ghost of Chandra Harper laughing at me. Poor John Moran, I thought. If he was haunting the inn, he wouldn't appreciate her company.

Chapter Twenty-One

Nowadays most people in Geneva Township think I'm called Chief because I'm the chief of police. My old friends know better. The "Chief" moniker was given to me by Dave Tedeski back in our early teens. Dave loved nicknames, and he slapped one on nearly every kid with whom we associated.

There was Stumpy, Scooter, Skip, Skeeter, the Stork—Dave was particularly fond of the letter S. There was also Dolph, Hammer, and Thumper, as well as Navajo, a kid who was actually Polish. Before Davey dubbed me Chief, he called me "Prez." I remember Shaky John asking Tedeski why he'd chosen that name. "It's not like he's presidential or anything," he'd complained. Dave had just laughed and said, "Cuz he lives in the White House, you dolt."

In fact, our house was white. So was our car, our garage, and even our dog. But Davey also knew my last name, of course, and he got a big kick out of the double entendre. Apparently, no one else appreciated the humor, however, because Prez didn't stick.

A short time later, when we were freshmen in high school, Davey renamed me "Chief." Not the Chief, just Chief. This time the name stuck, even though most people still had no insight into Dave's sense of humor. When I figured out why Dave had nicknamed me Chief, all I could say was, "Great Caesar's Ghost!"

But I liked the name myself, and from then on, I was always Chief. Maybe it was Dave's magical influence, but everybody seemed to accept it. Even people who knew my full name and didn't get Tedeski's joke seemed happy to call me Chief. And I was happy to introduce myself that way, to everyone I met, both here and down in Chicago.

I'd given Dave the nickname "Duke" after Duke Snider, the baseball great, but my friend was quick to steal that train and take it straight down another track. Dave claimed that he'd been given the name by none other than John Wayne himself. As the story went, Tedeski had met Wayne at a movie premiere. After a bit of chatting, John Wayne had said, "Young man, you remind me of me when I was your age, and I think it's only right that you're called Duke."

Of course, when Davey told that story, he spoke the words in a God-awful imitation of John Wayne, complete with the swaggering walk as an exit. Instead of the real thing, he looked like a drunken John Travolta from *Saturday Night Fever.* But my pal "Duke" was genuinely crazy about John Wayne, and he'd drag me halfway across Chicago anytime there was a chance to see a John Wayne Western.

Only one hero was bigger to Tedeski than John Wayne, and that was Superman. Duke loved all things Superman back in the day: the DC comic books, the reruns of the Superman TV show from the Fifties with George Reeves as the man of steel, and the Superman movies, of course, even the dismal last two of them. He knew every page and scene. His Superman comic book collection ran into the hundreds of issues, and he was always proud of it—even after he started carrying a gun for work.

It was Superman who was responsible for the near cashiering of Davey and some of his cohorts from the Chicago Police Department. Early in his career, when he was working the transit line detail, Davey and a few of his fellow officers pulled off what I like to call the Superstunt. To this day, it is heralded by Chicago's men in blue as one of the greatest pranks of all time.

Wearing plain clothes, members of the transit squad were patrolling the elevated train line, commonly known as the "L." They used decoys to nab the malcontents intent on committing robbery, assault, and various other acts of mayhem. The team usually set up their sting in high-crime areas. An officer in street clothes would lie on the platform or on a bench, pretending he had passed out from over-indulgence. If a perp robbed him, the transit boys would step in and make the arrest.

After months, the routine got boring, and the squad began to look for new ways to work the sting. Officer Iggy Kyrzuk began to dress as a woman in suggestive apparel, hoping to lure a groper or sexual deviant. Iggy stood about five-foot-eight and weighed in at a lean-but-mean one hundred and fifty pounds, so he pulled off the look pretty well, provided both the lighting and the criminals weren't too bright. In areas where homosexuals had been targeted for assault, Iggy occasionally posed as a well-heeled commuter of the gay persuasion—or a vulnerable metrosexual wearing too much bling. I couldn't tell them apart anyway.

One fine summer's night, Tedeski decided to raise the role-playing to a new level. Iggy had donned skin-tight designer jeans and a lavender silk shirt, along with a flashy gold watch and a neck chain. With his wallet bulging out of his back pocket and a navy-blue sport coat folded as his pillow, he slumped out on a bench. It was past midnight on a weekday, and most straphangers had already made it to their destinations. At last, someone took the "Iggy bait." A half-drunken perp purloined the fake Rolex, then stuck his hand in Iggy's pockets.

Suddenly, a hero appeared—and it was none other than Superman. Wearing tights and briefs, Dave Tedeski exploded through the metal turnstile, from which the bolts and pins had previously been removed. He swooped across the platform, his Super-cape flying behind him, then stopped and put his hands on his hips. "Unhand that man!" he commanded. Before the astonished perp could flee, Superman grabbed him by the wrist and twisted it rudely behind him, forcing him to the ground. The rest of the squad moved in to assist with the arrest.

At the arraignment in night court, the judge asked the accused man to describe the events of the evening. Of course the perp claimed he was innocent—that he had only meant to help the victim. "Honest, Judge, I was only trying to wake him up. But the next thing I knew, Superman was attacking me. I think he might've cracked my wrist when he threw me on the ground."

The judge frowned. "Excuse me, did you say Superman?"

The perp had been intoxicated, but not to the point of hallucination. He repeated his account, adding the bit about the flying cape and the exploding turnstile. The judge summoned the arresting officers into his chambers, along with the attorneys. Luckily, His Honor only gave Tedeski and the other officers a good scolding. But he made it clear that Superman had no place whatsoever in his courtroom. "Save your sideshow parodies for the Christmas party," he warned Tedeski.

Back at the stationhouse, the story spread fast. When it reached the top brass, the men received a second scolding—and the threat of suspension without pay if it ever happened again. It never did. Who could top it, after all? Tedeski's Superman story went down in the annals of the Chicago police, in all its hyperbolic glory. Over the years, I have heard myriad variations of the tale, all related to me by fellow officers who swore they were with Superman that night. But I know the real story. And I heard all the details of the plan directly from Dave Tedeski, the night before he pulled off the caper.

* * *

The murder of Chandra Harper had me thinking about Dave again—and remembering how much I missed his sage advice. Life had taken us in different directions, and it had been a while since I had spoken to Dave about work, my divorce, or anything else of much importance. I knew I should pay him a visit, and I promised myself I would do it very soon.

When it came to a criminal investigation, no one possessed a keener insight than Duke Tedeski. He taught me how to avoid the investigative pratfalls and gave me a number of good rules to follow. I'd never worked a homicide before Chandra's death, but Dave had, of course, and his step-by-step rules of murder were pretty simple.

In Dave's book of experience, the number one motive for murder was money—money someone had, money they owed, money somebody stood to gain. So Dave's number one rule was, Follow the money.

Rule number two: Consider the love angle, or sexual passion—including that gray area of love-hate relationships.

Rule number three: Consider money, love, or passion again.

Rule number four: If you're stumped, refer back to rules one, two, or three. All the other possible motives for murder—revenge, sociopathic pleasure, mistaken identity, et cetera—they just aren't as common as you'd think, Dave would always say. But money and passion? "They make the murder world go round and round."

Tyrrell's investigators were already tracking Chandra Harper's financials—looking into bank accounts, tax returns, insurance policies, property titles, and any other pertinent records that could be tracked electronically. No doubt they'd also be looking for Chandra's will, if she had one. So, I intended to do things the old-fashioned way and ask everyone who knew Chandra about her finances and personal life. Sometimes you need a tip to know which records deserve the most attention. And murders don't always revolve around the people who actually inherit—sometimes it's about the people who think they will.

Following Dave's murder rules, the next motive after money would be passion. John Ratz was the front-runner in that category—for now, at least. Considering Chandra's alleged sexual habits, the list of suspects was undoubtedly much longer, and it probably included lovers

I didn't know about. Naturally I'd turn a spotlight on her husband, who could have both money and sexual jealousy as a motive. The husband might even have paid someone to commit the murder, for all I knew . . . but I was getting ahead of myself.

I also considered the revenge angle. On Tedeski's list of motives, it wasn't a very likely scenario. But in this case, I felt it was still worth considering. If anyone could anger someone to the point of committing murder, it would've been Chandra Harper. She was so annoying that a lot of people would have liked to shut her up for good—and then claim temporary insanity.

Finally, there was the matter of "murder through mistaken identity." That, too, fell at the bottom of Dave's list of scenarios. But given the Navilio situation and Chandra's coincidental use of his suite, I couldn't rule out that possibility—not yet. What if Navilio had been the real target? I couldn't ignore the shots fired earlier at the bar and at the inn's sign, my strange encounter with Bigfoot—or the threats Zubeck had leveled against Navilio and the inn. And that made Ben Zubeck a suspect in the murder, too.

Chapter Twenty-Two

After I'd finished talking with Tyrrell in Chandra's room, I gave Shea a call and put him on Dumpster duty with Bert. There was a lot of groaning on the other end of the line, but I explained what Tyrrell wanted and why he needed help. "Looks like we're looking for a large blade or piercing object, probably a knife," I said. "Just imagine yourself tossing something like that after a murder and check out the obvious disposal sites—the Dumpster at Mars Resort, for example. He might've left on foot and gone down the shore to his car."

"Ya know . . .," said Shea, "it'd be pretty stupid to just toss it in the trash. Now, if I wanted to lose a murder weapon this time of year, I'd put it in a weighted bag and drop it down an ice-fishing hole," he said.

"Let's hope our killer isn't as smart as you are." I paused. "But while you're at it, do a little more looking around the inn and out on the ice itself. Just don't trip over any of Tyrrell's guys. He says they're short-handed, but they're never as short-handed as we are."

When I returned to L'Auberge, Professor Feri and most of the other writers were in the gathering room, drinking coffee and snacking on bagels. As before, only Greta and Ratz were absent. I'd arranged to use Chandra's original suite in L'Auberge as an interview room if I needed to talk with someone privately or on neutral ground. The electrical problem had been fixed, Debbie said, and that room was conveniently unoccupied, so it would serve the purpose well enough.

John Ratz was a good candidate for the murder, but I decided to leave him for later, until I'd armed myself with some information. Instead I started with Professor Feri, leader of the writer pack. I asked him to follow me down the hall to room 123.

Once we'd confirmed the preliminaries—his name, address, relationship to the victim, and so forth—I asked the professor to explain his whereabouts between midnight and 6:00 a.m. "It's strictly a routine question," I said. "You are not personally under investigation."

Professor Feri nodded. "I did not imagine that I was," he said haughtily, "because I can assure you that I was asleep in my room between those hours."

"Can anyone verify that?"

"Excuse me?"

"Were you alone in your room?"

He looked at me incredulously. "Yes, I was alone in my room."

"And you heard or saw nothing unusual?"

He smiled condescendingly. "I believe I have already stated that I was asleep."

I smiled back. "Just covering all the bases, Professor. Like I said, it's nothing personal."

Feri nodded curtly, but he relaxed again.

"So," I continued. "Can you confirm whether Chandra did her writing on a laptop computer? We're checking to make sure nothing is missing from her room."

"Indeed she did," he answered. "Both here at the workshop and at home, in fact. There are still a few writers who prefer to write longhand—it helps them feel the words, and resist the temptation to revise when they should be moving forward. I used to write everything longhand myself, but even I have given in to modern technology. You see—"

"Right," I said, cutting him off. "So, what kind of computer did Chandra use?"

"It's a Mac," he replied. "But I also know she writes longhand in her journal."

"You mean she keeps a diary?"

"No, I did not say a diary," Feri reprimanded me. "I said a journal. But I suppose one might say it is a quasi-diary, which she uses to organize her thoughts and observations, and capture the essence of the moment. Chandra is—excuse me, was—a uniquely intuitive individual. She was able to inculcate and discern knowledge from all things around her, be they animate or inanimate. Only a few blessed individuals whom I have known have had the ability to transcend mere relationships into a more powerful spiritual connection, which then brings individuals together into a finite equilibrium with Nature itself. Chandra was one of them."

I stared at Feri. I wanted to say I have no idea what the hell that means, but I'm pretty sure it's the biggest pile of psycho-babble bull I've ever heard. Instead, I said, "Tell me more about this diary—her journal, that is. Did you ever read it?"

"Chandra and I shared many professional moments together, which were also somewhat sensitive in nature. Yes, she occasionally read passages to me aloud, directly from her journal. At which times, I acted not entirely as her mentor in writing, but also as confrere of her letters . . . her confidant, if you will."

"You knew her pretty well, in other words," I said.

"Yes, officer, I knew her quite well, I believe."

"And as her confidant, did you ever learn of some activity or association that might have put her in danger? Something that might have led to her murder?"

"I can assure you, I did not."

"And as her writing mentor, do you have knowledge of the files on her computer?"

"Why, of course. Nearly everything Chandra wrote, apart from her journal, was submitted to me on a flash drive for review."

"Think carefully, Professor. Is there anything in those files that might have suggested she feared for her life—or more importantly, was there something that might have inadvertently put her in danger?"

Feri pondered for a moment. "If she feared for her life, I certainly wasn't aware of it. Chandra believed that her sister was murdered by her fiancé, but that case was officially closed some time ago, and there haven't been any new developments. Chandra made some accusations, and the matter became very unpleasant, yes . . . But to the best of my knowledge, it has been years since Chandra has had any contact whatsoever with the fiancé whom she accused. Moreover, Chandra's writings do not even focus on him, per se—they have more to do with her personal struggles to move on, to rebuild her own identity in the absence of her twin. She writes of several . . . shall we say, liaisons, but I don't believe any of them would have led to her murder."

"Liaisons with John Ratz, for example?"

"He was one of the men, yes. But as I said before, I don't believe that John Ratz has any connection to her murder. I urge you to look elsewhere—and not to take such a simple or unsophisticated view of Chandra's personal affairs."

"Thanks for the advice, Professor. I can assure you we're considering all the angles carefully. That's why I'll need to you to turn over all the computer files and papers that Chandra Harper has given you."

Feri looked appalled. "Oh, no, I could not possibly do that," he said. "They are not mine to give away."

"Yes, they are," I stated firmly. "Professor Feri, Chandra Harper gave those files to you. Now she is dead—and by not sharing them, you may be helping her killer escape punishment. You have no legal obligation to keep her writing secret, but you do have a moral obligation to cooperate. I assure you, I will treat the files as confidential material, and I will only use them as a tool to further the investigation."

The professor stared at me, still skeptical. Obviously he needed prodding.

"Please don't make me get a search warrant, Professor," I continued, "because I will. And then the only thing you will have accomplished is wasting precious time in this investigation." I stared at him directly. "Well, you'll accomplish one other thing, of course. You'll succeed in making yourself look like a suspect. If you hinder this investigation, I'll have to wonder why you would wish to do so. And then I will be forced to examine your own private concerns much more closely."

Professor Feri scowled at me, but after a moment, he let out a sigh. "I can assure you I have no wish to hinder your investigation. My assistant will make a copy of all the files I have from Chandra and give them to you straight away."

"Thank you, Professor," I said curtly. "I'm sure Chandra would appreciate it."

"Yes, well . . . for a rusticated gentleman, you can be very persuasive."

I said nothing, eyeing him until he twitched in his seat.

"Are those all of your questions?" Feri continued. "If so, I will have Evelyn get you those files now."

"Thank you. As I said, time is precious. Please tell her I expect them immediately."

Feri rose from the chair, but before he left, I posed one last question. "Professor Feri, as Chandra's confrere, as you say, did you and she ever sleep together?"

Feri's already ruddy cheeks flowered in an even brighter shade of red. "How dare you ask such a question!" he sputtered. "You have neither decency nor a sense of propriety!"

The professor had me there—when it comes to a criminal investigation, and a lot of other things, I am neither decent nor proper.

"I'll take that as a yes," I said.

Chapter Twenty-Three

Shortly after Feri had left the interview, Evelyn Durst handed me a red flash drive with Chandra's writings. The drive was tiny, but luckily there was an ID tag attached to the end to help me keep track of it.

I decided to talk to Greta next. I hadn't seen her up and about, so I went to Greta's suite and rapped lightly on the door. To my surprise, the door wasn't latched—it shifted a few inches inward under my knock. "Greta?" I called softly. When she didn't answer, I stepped inside.

The room was dim, the curtains drawn. I found Greta resting on the bed, sitting upright with her back against the headboard and her knees pulled up toward her chest with her arms wrapped around them. Her dark eyes were open, but she was staring into space. She had changed into blue flannel pajamas. There was a cup of tea sitting on the bedside table, and I could see the steam faintly rising. I waited in silence for a moment, then she spoke.

"Please, Chief, just tell me this is all a bad dream, and that when I wake up, Chandra will be waiting for me down the hall with the rest of our group."

"I wish I could, Greta," I said. "How are you feeling? Can I do anything for you? Get you anything?'

"No—but thank you, Chief. You're such a dear. I don't know what I would do if you weren't here to help me through this." She sniffled and finally looked in my direction. "I'm sure you're very busy, but can you sit with me for just a little while?" She patted the bed—the same bed I'd shared with her less than eight hours earlier.

"Sure," I said, pulling up a chair. "I've got a few minutes." I didn't tell her I was there on official business.

"I feel so sad," Greta continued, "and yet, I'm so grateful I met you. Last night was wonderful, and I know you felt the same. It was just like a dream. But then this morning, I woke up to this . . . horrible nightmare." She shuddered.

I put my hand atop her knee. "I'm sorry, Greta. I know you and Chandra were good friends."

"She was my best friend. And after her twin died, I became like her surrogate sister. We confided in each other; we shared everything. She could be frustrating sometimes, I know, but she really made me laugh. Have you ever had a friend like that, Chief?"

I nodded. "I'm sorry this happened," I repeated. Greta started crying, and I waited a moment for her to regain her composure. I handed her a tissue from the box beside the bed.

"Are you up to answering a few questions?" I asked. "You probably knew Chandra better than anyone else here, and I could really use your help."

"If it will help in any way, you know I will do it," she said, drying her eyes. "Ask me anything you want."

"You said Chandra confided in you. Did she have any enemies? I mean a real enemy, someone who would actually want to kill her."

"No, no one—except of course John Ratz. And . . . I don't think he'd plan to kill her, but maybe by accident? Or in a drunken rage? Is that what happened, Chief? Have you arrested him?"

I shook my head. "No. We haven't made an arrest yet. But we also haven't ruled out Ratz, so I'd like you to be careful around him. Don't spend any time alone with him, and keep your door locked—just to be on the safe side, okay?"

She nodded. "Okay, Chief," she said. "I'll be careful."

"In the meantime," I continued, "can you think of anyone else? Did Chandra meet anyone new recently? Or did she tell you she was afraid of someone—someone other than Ratz?"

"I can't think of anyone else. Not everyone liked Chandra, and some people found her annoying, but if being annoying was a cause for murder, we'd all be in danger."

I smiled. "Tell me more about Chandra's relationship with John Ratz. Did she love him, or was it just a diversion?"

"I don't know everything that happened behind closed doors, but from what I observed, Chandra thought of John as someone to pass the time with, nothing more. In fact, she often liked to have several men in her life at once, so she'd feel less lonely. But none of them was truly special to her—maybe not even her husband. The only time Chandra liked to be alone was when she was writing. The rest of the time she craved companionship. 'I must live among the living,' she used to say."

"And what about those other men? Anyone in the picture besides Ratz?"

"No, not at the moment—not as far as I know."

"Monday night at Kirsch's, you said Ratz was abusive to Chandra. I saw some of that firsthand, but were there other examples?"

"Not at first. Ratz never pummeled her with his fists or anything like that, but he was a control freak, especially in . . ."

Greta hesitated, as if she didn't want to tell me something.

"Go ahead," I said. "It could be important."

"Well . . . Chandra told me that Ratz was very domineering in bed. At first she liked it. Chandra's husband is a very nice man, but he's more . . . passive than Chandra." Greta lowered her voice, and I strained to hear. "Ratz was exciting to her, sexually speaking. She told me they played a lot of games. To me, it sounded as if Chandra was his personal sex slave. And for a while, she enjoyed it that way. But then it became too much for her, the relationship got out of control, and finally, Chandra told him it was over."

"When was that?"

"A few weeks ago."

"But he didn't agree to end it?"

"He seemed to agree, but you saw how he acted in the bar."

"How well do you know John Ratz yourself?" I asked.

Her eyebrows lifted. "I certainly don't know him the way Chandra did, if that's what you mean."

"I was just wondering what else you can tell me about him."

"Oh. Not much—and nothing that I haven't mentioned before. He's a war vet, and supposedly he's working on a book about Desert Storm, but I've never actually read any of his drafts. I don't like him, so I hardly ever speak to him. A while ago I agreed to meet him and Chandra for a couple of drinks down in the city, and Ratz got obnoxious."

"How obnoxious?" I asked.

"He thinks he's an authority on everything. Sports, politics, literature—you name it. The more he had to drink that night, the more of an expert he became, and the more argumentative he became. Chandra disagreed with him on something trivial, and he exploded and called her . . . well, a name I won't repeat. And then he said he'd have to school her when they got home. He lowered his voice and started smiling, pretending all was forgiven and it had been a big joke. But it wasn't funny. It was creepy."

"Did Chandra tell you what happened after that?"

Again, Greta hesitated. "Is it really important for you to know all the details? I mean, you saw how he was the other night, how aggressive he can be."

"At this point, we don't know what's important and what's not. It's possible a detail from that night in the city could have a connection to what happened here at the inn."

Greta sighed heavily, then related what Chandra had told her. “Chandra said that John made her stop at a liquor store on the way back to her condo that night. He even opened the bottle in the car. She tried to talk to him and calm him down, but he was fuming. As soon as they got in the door, he ripped off her blouse.” She swallowed. “And then he told her to strip off everything else, and in what order, and to lie face down on the bed and . . . he . . .” Tears started to tumble from Greta’s eyes, and she wiped them away with her fingers.

“It’s all right, I get the picture,” I said. Actually, I was more worried about the picture I was about to plant in Greta’s mind with my next question. But if Tyrrell was right—that Chandra might have allowed her killer into the room—I had to ask. “You said Ratz and Chandra played a lot of games before things got really ugly. I don’t suppose any of those games involved a weapon of any kind—a rope or a gun, or maybe a knife? Something from his commando days, maybe?”

Greta looked shocked. “Not that I know of,” she said. “And I do think Chandra would’ve told me that! Besides, what kind of friend to her would I be if I didn’t mention that kind of thing before now?”

“Sorry. Sometimes the questions are hard to ask, but they still have to be asked.”

“You asked for a reason, though,” she said. “Oh, God. How exactly did she die?”

“She was stabbed, Greta. I can’t say much more—and I’d appreciate it if you wouldn’t relate this to anyone else. But it’s not the horror scene you’re imagining. It looks as if Chandra may have even been asleep, after taking some pills.”

“Thank God,” Greta said. “I was really hoping that she hadn’t suffered.”

“Okay,” I continued. “So, after that night in her condo, Chandra told Ratz it was over?”

Greta shook her head sadly. “You’d think so, wouldn’t you? But she didn't—not until much later. She was so insecure. Chandra always needed a man in her life, even if it was Ratz."

"What about her husband? Wasn't he around?"

"Oh, Hector . . . He'll be so devastated. He's such a sweet man. He and Chandra are still married—they were, I mean—and they were very close, but they haven't lived together for a while. And he was out of town on a buying trip when the incident with Ratz happened. Chandra still relied on Hector a lot, though."

"Why didn't they live together?"

"It was a mutual decision. They loved each other, they just couldn't live together, that kind of thing." She paused. "Chandra once hinted that Hector liked other men. And she—well, she also liked other men."

"You mentioned a buying trip. What does Hector do for a living?"

"He owns an import-export business and a high end antiques shop. I've never seen it firsthand, but I understand it's quite successful."

"And Chandra never indicated they might divorce?"

"No. As I said, she relied on Hector. He was the most stable man in her life. I don't think she ever would have divorced him unless he asked her—or unless she found someone else to marry. But no one else was seriously in the picture."

"And what about Chandra, what was her financial situation?"

"She was comfortable, I know that much. Once she told me she'd inherited a little money from her parents, but I don't think it was a great fortune. In fact, it might be that Hector still supported her, at least in part. Anyway, she and I didn't talk about our bank accounts. Chandra thought it was gauche to discuss money."

"Okay, let's go back to Ratz. The other night you said he only signed up for Feri's workshop so he could be near Chandra. Do you still think that's true?"

"Yes, I do. During the last workshop, Ratz barely participated.

When we found out he had signed up for this session, both Chandra and I thought maybe something wasn't quite right, that he wasn't over her. And of course, we both knew about his issues with drinking. I wish . . ."

Greta let out another deep sigh. Her face was ashen, and she laid her hand on mine. "Chief, would it be all right if we stopped? I'm really tired. I think I just want to sleep a while now."

"Sure, no problem." I said. "I might have some more questions later, but they can wait. You've been very helpful, Greta."

"You know I want to help you. I'm just too tired to answer more questions now."

"It's fine."

"Maybe you should read some of Chandra's writing—it would tell you more about the men she knew, what her mindset was."

"I have a copy of her book from Professor Feri. He said Chandra also kept a handwritten journal, but we haven't found it yet."

"Really? That's odd. She kept that to herself, but it should've been in her room. I do have some computer files from her, though. Look over there on the table—there's a flash drive that Chandra gave me for review. The purple one is hers. It might have the same files that Professor Feri gave you, but it might have something new on it. You can take the drive if you'd like. I hope you'll return it sometime, but for now, it's too painful for me to read anyway."

"Thanks," I said. "You never know, the files might help."

Greta was staring off into space again.

"Will you be okay?" I asked. "I could send Evelyn Durst back to stay with you."

"No, that's okay, Chief. I just want to sleep a little while." She gave me a little smile. "Only this time, you don't have to wait 'til I'm asleep before you go."

I smiled back at her. I wanted to say "sweet dreams," but it seemed inappropriate.

As I left the room, I took the purple flash drive from the table. Beside it was the Starbucks coffee that Greta had offered me earlier. I needed a jolt, so I took a sip and immediately regretted it—the brew was as cold and bitter as the day. I left the cardboard-wrapped cup behind, pulling the door shut behind me and checking to make sure it had locked. Then I headed upstairs to find our Mister Rat.

Chapter Twenty-Four

As I headed upstairs in L'Auberge, I thought about the layout of the building. Ratz was in room 222, one of four king suites on the second floor. Each of those suites featured a spiral staircase leading up to a loft with a gas fireplace and a whirlpool tub overlooking the lake. A second fireplace was below, opposite the king-size bed. In short, these were rooms made for romance. I wondered whether Ratz had specifically requested his suite, and what he might have been planning at the time. He didn't strike me as the romantic type.

I rapped on his door and waited for him to answer. I heard a grunt, knocked again, and then finally Ratz, unshaven and unkempt, opened the door. He was dressed in sweat pants and a sleeveless undershirt, with the outline of his dog tags visible beneath it. Curls of dark chest hair peeked out above the neckline. Like last night, he wasn't wearing shoes or socks. The guy even had hairy toes.

"What do you want?" he asked, not bothering to conceal his disdain. He didn't appear to be broken up about the murder of his ex-girlfriend.

"I want to talk to you about Chandra Harper. Do you want to talk here or down at the station?"

"Don't give me that hard-ass crap, Chief—Feri told me you'd be coming my way. I've been rousted by a lot tougher and smarter guys than you—real professionals, over in the lands of sand. So don't think I'm going to crumble for some Barney Fife in Podunk, Wisconsin."

"Well, at least you know what state you're in. I'll mark you down as an uncooperative suspect." I thought about actually jotting it in my notebook, but I didn't think the notebook would have the same effect on Ratz as it did on the O'Malley brothers.

"Is that what I am, a suspect? Just because I had a little spat with Chandra doesn't mean I killed her. Hell, I've been even angrier with you, and you're still alive." He grunted. "Well, I guess you'd better come in then."

His face had changed from pissed-off to passive over the course of a few words. His room took me by surprise. Unlike the previous night, it was neat and orderly, like a military barrack. The bedsheets were tucked tight and folded over the cover. There wasn't an empty beer or soda can in sight, but a bottle of vodka stood on the bedside table.

"Want a drink?" he asked, pointing at the vodka.

"Isn't it a little early for that?"

"Not in Baghdad. Besides, it depends on when you go to bed," he said.

"And when did you go to bed?"

"I haven't yet."

"That's interesting. So where were you last night?"

He chuckled. "Right here, Chief. Right here." He walked to the bedside table and lifted the bottle of vodka. It reminded me of my own bedside table, and I wasn't happy about the comparison.

"A little hair of the dog, buddy?" Ratz asked.

"No, thanks, I'm on duty. But if you want one, go ahead." I was hoping it might loosen his tongue or turn in him into the raving lunatic I'd seen the other night. Heck, if I was lucky, he might even confess.

Ratz poured himself three fingers of Smirnoff and then lifted the glass, staring at the liquid. "So, let me see if I've got this right," he said. "You think I murdered Chandra just because I got a little drunk and unruly the other night. I get like that five times a month, Chief—and I haven't killed anyone yet."

"Maybe you just don't remember it," I said. "Do you remember last night?"

"Yeah, I do," Ratz retorted. "I'm never lucky enough to black out."

"Some of your writing classmates seem to think the reason you signed up for this workshop was to be near Chandra. Is that right?"

"There's some truth to that, I guess. But I'm here for the same reason everyone else is, to work on my book. I did think maybe Chandra and I could spend some quality time together, maybe patch things up and start over."

"Was Monday evening what you would call 'quality time'?"

"Look, pal, don't hold me accountable for what happened in the bar."

"Really, and who should I hold accountable then? The bartender for over-serving you?"

"No, I mean I'm responsible, but Chandra was also partly to blame. She comes on to me, she gets me all worked up so she can get her own needs met. And then she brushes me off like I'm some piece of crap. And then she does it all over again."

"I see. And did the poor little soldier boy get his feelings hurt?" I was trying to get him riled up, to see what might happen, but he only nibbled on the bait.

"Screw you. You want to have an intelligent conversation or not? I know I'm a suspect because I was close to Chandra, and let me tell you, I regret that relationship. I knew it wasn't a good mix—for me or for her—but I was attracted to her. And she was very attracted to me. She needed me."

"So, you think she needed to be abused and controlled?"

"Oh, geez. You've been talking to that bitch friend of hers, Grrrrreta. Talk about a control freak. She's the one who wanted to be

Chandra's Svengali, always manipulating her, trying to tell her who to see, what to do. In spite of what Greta probably told you, I was pretty good to Chandra . . . except maybe when I was drunk." He looked at the glass of vodka, which he still hadn't tasted. In what appeared to be a contrived scene, he held it up in the light, then pointedly set it down on the table, unsampled.

"I'll be honest with you, Chief," Ratz continued. "I'm not supposed to drink at all. For several months now I've been on antidepressants, and they don't mix well with booze. But I've had a tough time saying no to alcohol."

Unfortunately, I knew what that was like. "What type of drug are you taking?" I asked.

Ratz walked over to his valise and withdrew a container. "See for yourself." He tossed the bottle at me and I caught it.

I read the label of the half-empty pill bottle. Ratz had been prescribed a drug that I recognized as a serotonin reuptake inhibitor. It appeared to be the genuine article. The label read "third refill," which meant Ratz had been taking the medication for at least two-and-a-half months. When I was back on the CPD, sometimes it seemed everyone in my precinct was on a type of antidepressant, especially the wives. I was well aware how the medicine could take away that angry edge from the individual—except it didn't mix well with alcohol, which is really a depressant drug. The mixture could be potent and unpredictable, and it could have explained Ratz's behavior in the bar. The question was, how had he behaved with Chandra after that?

"You're right," I said. "You shouldn't drink if you're taking these."

"That's what I'm telling you. I wasn't at my best the other night, but I'm done being stupid. And that's why I finally decided I was really done with Chandra—and no, I did not kill her. In spite of everything, I liked her."

"When was the last time you talked with her, then?"

"I called her yesterday to apologize, and to let her know I wouldn't be bothering her again."

"And you didn't see her in person, go to her room? Maybe you got a little lonely."

"Like I told you last night, I've been staying clear of Chandra Harper since that little incident in the bar. If she got lonely, I couldn't say."

I thought about that. "Did you ever meet her husband, or anyone else she might've been seeing?"

Ratz shook his head. "It's not like I would've wanted to. She told me she and her husband were separated. And if she was seeing somebody else, she was smart enough not to tell me about it."

"How much did you know about her? Did you know about her past . . . or her financial situation?"

"I know that crazy story about her dead sister—everybody here does. And I know her husband must be pretty well off. Chandra had a real nice condo with a lake view, nice clothes, manicures and facials, that kind of thing. She took good care of herself."

"Except for seeing you, you mean."

He grunted. "Is that a question?"

"No," I conceded. "You said you were here all night. Can anyone vouch for that?"

He glared at me. "You mean, except for you or one of your little cop friends? Weren't you watching the inn all night after the shooting, like you said you would?"

He was right—that's exactly what I had told him I'd do. "And you were here, in this room, awake the whole night?"

"Pretty much. I couldn't sleep, so I was writing. I might've put my feet up around three-thirty or four o'clock, dozed until six, but it wasn't a deep sleep."

"And you never heard anything unusual?"

"Well, I heard you leaving here about three in the morning," he said smugly. "You tell me, is that unusual? I also heard you and Greta talking downstairs after you paid me your little visit, because I stepped into the hall. Then I heard your Jeep starting a little after three and looked out. I didn't hear anything suspicious after that."

I pulled out my notebook to jot a few things, taking a seat in the chair by the bed. It was partly a ploy to conceal my surprise—I couldn't let him ruffle me with details about my own personal life. "You're an observant man, Mr. Ratz. Too bad you didn't see the killer." I asked him a few more basic questions, confirmed his contact information, and emphasized that he and the other writers should stay close to L'Auberge for the rest of the day and avoid the lobby area.

"I'm not going anywhere," he said. "The room's paid up through Sunday."

"Good," I said. As I tucked my notebook back in my coat pocket, I felt something sharp. It was the plastic shard I'd picked up from the ice, out on the lake Monday night. I'd decided Ratz's feet were too small to be the ones that had kicked me in the head and body, but I wasn't completely sure what had happened on the lake that night, or whether a second person might have been involved. An idea occurred to me, and I surreptitiously palmed the shard as I stood up.

"I have some other people to question," I said, "but I'll also want to continue this conversation later. In the meantime, don't mix the booze and pills. And don't leave the area—because if you do, Judge Goggin will issue an arrest warrant and we'll give you a room at the jail. Trust me, it's not nearly as comfortable as this one."

"Yeah, yeah," Ratz said. "Anything else? I'd like to get back to work."

"No, that's it for now," I said. Then I reached under the edge of the bed and pretended to pick up the plastic shard. "This belong to you?" I asked casually. I held it up to Ratz.

"Don't think so," he said. "Maybe another guest or the housekeeper dropped it." His manner was genuine.

"What do you think it could be?" I asked, handing him the shard. "Some kind of plastic? Something broken?"

He studied the object for a moment, then said, "No, it's not plastic. It looks more like nacre to me."

"Nacre?" I asked. I didn't know the word.

"You know, mother of pearl, like you'd see on—" He abruptly handed the shard back to me. "Look, pal," he said tersely, "I don't know what you're trying to pull, but that's not mine."

"I'm not trying to pull anything. I'd just like your opinion on what it is and how it got here."

He glared at me. "Well, it looks like part of a knife hilt to me. But I think you knew that. And it's for damn sure not mine. So don't think you can plant it in my room and tie me to Chandra's murder."

I raised an eyebrow. "What makes you think Chandra Harper was stabbed? I don't believe I mentioned that."

Ratz's face was growing red. "Come on, Barney. You think the innkeeper and all the help over there at the restaurant could keep from jabbering to Feri and all of us over here? We got the murder news with breakfast. It doesn't take a genius to know Chandra Harper was probably stabbed. And it doesn't take a genius to see you're trying to set me up. What do you think—that you'll catch me in a lie? Make me crumble? I already told you, I don't scare easy, and I did not kill Chandra Harper."

I sighed. I didn't know whether Ratz was right about the shard belonging to a knife, but considering that I'd found it out on the ice roughly forty-eight hours before Chandra's death, it probably had no connection to the murder. Which probably meant I had just made my job more complicated. "It was a simple question, Mr. Ratz. Thanks for your time." I headed toward the door. "Like I said, we'll be talking again later."

"Looking forward to it," Ratz growled as he closed the door behind me.

Chapter Twenty-Five

In the city, there's a clear relationship between weather and crime. When summer heat is on the rise, aggression rises exponentially until finally it's too hot and the aggressiveness wanes. Family disturbances spike with the ozone levels, and you can track the rate of assault and battery right along with the rising humidity. Come winter, however, the crime rate plummets like the temperature, and during a blizzard, crime virtually flat-lines. I guess car thieves are just too lazy to dig a BMW out of the snow.

In a small town like Geneva, almost nothing happens in the dead of winter, especially not murder. But the moment somebody stabbed Chandra Harper in my quiet little home, "dead of winter" took on a whole new meaning. And I definitely didn't like it.

I headed back downstairs after leaving Ratz's room. The other writers were in the gathering room, and their lunch had just been delivered. After I'd confirmed that no one had any big revelations they were dying to share, I told them I'd finish up the interviews later in the day. Then I stepped outside to collect my thoughts and make a call to Shea and Bert. Their search of the Dumpsters and the shoreline hadn't turned up anything except their noses.

I asked Bert how he was holding up. It'd been a long night, and he had seen the body firsthand—that kind of thing usually has an impact on a person. On the other hand, I knew Bert was probably pumped up on adrenalin. He claimed he was fine, so I asked both officers to swing out to Zubeck's place together and see if he was home, then talk to him about his whereabouts last night during the time of the restaurant shooting and the murder.

"The guy seems lost in the wind," I said. "If there's no sign of him at his house again, see if you can find anyone who's seen him at his usual haunts. Try Herb's gas station—that's where Ronnie Frankel saw him last. Evidently Zubeck does a lot of jawing there."

As I ended the call, I took a seat on the wrought-iron swing beneath a leafless tree outside L'Auberge, placing my weary behind on the ice-cold metal. I was beat, and it wasn't even noon yet. I guess that's what happens when you follow an evening of drinking and gunfire with a sex cocktail and a chaser of murder.

I ran down the list of things I had yet to do. In the afternoon, I'd finish up the interviews with the other writers. I'd also talk with Hector Harper, Chandra's grieving husband, as soon as he arrived. At some point, I'd have to touch base with Tyrrell and tell him what I'd learned so far. I wished I had more to tell.

But first of all, I needed some lunch myself, and some intelligent discussion with a fellow officer whose mind I admired. I called Annie Madden and asked her to meet me at Gus Baldwin's place, Muddy's on the Lake.

I arrived first, and the joint was empty. Gus was placing a Bloody Mary on the bar for me before I even reached the stool. He must've seen me pull up and mixed the concoction while I was still in the parking lot.

"Here you go, buddy," Gus said. "I figured you'd probably need this."

"Thanks. I'm on duty, but I don't give a damn how it looks." I took a sip. "I gather you've heard the news."

"You mean, how someone shot up Kirsch's while you were there on a hot date last night—and then some woman got herself killed at the inn after that? You bet. That kind of news travels faster than you do, pal. It must be tough being chief of police in the new murder capital of the world."

I loved Gus, but he never passed up an opportunity to make a dig.

"I'm serious, Chief," Gus continued. "The way I figure it, we have maybe ten or twelve people living here all winter. So, even one murder puts us at a higher homicide rate than Detroit. It might even be higher here than in one of those cities run by the druglords down in South America. This could be your ticket to fame, Chief."

"I tell you what, Gus. If you ever want to play it safe and move to Medellín, let me know. I'll chip in a dollar for your plane fare."

Gus snorted. "This from the guy who won't pay his own dog's tab."

Thankfully, Annie Madden walked in and saved me from bantering with Gus. Before she could join me at the bar, I took my drink and pointed to an isolated table in the corner. As usual, Annie looked great. She was off-duty until later, but like a pro, she'd agreed to meet me and talk shop anyway. She was wearing faded jeans that fit her curves and showed off her long legs. She was athletic, but she walked toward me with the grace of a model working a fashion gig in Milan. My blood pressure rose with every step she took.

"How are you holding up, Chief?" Annie asked after we'd settled in at the table and ordered a couple of Gus's famous burgers. "Hard to believe all this is happening right here in our own little town." She wasn't excited like some tabloid reporter; like me, she was disgusted by the developments.

"I thought I'd escaped this kind of thing when I moved up here," I said.

"Well, it can't be exactly like Chicago. For one thing, I'm still working on the mysterious case of 'Who Stole Christmas?' You didn't happen to solve that one down in Chicago, did you?"

"Geez, that's right," I said. "We've still got the crèche caper.

Anything new?" I'd almost forgotten about the stolen nativity scenes, even though I'd made the case a top priority at our staff meeting yesterday morning. It already seemed like a year ago.

"Sorry, nothing new," Annie replied. "No one seems to know anything, and it's quiet at all the churches. I guess that's good, though. The whole thing seems pretty trivial compared to the murder. What do you have on that, Chief—any theories, any suspects or leads you can share?"

I gave Annie a run-down on all the facts and hunches I had so far. John Ratz was still at the top of my suspect list. Something told me he wasn't telling me the whole truth, and between the drinking and pills and personal issues, he might not know what the truth really was. Next on my list was Ben Zubeck. Then came Chandra's husband, Hector Harper, because he is, well, the husband.

"The evidence on any one of them seems pretty thin right now," I admitted. "It could just as easily be someone we haven't identified yet. I'm hoping Tyrrell's guys find something in the financials or phone records that points us in the right direction."

Annie sipped her Coke and pondered everything I'd told her. "The ex-lover as a suspect, I understand," she said, "and the husband, too. But Ben Zubeck? I know he's crazy, and he gave us that whole Carthage-must-be-destroyed speech about the inn. But what would he gain from killing Chandra Harper? Did he even know her? And why would he stab her? He strikes me as more of a gun nut."

"Those are all good questions," I said. "The murder publicity probably won't help the inn, but I don't think the killer had that outcome in mind." I explained that it might not matter whether Zubeck knew Chandra Harper, not if Navilio himself was the target. "Anyone who's familiar with Anthony Navilio's habits—his own employees or Kirsch's people, any of his regular business contacts, even his friends down in Illinois—all of them know his routine. Whenever he's at the French Country Inn, he stays in suite 303. And he usually stays up here for several weekdays, every week. Then he does a reverse commute and goes back to the city on weekends."

"In other words," Annie replied, "he stays in the same room this Harper woman was in."

"Right. Now, suppose Zubeck had decided to kill Navilio, but didn't know his target had left town. Zubeck might have figured that Navilio was still here because he saw the lights on in suite 303. If anyone was watching that suite from the lake, they would have seen some activity inside. And if they knew Navilio's habits, they'd assume he was there. No one would suspect that anyone else had been given that room—not on a winter weeknight when there were plenty of other vacancies at the inn."

Annie's hazel eyes were pensive. "If what you are saying is accurate—that the killer intended to murder Anthony Navilio—then you've opened up a whole new can of night crawlers."

"What do you mean?"

"Maybe Zubeck isn't the only one who would want to kill Navilio. What about Navilio's other potential enemies? That list could include his business associates down in Chicago, disgruntled former employees . . . anyone from an insulted banker to an under-tipped bartender, not to mention his wife, Kathleen. You said it yourself—it's usually the husband or the wife who does the crime. It's a good thing there aren't any English butlers involved. On the other hand, maybe that'd make it easier."

I laughed. "I was thinking Navilio's wife would know his whereabouts, maybe join him on that vacation in Italy."

"But we don't actually know that, do we? Maybe he and his wife are estranged or something. The point is, how much do we really know about Anthony Navilio?"

I shook my head and sighed. "At least we know he's still alive—by all accounts, anyway."

She laughed lightly. "You'll figure it out, Chief. Is there anything I can do to help? I've got some time this afternoon."

"Are you sure? I already owe you for helping me with Zubeck's eviction."

Annie smiled. "Are you kidding? It's not every day there's a murder to solve. I'd be insulted if you didn't let me pitch in."

I thought about my gut reactions at the murder scene. There was one thing still nagging at me. I asked Annie to see if she could get me a copy of *The Ox-Bow Incident* and drop it off at my house. "The book, not the movie. I already have the movie on tape." I explained how Chandra Harper's hand was resting on the cover of the book in death. "It's a long shot, and it probably means nothing, just like Tyrrell said. But I'd still like to take a closer look at that book."

"Not a problem," Annie said. "Anything else?"

I handed her the two flash drives. "Do me a favor and make a backup of these and drop one set back at my house with the book. If you've got time, feel free to take a look at what's on the backup. But keep the contents to yourself—they're private writings from the victim. If you notice any important differences between the files on the two drives, I'd like to know that, too."

"I probably shouldn't just leave these on your doorstep," she pointed out. "But I could leave things with Dorothy at the office."

"No, just leave everything on my kitchen table," I said. "There's a key for the back door under the plastic gnome next to the garage."

She smirked. "Sophisticated security system."

"Hey, no one has cracked it so far," I replied. "It's a holdover from my parents."

"Believe me, I get it. Most of the time I don't even bother locking my own door here," Annie admitted. "But with all that's going on, maybe I'll have to start."

We chatted a little more and ate our burgers. I told Officer Madden I'd square the extra hours on her timesheet, and that lunch was on me as a thank-you. As she headed off, I watched her go, enjoying the view, then walked up to the bar to pay the tab.

Gus was chuckling as he wiped a glass. "You're a damn fool, Chief, you know that?"

"Why, because I ate one of your burgers?

"Because that girl likes you," he said. "She must be a damn fool, too."

"Annie Madden? Officer Madden?"

"You see any other girl in here?"

I threw a twenty and a few ones on the bar. "You're seeing things, Gus."

"I always see things. Like the way you just looked at her leaving. Not that I blame you—she does have a pretty nice exit line."

"Well, that woman is my employee. And there are rules about that kind of thing."

Gus snorted in reply. "Damn fool," he repeated. As I reached the door, he called out one more time. "Say, Chief, what's the rule about drinking on the job?"

Chapter Twenty-Six

Hector Harper turned out to be a popinjay. His dyed brown hair was neatly combed and parted and held in place with just the right amount of hair gel and spray; his fingernails were meticulously manicured and buffed; and his expensive clothes were completely wrinkle-free. His fancy dress shoes were shined to a gloss so high he could've admired his own reflection, which he probably often did. It appeared to me that he had primped and polished himself for at least an hour before driving up to Walworth County. Most men, upon hearing of their wife's death, even an estranged wife, would throw on whatever they could find and drive posthaste to the scene. It was obvious Hector Harper was not like most men.

I found him sitting in the parlor between the lobby and the restaurant. He sat stiffly upright with folded hands, as if he were awaiting a job interview. Apparently he was just waiting for Debbie to bring him some tea and crackers. "Mr. Harper, the husband," she whispered in my ear as she bustled past me with a tray. "Our chief of police," she announced for Harper's benefit, in case he didn't recognize my uniform. She set down the tray and hurried back out.

Harper stood to greet me. "Hector Harper," he said solemnly, extending his smooth hand. He was the type who probably never got his hands dirty. "I understand there are no suspects in custody yet. Is that correct?"

"That's correct, Mr. Harper. I'm very sorry for your loss."

"Yes, thank you for the sympathy. Are you in charge here? I'd like to know what kind of progress you've made finding my wife's killer. What can you tell me?"

"We're doing all that we can, I assure you, Mr. Harper. I'm participating in the investigation, but the county sheriff's department is actually in charge of the case. Have you spoken with Detective Tyrrell, the lead investigator?"

"Yes, on the phone. He wasn't exactly a font of information. He explained that a room would be made available for me here at the inn, and that I should plan on staying overnight because it might take some time before I could see Chandra's body or have it released. Frankly, I'd like to know why that is." He cleared his throat and swallowed hard. "Naturally, I would like to see my wife and say goodbye. And I would like to make arrangements for the funeral."

"I'm afraid we have to wait for the medical examiner to release the body. It's standard procedure in a situation like this." I decided not to mention the autopsy in progress or describe any details of the murder at this stage. The stress of the day and Gus's greasy burger were a bad combination, and I was in danger of vomiting all over Hector Harper's sartorial display. He didn't appear particularly distraught over Chandra's death, but no doubt he would faint if I ruined his eight-hundred-dollar sport coat.

I offered to escort Harper to his room. Debbie had given him a first-floor king suite in the original lakeside guesthouse. The building was completely separate from L'Auberge, so it was a good choice. I didn't know how much Hector Harper knew about Ratz, or whether he even cared about Chandra's affair, but the less those two men mixed, the better.

Inside Harper's room, I raised the balloon drapes on the lakeside French doors to allow sunlight into the room and expose the view of the frozen landscape.

"Well, this is quaint," Harper said. "I certainly hope it's safe here."

He must have decided it was, because he immediately began to unpack his luggage. Evidently it made no sense leaving all those clothes in the cramped quarters of the suitcase—they might get musty and wrinkled. His heavily starched shirts were enveloped in cellophane bags, and his socks were folded as if they had only been purchased this morning. One might have assumed the bereft widower's suitcase had been packed for him by a gentleman's gentleman. From a side compartment, Harper pulled out a flash drive ensconced in a leather container and handed it to me.

"This contains everything I have from Chandra's work. I thought it might include something useful to you, perhaps a revelation of someone who may have wanted to harm her."

"Thank you," I said, pocketing the drive. That made three copies of Chandra's book I now had in hand. The woman was practically a best-selling author, albeit postmortem.

Hector finished his unpacking, then announced, "Thank you for your help, officer. If there's nothing else, I think I'd like to be alone now." He walked to the French doors and looked out at the icy, windswept scene.

"As a matter of fact, I wonder if you'd mind answering a few questions," I said. "It might help us if we knew more about your wife, and I'd like to keep the momentum rolling today." I eyed the room's small coffee pot. "I could use some coffee. Why don't I make us a cup or two?"

Hector cleared his throat again. "Make yourself at home."

I started the brew, and Harper fidgeted a bit, checked his watch, and stared out the windows. I took my time, composing my thoughts. The guy was an odd duck, and I wanted to handle him carefully.

Statistically speaking, when a wife is murdered, the husband usually did the crime. Even if said husband did not lay hands on the victim, he hired the man who shot, stabbed, drove over, choked, pushed, poisoned, or otherwise snuffed out the life of the victim. In a physical contest between the Harpers, I would've laid heavy odds on Chandra. Looking at Hector Harper now, I found it difficult to believe he had the necessary fortitude to carve a raw chicken for dinner, much less stab his wife—even if she were physically compromised. Nor did Hector appear the type who could successfully hire a thug to do the job, having few traits in common with bikers, drug pushers, or politicians. But when it comes to murder, there are often surprises. After all, like many viewers of courtroom TV, I was shocked to learn that O.J. Simpson had not stabbed his own estranged wife—or rather, that a jury of his peers had found him "not guilty."

My number one reason for suspecting Harper was money—which, of course, was the number one motive for murder in Tedeski's rulebook. The Harpers' financial relationship wasn't clear to me yet, but it seemed possible that Chandra might've been draining the guy dry. Maybe Hector had grown tired of it and wanted to save himself the expense of a messy divorce.

I motioned for Harper to take a seat at the small table and poured us both a cup of coffee. He crossed his legs and folded his hands in his lap, leaving my offering untouched.

"I understand you and your wife were separated," I began. "Is that correct, Mr. Harper? How long has that been?"

"For the past year," Harper replied. "It was a mutual decision. Chandra and I are—were—on very friendly terms. It was not a legal or formal separation. We simply decided to live apart." He swallowed hard. "I assure you, I still cared very deeply for my wife."

"When was the last time you spoke with her?"

"About a week ago. She phoned to let me know she'd be out of town, attending this workshop." He began ringing his hands as if he were holding a wet towel. "I certainly didn't know it would be our last conversation."

"Did she ever indicate to you that she felt in danger? Can you think of anyone who might have wanted her dead?"

"Honestly, no," he answered. "I adored Chandra, and everyone loved her. She was so caring and giving that people took advantage of her."

"What people took advantage of her? And in what way?"

"Chandra was very generous with her spirit . . . and her checkbook. You may not be aware, but Chandra saw many different men, and I fear some of them took advantage of her generosity."

"Did she mention anyone in particular?"

"I'm afraid not. I knew she was seeing people, some of them quite a bit younger. I didn't want to know the details. She seldom actually told me their names. And she never indicated that she thought she was in danger—not to me, anyway."

"How did you feel about these men?"

"Well, I certainly didn't like the fact that some might be using her, of course. On the other hand, she was probably using them as well." He paused. "It may be difficult for you to understand, but our marriage was not a traditional one."

"And how was it untraditional?"

Hector smiled. "We got along. We didn't live together, and we were no longer intimate in a physical sense, but we often chatted on the phone several times a week. We seldom saw each other in person more than once a month, however, except when Chandra needed something."

"Such as . . . ?"

"Emotional support, mainly. I loved Chandra, but she was very needy. She always had to have someone around her, someone paying attention to her. I think I was one of the few who gave her attention without expecting something in return."

"And what did the others expect?"

"As I said, Chandra was generous with her money. The men she would hook up with, her writing friends . . . when they'd go out together, it was generally Chandra who paid the bill. She never complained, but I was aware of it."

"Was Chandra a wealthy woman?"

Hector seemed uneasy. He paused, then answered, "Wealthy is such an arbitrary word. What qualifies one as rich these days? But . . . I would say Chandra was comfortable financially. She was well educated, and she did some charity work and fund-raising, but she did not need to work for a living. Her grandparents left her enough money to sustain her, as did her late parents when they passed on. As I said, she was comfortable."

"How comfortable, exactly?"

"Really, I can't say."

"But as her husband, wouldn't you know?"

"As I said, we did not have a conventional relationship. I had my own business, and I didn't trouble myself with her financial affairs. What Chandra did with her inheritance was her own concern."

"Was there a prenuptial agreement?"

"No, Chandra didn't feel that was necessary. And neither did I."

"What about a will? Did Chandra have one?"

Harper seemed amused, because he let out a laugh. I couldn't decide whether it was girlish or sophisticated. "Chandra might have had more wills than Howard Hughes," he answered. "It was all about the charity of the month with her. Once she told tell me she was going to leave most of her money to PETA. Then it was UNESCO, or her alma mater, Antioch College. If she actually changed her will as often as she changed her mind, I'd say her attorney was very well off. I have already given his name to Detective Tyrrell. Perhaps one of you should follow up with him."

"Thanks for the tip. Are you saying none of that money went to you, Mr. Harper? Under marital property law, surely you'd be eligible for something."

Hector cleared his throat again and looked annoyed. "As I've already told you, I don't know the exact details or figures. I do not need Chandra's money, and unlike the men she dated, I've never cared about it, either. For all I know, she spent it all on them."

"It's a rare person who doesn't care about money, Mr. Harper."

"In your world, perhaps," he said haughtily.

"All right. Let's say for the sake of argument, that Chandra still had her money. Is there anyone else who might have a claim on her estate? Another family member, perhaps?"

"I suppose she might have some distant cousin I don't know about, but Chandra had no other immediate family but me. Her only sister was dead. Ironically, Chandra thought she had been murdered."

"Yes, I've heard about her twin. And you didn't agree with Chandra about the murder?"

"I thought she might've been right, but who knows what happened? The police said there was no evidence against the sister's fiancé. Chandra was absolutely certain he was guilty, but I encouraged her to let it go and move on. Maybe I was wrong to do so . . ."

"Did you ever meet the fiancé—the man Chandra believed guilty of poisoning her sister?"

"No, I never met him. That ordeal happened before Chandra and I married."

"What about Chandra's other men friends, her lovers. Did you meet any of them?"

"I'm afraid I can't help you there either. I accepted those affairs, and I knew about them, but I most certainly did not involve myself in them directly. Now, if you'll excuse me, I'm getting very tired . . ."

"Just a few more questions," I said. "You stated that you last heard from Chandra a week ago, is that right?"

He sighed. "Yes. That's right, officer."

"And can you tell me where you were yesterday evening and early this morning?"

"Of course I can," he replied, as if offering me a grammar lesson. "I was at my apartment down in the city."

I noticed a slight tic below his right eye. "Can anyone verify that?"

He sneered at me. "Are you asking whether I have an alibi? Because let me assure you, I did not kill my wife. And I will not be railroaded by you."

"Mr. Harper, this is a murder investigation. I'm sure you understand why I must ask such questions of virtually everyone who was close to Chandra. I would be remiss if I didn't."

Hector cleared his throat again—a nervous habit, or a sign that he was developing a sinus infection. "Last night I returned to my apartment in Lincoln Park at roughly eight o'clock. I left again this morning just before six, when I went out for an early breakfast. My doorman would have seen me both times—in fact, I'm sure we exchanged pleasantries."

I did the math. It was not impossible for Harper to have been in Lake Geneva murdering his wife before breakfast, but it would have been very difficult. I asked him several more questions, and he answered them all in an equally terse manner, but he volunteered little additional information. Even as I went on to propose theories about other possible suspects, his answers amounted to a short "I believe so" or "I believe not."

I decided nothing more could be gained by questioning him before we'd looked at Chandra's will and other pertinent evidence, so I gave him a card with my cell number. "Just in case you think of anything that might be helpful . . . anything at all. Or if you have questions of your own. You can call me at any time, Mr. Harper."

I did not expect to hear from him anytime soon.

Chapter Twenty-Seven

After my encounter with Hector Harper, I headed back to L'Auberge to interview the rest of the writers. They were still in the gathering room, but they were no longer working. Instead they had decided to discuss the murder.

I chatted with them as a group initially, answering their questions as best I could and trying to put them at ease. Then I asked each of them to sit for a brief one-on-one interview in the empty suite at the end of the hall. If what I'd learned from Greta and Feri was correct, none of these other participants had a close personal or financial relationship with Chandra, so I didn't view them as prime suspects. Nonetheless, when ten people gather for a week at an isolated inn and one of them winds up dead, you can't overlook the rest of the pack. If this were an Agatha Christie novel, the characters could start dropping off like flies.

I'd observed six members of the workshop at length in Kirsch's bar: Greta and Chandra, John Ratz, and "the usual trio"—Professor Feri; his assistant, Evelyn Durst; and the Godfather fan, Emile Tavilion. Also attending were two other men, Robert Woolcott and Parker Benchley, who seemed very chummy. I'd seen them briefly Monday night, before they headed into town. The only other woman in the group was Alexandra Hale, a bored and well-educated housewife who'd joined Woolcott and Benchley on that jaunt. The remaining writer was Pharo Marks, a stooped, frail man in his eighties who kept to himself.

In some way or another, most of these people reminded me of

the "peculiar next-door neighbor" who appears on many a TV sitcom. All nine had agreed to stay at the inn until noon on Sunday, when the workshop was originally scheduled to end. For added "insurance," Tyrrell had informed them they were not to leave before that time without the express permission of his office or the district attorney.

I started my interviews with Feri's assistant, Evelyn Durst. Except for her thick eyebrows and large breasts, her appearance was unremarkable, but it was not unpleasant, and she had the aplomb of a woman twice her age. I remained baffled as to why she was devoted to a man like Feri. The professor had a room apart, in a cottage by the shore. Durst was in L'Auberge, but I had little doubt she was spending her nights with Feri.

I questioned Durst about the past workshops, and what she knew about the other members of the group. She revealed little I hadn't heard or guessed before. She did, however, confirm that Woolcott and Benchley were a couple. Hale, she said, was destined to be an Oprah star one day—with Feri's help, of course. I was pretty sure that would never happen—for one thing, Oprah Winfrey had announced plans to end her TV show and her book club—but I didn't want to burst Evelyn's bubble.

Woolcott and Benchley turned out to be the most ordinary members of the group, with none of Feri's pretentiousness. They were sharing a deluxe suite upstairs, at the opposite end of the hall from Ratz. Woolcott was working on a nonfiction book about Chicago activities during the civil rights movement. Benchley was writing a cookbook interspersed with first-person essays. They spent their evenings sampling different restaurants and bars in the area. They hadn't heard anything suspicious after midnight, including Ratz leaving his room.

Pharo Marks had noticed even less, which wasn't surprising given his age-related hearing loss. He was here writing a memoir about his days as an undertaker. He kept largely to himself after the group sessions because his health was failing.

A copper blonde in her early forties, Alexandra Hale was flighty and animated, assuring me twice that she had not left L'Auberge "even once" after midnight, that she was in bed during the time of the murder, and unfortunately knew "nothing at all" about anything useful. She did, however, rise to Ratz's defense. "The way Chandra Harper toyed with him was abysmal. It's a wonder he didn't blow up at her earlier." Hale appeared to find the subject of murder a little exhilarating—it was probably fodder for her bodice-ripper of a novel. It was fairly obvious she had a thing for Ratz herself.

I hadn't gotten my full eight hours of beauty rest the night before, and I had to rely on strong coffee to keep me awake through these sessions. For the most part, I found the writers rather dull. For their sakes, I hoped their prose was more interesting than their personalities.

And yet . . . when I considered this strange assemblage as a group, I was reminded of another whodunit by Agatha Christie. Maybe I didn't have to worry about the other writers dropping one by one, like the victims in *Ten Little Indians*—instead, maybe they'd all done the crime together, like the killers in *Murder on the Orient Express*.

When I met with Emile Tavilion, I was pleasantly surprised. He was the entrepreneur Greta had described as "interesting," and I had to agree. Tavilion was extremely enthusiastic about his book, *How to Build Wealth and Power Using the Business Principals of Don Vito Corleone, the Godfather*—a little too enthusiastic, perhaps. Every time I steered him away from *The Godfather* and tried to discuss something relevant to the investigation, he managed to shift the focus back again. By the time I'd finally ended my interview, I was sure that Vito, Michael, Fredo, and Sonny Corleone were all behind Chandra's murder, perhaps with the help of Luca Brasi.

I wrapped up the interviews shortly after four o'clock. No one claimed to know the whereabouts of Chandra's missing computer, but I hadn't really expected that. John Ratz still had the auspicious honor of topping my list of suspects. The housewife might have attacked Chandra out of jealousy, but based on the initial interview, Alexandra Hale didn't seem the type. Still . . . I might take a closer look at her later.

Greta Olsen was at the bottom of my suspect list, but I couldn't resist thinking about her and picturing how we'd spent the previous night. As a lover, she was intoxicating. With the cocktail hour swiftly approaching, I contemplated stopping by her room again, seeing if she felt up to a drink later. Then I thought better of it. I still had work to do, and under the circumstances, it wasn't a good idea to pursue her. Nothing like a murder to kill a good romance.

Feeling no closer to solving the case, I headed outside for a breath of fresh air. I hadn't heard from Shea and Bert about their efforts to track down Ben Zubeck, so I gave Shea a call.

"Where are you two?"

"You mean physically, or with the case?" Shea replied.

"Both." Shea liked to be a wiseacre, but I was too tired to complain.

"Physically, we're in the car, on our way back to the station. In regards to Mr. Zubeck, he wasn't home. In fact, it looks like they've moved out of the farm, or at least they've started to. It's like you said, he's in the wind."

"Did you stop by Herb's?"

"We did—and a few other places. And guess what?"

"Just spill it, Shea," I groused.

"Turns out Herb did see Zubeck yesterday. In fact, Ben Zubeck stopped by for gas . . . and he was pulling a trailer with a snowmobile."

"That's interesting."

"Yeah. According to Herb, Zubeck made a big point of saying he was out of town for a day or two. Seems he and his wife, Esther, have a single-wide trailer somewhere up north, where they go hunting and fishing. Looks like they're planning on moving up there full-time."

"Was Esther with Ben in the car?"

"Not according to Herb."

"And what time was that?"

"Around five or five-thirty, but Herb couldn't remember for sure. But you know what I'm thinking, Chief—I'm thinking maybe Zubeck didn't go up north at all. Maybe he just parked somewhere, then later he got on his snowmobile and paid a little visit to the inn, did some hunting down here."

"Could be," I said.

"Do you want us to look anymore? We heard Zubeck likes to hang out at Muddy's now and then. And Gus suggested we try Norman over at the Bayside—he and Zubeck used to be friends."

"Nah, you guys have had a long day—especially Bert. He must be running on fumes by now. I've got to check in with Tyrrell again, but I'll probably head home soon myself. Just bring Annie up to speed. She can stop by Muddy's later and see if Zubeck shows. Make sure Bert gets some rest so he's fresh tomorrow."

"Sure thing, Chief."

By the time I'd finished the call, my hands were numb. The temperature had dropped with the sun, and the shadows around the inn had changed from gray to purple. I was about to go back inside L'Auberge when I heard someone walking toward me. It was Greta, coming from the direction of the guesthouse, hands shoved in the pockets of her coat. She brightened as she caught my eye.

"Isn't it a little cold to be hanging out here?" she asked. "Or are you keeping watch on things, Chief?" She put her hand on my arm. "How's it going?"

"I was about to ask you the same." I cocked my head in the direction from which she'd come. "Were you over at Kirsch's? I thought they'd shut down for the night."

"No—I mean you're right, they're closed tonight, but that's not where I was. I was talking with Hector Harper. That poor man . . . I offered to help with the funeral arrangements and talk about Chandra. I really didn't want to, but he called me, and when I found out he was just sitting there in his room all alone, I felt sorry for him."

"I don't like the idea of you walking outside alone after dark."

"Oh, come on, Chief. It's not that dark. And it's Hector. He said you'd already met with him. So you know he couldn't hurt a flea." She glanced around, then stepped closer so our bodies met, and pressed her lips to my cheek. I was surprised how warm it felt. "Thanks for worrying about me, though."

"You must be feeling better."

"I am, thank you." She looked as if she might tear up again. "I'm still shaken, of course . . . but better."

I didn't know what else to say. I'm always at a loss for the proper words whenever there's been a tragedy; I struggle internally, unsure of how to help. I knew I shouldn't, but I found myself asking Greta if we could get together again, maybe have a drink later on. Luckily, Greta said no. She was smarter than I. She was also busy—she and some of the other members of the group were heading into Lake Geneva to commiserate with Hector Harper. And that was one party I had no interest in attending.

Chapter Twenty-Eight

With the interviews complete, I decided to head back home. On the way, I touched base with Tyrrell and summed up everything I'd learned. I promised him a written report later.

Tyrrell was in an uncharacteristically foul mood. He was still waiting on the forensics from the scene and the final results of the autopsy. Moreover, his other big case—the Hauftmann investigation—had hit a stumbling block.

"I thought your guys were close to solving that," I said.

"Don't rub it in."

Tyrrell did have a few updates on the Harper case, however. Preliminary results from the medical examiner confirmed that Chandra had been stabbed with a smooth-bladed weapon roughly three inches wide and ten inches long. Her system contained both alcohol and Ambien, a sleep aid, enough to make her very groggy at the time of her death. The financial updates were of greater interest: Chandra Harper had been rich, at least in the eyes of someone with my pay grade. Tyrrell's team had found bank accounts totaling just over two million dollars—with other assets yet to be discovered. It appeared most of this wealth would not be considered marital property, so it wouldn't go to Hector Harper unless it was stipulated in Chandra's will. Unfortunately, Chandra's attorney was vacationing in the Far East and he hadn't been reached yet.

"For all we know," Tyrrell grumbled, "the attorney arranged the murder with Navilio, they both paid John Ratz to do it, and now Navilio and the attorney are living it up on Chandra's money somewhere in Tahiti."

Naturally he wasn't serious.

I told him about the flash drives I had, and I offered to take a closer look at Chandra's literary efforts while I was at home that evening. He was perfectly happy to let me. "So far, I'm liking this Ratz guy as the murderer," Tyrrell said. "Turns out John Ratz had an arrest for assault after a bar scuffle a few years back. It wasn't prosecuted, but we have his prints. So, if we can match them to anything in the victim's room, we'll know he lied to you about not being there. I've got my guys running a deeper background check and seeing what else they can dig up on him. If you find anything in that stuff that Chandra Harper wrote, let me know."

"Will do."

I wasn't quite as sure as Tyrrell that John Ratz was our guy yet, but I didn't say so. The detective and I agreed to touch base again tomorrow, unless something broke sooner.

When I walked into my kitchen, I saw that Annie Madden had stopped by as promised. The flash drives containing Chandra's writing lay on my kitchen table. Beside them was a hardcover copy of the novel *The Ox-Bow Incident*. My helpful assistant had tracked it down at the local library. There was a little note attached: "It's due back in two weeks, but I know you'll figure things out before that. —Annie."

I wished I had her confidence.

I made another pot of coffee and fired up my home computer. When I plugged in the little USB flash drive from Feri, I immediately I hit a wall: I couldn't open the files on my PC. I tried the second drive, and the third—all the same. I'm completely hopeless with all things electronic. I had just figured out how to set the timer on my ridiculously expensive and now-prehistoric VCR when DVDs suddenly came along and made my entire movie collection obsolete. I'm even worse with computers, and before they came along, I had been perfectly happy with my IBM Selectric.

Fortunately, I know a kid named Nathan Smith. Nate is a teenager who still lives down the road from me. He's especially fond of Dawg, so he helps me out with him from time to time. More importantly, Nathan is a wiz at all things tech. He's also very patient, and he explains things slowly while I jot Post-its and stick them all over my computer. At times I think it would be easier for me to learn nuclear physics.

I knew Nate would be home from school by now, so I called for help. He came right over with his trusty laptop in his backpack and an iPod in his pocket. The kid probably had a Blackberry, too. Nate had the problem fixed in five minutes. He gave Dawg a friendly ear-tussle, then headed back out, adding he would be home all evening if I ran into trouble again. "You can text me, Chief," he said with a grin. "Oh yeah, right—maybe just send a smoke signal."

The first drive, from Professor Feri, contained several hundred pages from Chandra's book. I realized these files were going to take a substantial amount of time to read, so at first, I tried to skim them. I quickly reached a section that described Chandra's breakdown after the death of her twin sister. The twin was named Cassandra. Chandra and Cassandra. I shook my head. Some parents should not be allowed to name their own children.

The next chapters described Chandra's descent into depression after her sister's death. She climbed back toward sanity, she claimed—but not until she realized the death was not a case of accidental botulism poisoning, but rather a deliberate murder by the fiancé, a.k.a. the master chef Alden Torrence. Chandra was certain that Torrence had placed the deadly culture in Cassandra's food. Her proof was sketchy—it was more like sisterly intuition. The motive was money, Chandra believed. Though the couple had not yet married, Cassandra and Torrence had several assets in common, including real estate. Torrence had inherited all of it. Chandra also asserted that Torrence had been jealous and abusive toward Cassandra. For this, Chandra felt guilt, because she did not convince her sister to leave her abuser. Instead, Chandra had complained directly to Torrence, which only made Torrence angrier and more jealous, strengthening his motive for murder. As for means and opportunity . . . Torrence was a chef, and he taught at a culinary institute—surely he could have manufactured the botulism culture and found a way to introduce it into Cassandra's sushi.

As Chandra dug deeper into the fiancé's life, her obsession grew, and her theories became even more far-fetched. She scoured newspaper accounts and police reports, looking for other examples of botulism, accidental poisoning, or even fatal encounters with E. coli. She zeroed in on three victims, all female. Like Cassandra, all had light complexions and blonde hair, and they were of similar age. Furthermore, all the deaths had occurred in northern states. That fact was very important to Chandra—and it was enough for her to believe her sister's murder was not an isolated incident. Alden Torrence was "a man of the North." Earlier, when Cassandra had indicated a desire to move to Florida, Torrence had refused because he could not tolerate warm climates. In fact, after he allegedly murdered Cassandra and his three other victims in the Upper Midwest, he "fled to Canada"—as Chandra described—and then moved to Alaska.

I could see why the police had never taken her seriously: Chandra's evidence was far from conclusive. But the three other victims were real enough, and Torrence, according to Chandra, could have known all three—although she was only able to confirm intimate contact with one of them. Even so, I could understand why she had come to view Torrence as a serial assassin. Statistically, what were the odds that a single chef would sleep with two or more women who subsequently died from food poisoning?

As Chandra's book continued, she became all-consumed by the loss of her twin. Eventually, she lost track of Torrence's whereabouts.

She abandoned her search and began a downward spiral into loneliness. To ease her pain, she sought solace wherever she could find it, often in the arms of strong-willed men who dominated and often abused her. Occasionally, she took the upper hand, only to find that she had very little control over anything.

I took a short break from reading, stood up and stretched, then looked at my watch. It was already ten o'clock. I didn't know how much more of this "light reading" I could take, but I decided to keep going.

As I continued, it became apparent that putting words on a page was therapeutic for Chandra. Though much of the writing was sad, the vivid descriptions of her sex life would make even a ribald man blush. Not all the encounters were abusive. One involved an unnamed woman whom she'd met in a bar, as well as the woman's husband. Good or bad, those relationships were clearly the vehicle that Chandra used to subdue her inner demons. Unfortunately, they often unleashed new ones in the process.

I hunted for a description of Ratz. She hadn't used his real name, but he was obviously "the warrior" near the end of the book—the physical descriptions matched. Ironically, he played a comparatively small role, and there was nothing incriminating in her description—no knife-wielding threats, for instance. Chandra did write about the ugly Chicago encounter that Greta had described. Greta's version bordered on rape—she'd told me Ratz had punished Chandra with rough sex just for contradicting him in a conversation. In Chandra's own account, she had a "safe word," a term used by S&M aficionados. But Chandra and Ratz weren't into whips and chains, and her so-called "safe word" was no. If she had simply said no, she reasoned, "the warrior" would have stopped. But she did not say no. She could not bring herself to do so.

I continued delving through the pages of Chandra's writings. I was beginning to appreciate Chandra more now, postmortem, than I ever had antemortem. Besides the book, there were several short stories and poems, some sweet, others fatalistic. Not one of them was illuminating, however. The flash drive from Feri also included a file of his own pedantic notes and editing suggestions, which were equally unenlightening.

Dawg began to paw at the back door. I rose and stretched, then let him outside. After four hours, I'd barely finished the files on the flash drive that Feri had given me. The other two drives were largely untouched, but they appeared to contain most of the same information. I now had more insight into the life of Chandra Harper than I had ever wanted to have. Unfortunately, I still didn't know who killed her.

Weary of reading, I decided to switch gears. I broke out the Visine and vodka to prepare myself, then linked my camera to the computer so I could upload the crime-scene photos and have a closer look. I glanced at my watch again. It was probably much too late to call Nathan, but luckily, I managed not to screw things up with the photos. One by one, images of the murder scene flashed across my computer monitor as they loaded. I was glad Nate hadn't had to see these gruesome images.

I pored over the photos for another hour, looking for any kind of relevant detail, any piece of overlooked minutia that, when finally noticed, would point me toward the killer. I learned nothing. My eyes were burning, and I was almost out of Visine. I pictured myself putting a cool slice of cucumber on each eye for relief—it always seemed to work when women did it on TV. I'd never actually tried it myself, and I had no cucumber, so I poured another jigger of ice-cold vodka and held the glass to my eyelids before I downed it.

Then, finally, I shut off the computer and headed to bed, utterly defeated. Twenty-four hours earlier, I had escorted Chandra Harper to her suite and assured her it was safe. As I drifted off to sleep, I knew she'd be complaining about that in my dreams.

Chapter Twenty-Nine

April is the cruelest month, wrote Nobel laureate T.S. Eliot. What did he know? The man was born in St. Louis, but he lived in foggy London most of his life. For Wisconsinites, January is the cruelest month. True, there might be the occasional cold, bright day when the sun shines directly into your soul, promising a new year filled with optimism and idealistic resolution. For the most part, however, it's a month of postponing dreams, slipping on sidewalks, and enduring bleak, bitter days that bite to the bone as you fantasize about a trip to the South.

I often say I like the cold, but this winter felt especially grim. I awoke to another pounding headache, and the day was as gray as my complexion. I'd come back to this house in this once-quiet small town to recapture the untroubled days of my youth. Instead I was feeling low and incompetent—and completely stuck. And I was not just stuck in terms of every crime I suddenly had to solve; I was stuck in life. Quitting my job was hardly an option—my next law-enforcement post would probably be some flea-bitten town in the north woods, a place too quiet and cold even for me. I was heading toward a Bloody Mary and a good wallow when I was nagged by the words of an old friend: "If you want something done," he'd say, "give it to a busy man."

And he was right. It was time for me to get busy, do my job, and solve the murder of Chandra Harper.

I set the coffee brewing and made myself some eggs, then turned on the computer and returned my attention to the crime-scene photos. Tyrrell had given me a copy of the official photos to supplement the shots I had snapped myself. They were sharper than mine, but apart from confirming the scale and measurements of certain items, they didn't appear to show anything different. I pulled out my notebook and began jotting details and questions—reviewing who the current suspects were, what they'd said in the interviews, all the specifics we knew so far and had yet to confirm about the crime.

Chandra had died sometime between three-thirty a.m. and six o'clock. Her attacker had used a large, bladed weapon. There were no signs of forced entry, so her assailant may have had a key, or Chandra could have admitted the killer into the room herself. There was no indication the lock had been picked. I didn't think Chandra had coincidentally forgotten to lock her door on the night of her death—because even if she had, that still left the question of how the killer got into the building. I also doubted the killer had been hiding there in her suite, waiting until Chandra fell asleep—I'd checked the room myself around midnight, and there weren't that many places to hide.

My notebook was filling up fast, with almost a hundred entries. I reread them, this time out loud. Only one idea seemed worthy of speculation.

Detective Tyrrell had assumed the bloody finger marks on the carpet were made by Chandra as she tried to reach for her purse, which contained her cell phone. As she reached, she scattered the items off her bedside table. Her hand had fallen atop the novel, *The Ox-Bow Incident*, strictly by chance. At least, that's what Tyrrell had surmised. I speculated differently.

At our first meeting, Chandra had been aghast when I said I preferred to glean information from movies instead of books. In fact, I've learned a lot about history, geography, and biology from motion pictures, along with a lot of needless trivia. Of course I realize that movies "based on a true story" are notoriously loose with facts, but if I ever doubt the reliability of something, I use Google, the one computer function I seem to have mastered. Oliver Stone's movies, especially *JFK*, make me crazy, so I no longer watch them. They're filled with Stone's conjectures, which are impossible to verify.

But I wasn't researching a decades-old assassination plot, I reminded myself—I was investigating a day-old murder. Although my theory might have been just as crazy as one of Oliver Stone's, I believed that Chandra Harper was attempting to give someone a clue about her murder when she put her hand on the cover of *The Ox-Bow Incident*. And that someone might have been me.

I carefully clicked my way out of the photo software, then went to Google to search for a movie website. I had seen the movie version of *The Ox-Bow Incident* several times, but not recently enough to recall the small details.

The Ox-Bow Incident is a Western set in Nevada during the 1880s. Based on a true story, it stars Henry Fonda as Gil Carter, a cowboy and drifter. Henry Morgan plays his sidekick. After the murder of a local rancher, a large posse is assembled to pursue the killer or killers and bring them back to town. Fonda is among the riders. The posse eventually comes upon three suspicious men, played by Anthony Quinn, Dana Andrews, and Francis Ford. After a contentious debate, the posse members decide to hang all three of the accused. Only Fonda and a few others object, but they're outnumbered. As the movie ends, the sheriff arrives, too late to stop the lynching. He carries news: There had been no murder after all—only a shooting. And the three men they just hanged were all innocent.

I found a good summary of the movie online and jotted a page of notes. So far, I had no idea whether those details meant anything in terms of Chandra's murder. I realized I would probably have to watch the movie again. And, I'd have to read the novel, or at least skim it. There were bound to be details there that weren't in the movie, maybe even some key differences. I could still see—and hear—the image of ghostly, undead Chandra at the murder scene, rising up from her body just to harp at me about my illiterate ways. I knew reading the book was the only way I'd ever shut her up.

I glanced at the kitchen clock. It was still early, but it was a lot of homework for something that could possibly lead me on a "wild goose chase," as they say in the old Westerns. I picked up the phone and checked in with Dorothy. She was relieved to report that no further murders had occurred in the township overnight, and there was not a single new incident to report from my officers. "Maybe things will get back to normal soon . . . right, Chief?"

I hoped Dorothy was right. I told her I'd be working at home if anybody needed me, then cracked open my new library book. It was a good thing Annie had checked it out on my behalf. I hadn't been to the library for so long that I wasn't even sure I had a valid card.

Chapter Thirty

Reading *The Ox-Bow Incident* was a more difficult task that I had expected. I thought I'd breeze through it. After all, it was a Western, not old-English Lit. But it wasn't like *Shane* or *True Grit*. In the illustrious words of Chandra Harper, the novel was a "complex morality tale," with the emphasis on complex.

I called the only bookstore in Lake Geneva and asked if they carried *Cliffs Notes* for the novel. Of course they didn't, and I felt embarrassed for asking. It reminded me of my days back at Saint Isaac Jogues Grammar School. Once I'd had to write a report on *Johnny Tremain*, a novel about the Revolutionary War. It was due on a Monday morning, but I'd procrastinated. On Saturday, I called my friends for help and came up empty. Then I tried to find the corresponding *Cliffs Notes* and came up empty again. I even checked the TV Guide, hoping by some miracle of miracles that *The Wonderful World of Disney* was showing the movie version. I did everything short of calling the author, Esther Forbes—or actually reading the book. On Sunday afternoon I finally skimmed it, then bulled my way through the report, relying heavily on the back cover for insight. I got an "F"—and a letter to take home to my parents.

I didn't want to fail with this case, and I was running out of time, so I stretched out on the sofa and started reading again . . . and promptly nodded off. I forced myself to sit up and try again, skimming the pages of *The Ox-Bow Incident* with my finger. The more I skimmed, the more I doubted my harebrained theory about Chandra's "final, finger-pointing, dying clue." I reached the end of the book, then rustled up my copy of the movie. I prepared to stick it in the VCR, praying the aging machine wouldn't eat the tape.

On a whim, I phoned Greta, the tape still in my hand. The invitation I extended sounded ridiculous even to me: basically, I asked if she wanted to spend some quality time alone with me and Dawg at my cluttered house, searching for clues to her friend's murder by watching a movie filmed in 1948. She declined, but all was not lost—when I said I was planning to swing by Kirsch's later to speak to the staff and have a drink around happy hour, she offered to join me for a cocktail. I promised to call her room when I arrived.

My stomach grumbled loudly just then, and I realized it was past lunchtime. I decided to fix myself the perfect movie-watching snack: I fried several slices of bologna in a large amount of butter, then slapped them between two slices of Jewish rye—after I'd swabbed the rye in the melted butter at the bottom of the pan. A tall, cold glass of two-percent milk accompanied my repast. Greta didn't know what she was missing. She'd probably thought my invitation had only meant some microwave popcorn and a diet ginger ale.

The milk complemented the fried bologna the way a fine Cabernet complements filet mignon. The only thing missing was a side of baked beans. The movie was good too, as entertaining as I'd remembered. When the credits rolled, I retrieved the list of character names I'd jotted earlier and compared the movie characters to the names in the book. Fonda had played Gil Garter, and Harry Morgan was Art Croft. Other characters included Major Tetley, Poncho and Sparks, and Rose Mapen. Anthony Quinn was Juan Martínez, a Mexican gambler using an alias. But unless a Mexican gambler had murdered Chandra—or perhaps an Aztec-Irish-Mexican-American man like Quinn—neither the movie nor the book told me anything new. In fact, it drew me to the same conclusion that Detective Tyrrell had already indicated: the book was meaningless to the investigation, and Chandra Harper's fingers were probably just trying to reach for her purse and cell phone.

My suspect list hadn't changed: Ratz was on top, seconded by Chandra's husband and Ben Zubeck neck and neck. Alexandra Hale was a very distant third—maybe she'd wanted John Ratz all to herself. The list after that included everyone else besides Zubeck who might have wanted to kill Navilio but who was stupid enough to kill Chandra Harper by mistake. It was probably a hundred names long, but for brevity's sake, I'd never written it down.

As the video started to rewind, it made a squeaking sound, which quickly escalated to squealing and scrunching. By the time I reached the machine, little loops of tape were sticking out of the slot like shreds of meat in a badger's mouth. I tried to wrestle it out, but the tape was completely stuck. The eject button did nada, and the display was dead. I cursed. At least I'd had a chance to watch the movie, but it was a good bet it was the last one this machine would ever play.

The afternoon was waning, and I wasn't fit for public consumption. To save time, I brushed my teeth while I took a hot shower. I banished the bologna breath by swirling a hefty shot of mouthwash, then spat it out on the shower floor, hitting the drain dead-on. I felt refreshed and revitalized—and ready to join Greta at Kirsch's. But first, I had a little side trip to make. It was time to pay a visit to a character called Norman at the Bayside Motel, and to hear what he could tell me about Ben Zubeck.

Chapter Thirty-One

Wrapped around a quiet cove, the village of Williams Bay lies just over the wooded ridge that separates Como Lake from its big sister, Lake Geneva. Before the last Ice Age reshaped the terrain, the two lakes were connected. Apart from the historic Yerkes Observatory and a handful of restaurants and shops, the village is mostly residential, and the local officials seem to like it that way. There is no McDonalds, no big-box store, not even a grocery store.

The village does have an inn or two, however, one of which is the Bayside, a 1950s vintage Mom-and-Pop-style motel located just outside my jurisdiction. Locals affectionately called it the Bates Motel, after the building in the Hitchcock thriller *Psycho*. Although the establishment bore some resemblance to Hitchcock's setting, the clincher was the manager, a crusty codger whose surname happened to be Bates. His first name is Michael, but all the locals call him Norman, including me. He's a local historian and a clearinghouse of current scuttlebutt, and I often check in with him when I want to hear what kind of rumors are floating about.

That day, I wasn't interested in the usual sordid gossip—I wanted to know whether Norman had heard anything about Ben Zubeck. As I descended the hill toward the Bay, I passed one of my favorite landmarks, a white igloo-shaped building known as Daddy Maxwell's Arctic Circle Diner. It was a popular hangout, but it wasn't the kind of place you'd ever see the big rigs line up. And in my book, that was a good thing. Contrary to popular wisdom, truckers do not know the best places to eat. If you want advice on a restaurant, pay attention to the reviewer's nationality instead of his profession. If he's Irish or English, ignore the advice completely. If he's Russian, German, or Polish, take his advice with a grain of paprika. When it comes to food and restaurants, only Italians give consistently good advice; ergo, only Italian truckers know where to eat.

As I continued toward the Bayside Motel, I formulated the questions I'd ask my source. Norman Bates was like a "streetwise" character from a Seventies cop show—the kind who knew everything from where Jimmy Hoffa was buried to who really killed John F. Kennedy to whether a certain bar matron was truly a blonde. In the real world, no street source is ever half that wise or well-informed. Even so, I was counting on Norman to give me some inside dirt on Ben Zubeck. I doubted Zubeck was actually Chandra Harper's killer, but I did believe he was behind the restaurant shooting—and it was a pretty big coincidence that both events took place on the same night. The possibility of a connection was still bothering me . . .

Norman must have seen my headlights as I approached the motel, because he opened his front door and invited me into his home as soon as I stepped out of my vehicle. His domicile was a modest cottage flanked by two matching buildings on either side. All had brickwork along the base, with white siding above. Each of the other buildings housed a pair of motel rooms.

"Welcome, Chief," he called. "Better get yourself inside before I lose all my heat." Norman was an Irishman in his early seventies. He was lanky and tall, though his height was diminished by a slight stoop. He always wore a navy-blue knit cap in winter. His face was ruddy and weathered, and though he had a full beard along his jaw, there were thick white bristles where he occasionally shaved his upper cheeks. I could never decide whether he looked like a New England fisherman or a retired IRA member.

"What brings you here today?" Norman asked.

"Oh, just looking for the word on the street, and maybe a history lesson," I answered, stamping the snow off my feet and hurrying through the door.

Like the French Country Inn, the Bayside Motel was owned by Anthony Navilio. That fact wasn't widely known, but I thought Ben Zubeck might be aware of it. And that meant Zubeck might've been giving Norman Bates some trouble, too, or at least an earful.

Norman gestured toward the couch in his small living room, which smelled of stale cigarette smoke. Bookshelves lined the wall behind the overstuffed brown couch. As I took a seat, the couch springs creaked, and my rear sank about six inches lower than my knees.

Norman headed toward the fridge. "Want a beer, Chief?"

"Actually, I'm on duty," I said.

"Your point being?"

I smiled but didn't answer. Norman was already grabbing the handle of his small white refrigerator, which was visible from the couch. His home was essentially a suite with a kitchenette—only the bedroom and a tiny bathroom were separate. The fridge shook when he opened it, and all the bottles clinked inside. He popped the caps from two Smithwick's and handed one to me. I thought about asking for a glass, but judging by the pile of dishes towering above the rim of the sink, I doubted he had a clean one.

The bottle was colder than the ice on Lake Como. "I'll bet Irish truck drivers know the best places to drink beer," I said.

"Pardon me?" Norman replied, taking a swig.

"Nothing—just mumbling to myself. I tend to do that a lot."

"I've noticed."

Norman settled into the cracked leather easy chair that was perpendicular to the couch. The lamp table beside him held an ashtray and a pack of unfiltered Chesterfields. Newspapers and books were scattered across the coffee table, along with one black sock.

"So, Chief, did you come here today to mumble, or is something particular on your mind? Like maybe a murder at the French Country Inn?"

"What've you heard about that?" I asked.

"Just the basics. If you'll pardon the expression, it's been real dead around here. I've barely been out of my house for a week, and nobody's been calling me about much of anything. But I've heard that a lady from Chicago was killed in her room over there while she was sleeping."

"That's about the size of it," I said.

"That kind of killing, it sounds like something personal to me. Any leads?"

"Nothing worth sharing."

"It's a damn shame, though—especially for that woman. Between the murder and the shooting at Kirsch's, Navilio is having one hell of a week over there."

"Have you spoken with your boss lately?"

"No, but Navilio and I never talk much directly unless there's a problem over here. I just send the bills and the balance sheet to his assistant."

"So, you haven't had any problems yourself? Crank calls, threats, that kind of thing?" I didn't bother to ask whether anyone had been murdered in their shower. He'd heard that joke a million times before.

"There's always my prostate problem," he said. "I could tell you about that if you want."

"No, thanks. I was thinking you might've had some contact with a man named Ben Zubeck."

"Not lately," Norman said. "But I know him. You don't live here seven decades without at least knowing that fellow's name. Zubeck is a little rough around the edges."

"How rough, would you say?"

"Rough enough to kill someone, under the right circumstances.

He's calmed down some in the last ten years, but I still wouldn't want to be on his bad side. Which, of course, is where you now happen to be."

I stared. "What do you mean by that?"

"Didn't you serve him those eviction papers?"

"That's right," I said. "I thought you hadn't heard any news this week."

"That wasn't news—I knew the eviction was coming. Ben has been struggling for a while. And I knew Navilio had his eye on that property. I wasn't surprised to hear Zubeck is making threats against the French Country Inn."

"Do you think he'd act on them?"

Norman stroked his beard, which was streaked yellow from tobacco. He took another swig of his beer before he answered. "You know, I knew Ben pretty well when he was a teenager. I'm older than he is, but not by that much. He's always had a crazy streak. I can't see him killing some tourist he didn't know, but the shooting at Kirsch's? Sure, he might do that. I'd watch my step with him, Chief."

"Thanks, I will."

The phone rang. It was sitting on a Formica-topped table by the door, which held yet another ashtray and some notebooks. Norman grunted and went to answer it. He picked up the receiver and glanced at the caller ID, then frowned.

"Hyello," he said.

To keep myself occupied, I picked up a book from the coffee table and started leafing through it. It was about Chicago's gangster history, with photos of Capone, Bugs Moran, and John Dillinger.

As Norman listened to the caller, his face showed growing annoyance. The voice on the other end sounded like a chipmunk to me. Finally, Norman interrupted. "Yeah, yeah, I remember you. You've called three times already. But like I told you before, I'm only gonna sell you the one with the one nut." Norman paused and listened to more chatter. "No, the one testicle." More chipmunk chatter. "Listen, pal, I've changed my mind. Don't ever call me here again." He hung up the phone.

I lifted an eyebrow. "You in the testicle business now, Norman?"

He grinned. Despite all the smoking, his teeth were in good shape—he didn't skimp on the Pepsodent. "Why, you need a spare?"

"No, I'm good. What was that all about?"

"Oh, a friend and I have a little dog-breeding business on the side. We breed Bernese. We get a thousand dollars a pup, and that guy would've paid, even for the imperfect testicles, but I won't do business with a moron. It's not fair to the dog. You ever heard of a Bernese, Chief?"

"You mean béarnaise? Like the steak sauce?"

"No, I mean the dog, as in Bernese Mountain Dogs. They're related to the Saint Bernard. Great dogs. You ever need another four-legged deputy, give me a call. Want another beer?" he asked, grabbing a second one for himself.

"No, still good, but thanks." I wasn't here to discuss dog-breeding or testicles, so I steered Norman back to the subject at hand. "Tell me more about Ben Zubeck. When was the last time you two spoke directly?"

Norman stroked his beard again with his thick, gnarly fingers. "Oh, gee . . . at least a year ago. We used to have a beer together once in a while at the old Keg Room, but I haven't seen much of him since the Keg burned down."

"Have you ever witnessed his mean streak firsthand?"

"Oh, sure. Whenever he thought someone wronged him, even just a little, he could go after 'em with a vengeance. One time I saw him take out two jerks from Illinois after they insulted a local lady. That fight was over before it even began. Zubeck never said a word—he just stood up and flattened the two guys before they had a chance to defend themselves. Someone called the cops, but then everyone in the place said the two losers started the donnybrook."

I hadn't heard the word donnybrook in years. "Zubeck has a history of more than just bar fights," I noted.

"Yeah, I heard about some other things, but you asked what I'd seen firsthand. I didn't actually see any of the other stuff." He pointed at the book in my hand. "You like hearing about the local history and Chicago stories, right? I've got another one that might interest you—it has a lot of stories about the French Country Inn. You can borrow it sometime if you'd like. I've actually highlighted all the passages that mention Lake Geneva and the Lake Como Hotel, so you wouldn't even have to read the whole thing."

"Much obliged," I said. "My plate's full right now, but maybe I'll borrow it another time."

"You ever heard of a guy named Jimmy Murray?" Norman asked.

"As a matter of fact, I have. He was that Chicago small-time crook who was involved in the big train robbery during the Thirties."

"The Rondout robbery, only it was 1924. Murray was involved in all kinds of crimes and schemes, and he generally got away with them. He was sentenced to thirty years for the Rondout heist. Five years later, his wife, Rosy, cut a deal with the Feds and handed over nearly four-hundred grand—supposedly his part of the take. Whaddaya know, they let him go. But Murray still had quite a bankroll."

"What makes you say that?"

"He owned a lot of properties. He bought a house on Le Moyne Street down in Oak Park and he owned several other homes outside Cook County, including a lake home near Waconda. He also spent about thirty grand building a restaurant called The Rainbo Barbecue, down on the corner of Harlem and North Avenue."

"Was that on the Chicago side?" The corners at North and

Harlem were in four different jurisdictions. One corner was Chicago, the others were River Forest, Oak Park, and Elmwood Park.

Norman took another big swig and thought a minute. "I'm pretty sure Murray's joint was on the northeast corner, but there are conflicting stories. The address was 7190 West North Avenue, I think—so, that would make it in the Galewood district of Chicago."

"I've heard the owner of the Lake Como Hotel was tied in pretty tight with Murray. Is that right?"

"You mean Hobart Hermansen. Yeah, he knew Murray, and they both knew Dillinger and Baby Face Nelson. Dillinger hid out at the Rainbo a number of times—the second story of the building was set up for it. So did his gang members, including his good buddy Tommy Carroll. Nelson hung out there, too. In fact, it was Murray who introduced Baby Face Nelson to Hermansen. Now there was a guy you didn't want to cross—Nelson, I mean, though Hermansen was no marshmallow himself." He scratched his beard. "You got a few minutes? I got something I want to show you."

I checked my watch. Happy hour was already in full swing at the French Country Inn, and I needed to move on soon. "A few," I said. "Then it's back to work for me."

"Hang on a second." Norman disappeared into his bedroom, then returned with a small plastic bag. "Tommy Carroll was a member of the Dillinger gang. He carried a book of matches from the Lake Como Hotel as an unofficial gangland calling card."

He handed me the plastic bag. In it was a blue matchbook cover, obviously very old. The front side read HERMANSEN'S LAKE COMO HOTEL. Underneath that was a telephone number, 5-7891, then the address, simply P.O. LAKE GENEVA, WISC. The back of the matchbook featured a drawing of a muskie jumping out of the waters of Lake Como and the name THE MUSKALLONGE.

"I'm impressed, Norman. Is this one of the actual calling cards?"

"Sure it is."

"How'd you get this?"

"A friend," he said cryptically.

I stared at it. "What's The Muskallonge? That's not how you spell the name of the fish."

"I think it was the name of the hotel's drinking establishment—you know, like the Muskie Lounge. As I was saying, a matchbook from the Como Hotel was like a calling card. It let people know you were part of the inner circle, you were an okay guy. The Dillinger gang used Hermansen's place as a safe house in Wisconsin, and Murray's joint was their safe haven in Chicago."

"I like the matchbook story," I said. "It's like they had a secret fraternity handshake, only they slipped the other guy matches when they shook."

Norman pointed to a book on the coffee table: *Don't Call Us Gun Molls: Women of the John Dillinger Gang,* by Ellen Poulsen. "That one tells the whole matchbook story. It also talks about how the Dillinger gang would come up here to Hermansen's place," Norman continued. "Baby Face and his wife, Helen, usually stayed in the main part of the hotel, but Tommy Carroll, the matchstick man, liked to stay in a cottage by the shore with his moll, Jean. I think Navilio calls it The Petite Aubergine or somethin'."

"Le Petite Auberge," I said. "It's right by the shore. Easy to get in and out of by boat . . . or car or rail. The train tracks ran right past the inn."

"You know who else you should talk to? Clam Chowder," Norman said.

"About what? Ben Zubeck or the murder?"

He looked annoyed. "About the gangster history."

I was getting ready to leave when the phone rang again. Norman went to answer it, glancing at the receiver before he spoke. "Reservations, yes, this is the reservationist." His friendly, professional tone sounded nothing like his usual speaking voice. He paused. "The eighth and ninth of next month? I'll check the computer for the availability of those dates for you. Please hold."

He put his palm over the receiver and looked in my direction. "This'll just take a second." He continued the phone conversation. "I am terribly sorry, but we are fully booked on those dates." Without allowing the person to make another inquiry, Norman added, "But please keep us in mind for another visit."

He hung up the phone. "I wish people would just leave me alone during the off-season."

"I know how you feel, Norman." I stood and handed him the bag with the matchbook. "Thanks for the beer and the stories, but I'd better be off now. Maybe I'll swing back and pick up those books another time."

"Suit yourself," Norman said, sounding a little disappointed. "You remember what I said, though."

"About Jimmy Murray, or Clam Chowder?"

"About Ben Zubeck. I'm serious now, Chief. You watch your step with him."

"I'll do that, Norman," I said, heading out into the cold and dark. "You can be sure of that."

Chapter Thirty-Two

Sooner or later, everyone comes to Kirsch's at the French Country Inn, and tonight the usual suspects were all in the bar. As I walked in, I immediately spotted Ron Frankel and his buddy Kirsch, along with bartenders Rick and Roy, who appeared to be off-duty because they were on the same side of the rail as their boss. Professor Feri, Evelyn Durst, and Emile Tavilion had taken their favorite positions at the far end of the copper-topped counter. A half-dozen patrons, all locals, occupied the rest of the barstools, and several people were standing behind them. In fact, the place was packed, which was unusual for a Thursday night during the off-season. Murder draws a crowd, I thought.

Mary Haggermaker and Patti Goff, the current innkeeper and her predecessor, respectively, were sitting at a table in the corner near the fireplace. As soon as Patti spotted me, she waved me over. I knew she probably had some outlandish theory about the murder that she wanted to share, but I was here to listen, after all, so I returned a quick greeting from Ron and Kirsch, then walked over to the women.

"Good evening, ladies," I said. "What brings you here tonight?"

"As if you couldn't guess," Mary replied. "We've had a couple of trying days around here, and Patti was nice enough to come in to help us out. We thought we'd blow off some steam and find out what the latest word is."

"Looks like a few of your friends had the same idea," I said.

"Well, everyone is curious," Mary said. "And Detective Tyrrell hasn't been all that forthcoming. So, what can you tell us, Chief? Any leads yet?"

"Sorry, but I can't discuss the investigation."

"Oh, bull," Patti said in her usual imperious tone. "Then why are you here, Chief? Sit down, please. I have a couple ideas about the murder that I'd like to share. Assuming you'd like to hear them?"

I smiled and sat down. I always got a kick out of Patti. "Shoot," I said.

"Okay, first of all, do you think the killer might have intended to murder Tony Navilio instead of Chandra Harper? Suite 303 is the suite he usually stays in."

"It's a possibility. We're pursuing that angle, along with a number of others that seem more likely. I can't give you any details, though."

I thought Patti would be pleased that I hadn't totally crushed her theory. Instead, she looked as if a winning lottery ticket had just blown out of her hand and disappeared down a sewer grate. "Boy, I was really afraid of that . . ." she muttered, fishing in her purse.

"I don't think you have to be worried, Patti," I said.

She twisted her face. "Why wouldn't I be? Tony was my boss for years, you know. And if he was the target . . . then maybe the killer will be back."

"It's a big leap, Patti. We're not a hundred percent certain yet, but in all likelihood, Chandra Harper was the intended victim."

"Well, maybe you won't think it's such a big leap when you see this," she said. She pulled a folded sheet of yellow legal paper from her purse. "I've compiled a list of people of interest that you might want to check out." She carefully unfolded the paper and smoothed it on the table. "Now, I've listed them in two columns. Column one has all the people with whom Tony regularly does business. Mary let me go through all the files in the office so I could be thorough. I searched the computer, his office correspondence, contracts, proposals, and every other place I could think of."

I raised a hand to interrupt her, but she was on a roll.

"Now, the second column is more important," Patti continued. "Here, I've listed all the people with whom Tony has had some kind of a dispute—either they were angry at him, or he was angry at them. Or both. And . . ." She tapped the sheet. "I've added a little note here in the margin as to why."

I glanced at the sheet. The second list was much longer than the first.

"Look's like he's made a few enemies," I said. "It's good work, Patti, and I appreciate the effort, but I can't really use this. Did you have Navilio's permission to gather this information?"

"Well, no . . . not directly." She looked dejected. "But I've had access to all his files before. And I don't think he'd mind—after all, it's his safety . . ."

"I'm sorry, Patti. This isn't the way we do things. But you could make up a new list of people for me—a short list of the people you personally suspect—and then give it to me tomorrow."

Her face brightened. "I'll do that, Chief. Hey, is it just me, or is it cold in here?" It was Patti's trademark line. Mary and I both answered that we were plenty warm by the fire. I was about to make my excuses and head toward the bar when I remembered one of the big question marks in my notebook.

"There's something else you could do to help with the investigation," I said to Mary. "You, too, Patti."

"Sure, Chief," Mary said.

"I'd like to know about your procedures with the room keys for the inn—where you keep the spares, who might have access to them. Can you show me?"

Mary looked disappointed. "Detective Tyrrell already went through all that yesterday."

"Let's go through it again," I said patiently. "It'll only take a minute."

Mary and Patti led me back to the lobby, where Mary pointed to a locked compartment behind the desk. "The individual keys to the guest rooms are in there," she said. "We only open that box to give out a key or to put one away," she said.

"Is there a master key for the rooms?"

"I have one, which I keep with me at all times," Mary said. "Even at home. But we keep another one hidden in the front closet under the stairs, just in case a guest loses a key or gets locked out of their room when I'm not here."

She showed me. It wasn't obvious—you had to rummage in the closet to see the hook that was holding the key—but since the closet itself wasn't locked, the key was accessible. "Who knows about this key?" I asked.

"Just me, Tony Navilio, and Jim Kirchschlager. And some of our staff. The lead bartenders know about it, too—they help out whenever a guest has a problem late at night, after the desk clerk is gone." She looked uncomfortable. "Honestly, Chief, I know it sounds like a lot of people. But not one of them would have anything to do with the murder. They're all trustworthy."

"I'm sure they are," I said. "What I'm wondering is, could someone else have seen one of them take out this key? Then that person would know about it, too."

Mary thought for a moment. "I doubt it. We haven't had a guest locked out of their room since last summer. And it's not like we give people a tour of the closet, you know. We're careful."

Patti frowned at me. "I like my theory better than yours. Except for the part about Tony Navilio being the target, of course."

"I'm not offering you a theory, Patti. It's an inquiry. And I appreciate the help."

We headed back to the bar together, but the two women seemed happy to be rid of me, so I left them at their table. One of the friendly locals, a large man by the name of Frank Murphy, grabbed my arm as I walked past his bar stool. He smelled of beer, whiskey, and cigar smoke.

"Hey, Chief," he said, "I've been meaning to call you. I have a theory for ya about who killed that woman."

I looked at the hand still gripping my arm, then gave Murphy a hard stare. He was an amiable Irishman who seemed to get along with just about everyone, but he had an intense dislike for Italians. If Chandra Harper had been Chandra Harperino, Murphy would have been my prime suspect based solely on his anti-Italian bias. Thankfully, I was Scotch-Irish-Italian, and that made me at least a half-decent guy in his book.

Murphy let go of my arm. He seemed ruffled by my lack of response. "Sorry, Chief. But did ya hear me? I think Navilio might've murdered that Harper woman."

I was actually relieved—I'd been certain Murphy was going to tell me all about a sleeper cell of Italian terrorists who'd been conspiring to commit murder and take over the local government. "Okay, Murph. I'll bite. What makes you think Navilio is the culprit?"

"Those Eye-talians are a cagey bunch," he stated. "I think Tony Navilio himself killed that poor lady just to improve his business. In this economy, you have to be creative." Murphy was born and raised in Walworth County, but when he drank, he inexplicably acquired an Irish brogue.

"How does a murder lead to an increase in business?" I asked. "Seems like it'd be the opposite."

"How naive can you get, Chief? This is the age of bad behavior—you know, Jerry Springer? Paris Hilton? You heard of them, right? They're famous. And what did Paris Hilton ever do besides screw her boyfriend on video and kiss her Chihuahua? It's nuts, I tell ya, but in this day and age, a lot of folk are fascinated by nothin' but bad behavior." Murphy's brogue became thicker as he pontificated. "Look at Jerry Springer," he continued. "Every day, that fella has a new piece of trailer trash on his show, just—"

"Now, Murph," I interrupted. "A lot of good people live in trailers, too."

"Ya know what I mean. He never has anyone on that stage who has accomplished anything, just low-bellied trash, hopin' to become famous for their bad behavior. But don't let the name fool you—he's really an Eye-talian."

"Who, the low-bellied trash?"

"No, you idiot, Jerry Springer."

"I thought he was a Cincinnatian."

"Hey, I'm dead serious. He's an Eye-talian. And their kind is very tied in with the bad-behavior group. It's the dummying down of America, I tell ya."

"Well, you might have something there . . ." I interjected, but my humor was lost on Murphy. I could've mocked him outright and he wouldn't have noticed.

"I do," he agreed. "If you check up on Navilio's business, you'll see. He's havin' some big financial troubles—I'll just bet you. This murder is his way of increasing his business. Remember, Chief, there's no such thing as bad publicity. People will come to this inn just because there was a murder here." The Irish brogue was getting thick. "It's foakin' brilliant, I tell ya," he said. "Foakin' brilliant."

I thanked Murphy for his help and declined his offer to have a drink with him. One more Irish whiskey and the man would start swearing in Gaelic.

Through the corner of my eye, I could see Frankel and Kirsch waving me over. I moved in their direction before Murphy could grab my arm again.

"Jim, Ronnie," I said. "Good evening, gentleman."

Kirsch raised a glass. "Good evening to you, too. So, Ronnie and I have been thinking about this murder for you, and we've come up with a good—"

"Theory?" I offered.

"Okay, a theory. We could call it that, don't you think, Ronnie?

"Sure, it's a theory," Ronnie said. "But it's a good one. Are you listening, Chief?"

I nodded. "I'm all ears."

"Okay, then," Ronnie continued. "Now, Tony Navilio is the quintessential businessman, right?"

The phrase "quintessential businessman" was not exactly how I would have described Navilio myself, but for the sake of brevity, I said, "Sure."

"Kirsch and I think that one of Navilio's competitors might've killed this lady," Ronnie continued.

"And why would they do that?"

"To drive the French Country Inn out of business, of course. Maybe Navilio's business has been so good that another hotel owner—or maybe even a consortium of hotel owners—has decided to knock him down a peg."

"Why not just burn the place down?" I asked. As soon as I'd said it, I regretted it. I didn't want to get sucked into another preposterous conversation. Then I reminded myself I was at the bar to listen.

"We thought of that," said Kirsch, "but then Navilio would just rebuild with the insurance money, and everything would be brand new, and business would be even better than before. But with a murder, Navilio goes belly up."

I was dumbfounded, so I said nothing. Finally, Frankel couldn't stand it. "So, what do you think, Chief?"

"I didn't think you were actually serious. Wasn't it you who warned me about Ben Zubeck after you saw him at Herb's gas station? Wouldn't Zubeck be a more likely suspect?"

"Well, that makes no sense at all. Zubeck probably would have burned the place down to hurt the business. But he wouldn't have killed this woman, would he?" Frankel raised a brow. "Is that what you think, Chief?"

I shook my head. "Nope. I think the Eye-talians are behind the whole mess. And I think it's time for me to call it a night."

Once outside, I cracked a smile. I'd been prepared to hear some improbable theories, but not this improbable. It was still early, and I wasn't sure what I wanted to do with the rest of my evening. I had promised Greta I'd call her for a drink. But the truth was, I wanted the drink without her company. Sure, if she and I got together, it might lead to another exciting romp in bed. But I was tired of thinking about the murder. And I knew if I saw Greta, it would be impossible not to think about Chandra Harper.

I hesitated, then phoned Greta to cancel. I didn't want to be a total jerk and just stand her up—or have her calling me later in a huff.

To my relief, Greta didn't sound too disappointed. She said she was tired anyway and not in the mood for hanging out at Kirsch's. "I'll probably just turn in early," she said. "Another time, maybe?"

"Absolutely."

Although I didn't want to see Greta, I also didn't want to spend the rest of the night alone. I left for home, taking a very slow, circuitous route.

Chapter Thirty-Three

By the time I reached my house, my intuition was telling me there was more to this case than I realized. I was missing something—something that had nothing to do with the forensic results or any of the other information Tyrrell was still gathering. Trouble was, I was suffering from burnout. I dreaded the things that awaited me in my kitchen: the photos of the crime scene, Chandra's depressing writings, and all the other unpleasant thoughts that had already filled up my day. You can only think about such things for so long before they become an obsession—and drive you over the edge.

I decided to get some fresh air by walking to Muddy's for a drink. Dawg knew exactly what I had in mind. It's uncanny, but he often knows what I'm thinking before I do. Okay, so sometimes he probably guesses by the type of clothes or shoes I put on. If I change into running shoes, for example, he knows it's time for a jog. Boots mean a hike in the woods; heavy boots with deep treads, a walk in the snow. A flannel shirt with down vest means I'm off to Muddy's. But tonight I wasn't wearing a flannel shirt, and Dawg still knew my plan.

"What do you want, pal?" I asked. He just sat down and stared at me with his big round eyes, willing me to take him along.

"You look like a cartoon character, do you know that?" Of course he knew—I told him that all the time.

"Tell me what you want, Dawg," I said. "Do you want to go to Muddy's?" He barked several times and jumped up on his hind legs.

"Good boy. Okay, now answer this one: Who killed Chandra Harper?"

Dawg cocked his head, then sat down in front of the door and stared at me over his shoulder.

"I hear ya, pal," I said. "I'm tired of talking about the case myself."

So we were off to Muddy's, where I could get the murder off my mind. It didn't matter if the place was crowded. Muddy's is the kind of joint where a guy can be surrounded by other people and still enjoy being alone, but not lonely.

The bar had a dozen customers. Gus Baldwin was his usual curmudgeonly self, hurling verbal barbs at me and his other patrons. We all loved it, though, even when the insults were personal. Gus offered to buy my first drink, saying I deserved it because I am "one hell of a cop," keeping the township safe. "Congratulations, Chief," he said. "No one has been murdered for at least thirty-six hours."

Booze always tastes better when someone else pays for it, and my free vodka was no exception. This one tasted especially good because Gus had poured me a top-rail brand instead of the leftover summer rotgut he serves to most of the tourists. As I nursed my drink and fought to keep the murder out of my thoughts, a local guy who I barely knew and whose name I couldn't remember sat down beside me and started to chat as if we were lifelong buddies. Fortunately, he did not bring up the Harper murder. Instead he spoke of an equally odious topic: the Green Bay Packers. I tried not to listen as he rambled on about all the lost opportunities of the past football season. After a few minutes, however, I was desperate to escape. As if on cue, the man changed his one-sided conversation to a new topic, one just as boring to me as the first: deer hunting. As he described his last big kill and all the lost opportunities of the previous hunting season, I seriously contemplated suicide. Then I was rescued by Officer Burr.

"Chief, I've been looking all over for you," Bert said excitedly.

"Did you try the phone?"

"It must be turned off."

"It is. And that should tell you something, Bert—one, that I think you and Shea can handle things, and two, that I need a little time off to clear my head so I can start fresh tomorrow. So, unless there's been another murder or you've spotted a flying pig overhead, you can turn right back around and leave me here with my good buddy what's-his-name. We were just having a spirited discussion about whether it's preferable to shoot a deer with a rifle or a bow and arrow."

Bert stepped closer and lowered his voice. "Chief, Dorothy just called. They caught the nativity thief red-handed at Saint Sabina's. Shea's over there now and Dorothy thinks you oughta handle it."

"Dorothy does? Is the thief dead? Has anyone been murdered?" I asked.

"No, sir, but it's—"

I interrupted before Bert could say another word. "If there is no dead body, you and Shea can handle everything just fine."

Bert leaned into my ear and whispered, "You're gonna want to hear this." To my surprise, he also tugged hard on my arm, pulling me off the barstool and away from the prying eyes and ears of the other patrons.

"You better be right about that, Bert," I said.

"Chief, listen. I wouldn't bother you, but it's Heavy Mullins. He's the thief. He's over at Saint Sabina's church with Shea and Father Sabatino. And that newspaper guy from the Janesville Chronicle is there, too. In fact, he's the one who called it in."

"What the heck is a crime reporter doing at the church this time of night?"

"I don't know. Praying maybe. Or just prowling around. The point is, Father Sabatino decided not to turn Heavy over to Shea. He won't even let Mullins out of the church—he's claiming sanctuary, whatever that means. Now Shea's really ticked off and threatening to arrest the both of them."

"Heavy and the reporter?"

"No, Heavy Mullins and Father Sabatino. It's getting crazy, Chief. Please, come with me."

Gus saw that something was up, so he offered to keep an eye on Dawg for me, then Officer Burr and I were on our way to Saint Sabina's church. I couldn't believe what I was hearing from Bert. Of all the possibilities, it was Patrick O'Brien, the crime reporter for the Janesville Chronicle, who'd seen someone attempting to steal the nativity scene from the church lawn. O'Brien had called the stationhouse. As soon as Officer Shea had arrived, Father Sabatino escorted Mullins into the church proper and declared sanctuary. He was refusing to let Shea come in and arrest him.

I was sure Bert was either exaggerating or mistaken. The story didn't add up—Father Bob and Heavy Mullins were two of the nicest, most easygoing guys a person could meet on this Earth, and probably in Heaven as well. The two were well respected in the community, and they were good friends, having known each other since childhood. In fact, I'd known them back then, too, and I used to pal around with Heavy on occasion. Some people changed with age, but Heavy Mullins was still one of the most honest and respectable guys I knew.

When we were teenagers, Dave Tedeski and I and some of our friends went through a phase where we started drinking, cavorting, and causing all kinds of ruckus. Heavy Mullins had refused to participate in any of it. We started calling him "the forty-year-old teenager" because he was so serious and straight-laced, and he never did stupid things like the rest of us. Of course, at the time we didn't know how stupid some forty-year-olds can be.

Heavy's real name was Joby. It's not a very common name, but as luck would have it, there was another local guy named Joby Mullins. Back then, Heavy was a little big, so everyone called his counterpart

Skinny, and we called our Joby Heavy. As the two grew up, Heavy lost all his prepubescent fat. These days Skinny has piled on the pounds, and Heavy is thin, but we still call him Heavy.

As a teen, I'd come across Bob Sabatino occasionally, but I didn't know him as well as I knew Heavy. However, I did know that he had grown up to become one of the most admired religious leaders in our community. So I was puzzled as to why Heavy would target his church. Or any of the other churches that'd been robbed, for that matter.

Bert was talking as we drove. "What exactly does sanctuary mean, Chief? I mean, I've heard of it, but I don't know where it comes from."

"It's a pretty old term," I answered. "In medieval times, criminals or fugitives could seek asylum from authorities by hiding in a church or rectory. Effectively, they were immune from arrest—at least for a while. The church was their protectorate. So, Father Bob is protecting Heavy Mullins by keeping him inside the church and not allowing him to go with Shea."

As we pulled up to Saint Sabina's, I saw Officer Shea's squad car out front with the emergency lights blinking. A tan SUV was parked beside it, and the reporter was photographing the license plate. Shea was standing on the cement stairs that led to the side door adjacent to the main altar. I motioned for Bert to go stand with him, then I walked over to the squad and turned off the flashing lights.

The reporter confronted me like a yapping dog. "What's the story, Chief? Is the thief still inside? Has he made any demands? What does Father Sabatino have planned?"

I pointed at a spot on the sidewalk. "Wait here," I commanded. "If you cooperate, I promise I'll talk to you later." He obeyed, and I continued on toward the church.

Shea was grumbling something to Bert near the side door, then he looked up at me, red-faced. "Why'd you turn the lights off, Chief?

Protocol says we are to have the emergency lights flashing in this type of situation."

"Forget the protocol tonight, Jerry," I said. "I don't think we'll be doing this one exactly by the book."

"But Chief, there are witnesses. O'Brien from the Gazette took pictures of Heavy, for Pete's sake. And then there's Father Bob and you and me, Bert Burr—this whole thing is a mess."

"Look, I know Father Bob and Heavy Mullins," I said, heading up the stairs. "Let me worry about this. You wait here with Bert, and I'll sweep up the mess. Meanwhile, keep an eye on O'Brien over there, will you?" I paused at the door and turned. "And Shea . . ." I added.

"Yeah?"

"Play nice with the reporter. We don't need any more problems to clean up."

The church was dim as I entered, but I spotted Heavy Mullins sitting in a pew halfway down the aisle from the altar. His back was to me, and his head was hanging low. I stopped long enough to genuflect and make the sign of the cross, then slowly approached. I was still six pews away when, from out of nowhere, Father Sabatino appeared and bumped his sizable physique directly against my body. I was shocked. We stood chest to chest for a moment, then Father Sabatino spoke in a low, menacing voice.

"You are not taking him in, Chief. Do you understand me? You are not arresting Heavy for this—not tonight, not any night."

Father Bob's eyes burned into me. He looked more like a determined prizefighter than a kindly man of the cloth. Except for his graying hair, Robert Sabatino hadn't changed much since high school; he was still tall, burly, and athletic, though he had two arthritic knees, courtesy of his days as a first-string linebacker. After high school, he'd turned down a football scholarship to enter the seminary up at Saint Peter's College.

I held up my hands in mock surrender. "Take it easy, padre. I'm just here to talk. I'm sure we can work this out."

"This is not Chicago, Chief, so don't treat it that way. I have already talked to Heavy. He still has all of the crèches in his garage. He will give them to me, and then I will return each and every piece to its rightful owner. No one has to know Heavy was involved except me, you, and God. And Officer Shea, of course."

"I wish it were that easy, Father. What do we do about O'Brien—you know he'll want his story."

"I'll talk to him; he's Catholic. But if he tries to write this story, you and I will just say it's false. People will believe us—we have a lot more credibility than some damn reporter."

I could not believe I was hearing these words from a Catholic priest—not this priest, anyway. "Father, get a hold of yourself," I said. "Are you going to lie about a crime?"

"For Heavy Mullins's sake, I will. And you will too, right?"

I didn't hesitate. "I would—if I thought it would do any good here."

"Yeah, well you let me worry about what's good and what's bad."

All I could think was what a mess . . . and how could I spare Heavy Mullins and his wife any more pain than they had already suffered? A week before Christmas, they had lost their only son, Jake. Just twenty years old, Jake Mullins had been serving as a marine in Afghanistan. Against his parent's wishes, he had volunteered for another tour of duty, and he'd shipped out in December. Jake had believed he was doing something constructive, that serving in the military was his purpose in life. One week later, he was killed. He died instantly when a sniper's bullet pierced his neck. Merry Christmas, Mr. and Mrs. Mullins, your lives will never be the same.

The news had crushed Heavy and his wife, Luna. Now Luna was on the verge of a nervous breakdown, and people thought that

Heavy would die of a broken heart. I used to wonder whether it was actually possible for that to happen—until I saw Heavy at his son's wake and funeral. He was burying not only his son, but his closest friend.

Father Bob motioned for me to sit down at the back of the church. In a low voice, he explained that Heavy had confessed to stealing all the nativity scenes, and that he'd done it because he was mad at God for taking his son. He had planned to burn all the crèches, but in spite of his anger, he just couldn't bring himself to do it. So, he'd kept all the items locked in his garage.

Father Bob and I formulated a plan. We agreed that an "anonymous donor" would deliver all the stolen nativity scenes to Saint Sabina's church later that night. The father would call it in and we'd note his discovery. Then Bert and Shea would sign the report, and the case would effectively be closed.

I went back outside and called everyone else into the church. Heavy remained in shadows near the altar, kneeling in prayer. Father Sabatino and I explained the situation, and with a little coaxing, Officer Shea agreed not to pursue the matter and not to tell anyone what had really happened. Officer Burr didn't need any prompting to go along with the plan; he admired the Mullins, as we all did, and he had no stomach for escorting a bereaved and good-hearted man to jail.

The reporter was not such an easy sell. When I told him we weren't making an arrest, and there was nothing to report beyond the recovery of the stolen goods, he dug in his heels. Pat O'Brien had stumbled upon a good story, he had taken photographs, and now he realized he might have an even juicier tale—the conspiratorial cover-up of a crime by a police chief, his fellow officers, and a Catholic priest.

"I have a job to do here, Chief, and I plan to do it," O'Brien said. "Come hell or high water."

It was the wrong thing to say, because Father Sabatino suddenly threw a punch at O'Brien. Luckily, O'Brien lurched back and Bert caught Sabatino's arm just before it connected. I found myself looking up at the Madonna and furtively checking for her reaction.

Then Bert Burr astonished me by declaring that he'd seen O'Brien take a swing at the priest, and threatened to place the reporter under arrest for assault. When O'Brien protested and looked at me for help, I shrugged. Emboldened, Bert announced that O'Brien would soon be a marked man in all of Walworth County, and in Rock County, too, because "we cops stick together like a flock of migrating geese, and we all hate newsmen just as much as we hate politicians."

I put a hand on Officer Burr's shoulder. "That's enough, Bert," I said. "Look where we are. Nobody hates anyone here. I'm sure O'Brien is just trying to do his job, and I'm sure he'll come to see the light. Right, O'Brien?"

Eventually, the reporter agreed to go along with my plan—after I'd promised him an exclusive on the Harper murder. But I also believe Heavy Mullins's broken spirit and sad face helped sway O'Brien to my way of thinking. That, and a promise from Bert that if the reporter ever broke his word, Bert would hunt down O'Brien like a mangy dog.

Then we all placed our hands atop one another, including O'Brien, and swore before God and the crucifix that we would never reveal what had really occurred on this night at Saint Sabina's church. I looked at the sincerity in everyone's eyes, and I knew I would never have to worry. Our story would remain a secret forever.

Chapter Thirty-Four

After I'd squared things away at Saint Sabina's church and arranged for the transport of stolen goods from Heavy's garage, I went back to Muddy's to pick up Dawg. I turned off Highway 50 and descended the steep hill toward the lake on autopilot, and as I pulled into the parking lot, I had an overwhelming sense of déjà vu. My ex-wife used to say that living in Geneva Township was like being in the movie *Groundhog Day*: somehow you always wound up in the same place with the same people. Only instead of a waking up in the same bed like Bill Murray, I was bellying up to the same bar a little after two a.m., looking for an escape from everything that ailed me.

The parking lot had cleared, and the saloon was almost empty inside, except for one elderly gentleman. He was seated at the end of the bar with his back to me, wearing gray wool pants and an out-of-fashion gray fedora. He didn't turn as I entered, but I recognized him by the hat—and his posture. He sat straight as a marine recruit attempting to please his drill instructor. His pose belied the fact that he was pushing ninety years of age.

His name was Clement Schauder, but everyone called him Clam Chowder, except yours truly. Old Clem looked pretty spry on the outside, but inside, he was a mess. Rumor had it that every organ in his body once belonged to someone else. More than one source informed me that the man had received a heart-and-lung transplant only months after he'd received a kidney donated by his nephew, who was paid a hefty sum for the thoughtful gesture. In typical Lake Geneva hyperbole, people said only two of his organs were still original: his brain and his penis. I wasn't sure how much was true—he probably had at least one transplant—but it hadn't slowed him much. Evidently, it hadn't slowed his drinking much either.

As I sidled up to him at the bar, I encountered the aroma of gin and manly cologne. "Howdy, Clement," I said. "Have you seen Gus and my dog?"

"They're in the back, having a late-night snack." Clem turned and gave me a grin. His face was wrinkled, but his dentures were new and bright. "I'm in charge while Gus is gone, so help yourself to whatever you'd like."

"Thanks, don't mind if I do," I replied.

As I poured myself a vodka on the rocks, Gus pushed open the kitchen door, and Dawg padded out, wagging his tail. I gave him a little pat and he curled up behind me.

"I see you're stealing my liquor again," Gus said with a growl.

"No, sir," I retorted. "I'm confiscating your stock. I'm sure you realize that it's a capital offense to serve liquor after two a.m. in these parts."

"Who am I serving? The till is closed and you helped yourself. And Clam isn't drinking—he's getting a transfusion. Whenever his red blood count gets too high, he needs to thin it down with cheap gin. His liver used to belong to Al Capone, you know—or was it Frank Nitti, Clam?"

Clem grunted. "It sure isn't Capone's. That guy died full of syphilis."

"Then whose liver is it?" Gus asked.

"The docs told me it belonged to the poet Dylan Thomas. I should've sued his estate, because the damn thing's defective. I'm always a wee bit tipsy when I awake after a night of serious drinking."

"Nah, it can't belong to Dylan Thomas," Gus said, pointing to the picture of Thomas on the wall. It was hanging in Gus's photo gallery of famous literary figures, opposite the gallery of famous gangsters. "He died of alcohol poisoning at the Chelsea Hotel in New York. As the story goes, he drank forty-five shots of Irish whiskey before he went up to his room. And then, to borrow a phrase from our departed Irish poet, he went gently into that good night."

"There you go," Clem said. "That's why his liver is defective."

"Wasn't Dylan Thomas Welsh?" I asked. "I heard he actually died of pneumonia."

Gus ignored me. "There's one thing I've always wondered about the Irish," he continued. "They love potatoes, right? Boiled, mashed, scalloped, fried—you name it, they love it. They even give spuds Irish names, like potatoes O'Brien. So why aren't there any Irish vodkas? Vodka is distilled from potatoes. You'd think the Irish would have a whole panoply of vodkas."

"I don't know, Gus," I said. "I'm not even sure what a panoply is. But the Irish make some pretty good whiskey, so maybe that's enough." I pointed at the bar clock. "Do you need us to get out of your hair anytime soon?"

"Nah, you guys relax—just don't drink me dry. I've got to change out some kegs in the basement and do a minor repair, then maybe I'll come up and join you for a nightcap." He locked the front door and turned off the neon signs in the window. Then he hoisted a trap door behind the bar and disappeared down a narrow stairway, leaving me alone with Clem.

"Tough business over there at the French Country Inn," Clem said.

I sighed. "If you don't mind, Clem, I'd rather take a break from talking about the murder."

"Suit yourself," Clem said, deflated.

There was an awkward pause, then I remembered what Norm at the Bayside Motel had said to me earlier about Clement Schauder. "Say, Clem, you're kind of an expert on the local gangster history, right?

Bugs Moran, Baby Face Nelson, John Dillinger? I heard you know some stories about those guys spending time at the French Country Inn."

Clem's eyes started to glisten as if they were moving back in time, perhaps to his youth. "I know a thing or two."

I did the math in my head. Clem would've been about twenty years old in the early 1930s. "Do you remember when the inn was called the Lake Como Hotel?"

"I do," he said with a twinkle in his eye.

"Is that so?" I said. "Did you know the owner of the inn back then, Hobe Hermansen?"

Clem chuckled, and I was taken aback by his answer. "Oh, I knew him. I knew him very well. I was Hobart Hermansen's personal driver."

* * *

Sipping his glass of gin, Clem sat quietly, waiting for me to give him a nudge before he would spill a story I had no doubt he was eager to tell. He'd probably honed his presentation through the years.

"So, you were Hobart's personal driver," I said.

"Yep, and a fine man he was. Very generous to those he liked. A real character. Yes, sir, he was a real character."

Clem stared at his now-empty rocks glass. "Pour me 'nother," he commanded.

"Ice?"

"No, thanks."

As I leaned over the bar top to reach for the bottle of Beefeaters, Gus poked his head up through the trap door like a badger popping out of his hole. "Hey, I said you guys could relax—not drain me dry."

"Don't worry," I said. "I'll pay for it later."

Gus growled and disappeared again.

With a new glass of gin in hand and the prospect of a few more in sight, Clem seemed ready to talk. "So," he said, "you're interested in the old gangster stories. What would you like to know?"

"Anything, everything."

He flashed a grin. "Now, lad. Gus doesn't stock enough gin for me to tell you everything. But I'll tell you this much . . . You know the room at the inn where that woman got herself murdered Wednesday night?"

"I'm familiar with it," I said, fearing he had a murder theory of his own.

"Well, that room has seen its share of history. You wouldn't catch me staying there."

"What do you mean? Was somebody else killed there?"

"I'm not saying yes, I'm not saying no. But here's something only a few people know: the Feds were holed up in that very same room in November of 1934, waiting for Lester Gillis—that's Baby Face Nelson—to show up. And when he finally did, it was the last day Baby Face ever drew breath. They shot him in a car chase down across the state line. 'Course, Baby Face being Baby Face, he took out a few lawmen before he died."

"Are you saying Hermansen set up Baby Face Nelson?" I asked, incredulous.

"Depends on your point of view. The Feds found out that Baby Face was headed to the Lake Como Hotel on their own. Hobart just gave them the room, so they could lie in wait. He was in a pretty tight spot."

"But weren't Hermansen and Baby Face friends?"

"I wouldn't say that, exactly, Nelson being a psychopath. Hobart made him feel comfortable, like any good innkeeper would. But Nelson liked it at the Como Hotel, sure he did. He and his gang holed up here plenty of times. Baby Face and his wife, Helen, were especially fond of that little cottage right down by the waterfront."

"How old were you in 1934? Were you already working for Hobe?"

Clem smiled and dodged the question. "I didn't start working for Hobart 'til later, which is probably a good thing. Nineteen-thirty-four was a dangerous year, yessir it was, especially for the lawmen and their prey. John Dillinger was shot dead in '34. Right before that, they got Tommy Carroll then—"

"And Hobart Hermansen was in the middle of all this somehow?"

"You know, Chief, I don't want to talk about Hermansen. He was good to me personally, and he didn't talk much about his friends, which is probably why they trusted him. But I can tell you how Baby Face Nelson met his end."

"Sure," I said. "Why not?"

"Well, first you have to understand the whole cast of characters. On the one hand, you've got Lester Gillis, which was the real name of Baby Face Nelson. Lester was a Chicago kid, a mama's boy. His dad committed suicide when he was young, but by then he was already a thief and a delinquent, on his way to bigger robberies and all sorts of other mayhem. And then you've got Dillinger, an Indiana boy who's a much better bank robber. He's Public Enemy Number One, but he isn't a trigger-happy killer like Baby Face. The two of them join up early in the spring of '34, after Baby Face helps spring Dillinger out of jail—and then they're together in a gang."

"Who's in charge?" I asked.

"Depends on who you ask. Dillinger got the credit, but Baby Face only did what Baby Face wanted—my bet's on him. Either that, or he was the loose cannon in the new gang. Are you with me?"

"I'm with you," I said.

"Okay then. The Feds were focusing on Dillinger at first. They got a woman named Anna Sage to help them out. She was a Romanian running prostitutes, so they leaned on her. She and Dillinger and another woman all walk out of the Biograph Theater in downtown Chicago on the evening of July 22, 1934. Dillinger is in disguise—he's had some plastic surgery, in fact. He thinks he's just enjoying a night out at the movies, struttin' with two dames. Except Sage signals the Feds to confirm who she's with, and what-do-you-know, Dillinger is shot dead in the street. Anna Sage is wearing this orangey-red skirt, so they'll know it's her."

"The famous Woman in Red," I said.

"So you do know a thing or two."

"A thing or two," I allowed. "So what about Baby Face?"

"He wasn't there, of course, or things would've been a lot bloodier. As a matter of fact, he might've been up here at Lake Como at the time. But who's telling this story, you or me?"

"Sorry," I said. I topped off Clem's glass with a splash of Beafeaters by way of apology. Then I topped off my own glass with Grey Goose. Right on cue, Gus stuck his head into the barroom as if he had been alerted by some secret alarm.

"Don't worry, I'll pay," I said.

Gus grunted and went back to whatever he was doing in the basement.

Refueled with gin, Clem continued. "Okay, so where was I? About a month before Dillinger got shot, Nelson and his wife were staying at the Como Hotel, along with some of the gang. There are two big names you should know: Tommy Carroll and John Paul Chase. Carroll was an ex-boxer and a real good-lookin' man. He'd served time for armed robbery, but he was out by '31. He was a good wheelman. John Paul Chase was a liquor smuggler from California. Baby Face met him out there, in Sausalito. Chase was a little simple-minded, but he was absolutely loyal to Baby Face. All these guys got around the country, covering thousands of miles in their shiny automobiles—they didn't just stick to Wisconsin and Illinois. And they liked to travel with their molls or girlfriends—or in the case of Baby Face, his wife. He was real devoted to Helen Gillis."

"But they were all at Lake Como about a month before Dillinger got shot," I said.

"About that time, yes. Like I said, they came here a lot. They also met up here in the spring of '34, right after the big shootout at Little Bohemia. You heard of that, I assume?"

I shook my head.

"Well, just be glad you've never screwed up anything as bad as the Feds botched their raid up there. But it puts things in perspective—explains why the Feds were so red-hot for Dillinger and Nelson by summertime."

"Up there?" I asked. "Where was the raid?"

"At the Little Bohemia Lodge. It's a resort up near Rheinlander. Dillinger, Tommy Carroll, Nelson and Helen, and a bunch of the gang were all holed up there in April. You can just picture it—they're enjoying the scenery, putting their feet up . . . Then one day the Feds show up and the guns start blazing. The Feds kill a bunch of innocents by mistake, and then it's a standoff that lasts for hours. It ends with just Helen Gillis and the molls walking out to surrender. One of them is even clutching her little pet dog, begging them not to shoot. The gang members were all gone, though—they'd already sneaked out the back and got away clean. Of course, Baby Face did kill three people himself, stealing cars as he left the area—like I said, he was trigger-happy. A while later, Baby Face and Helen met up again for some quality time at the Lake Como Hotel. Some of the gang was there, too. And you know what? The Feds botched it again. After Little Bohemia, they had Helen in custody. They could've tailed her, but they didn't—they had no idea she broke parole and headed down here to Como. So, they didn't figure out Lake Como was one of Nelson's favorite hideaways—not until later, in November of that same year."

"And that's when they were here, waiting for him."

"That's right. But don't interrupt." He shook a bony finger at me and I held up my hands in surrender.

"So, where was I?" Clem continued. "It's early June, and the gang comes back here to Como to hole up with their lady friends again. But Tommy Carroll's girlfriend hates Baby Face, and the feeling is mutual, so things aren't pleasant. Tommy and his girl leave early and head down to Waterloo, Iowa. It was a bad place to go, though—you know why?"

"Uh, because he meets his Waterloo?"

"You got it. Carroll gets caught in a shootout with the police down there on June the Seventh, and he takes five bullets. A few hours later, Tommy Carroll is done leaking blood and he's a dead man. Nelson gets the news while he's at the Lake Como Hotel. John Paul Chase was up here then, too." He paused and lifted his glass. "I'm getting thirsty again. Don't know if I can go on."

"Please do," I urged, refreshing his gin. This time Gus didn't poke his head up to complain. I wondered if he'd had a stroke or something in the basement.

Clem resumed his tale. "Okay, so now Tommy Carroll is dead. Come July, Dillinger is dead, too, and Nelson goes so far underground that only a termite can find him. But come Labor Day weekend, where do you think Baby Face and John Paul Chase decide to get some R&R?

"The French Country Inn—I mean, the Lake Como Hotel?"

"You got it. Baby Face's wife, Helen Gillis, is there too, and Chase brings along his girlfriend, Sally Bachman. She'll be important later when we get to the good part of the story." He grimaced. "Hang on a minute—I gotta take a pee. You get to be my age, that kind of thing happens more often."

As he eased himself down from the bar stool, he appeared to be struggling, so I put out a hand to help. He slapped it away. "Do I look like a damn cripple?" he snapped. His posture changed to a slump as he shuffled toward the john.

I was contemplating a raid on a jar of olives to go with my vodka when Gus popped back up the stairs with a wrench in his hand. "Damn plumbing. This building's too old," he said. "Where's Clam?"

I nodded toward the bathroom. "His plumbing is old, too. But he's not done with his story yet."

Gus chuckled. "Guess we'll all be here a while." He tucked back below, and after what seemed an eternity, Clem reemerged, struggling to zip up his fly. Once he was back on the bar stool, he grunted, took a sip, and started talking again.

"Okay, so this Sally Bachman is Chase's girlfriend. She overhears Nelson and his pals talking about coming back here to the inn sometime in October or November. In fact, they're thinking they might just spend the whole winter at Lake Como. It's a perfect place because it's so quiet. But first, they head west to California. Meanwhile, the Feds are chasing their own tails.

"Then the Feds catch their big break. Sally Bachman gets herself arrested in Sausalito. John Paul Chase is from California, remember. Of course, Chase himself never would've betrayed his best friend Baby Face, but Bachman isn't so loyal. She tells the G-Men about a lakeside hotel somewhere near Chicago, where Nelson is heading for a winter stay. But she's got a problem with geography, and she's not sure whether the resort is in Wisconsin or Illinois. And she can't even recall the name of the inn. But then she draws a little map showing a long, narrow road leading past the woods to a property alongside a lake, with the railroad tracks running right alongside the hotel—she even gives an accurate description of the buildings and the layout of the place, she's so helpful. And then she remembers Hermansen's name, more or less. And that's enough."

"They find the inn."

"Right. And when the Feds check up on the owner, Hobart Hermansen, they find out he has connections to the Chicago underworld, primarily through his wife's ex-husband, Bugs Moran. And they know he's connected to Jimmy Murray."

"The guy behind the Rondout train robbery," I said.

"Right—but don't get me sidetracked. Anyhow, Murray is slick. He's kind of a facilitator, you might say. He's the one who recommended the Lake Como Hotel to Nelson as a place to hole up in the first place. And sure, Baby Face had a lot of good times here. But if he wanted to survive, he shouldn't have come back in November of '34."

"But Nelson did come back to the inn."

"He did."

"And that's when the Feds were here waiting for him."

"You got some kind of disorder? You keep flapping your trap."

"Sorry," I said. "So what happened? Was it like Little Bohemia?"

"Not even close. First of all, the Feds send three guys up here to wait for Baby Face and his gang. Agents Metcalfe, McRae, and Winstead. They don't know exactly when Nelson is gonna show, but they've got a plan: They're gonna ambush Nelson and anyone with him."

"In other words, they don't plan to arrest him."

"No, sir, they don't," Clem said excitedly. "This Winstead agent is packing a .357 Magnum and a couple of high-powered scope rifles. So he's not planning to arrest Baby Face Nelson—he's gonna kill the sonofabitch!"

Clem paused to catch his breath and take a few more sips of his drink. His words were beginning to slur, but thankfully, he'd slowed his alcohol intake. I didn't want him to pass out before he finished the story.

"So, the agents get here in early November. They tell Hobart they want to stay in his house or in the room above the lobby—the one Navilio uses for his office now. Hermansen gives them the room. And then they wait . . .

" . . . until the afternoon of November 27. One of the agents, I think it was McRae, heads into town to stock up on some groceries. Naturally, he takes the only car they've got. Of course, while he's gone, who do you think shows up in a black Ford V-8? Nelson and his wife, Helen, with John Paul Chase in the back seat. Nelson gets out, real nonchalant, with his .38 automatic tucked under his jacket. He says howdy to a guest on the porch, asks if Hobart Hermansen or Eddie Duffy are around."

"Eddie Duffy?"

"Hobart's handyman and gofer. Real nice fellow, too—he told me a lot of this stuff. Okay, so the guy on the porch says he hasn't seen Hobart or Eddie. But you know what? The guy on the porch is Agent Metcalf, with his head where the sun don't shine. By the time he realizes it's Nelson, Nelson has smelled the trap, and he's already driving away. Agent Winstead takes a shot at the car from an upstairs window, but of course he misses.

"So now, Nelson is fleeing toward Chicago on Highway 12. Meanwhile, the agents have called their boss, and half of Chicago has been notified about Nelson's black Ford V-8, and they've got the plate number too. Two FBI agents, Bill Ryan and Tom McDade, are speeding north when they pass Nelson on the road near Fox Grove."

"Your memory for detail is amazing, Clem," I said.

"Yeah, well my brain is about the only thing still working right. But let me finish, will ya? I haven't got much longer to live—and neither did Baby Face that day. Agents Ryan and McDade speed right past Nelson's car, heading the other way. The agents hit the brakes and make a U-turn to follow—but Nelson makes a U-turn, too, charging them head on. It's like they're a couple of jousting knights."

"Or they're playing chick—" I started to say, but Clem shot me a look and I stopped talking.

"Now we've got us a real gun battle." Clem held up both hands, pointing two fingers like pistols. "It gets crazy. At one point, things turn around and Nelson starts chasing after the Feds and shooting at their car from behind. Bullets are flying, glass is breaking, smoke is streamin' from the engines. Agent McDade floors it and spins off the road. Nelson keeps going, but then another car with two more agents comes barreling up behind him. Chase starts shooting at them through the rear window, or what's left of it. Baby Face puts the pedal to the metal, but his car is full of holes and it's bleeding out fluids, and it's having none of it. So he's forced to pull over just outside Barrington.

"He orders Helen out of the car and she runs for cover. Baby Face makes his final stand, with Chase backing him up. Agents Cowley and Hollis are the guys on the scene. It's a damn war. There are only four shooters, but about thirty witnesses have pulled over on the side of the highway. Hollis takes one in the head, and Cowley gets seriously wounded. So does Baby Face, but he still manages to steal the agents' car, transfer a bunch of guns from his own crippled car, pick up Helen, put Chase in the driver's seat . . . and then they're off again."

I said nothing, rapt.

"Baby Face knows he's dying. He's bleeding bad, so you know what he does? He tells Chase and Helen to take him to a priest."

"He's Catholic?"

"Don't know, but he has a lot to confess—including the death of Hollis and Cowley. During the standoff, Nelson took a slug in the gut and kept right on charging just so he could be sure to take out the second man. Both agents had families. As a matter of fact, so did Baby Face—he and Helen had two kids."

"So, do they get him to a priest in time?"

"Not just any priest—it's a priest Baby Face knows. But when they meet up with him, the priest acts twitchy and they don't trust him. Baby Face is barely hanging on, so Chase and Helen wind up taking him to a house in Wilmette that was owned by Jimmy Murray. Jimmy isn't living there himself, and I guess the woman who answers the door has a pretty big shock when she opens the door. They take Nelson to a bedroom."

"And then?"

"Then it's finis. Nelson died there later that night. He had a total of seventeen bullets in his body. Near dawn, Helen and Murray wrapped his body in an old Indian blanket, then dropped it off at a cemetery. The police found his body after a couple hours or so—they must've been tipped."

"Whatever happened to John Paul Chase?"

"Now, that's kind of funny. He walked right into a Chicago police department and filed the paperwork for a chauffeur's license, then got himself a job driving a car out to Seattle. But the Feds eventually caught up to him in California. They sent him to Alcatraz for a long time, then moved him Leavenworth. He served about thirty years."

"What about Helen?"

"You know, Chief, I'm not sure, but I think she got sentenced to a year. She was only twenty-five when her husband died, so I suppose she lived her life after that. I read a newspaper story where she gave an account of her last day with Baby Face. Of course, it didn't quite match what else I've read . . . But I'm tired of talkin' now, Chief. You want to know more, you should read a book or two yourself sometime."

"Thanks for the tip," I said. "And the stories."

Gus climbed up from basement, wiping his hands on a rag. "You guys still here?"

"Not for long," I said. "I'm calling it a night."

I offered to give Clem a ride home, but he declined—he said he didn't like riding in police cars. Gus said he'd take him. I whistled for Dawg, then tossed a twenty and a ten on the bar. Then I headed home, leaving Clem to ponder the past and stare at his tumbler of gin.

Chapter Thirty-Five

I awoke with a start just a few hours after I'd gone to bed, with thoughts of Ben Zubeck swirling through my brain. I wasn't sure of the time, only that it was still early and I was still tired. In fact, I wasn't even sure what day it was. I only knew it wasn't Wednesday, the day Dorothy had phoned me about the murder. I made several calls, then went back to sleep before I arose a second time, several hours later.

The previous night had not been my finest in law enforcement. The visit to Kirsch's had been a fiasco in terms of leads, but at least I'd learned something new about the way the staff at the inn handled their keys. And the business with the nativity scenes was over—or so I hoped, but I was pretty sure the reporter would keep his mouth shut. He was eager to get that murder-story exclusive I'd promised him.

As for the murder, Tyrrell was moving ahead with his theory about John Ratz. In our morning conversation, Tyrrell had informed me that Chandra Harper's phone records showed considerable contact between the two lovers in the days leading up to the murder, mostly one-sided, from him to her. A tech was now examining Ratz's clothing for traces of blood. If it showed anything, they'd test it for type and DNA. Ratz had cooperated fully with the search, which told me that he wasn't handing over anything that he believed would incriminate him. If he had stabbed Chandra, he probably would've disposed of any clothing he wore to do it, along with the knife, just as Shea had suggested—by tossing it down an ice hole in the dead of night. Unless, of course, Ratz's drug problem had impaired his judgment and caused some memory loss, which was part of Tyrrell's pet theory. Tyrrell believed Ratz either was in serious denial, or he didn't fully recollect the events of that night.

Meanwhile, I was tired of wondering if and when Ben Zubeck might decide to reload his rifle or fill up a gas can and "go Latin" on me, turning the French Country Inn into his personal version of Carthage. But on that count, at least, I had a plan. Admittedly, my plan was about as crazy as Ben Zubeck himself, but it was a plan nonetheless. In one of my early-morning phone calls, I'd instructed officers Madden and Burr to track down Ben and Esther Zubeck and bring both of them in for questioning as soon as they were located. And then I simply waited.

We got lucky—the pair was spotted at Herb's gas station around one p.m. A short time later, my officers and I apprehended them at their old farmhouse, where the Zubecks had been loading up a few boxes in preparation for moving. To everyone's surprise, Ben Zubeck agreed to go the stationhouse for a chat without putting up much of a fuss, except for the usual verbal tirade.

At the stationhouse, I told them they weren't under arrest, but I advised them of their rights. Both suspects declined to have an attorney present. I teamed up with Annie Madden to interview Esther first, and told Bert Burr to keep the husband company for a while. I had to think that after spending an hour alone with Bert, Ben Zubeck would be crazy enough to admit to anything, including the abduction of the Lindbergh baby.

Esther Zubeck was a hard nut to crack. Meaning, she turned out to be a certifiable nutcase, just like her husband—except she was a lot better at keeping her mouth shut. I could get no useful information from her whatsoever. She did, however, spit on the floor and say "I got nothing to say to you" at least a half-dozen times. Annie and I tried a little good cop/bad cop, with Annie being good. Meanwhile I insulted Esther, mocked her, and even questioned her femininity, which wasn't hard—she looked like an ox. I sneered, leered, and jeered, then at the very end propositioned her, all to no avail. By then Annie was struggling to keep from laughing at me, but she managed to play it straight. Esther Zubeck remained stubbornly stoic. She never even blinked. The only time I fazed her was when I said I knew Ben had done the shooting and the murder—and that I'd find a way to pin both crimes on him if it was the last thing I ever did. "You be sure to let him know that," I said. Esther opened her mouth as if she finally had a good retort, but then she clamped her jaw shut again.

Having gotten nowhere with the missus, I unleashed my interview skills on the mister. I was hoping he'd been driven one step closer to surrender by the torturous ramblings of Officer Burr. Annie accompanied me into the room, but this time, I asked her to play the silent type, going along with whatever happened.

Zubeck reluctantly shook my hand when I extended it to him. His own hand was as big as a catcher's mitt and as rough as sandpaper. I glanced at his shoes. They were old work boots—and definitely big enough to leave a dent in my forehead. He was as ugly and mean-looking as his wife, but he was a lot more talkative.

"Why'd you bring me and Esther down here, anyway?" he demanded. "We didn't know that woman who got killed—we never even met her."

"You've made open threats against Anthony Navilio and the French Country Inn," I stated. "That woman was killed in Navilio's own suite. It's a pretty big coincidence, don't you think?"

"If she was in his suite, then why aren't you asking Navilio about her murder?"

I was embarrassed by Zubeck's question. The truth was, I'd yet to speak with Anthony Navilio—and I'd never even checked on the story about his vacation. I considered firing myself and putting Ben Zubeck in charge of the investigation.

"Never mind about Navilio," I said. "He didn't do it. Besides that, we have every reason to suspect that you're the one who shot up Kirsch's restaurant Tuesday night."

"Me?" he replied. He chuckled. "That's rich."

"Why is that?"

"Hell, I could shoot a hemorrhoid out of a man's ass at five hundred paces. If I was the one who shot up Kirsch's, there would have been a dozen dead bodies lying around, including yours." He grinned at me. "If you were there, of course. Since I wasn't, I wouldn't know."

"Oh, I was there," I said. "Question is, where were you at the time? But we both know the answer to that, don't we, Ben?"

He scowled. "I drove up north to stay at our trailer that night."

"Any particular reason?"

"I was just checking in on the place and hauling a few boxes up there. In case you haven't figured it out yet, asshole, we need a new place to live."

"Where's this trailer you have?"

"Past Tomah, about three hours from here."

"Did anybody see you up there?"

"Prob'ly not. We've got twenty acres and nobody's around up there now."

"Did you stop for gas, use a credit card?"

"I paid cash."

"So, what you're saying is nobody saw you, and nobody can vouch for your whereabouts. Sounds like a pretty thin alibi, Bennie."

"Hell, I don't need an alibi."

"And why is that?"

"'Cuz you're so goddamned stupid, you couldn't find a duck in a flock of geese, that's why, you big-city piece of crap!"

I paused, only slightly ruffled and determined not to show it. "That's right, I am a big-city cop. That means I don't need to worry about your side of the story. I'll just manufacture the evidence I need." That was a lie, of course, but it was all part of my nefarious plan.

"Like I said," Zubeck continued, "you're a piece of crap. But your shit won't stick to me, Chief." He said my name as if it were the worst insult of all.

"Oh, it'll stick. But I won't just put you away, Ben," I continued calmly. "I'll get that wife of yours, too. Before you know it, she'll be up at Delafield. You know what's in Delafield, right? The Women's Correctional Facility. Esther will have a great time up there with her fellow dykes. Hell, she'll probably even thank me for the favor."

It was the straw that broke the crazy's back. Zubeck lunged across the table, trying to land a right hook. I was ready; I simply stepped backward, eager to block his next punch and land one of my own. To my astonishment, Zubeck didn't make that move—Annie didn't give him the chance. She sprang out of the corner like a panther, clobbered his shoulder with her nightstick, then pulled the weapon hard against his neck and dragged him back into his chair and held him there in a choke hold, all in the span of about one second.

Zubeck was just as astonished as I was, because he sat there with his hands raised in surrender, wheezing and gasping for breath.

I shot Annie a look and she released him. "Sorry, Chief," she said. "I guess I got a little excited."

"Are we all calm now?" I asked.

Zubeck glared at me, wheezing and breathing hard. As soon as he could speak again, he jabbed a finger at me. "You leave my wife out of this, you skunk," he rasped. "At least I have a wife. And she's a good one, not like your own bitch-whore, who was screwin' every other guy right under your own nose. But we can't really blame her, can we? Look who the bitch-whore was married to."

I hadn't expected my ex-wife to be part of this conversation. Zubeck's tactic had probably hurt me more than any insult about Esther had hurt him. And, unfortunately, he was right—my ex had been screwing every Tom, Dick, and Dick she could get her hands around. It was one of the reasons I'd left Illinois and moved up here to Wisconsin.

Then I realized I was a victim of my own success. My plan was to make Zubeck angry—to get him so hot and fuming that he'd make a mistake and come after me personally, and soon. Better me than the inn or its guests, I reasoned, and better on my terms than on his. Ben Zubeck had a history of hot-headed violent reactions, and I didn't think he could resist making a move against me if I got him angry enough to strike. In essence, I was poking a rattlesnake. I decided to poke a little harder just to seal the deal.

"Tonight, Bennie Boy, I am going to go home, put my feet up, have drink or two to celebrate, and relax the whole evening. I'm going to sleep like a baby. But you aren't going to have a moment's rest," I said. "We're closing in on you—you and your little Estie. You two are going away for a long, long time. Well, as much time as you've got left, anyway. Let's face it: you're an old man, Bennie, two steps from worm food."

Zubeck sat there for a minute, eyeing me with malice. When he spoke, he seemed calm, but there was a threat behind every word. "You can spend the whole night inspecting your own ass for all I care. I'm done talking to you. You either arrest me and Esther now, or you let us go. If you had any kind of proof at all, you piece of crap, you would've booked us instead of bringing us in here for questioning."

He was right, of course. I let them both go a few minutes later, but I'd gotten the reaction I wanted. The question was, would the rest of my plan go the same way?

* * *

The snowmobile is a modern-day chariot, with horsepower instead of horses. In my brilliant plan, I would be the charioteer Ben Hur. I would ride my Yamaha 350 into battle and conquer Ben Zubeck on the icy surface of Lake Como or on the snow-covered plains and hills that surround it.

If my instincts were correct, Zubeck would do a repeat of Tuesday's drive-by shooting at Kirsch's restaurant, when he'd used me and every other patron for target practice. Only tonight, he'd go directly after yours truly, the bad cop who'd insulted him and his dear wife and therefore deserved whatever punishment Zubeck could dish out.

This time, I'd be waiting for him. And so would a few of my friends.

Earlier I had set up a trap using all my men—plus Annie, of course. I had also enlisted the help of three trusted members of the Salty Dog Snowmobile Club, each with military experience. Bert was assigned to tail Ben Zubeck and keep an eye on him wherever he went. The rest of us agreed to split up. One team kept watch on my house. The other guys were posted along the most likely escape route.

It was a wicked night. The winds were gusting, and the impending snowstorm blocked out the moon and stars, leaving us squinting at the dark through watery eyes. If my plan were to fail, I would've wasted a lot of manpower, but I knew the participants wouldn't mind—provided none of them got shot or froze to death.

A few minutes after nine o'clock, Bert called my cell phone to report that Ben Zubeck had left his house by snowmobile. A short time later, Bert reported that Zubeck had arrived at Muddy's and gone inside, where he was currently pounding down boilermakers as if Gus had just made the last call.

Meanwhile, I was sitting atop my trusty snowmobile on a knoll, surrounded by evergreens and bare shrubs, across from an easy access-point to the lake. My house was in full view about one hundred yards away, with lamps lit, fireplace ablaze, and the television flickering in the big living room window. I'd set up a dummy so it was stretched on the couch, barely visible except for the feet perched on a coffee table. For all practical purposes and to all passersby, it appeared to be a normal evening at ye olde homestead.

Bert called me a half-hour later with an update: he'd peeked through the window of Muddy's, and Zubeck still appeared to be comfortable at the bar. "Looks like he plans to be here a while," Bert said. I radioed the crew to hold their ground and be patient—I was sure Zubeck would make his move tonight. He was just fueling up.

Another half-hour passed. I thought I heard the distant whine of another snowmobile, but when I removed my helmet, it was only the wind, whistling through the trees. It sounded like banshees on Halloween night. My face and ears were raw, and I wondered if my stakeout compadres were as cold as I was. I waited patiently.

And then it happened.

I heard the dull roar of an engine, and this time, it was definitely not the wind. A moment later, I saw the silhouette of a husky snowmobile rider speeding into view. The rider was dressed in black from head to toe. He slowed just enough to brandish a rifle at my house. Three rapid shots exploded from the weapon, then my would-be assailant raced onward toward the lake.

The chase was on.

"Damn, it Bert!" I exclaimed out loud as I fired up my sled. "How the hell did he get past you?"

But I knew there'd be time to chastise him later. My Yamaha 350 was already speeding forward with the throttle full-bore, as though my sled had a mind of its own. My quarry was racing away with no headlight, and he was quickly getting harder to see. I spied the halide lights of the Salty Dog trio, approaching fast from the west. As the dark rider started across the wide-open ice, Jerry Shea appeared from the east like the lone ranger in his four-wheel-drive SUV, trying to cut off the shooter's path. The big vehicle was not nearly as maneuverable as a snowmobile, however. The dark rider abruptly changed direction and veered toward my path. In the next moment I was racing with him side by side, both us at still at full throttle. The faceplate on his helmet masked his expression, but I could picture Zubeck's maniacal grin. His padded suit covered him from head to toe. One gloved hand was on the steering column. The other hand held his rifle, which he raised and swung toward me. Few people can fire a rifle one-handed without missing or cracking a wrist, but I figured Zubeck might be crazy enough to try it, so I immediately eased off the throttle and fell several yards behind.

When no shot erupted, I accelerated until I was once again neck and neck with my competitor. This time, he maneuvered close and tried to shove the rifle into the revolving tracks of my sled. The rifle tip hit home, but the weapon was torn from his hand and left behind as we sped on.

Next the driver swerved, as if he would smash his snowmobile directly into mine. I swerved to avoid him. He swerved again and rammed into me, but by some miracle we managed to keep racing forward. Then I saw the three remaining members of my crew, just ahead and riding toward us. We had the culprit completely surrounded.

The shooter made one last, desperate move to escape: he drove straight at the sleds of two of the Salty Dogs, playing the old hotrod game of chicken. The Dogs split off at the last second, and the shooter was free of them—but not free of Shea. The SUV roared in from the side, clipping the back of the perp's sled and jolting it. The rider went airborne, his dark form sailing in slow motion, then he hit the ice and began tumbling and sliding like a rag doll. His machine slid onward ahead of him, carried by momentum. In the next instant, Officer Shea was cranking the wheel hard and the SUV was swerving, and I held my breath as two wheels lifted, but Shea somehow managed not to roll the SUV or run over the downed man.

The posse of sleds skidded to a halt and all my officers leaped into action, drawing their weapons and slowly advancing on the motionless body. Officer Burr was nowhere in sight, but I knew if he were present, he would have yelled something like: "Freeze! You're on thin ice, fella!"

Cautiously, I approached the quarry, who was starting to moan and attempting to roll onto his back. I breathed a sigh of relief—I hadn't wanted Zubeck to be paralyzed or killed, just apprehended. I winced as I grew near. The fall had ripped open parts of his padded suit, exposing patches of raw, bloody skin to the cold. When I was certain that all the fight had gone out of him, I helped him sit up and remove his helmet.

My snow posse and I were struck dumb. It was the shooter, all right, but it was not Ben Zubeck.

Chapter Thirty-Six

Dawg was very happy to see me when I got home that night. He knows whenever I'm in danger—and of course he'd heard all three shots from the basement of my house, where I'd stowed him away for safety. In retrospect, I should've left him with the wife of one of the Salty Dogs, and I owed my cartoonish canine a great big apology by way of a great big piece of bologna.

I was very glad to be home in one piece myself. I had predicted that I would upset Ben Zubeck enough to make him come after me, and I was half right. A Zubeck had come after me, but it wasn't Ben. The gun-toting devil on the snowmobile was none other than his wife, "Little Estie."

Esther Zubeck had taken quite a tumble on the ice, so we escorted her directly to Lakeland Hospital, where doctors confirmed that her injuries were not severe. Her tongue, however, had been significantly loosened. Between vitriolic outbursts, she revealed her version of the truth: She alone had shot up the sign for the French Country Inn, and she alone had shot up the restaurant, doling out punishment where punishment was due. According to her, Ben had mellowed in his old age, and when he'd failed to turn his threats into action, she'd taken matters into her own hands. She claimed she'd been staying at her sister's house on Tuesday night, out near Highway H, when Ben went up north to their trailer to take up a load of boxes and do a little snowmobiling. I wasn't sure whether Esther was just covering for Ben on the sign or the restaurant shooting, but I knew one thing for certain: she alone had fired on my house.

Meanwhile, Ben Zubeck had continued guzzling drinks at Muddy's right up until the time we picked him up. When we'd informed him what had happened to Esther, he'd thrown a punch at Shea. So, we had him for assaulting a police officer, plus drunk and disorderly. A short time later, Mr. Zubeck was brightening a cell at the county jail with his cheerful disposition. I was fairly certain he'd known what Esther was up to that night—and during the restaurant shooting—even if he hadn't participated directly. And I wanted both Zubecks tucked away safe and sound until we could sort things out.

It was well after midnight by the time I'd wrapped things up completely. In lieu of a commendation, I'd bought several rounds of drinks for the Salty Dogs. Then Bert stopped by my house to help me nail some plywood over the shattered window. Luckily, only the small side window had been breached, not the big picture window in the middle. The second shot had taken out my porch light, and a third had lodged in the painted fir siding.

"Wish I could've been more help to you earlier," Bert said. "Guess you can ignore that voice mail I left you."

Just as the posse was leaping into action, Bert had given me a call to complain that he was still freezing in the parking lot of Muddy's while Ben Zubeck was inside, getting falling-down drunk. "Maybe we should just call off the sting," the message continued. A minute later, Bert had finally heard the snowmobiles roaring across the lake, but he'd kept to his post. After all, I'd told him to stick to Zubeck.

As we finished up the window repair and Bert drove away from my house, I realized where I'd made my biggest mistake in all this. Dave Tedeski had tried to teach me well, but his pupil hadn't listened. "Always concentrate on the top of your suspect list," Davey would say, "but never take your eye off the bottom. You never know when something, or someone, will turn your world upside down."

In other words, the person you least suspect for a crime is often the real culprit. And in this case, I hadn't even bothered to draw up a list of suspects—I'd just surmised that Ben Zubeck was the restaurant shooter, the way Tyrrell was currently working his angle on John Ratz. If I'd thought just a little bit harder, I would've realized that Ben Zubeck's wife had exactly the same grudges and motives as Ben did. She even could've been the one who kicked me in the head Monday night—her feet were certainly big enough.

Tomorrow, I would try to establish without a doubt which Zubeck had fired into Kirsch's restaurant, and whether either one of them had played a role in the murder. I tried to picture Esther stabbing Chandra Harper. It didn't feel right, but I'd have to at least be open to the possibility. In the meantime, some of the pieces of my life were falling into place again, as if the world were slowly righting itself. I wondered what would happen next to turn it back upside down.

Chapter Thirty-Seven

With the Zubecks in custody, one might have thought I'd call it a night. I was officially off duty, after all, and I'd intended to head for bed. But I was wired and wide awake and thinking about all of life's little mysteries: the past and future, Greta and Annie . . . and Who killed Chandra Harper?

So, I filled my Thermos with fresh coffee and went out for a drive. I do some of my best thinking behind the wheel, prowling the quiet back roads and the dark and lonely lanes. As my thoughts turned toward the murder, I found myself pulling into a familiar parking spot, directly across from the French Country Inn.

I sipped my coffee and stared at the buildings along the shore. All seemed quiet again. The windows of the guest rooms were dark, including that of Hector Harper in the long guesthouse close to the lobby. Even John Ratz, to the west in L'Auberge, seemed to be sleeping. I really wasn't expecting any trouble tonight—we'd filled our quota for the week. And yet, I wouldn't have been surprised to see a black Ford V-8 drive up to the lobby with a ghostly Baby Face Nelson at the wheel. There hadn't been this much action at the inn since the days when he and Bugs Moran used to come here to gamble and drink.

As I ruminated on the current state of affairs, I spied movement a few paces from the door to Hector's suite in the guesthouse. It was a man, small build, bundled up against the cold. He had a flashlight in his hand and was cradling a cardboard box. It took a moment, but I recognized the blaze-orange cap and the black-and-red checked coat.

It was Santiago, the all-around prep cook, stock man, dishwasher, and gofer. The guy had a deep fear of "loco" hunters, so he wore red and orange from September to May. Originally from northern Mexico, Santiago was one of Kirsch's most trusted employees. Kirsch liked him because he worked hard and had a knack for doing whatever needed to be done. Many a time, I'd seen Santiago moving supplies between Kirsch's restaurant and the side door of the guesthouse, which led to a laundry and a basement storage room. I'd also seen Santiago working at night after the restaurant had closed, and I had questioned both him and Kirsch about it before, so his actions tonight weren't entirely suspicious. Nonetheless, I decided to watch a while and speak to Santiago when he came up from the guesthouse basement. I wondered whether anyone had questioned him about what he might have seen or heard on the night of the murder.

I watched and waited. Several minutes passed, and still no Santiago. If the liquor storeroom had been in the guesthouse basement instead of below Kirsch's restaurant, I might've suspected Santiago was enjoying a nightcap. But as far as I knew, the guesthouse basement only held the inn's laundry as well as extra storage for cleaning supplies, nonperishables, and assorted equipment.

I stepped out of the car to have a closer look. As I crossed the road, I heard a racket near the side parking lot of the restaurant—on the opposite side of the property and a good hundred yards away. When I hurried over to investigate, I found Santiago again, tossing some garbage bags into a Dumpster with his back to me.

"Buenas noches," I said, shining my flashlight in his direction. Santiago had been helping me with my Spanish, but even with his heavy accent, he did a much better job with my first language than I could do with his.

Santiago jumped about a mile high. "Dios mío! You scared me, Chief. I thought maybe it was that loco guy who shot the restaurant."

"Lo siento. Didn't mean to sneak up on you. And we have

the shooter in custody now, so you don't have to worry about that problem, at least."

"Is there another problema?" he asked warily. "I am working here. I am doing nothing wrong."

"It's okay, amigo. I was just parked over there watching the inn." I pointed toward my Jeep. "I saw you walk over from the restaurant to the basement carrying a package. What I can't figure out is, how did you get all the way over here without my seeing you again?"

Santiago glanced at his feet nervously. "I just take some cans and things over there. I do nothing wrong."

"I'm not saying you did. But I never saw you leave the basement of the guesthouse, and the next thing I know you're way over here, on the other side of the restaurant. How did you do that?"

Santiago put his head down and began to mumble something to himself in Spanish, but I couldn't make it out. I tried to reassure him, but he kept mumbling, and I was beginning to lose patience.

"You know what, amigo? There's going to be a problem after all—if you don't explain to me what's going on here."

"Por favor," he said. "I don't want to get in any trouble."

"Get in trouble with who? If you don't tell me, you'll be in much bigger trouble with me."

"With the chef, Chief."

"Excuse me?" His accent was so thick it sounded like one word.

"You know, with the chef. Chef Drew. He says it will be big trouble for me if I tell anyone about this."

"If you tell anyone about what, amigo?"

"The socavón."

"The soca-what?"

He raised his hands and looked skyward as if praying that God might help me get the translation. "Socavón. You know, socavón . . . el paso subterráneo . . ." He made a shoveling motion as he kept groping for the word, then said, "The tunnel."

"There's a tunnel between the two buildings?"

"Sí, a very old tunnel. But Chef Drew say I must never tell, or go through the tunnel, or he will call Homeland Security and have me deported to Chile."

"Aren't you from Mexico?"

"Sí, yes, but Chef Drew, he gets confused. And he is not here now, and it is very cold, and so I use the tunnel to go back to the restaurant." Santiago began to shiver, although I wasn't sure whether it was from fear or from the biting wind.

"Okay, let's go inside. You're going to show me this tunnel."

Santiago let out a deep sigh, then acquiesced. "Okay, Chief."

He led me through the back door and into the restaurant kitchen, then down a flight of stairs to the basement, where I found myself in a cluttered storage area packed with mountains of canned goods and towers of stacked chairs. The room also held a reach-in freezer and an ice machine and the entrance to Kirsch's wine cellar, which, I noticed, was securely padlocked. Beyond that were a lineup of employee lockers and a portable clothes rack for the chef's uniforms—gray hound's tooth pants and several starched white jackets. Santiago led me past the wardrobe and down a narrow aisle. The floor became damp in one spot; it appeared the water softener's discharge pipe did not quite reach all the way to the sump pump. The passage grew dark as we ventured farther from the stairs, and I switched my flashlight back on. At the far end of the basement, a concrete wall met the back end of a walk-in cooler. Santiago pointed toward the shadows, and I spied a narrow gap in the wall. I shined my light on it. The opening looked barely tall and wide enough for a child to squeeze through.

"Follow me, Chief," Santiago said. Then he bent down and entered the darkness headfirst. My guide was agile, thin, and small in stature, and he had no trouble slipping into the tunnel. I was not sure I could follow him without getting stuck, but I managed to contort and squish my much-larger physique through the opening, grateful that the dirt-floored passage just beyond was less constricting. Even so, it was barely as wide as my shoulders and less than five feet high. Anyone with claustrophobia—or a fear of spiders, for that matter—would've panicked.

Santiago held his pen-sized flashlight in an outstretched hand and moved ahead easily as I stooped and plodded behind him, shining my own light at the surroundings. I guessed we were now somewhere below Kirsch's dining room. The tunnel extended through a dirt-floored crawl space. The beams and floor joists were laced with cobwebs overhead. The so-called "tunnel" was a dug-out channel, which dropped the dirt floor a few feet lower and allowed us to walk, though still stooped. As we moved forward, I realized a labyrinth of old side tunnels and walkways crisscrossed the entire crawl space, though most were filled with wood planks and other debris, or they had caved-in and were no longer usable unless you were on your belly.

My lower back began to ache from stooping, but when I tried to straighten, my forehead cracked against a wooden beam. I swore out loud.

"You okay, Chief?" Santiago asked.

"Yeah, I'm fine. Keep going." I felt like Danny the Tunnel King, Charles Bronson's character in the movie *The Great Escape*.

The tunnel descended, then finally, we hit a wall. We slipped through an opening at one end and found ourselves in a chamber with almost six feet of headroom. The floor was cobblestone, and the walls were brick and mortar. After the tunnel, it felt like Grand Central Station. I looked around and saw crates packed with dirty green bottles, small boxes of thingamajigs, and some bent copper tubing, which appeared to be the remnants of a homemade still. In a corner, three cobweb-covered oaken barrels lay on their side. I remembered Greta's tale about the speakeasy that was here during Prohibition. This area was probably an old gin mill, where Hobart Hermansen and his cronies had brewed beer or distilled alcohol when other bootlegging options dried up. I'd also heard about planes that would land on the lake in winter and deliver boxes of liquor. This tunnel system was a good way to hide all sorts of things, including criminals making their escape.

"Where does this lead?" I asked Santiago, shining my flashlight through a second small opening that was chiseled through the brick wall.

"The laundry below the guesthouse," Santiago answered. "And este . . ." he said, pointing to the opposite wall, "es una vía to the lobby." He shined the flashlight beam on the opposite wall from where he was standing, but I saw no opening.

"Dónde?" I asked. "I don't see it."

He walked several paces to the wall, then appeared to pass directly through the bricks and out of sight. When I followed, I saw that it was a trick of the eye. The first brick wall was incomplete. Roughly a foot behind it stood a second brick wall with an identical surface. They overlapped, but there was a narrow gap, so you could slip around the end of the first wall and then slide sideways between them.

I peered through the gap but saw only darkness. Then Santiago turned his head and grinned as he flicked on his flashlight under his chin. "Boo, Chief." I pulled my gut in as tightly as I could and squeezed through the narrow slot behind him.

We turned again, and found ourselves in another low-ceilinged, dirt-floored maze. The tunnel floor sloped upward. We traveled a few yards, and then the tunnel appeared to hit a dead end below a four-foot-high ceiling. A crude step was cut into the dirt wall. Santiago pointed up, carefully lifted several planks from the wood ceiling, and slid them aside one by one. Then he climbed out of the tunnel.

He reached back with his hand to offer assistance. I took it and followed, and found myself standing inches away from him inside a closet—the same closet that Mary Haggermaker and Patti Goff had shown me the previous evening. We were under the big oak stairway.

Santiago reached forward and turned the door handle, and then we were standing together in the lobby of the French Country Inn.

"Amazing," I said. "Utterly amazing."

Chapter Thirty-Eight

In some ways, the Harper murder investigation was simplified by my knowledge of the tunnels under the French Country Inn. We'd been challenged by the fact that the killer had not forced his way into Chandra Harper's room—which led us to believe that he either had a key to both the lobby and Chandra's suite, or the victim herself had let him in. But none of the other guests' keys would open the door to the lobby when it was locked for the night—only Chandra's key did that. Which left only three probable means to gain access to the building after the bar closed: the inn's master key, a restaurant key, or Chandra herself.

Unless, of course, the killer had entered the building through the tunnel system. If I made that assumption, the suspect list became shorter. It included only those who knew about the tunnels. I did not suspect Santiago—though experience told me I couldn't absolutely rule him out. When I asked him who else knew about the tunnels, he said, "only Chef Drew and Kirsch."

I wondered whether Santiago was right about that. The tunnel access in the closet was hard to spot when the floorboards were in place, so it was possible. Even if anyone realized the boards were loose, they might just think they hid an ordinary crawl space. I suspected Navilio might know about the tunnels—after all, he'd been involved with the building renovations. But I didn't think that he or Kirsch or Santiago had anything to do with the murder. There was no established motive for any of these men.

And that put "Chef Drew" right at the top of my tunnel-crawling-suspect list. I wasn't certain of his motive, either, but my gut told me Andrew Turkley was guilty of something. He was, after all, a chef.

I freely admit it: I have a bias against professional chefs. They're all geniuses. If you don't believe me, just ask them. Sure, many of them can be great storytellers, knowledgeable about food and wine and every other subject. They can also be very generous in offering free drinks and appetizers to their friends, especially at the restaurant owner's expense. But when you work with those same chefs, it's a different story.

Tedeski and I learned that firsthand when we did several stints in Chicago restaurants during our youth, before we were cops. In every case, the head chef was a smug, arrogant bastard who never accepted responsibility when something went wrong, but always took credit for any success. Working in the restaurant business had taught me one valuable lesson: Never work in the restaurant business.

Before I left the lobby of the inn, I asked Santiago to keep our little tunnel-crawling expedition a secret, and he was happy to do so. He informed me that Chef Turkley was expected back in the restaurant at ten the next morning. I went home and grabbed a few hours of shuteye, but as soon as I awoke, I phoned Dorothy and asked her to start a background check on Andrew Turkley. When she asked why, I told her it was just a hunch—but I wanted her to pursue it quickly and quietly.

Then I headed back to the inn and waited in the main dining room at Kirsch's restaurant, in front of the fireplace. Of course, the chef was late. In Cuisine Class 101, chefs are taught to keep the "common people" waiting.

I thought about the tunnels and what they meant. A person could duck through the side door at the guesthouse, head down the stairs to the basement laundry, then make their way through the tunnels to reemerge in either the lobby of the inn or the restaurant kitchen, without ever being seen. Getting through the utility door of the guesthouse wasn't much of a challenge. Under the cover of darkness, an intruder could surreptitiously move along the lakeshore, dart under the balcony, and enter the door to the basement stairway. According to Santiago, that particular door was usually unlocked. "No one steals the toilet paper or towels," he'd explained. Moreover, a spare key to that door was kept on the sill directly above it, the first place even an amateur crook might think to look. The tunnel opening in the laundry room, however, was not obvious. There was a virtually unnoticeable passage behind a hot water heater. From there, a person had unfettered access to the underbelly of the property—and to the building that held the lobby, the restaurant, and suite 303.

The tunnel access under the kitchen was not quite as easy to reach unobserved, but it was still doable—even during working hours. Any restaurant employee, from bus boy to bartender, could head down to the kitchen storeroom after making some excuse, move to the lobby, and quickly head upstairs to suite 303 with no one knowing where they'd gone. During the off-season, the lobby was usually empty after ten p. m., with only the desk lamp and a table light softly glowing. More importantly, at that hour, the front door was locked and the desk was unmanned.

If I assumed the killer had used the tunnels, my next task was to determine who he was trying to kill—Navilio or Harper. Then I had to obtain enough evidence to hang the son of a bitch. Right now, my money was on Turkley trying to kill Harper, but why?, I wondered. What was his motive?

With an air of importance and the scent of cheap cologne—both of which arrived seconds before he did—Chef Andrew Turkley finally entered the dining room at precisely 10:42 a.m.

"How are you doing, Chef?" I asked.

"I'm holding up all right, considering everything that has happened," Turkley said. You'd think he was the victim. "No offense," he continued, "but I don't like the police crawling through my kitchen and my restaurant."

"None taken." I didn't bother to point out that it was Kirsch's restaurant, not his. "I'm here because I have a few questions I'd like to ask you. Would you sit down a minute, please? It's very important."

He hesitated, but he sat. "Sure," he said. "I wouldn't want you to think that I'm not cooperative."

I launched right in. "First of all, did you by any chance know the victim, Chandra Harper? Had you ever met her before, maybe when she made a prior visit to the inn? Or earlier this week, perhaps—did you and she chat in the bar?"

"No, no, and no. In fact, I never once laid eyes on her, alive or dead."

"You might have known her by her maiden name, Chandra . . ." The maiden name escaped me and I leafed through my notebook.

The chef looked annoyed. "It doesn't matter what her maiden name was. I told you, I never met her. I've never known anyone by the name of Chandra."

" . . . Collins," I finished. "Her name was Chandra Collins." I gave him one of my own annoying little looks, which meant *I will tell you if it matters or not*. "I haven't seen you around the last few days. Where have you been, Drew?"

"I've been around. I've just been very busy lately. I've been spending a lot of time in the kitchen, and I haven't had a chance to mingle with the customers the way I usually do. I trust you enjoyed your dinner the other night, though."

"I did," I said. "Why are you so busy? It's the off-season. Even with the writing group staying here, business is pretty dead compared to summer."

Chef Drew puffed up his chest. "Do you really think a chef's job is limited to cooking on demand for a few patrons? I have myriad responsibilities. There are new menus to create, recipes to test, ingredients to procure, vendors to contact, budgets to balance—most people will never understand what it takes to be a successful chef."

I smirked. "Life is tough all over."

I continued with a barrage of questions, but the chef steadfastly denied that he had known Chandra Harper or that he had been at the inn at the time of the murder, although he didn't have an ironclad alibi for that time, either—he was in bed, asleep and alone, he said. I felt a change in approach was in order, so I apologized if I'd offended him, explained I'd been under a lot of pressure lately. Then I asked if I could have a Bloody Mary. Together we walked to the bar, and our conversation became more relaxed as he mixed me the cocktail.

"Aren't you on duty?" he asked. "Not that it matters to me of course."

"I'm always on duty," I said. "And I know it's early, but I need a little heat in my boots to keep me going all day."

He smiled and handed me the drink, and without hesitation I took a gulp. I cleared my throat. The chef was heavy-handed with the horseradish sauce and Tabasco, but that was just the way I liked it. I took another swallow.

"Ah," I said. "It's perfect. You know, I usually like the cold and snow, but right now, I wish I were drinking this on a sandy beach somewhere down in the Caribbean."

The chef laughed. "You and half the people around here." Then he said something else—a thirteen-word statement that rang a bell in my head and told me unequivocally that he had murdered Chandra Harper.

* * *

The number thirteen has always represented bad luck, and those thirteen words uttered by Chef Turkley were surely bad luck for him. When I said that I wished I were drinking in the Caribbean,

Turkley had replied that everything south of Illinois was just the tenth circle of hell to him. And then he'd clinched it with thirteen words: "I despise the south—can't tolerate heat. I'm a man of the north."

In her writings, Chandra Harper had provided one obscure but critical detail about Alden Torrence, her sister's fiancé and alleged poisoner: Torrence was a man of the north. When she had tracked Torrence after her sister's death, Chandra had focused her search on the north—because Torrence was unable to tolerate hot weather. He had refused to move south when Cassandra had suggested it.

The evidence was thin at best, but my gut told me Alden Torrence and Andrew Turkley were definitely one and the same. Chandra had been a royal pain in the behind to me—a person she'd just met and perhaps even liked. I could readily imagine how Torrence saw her. To him, Chandra wasn't just a harpy, she was the she-devil incarnate. She was also a threat to his livelihood—whether or not he had actually killed Cassandra,. She had harassed him and sullied his reputation, prompting his moves to Canada and Alaska. After that, Chandra had lost his trail, he'd changed his name, and he was rid of her for a while. Then, suddenly, their paths had crossed again by chance, here at the inn, and he'd decided to get rid of her once and for all. All I needed to prove my theory was some physical evidence—preferably a clear link between him and the murder weapon, or something else that put him at the murder scene.

I thanked Chef Drew for his assistance and apologized for any convenience. To reassure him, I repeated that I'd been under a lot of stress lately. I didn't want him getting jumpy. Then I hurried out, phoning Dorothy on the way. She confirmed it: Alden Torrence and Andrew Turkley were the same man, sharing the same skin and using the same social security number. Moreover, Torrence's fingerprints were in the system. He'd been booked for a drunk-and-disorderly charge twelve years ago—after he'd gotten into an intense public argument with Chandra Harper. My next move was calling Tyrrell, so we could arrest Turkley on suspicion of murder. If we were lucky, the chef's fingerprints were also in suite 303—and on some personal item owned by the victim—giving us ample cause for a search warrant for Turkley's home, car, and anywhere else we needed to look.

Chapter Thirty-Nine

Turkley was squirming in his chair like a schoolboy in the principal's office, caught red-handed with a spitball shooter while trying to explain why he could not possibly be guilty. His behavior could not have pleased me more. In fact, I was only a degree or two short of outright gloating—not just because I'd gotten the better of an arrogant chef, but because I had managed to solve the murder of Chandra Harper. Naturally, Tyrrell had made the actual arrest, and we were now on his turf for the interrogation. Tyrrell was in charge, and the sheriff's department deserved its due. But after years of being called Barney Fife, rent-a-cop, and even Chief Cuckold behind my back, I was happy to have the small-town spotlight shined upon me. And Tyrrell had graciously consented to let me lead the interview.

Chefs love to give each other awards. It's usually for things like "most creative menu," "best new restaurant," or "most talented dicer of East Asian eggplant." But if there were an award for "best acting by a chef who killed a patron to keep her quiet," it would have been named the Drew Turkley Award. Heck, I would've carved a little Oscar statue out of a zucchini and presented it to him myself. Turkley was brilliant in his denials—at least, he saw it that way himself. He had confessed to virtually everything, including owning the murder weapon and being in Chandra's room at the approximate time of her death. He'd even admitted that he'd taken the knife right out of her back to dispose of it. But he steadfastly insisted that someone else had plunged the blade into her.

"Okay, let's go over this again," I said, ignoring Turkley's groan. "You've stated you were in Chandra Harper's room at approximately three-thirty a.m. on the night she was murdered. Is that correct?"

"Yes, that's correct. But I did not kill her."

"And were you aware that Chandra Harper was Cassandra Collins's twin sister, and that Chandra believed that you poisoned her twin?"

"Of course I was. How could I forget that? Chandra Harper was my personal nightmare. But I repeat, I did not murder her. Nor did I murder her sister Cassandra. I mean, come on, would I actually risk my good name and well-deserved reputation by giving someone a case of botulism?"

"I don't know," I responded, "but I'm not sure it's relevant to this crime. We found the victim's laptop computer, her diary, and the murder weapon all buried in a snowdrift behind your house. Your prints are on the weapon, which is your own chef's knife. And you've admitted that you took these items from the scene. It doesn't look good for you, Drew."

"I know what it looks like, but the truth is on my side. I did not kill Chandra Harper. Like I've told you a million times, she was already dead when I went to her room."

Incredibly, Turkley had waived his right to have an attorney present—even after we'd presented him with all of the proof we had accumulated against him. I attributed it to stupidity and extreme arrogance.

"I am innocent," he stated. "And as I said before, eventually even you will figure that out. You may be a hick, Chief, but at least you're an honest hick."

It seemed impossible to disabuse the chef from his patently bogus story. We allowed him a few minutes to gather his thoughts. Tyrrell even brought him a can of diet cola. Then we started all over again, looking for any change or inconsistency in Turkley's incredible account of the events leading up to the murder.

"It was Sunday night," Turkley said. "That's when I first knew the world had turned upside down. I was working in the kitchen, and then I went into the dining room to schmooze the patrons. Some of the guests from the writer's workshop were at the bar. At first, I just heard her voice—you don't forget that kind of horror. And then I spotted her. It was Chandra Collins, all right. I recognized her immediately. Even so, I couldn't believe it was really her—I hoped it was a look-alike, or I was just seeing things. She didn't see me, though; she was too busy talking to this dark-haired woman. I recognized that woman, too. She'd been to the inn a few other times, doing some kind of research. Navilio and Kirsch had given her a tour last summer. So, when Chandra left, I engaged in casual conversation with the lady, Greta-something. She was kind of flirty with me—a lot of women have a thing for chefs, you know. So I bought her a few drinks, and she told me everything I wanted to know about Chandra Collins, now Harper, including what room she was staying in. I also heard about the tell-all book Chandra was writing about her sister's death—and about me—and how Chandra had never stopped looking for her sister's supposed killer."

He took a sip of the cola. Sweat beaded on his forehead, even though the room was not noticeably warm. Then he nervously passed the cola can back and forth from hand to hand.

"Why didn't you just leave town, before Chandra spotted you?" I asked.

"I thought about it. But Kirsch is going to pay me my year-end bonus next week, and I need the money. Plus, I'm tired of moving. I like it here. So, I admit it: that night I decided I would have to get rid of Chandra before she recognized me—and before she made my life a living hell all over again."

This part was new, and to my dismay, Tyrrell jumped in on

Turkley's monologue. "Are you now admitting that you killed Chandra Harper?" he asked.

"No, I didn't say that. I said that I'd decided to do it. I wanted to kill her, but there's a big difference between that and actually killing her."

Turkley put his head down and ran his fingers through his hair. It was the best job of method acting I had seen since the last time I watched Marlon Brando in *On the Waterfront*. I half-expected Turkley to use Brando's trademark line, "I coulda bin a contenda."

He continued. "I was desperate, I admit that, too. And maybe even a little paranoid. At first, I didn't think Chandra knew I was working here at the inn, but then I thought, what if she does know? What if she's playing some kind of sick game before she moves in for the kill? Hell, she probably killed herself just so she could frame me for the murder."

Tyrrell snorted. "You're not suggesting she stabbed herself in the back."

"Okay, so maybe she didn't stab herself, but she was here, in my restaurant—there was no denying that. And that bitch was a nightmare. I wouldn't wish her on my own worst enemy. Then Monday night she had that argument with the writer in the bar. It was like a sign that I should make a move on her. I figured the guy in the bar would be the perfect suspect, the jilted lover with a violent temper. So later, I went over to Chandra's room in L'Auberge. I planned to strangle her or maybe suffocate her—but obviously I didn't do either one."

"How did you get in?" I asked.

"I used the master key from the closet in the lobby."

"Who told you about the key? Mary Haggermaker?" I knew she hadn't—I just wanted to see if the chef would lie.

He shrugged. "I guess Kirsch mentioned it."

"So, you used the key to get into Chandra's room at L'Auberge. Is that correct?"

"Yeah, I just told you that."

"What did you see when you went inside?"

"Not much—she'd already moved over to suite 303 above the lobby, but I didn't know that then. As I was leaving, though, I spotted this little shard of something on the floor, and I picked it up. Then I had this really sick feeling—it looked exactly like the hilt from one of my own knives. I was sure Chandra Harper was leaving me some kind of message—that she was messing with my head, and she was closing in, and somehow she was going to frame me for her sister's murder after all these years. I thought it was even possible she planned to kill me."

"Really. So what happened next?"

"You know what happened. I hung around outside the inn, trying to figure out which room Chandra Harper had moved to, and what I should do next. That's when I got attacked by you, Chief. It was you, right? Sorry about your head, but a guy has to defend himself. I thought maybe you were somebody Chandra had hired to do me in. I didn't know it was you until after I'd kicked you. It was dark, and you weren't wearing your uniform."

"Yeah, it was me." I felt chagrined because the chef had gotten the better of me that night. Served me right for wearing dress shoes. "Keep going."

"Okay, so I started to rethink things, and I got scared. It's easy to say you're going to kill a person, especially when you hate their guts, but actually doing it is another thing entirely. The only thing I've killed with my own hands is live shellfish."

Tyrrell looked at me. He wasn't buying Turkley's story any more than I was.

"So," I said, "if you decided not to kill her, then what were you doing in suite 303 the next night, precisely at the time of the murder?"

"It wasn't precisely at the time of her murder—it was right after," he protested.

"And you were there because . . ."

"Because I'd spent the whole damned day worrying about what she had planned, how she would ruin my life. And okay, I admit it, I thought to myself, I've got no choice—I've got to kill her. Only now, it was going to be a little easier, because she'd moved to 303, where she was all by herself. And, I knew I could use the old tunnels from the Sewer to get in and out without anybody seeing me."

I had told Tyrrell about the tunnels, of course, but I hadn't referred to them as sewer tunnels. We both simultaneously said out loud, "The sewer?"

Turkley explained. "The Sewer" was the name of the old speakeasy and gambling den that was here at the inn during Prohibition. "Kirsch told me about it. He even told me about the old tunnels they used back then."

"Did Jim Kirchschlager show you the tunnels?"

"No, he thought they were unusable and mostly sealed up or collapsed. And he said whatever was left wasn't safe. But then Santiago showed me they were still passable—he probably has more experience with that kind of thing."

I let the remark slide. Santiago was a legal immigrant, and I doubted that he'd crossed the border underground.

Turkley rubbed his eyes and sipped his diet Coke. "Where was I?" he asked.

"You were about to break into Chandra Harper's room," Tyrrell said, "because you wanted to kill her."

"Yeah," Turkley said. "That's right, I did want to kill her, but I didn't do it. And when it comes down to it, I probably could never have done it myself." He took a swig and exhaled. "But hey, luckily I didn't have to. As fate would have it, somebody had already taken care of my problem. I guess the gods were smiling on me."

For a moment I wanted to reach down Chef Turkley's throat and pull his bowels out through his mouth. His characterization of the murder made me sick. The guy was a sociopath. "Yeah, lucky break,"

I muttered. "So, tell us exactly how you reached Chandra's room, and exactly what you saw and heard at that time."

"Well, I didn't hear anything. I went back to the inn around three-thirty in the morning, maybe a little later. I walked along the lakefront, on the ice. I didn't want to risk being seen going in through the restaurant. So, I went down into the laundry in the guesthouse, then I went through the tunnel and came up in the lobby of the inn. From there, I picked up the master key and went up to Chandra's room. I don't mind telling you, I was sweating bullets. I was sure she'd be waiting for me with a knife in her hand, ready to pounce."

"Why would you think that?" I asked. I thought Turkley might be delusional.

He hesitated, but only briefly. "Because I made another stop first in the tunnels," he continued. "I went up to the kitchen and took a carving knife from my set. I'd already noticed that a paring knife was missing the day before—I figured that's where the shard I found in L'Auberge had come from. But the night Chandra died I saw that another knife was missing—my best chopping knife. I figured Chandra had taken it herself." He shrugged. "Guess I was wrong, because I found it stuck in her back when I finally got to her room."

Tyrrell was losing patience. "So, you didn't stab her," he stated, "but you expect us to believe that someone else stabbed her with your knife, just minutes before you entered her room, ready to stab her with yet another knife? Great defense, Turkley. A jury is going to take about five minutes to convict you for murder. You might as well come clean and admit you did it. It'll save all of us a lot of time."

Tyrrell's bulldog approach had no effect—other than to make Turkley roll his eyes, flip Tyrrell the bird, then glare at him in silence.

"I'm curious," I said. "Why did you take the knife from Chandra's back? Why not just turn around and leave—if you were so scared, as you say."

"It was my best knife," Turkley replied snidely. "Oh, come on, that's a joke, Chief. Isn't it obvious? Someone wanted to frame me, and I couldn't let them get away with it. So, I took the knife and the laptop and her notebooks and whatever else she might have left behind to finger me."

"In other words, you were the victim," Tyrrell said, "and Chandra was framing you."

Turkley looked disgusted. "Someone was framing me. You figure it out, smart guy."

"All right," I said. "So you grabbed the computer and her notebooks, and the bloody knife, and you high-tailed it out of there. How did you leave?"

"The same way I came in," he said. "Through the tunnel."

"And you neither heard nor saw anyone else around the inn?"

"No one."

"Why didn't you just get rid of the evidence?" I asked. "You're an intelligent guy, right? You must've realized it could come back to haunt you."

"I thought about it. At first, I was going to throw everything in a hole in the lake, but I wanted to do it right, wrap it up and weigh it down so it'd be gone forever. That night I didn't have enough time—I just wanted to get the heck out of there. Then, I started wondering if maybe I should keep it, because it might help me out sometime—maybe it showed who really killed Chandra. Last night I changed my mind again, and I was going out on the lake to dump everything. But wouldn't you know it, there was a big ruckus with a bunch of snowmobiles. So, I figured I'd try again tonight on Lake Geneva, which is a lot bigger and deeper. Guess I won't get the chance."

"Guess not," I said. I sighed. I couldn't think of any more questions to ask Drew Turkley, and I was tired of listening to his answers. Tyrrell was right—we didn't need his confession to get a conviction on this one.

I stood up to leave. "You might want to rethink that lawyer, Turkley."

"You don't believe me?" he said, as if that were impossible. With one final, heartfelt plea, Alden Torrence, a.k.a. Andrew Turkley, reached down deep within himself to muster all his phony sincerity and convince Tyrrell and me of his innocence.

"I did not . . . kill . . . that woman," he insisted.

I think he even had tears in his eyes. If he hadn't sounded like a certain ex-president, I actually might have believed him.

Chapter Forty

I was feeling pretty good about things for a change, and I thought I'd reward myself with some much-needed R&R that evening. I considered calling Greta, but I hesitated—I wanted a nice evening, yes, but one that was quiet and uncomplicated, without a single mention of Chandra Harper's murder or all the developments in the case. I phoned Bert Burr instead.

"Say, Bert, do you have a VCR? Mine's broken."

Bert was feeling uncharacteristically cocky that morning. "Sure, boss. It's right here next to my eight-track player, my leisure suit, and that bottle of Galliano I keep just in case somebody like you wants a Harvey Wallbanger."

"Don't be a wise guy—I get enough of that from Shea. I just thought maybe you'd have one of those VCR/DVD players."

"Sorry, Chief, can't help you there. What do you want to watch, *Debbie Does Geneva Township*?"

"You're a real riot, Officer Burr. Actually, I have this great documentary on trains, and it's still in the cellophane wrap. I was hoping to finally watch it and give my mind a break from everything else. But I've got a broken VCR, about twenty boxes full of VCR tapes, and a total of three DVDs that I've already seen way too many times to count."

"Do you want to just borrow one my movies? I have a whole collection."

"No, thanks—especially not if it's the Debbie series. I really wanted to watch this particular tape about the trains."

"Why don't you call Annie, Chief? I think she has one of those VCR/DVD combos. She'd probably let you borrow it."

"Thanks, Bert. Maybe I'll do that. See you tomorrow."

I hung up and stared at the phone. I didn't really want to impose on Annie Madden. Or maybe I was just embarrassed to be stuck with a DVD player when I owned hundreds of VCR tapes. I would've bought one of those combination players myself if I had realized they existed and understood that my old VCR would break down just two months after I'd finally bought a DVD player. I swear, I'll never again buy any type of modern technology without being accompanied to the store by a tech-savvy teenager.

I called Annie Madden. She answered before I could change my mind and hang up. "Hi, Annie, how are you this evening?" I asked, trying to sound casual.

"Um, I'm great, Chief. How are you? You must be thrilled to have a murder suspect in custody. So, it looks like Chef Drew really did it?"

"We still have a few loose ends to tie up, but it looks like an open-and-shut case."

"Well, it must feel great." She paused, but when I said nothing further, she asked, "Why'd you call, Chief? I hope it's not because you need me to work tonight. I'm afraid I've got plans."

"Uh, no, I don't need you to work." I felt a pang of jealousy, which I had no right to feel. She probably had a date. And why wouldn't she? Annie Madden was gorgeous, there was nothing between us but work, and I had absolutely no say about her personal life. And yet, it was as if I'd time-traveled right back to eighth grade, and I was watching an episode of *The Partridge Family* after school. Back then I'd been so smitten with Laurie Partridge that I got jealous whenever some teenage blond surfer-guy was hitting on her. I'd actually throw a pillow at the TV. I could never quite understand why I became so worked up over a girl in a sitcom, but the feeling was there nonetheless. To this day, I feel like throwing something at every blond-haired surfer dude.

"This isn't a work call," I explained. "It's just a personal favor—but that's okay, sounds like you have a hot date tonight."

Annie laughed. "Only if that's the personal favor. What exactly did you have in mind?"

I was struck dumb. "Um . . . well . . ."

Annie laughed again. "You're an easy target, Chief. But I do have plans. I was just about to head to my mother's house to take down her Christmas tree. I know it sounds silly, but I've already cancelled on her once, and I promised I'd do it tonight. She's getting up in years, and she hasn't been doing well lately."

"I took my own tree down the day after Christmas."

"God forbid," Annie said with a hint of mock horror in her voice. "My mother always keeps her Christmas tree up at least until the sixth of January. That's the day of the festival of the Epiphany, when the Baby Jesus is revealed to the Magi. You just can't take it down before that."

"Well, once I kept own my tree up until March, so maybe she'd forgive me for this year's sacrilege."

"Maybe," Annie said, "but let's just not tell her. So, you mentioned a favor?"

"Bert thought you might have something that plays movies on tape."

"A VCR, you mean?"

"Right, a VCR."

"Sure, I've got a combination player. I have a lot of old movies on tape that I still like to watch."

"Would you mind if I borrowed your machine tonight? I have this documentary on trains, but my VCR is broken, and I'd really like to watch the tape. The problem is, you'd have to come over and hook up your machine for me. I'm hopeless."

"Oh." She paused. "I'm really sorry, Chief, but I don't think I have time for that. My system is all interconnected behind the furniture, and it's hard to get to the wires and cables. It'd be a hassle to unhook the machine and haul it over there."

"Well, if you can't help me . . ." I put a little self-pity into my lament.

"Oh, cut it out, Chief. Whining doesn't suit you. Why don't you just watch the tape over here at my place? You can have the whole house to yourself. There's even beer in the fridge. I'll leave the door open, throw a log on the fireplace, and you can make yourself at home. In fact, if you don't tell anyone where you are, then no one will bother you here."

That sounded like a much better prospect than calling Shea for help. "Are you sure it's okay?" I asked.

"Positive. I'm leaving for Mom's in ten minutes. If you're done with your tape and want to leave before I get home, just make sure the door is closed tight, and keep the outside lights on."

"Thanks, Annie, you're a life-saver."

"Well, I am trained to do CPR. How soon will you be here?"

"About fifteen minutes."

"I'll be gone by then, but like I said, just make yourself at home."

* * *

When I stepped inside Annie's house, the smell of popcorn filled the kitchen. The setup was just as she had described: cold beer, a wood fire ready to go, and the pièce de résistance: fresh popcorn with a little ramekin of melted butter on the side. She'd stuck a Post-it to the bowl: "Congratulations on the arrest. Enjoy the popcorn." She'd also stuck two jumbo-size Post-its on the VCR, with step-by-step operating instructions that even a six-year-old could've followed. She must've thought I was a real dimwit.

I lit a match and started the fire, which she'd prepared for me like a Girl Scout. I smiled, opened a Rolling Rock beer, and helped myself to a handful of popcorn as I watched the fire quickly catch hold. And then I did what any red-blooded, unscrupulous investigator would do: I snooped. I couldn't stop myself from poking around Annie's house, just a little. I didn't fondle the contents of her underwear drawer or do anything perverted like that, but I did open her medicine cabinet and peek into her bedroom. Her home was meticulously neat and well organized—couch cushions straight, countertops crumb-free, rugs recently vacuumed. The bedroom smelled sweet, and the bed was made perfectly. It was the antithesis of my own home.

Next to Annie's television set was a tower filled with DVDs. There were a few too many chick flicks for my taste, but she owned plenty of action movies and several excellent dramas. I was also impressed that Annie had a fair amount of classics, including several film noirs and a collection of films by Alfred Hitchcock, my favorite director. She also owned copies of *King Kong*, both the 1933 version, starring Fay Wray and Bruce Cabot, and the abysmal 1970s remake.

"Hmmph," I said out loud. I beat one hand against my chest and sniffled. I love the classic *King Kong*, though I've always felt sorry for the ape. I mean, there he was, a godlike king of his own uncharted island, with a steady supply of fresh young virgins that would've made a Hollywood producer jealous. Then he gets kidnapped and brought to New York, and he can't make it there. All Kong wants is his lovely Fay Wray and a one-way ticket home, but he doesn't get home, and he doesn't get the girl of his dreams. It's a great love story—not quite on par with *An Affair to Remember*, but in some ways more touching.

I put my train tape in the VCR and managed to get it going

on the first try. "Great Caesar's Ghost!" I exclaimed. "Chief, you have finally mastered the video cassette player! Too bad it's already obsolete."

I searched the refrigerator for another drink. A beer in someone else's home always tastes colder and better, and the second one was as good as the first. The tape I was watching featured all the famous trains: the Empire Builder, which traveled from Chicago to Seattle; the Twentieth Century Limited, the greatest express from New York to Chicago; and of course, the great European trains such as the Orient Express. I finished the second beer about two minutes into the tape. I hit the "pause" button, then helped myself to a glass of Dry Sack sherry. Annie kept a bottle on the buffet in her dining room. Maybe it was the stress of the past few days, or the two beers and the sherry, but ten minutes after the first train had left the station on the TV screen, I fell sound asleep on the couch.

* * *

I had the most incredible dream.

The room was dark, but the fire was burning more brightly than when I'd first stretched out on the sofa. The warm red glow illuminated the figure of a beautiful woman, who stood before me. A white towel was wrapped over her hair, and another covered her body.

I reached up and stroked her thigh. It was a good fantasy; she didn't pull away. In fact, she made a murmur of contentment.

"Mind if I join you on the couch?" she asked. Both towels fell away, then the naked silhouette of the woman stretched out over me and pressed her lips to mine, and our tongues danced like the flames in the fireplace.

"I have wanted to kiss you since the first time I laid my eyes on you," Annie Madden said to me. "Did you know that?" She didn't wait for an answer. Instead, she kissed me again, harder this time. I reached up with one hand and touched her right breast, while my other hand followed the curvature of her body until it reached her inner thigh. Her body shuddered in pleasure, and I believed she might have an orgasm, but instead she rose and took my hand, pulling me from the sofa.

It was no dream.

I followed her to the bedroom, leaving a trail of discarded clothes. Her bedroom, like her body, was warm and feminine. The coverlet had already been neatly furled over, as if a maid had provided turn-down service.

We tumbled onto the bed and Annie kissed me over and over again, on my neck and chest and cheeks, then she came back to my lips, and all the while our hands explored each other's bodies. Her skin was remarkably soft and sensual for a woman I knew to be so athletically tough on the job, and her breasts were more delicate than I had imagined. I reciprocated each of her movements and kisses, and then gently, she climbed on and guided me into her. We moved together as one until we reached mutual satisfaction, then we lay in silence as we both drifted off to sleep, Annie first, and I, a few moments later.

Chapter Forty-One

When I awoke a little later that night, I looked at Annie's soft, beautiful face and thought about how much I cared for her, and how unexpected and wonderful this night had been. I did not regret what had happened—I had no remorse at all. Yes, I was still her boss, but some things are more important than political correctness. I told myself we'd just have to figure out how to deal with the situation in the best way possible, and try to keep our relationship under wraps until we did. And if she changed her mind about me and decided to sue me for sexual misconduct . . . well, it still would be worth it.

Her face told me that wasn't going to happen, though—at least not today. My left arm was trapped beneath her head, and I slowly slid it out from underneath her, stopping each time I thought she might awaken. Once free, I ducked into the bathroom and threw on my clothes, then went outside to move my car. When I returned, Annie was sitting on the sofa with a flannel blanket wrapped around her.

"I heard the car and I thought you were leaving," she said evenly. I couldn't read the tone in her voice, but it wasn't light.

"No, not hardly. That wouldn't have been very gentlemanly," I said, hoping to reassure her that I wasn't the type of boss who darts home moments after an orgasm. "I just thought I should move my car around back, away from prying eyes and patrolling officers."

"Good idea."

"Did you really mean what you said to me?" I asked.

"About what?"

"About wanting to kiss me the first time you saw me."

She seemed to relax a little. "Oh, that. I don't mean it was love at first sight or anything corny like that, but I did want to kiss you the first time we were introduced at the station. Maybe you looked like you needed it."

"Gee, thanks."

She smiled. "Well, it's the truth. But it was for my sake, too. What about you, what did you think the first time you saw me?"

"Honestly? I remember thinking how beautiful you were, but I didn't think about kissing you. I would have to say Bert Burr was the first officer I ever wanted to kiss."

We both laughed, then she chided me for always resorting to humor when the situation called for a serious moment. I told her I hadn't noticed that I did such things.

"Care for another cocktail?" she asked. "I noticed you like my sherry."

"Thanks," I answered. "I'll take a glass on the rocks. Sherry relaxes me, but it's not as strong as the vodka I usually drink when I'm really nervous or anxious."

"It's been quite a week, hasn't it?"

"It sure has. I moved up here to get away from serious crime and aggravation. I wouldn't have expected this kind of week in July, much less January."

"I hope I at least took your mind off things."

"You did more than that, believe me, Annie. And I think you know it."

I was going to broach the subject on how we would continue to work together now that we had slept together, then I decided against it. I wanted to keep on sleeping with Annie, and it would take a lot of effort to create any kind of even playing field. But I couldn't ask her to quit her job, and I couldn't exactly quit mine.

She leaned over and gave me a long, hard kiss that told me she didn't want to worry about police work and protocol either. I reached under the blanket and caressed her breast, then she snuggled next to me, continuing to kiss me as if she thought I might be about to leave for the night and she wanted to change my mind. For a moment we huddled together in silence. Then she asked me what I was thinking about.

I didn't want to tell her. "What do you think I'm thinking about?"

She sighed. "My guess would be Chandra Harper. Here I am, totally naked and right next to you, and you're thinking about a dead woman. You're going to give me a complex."

"I'm sorry," I said. The fact was, my mind had drifted back to Chandra Harper, and the long interview with Andrew Turkley. I decided to change the subject, and asked Annie about the visit to her mother.

She rolled her eyes. "Oh, that's sexy—ask about my mother." She gave me a brief description of her not-so-exciting evening, then inquired about my train travelogue.

"I missed the whole thing," I said. "I fell asleep after ten minutes."

Annie decided we should watch the tape now, so she pressed the "play" button on the remote control, and we viewed it together, occasionally kissing and fondling like two teenagers in the balcony of a movie theater. I hadn't realized how much trains and sex had in common before that night. Sure, I understood the sexual symbolism, but it had never resulted in quite the same reaction before. Annie was naked beside me, and all those locomotives were going back and forth on the TV screen, in and out of tunnels. Then they'd let off steam from their chimneys and have to stop for some water. Then the locomotive would build up more steam, and it was in and out of the tunnels again. The whole thing was making me crazy with lust and desire, and after about forty minutes of train documentary, we both had a full head of steam. I led Annie back to the bedroom and let her take another ride on my locomotive, even though she hadn't purchased a roundtrip ticket.

It was still dark when we awoke again, but the sun was trying to pierce the gray clouds of dawn. We dressed, and Annie put on a pot of coffee and asked if I wanted breakfast. I declined, stretched, then yawned.

"You know, I feel really refreshed," I said. "Even though we only took a few naps last night, those were the most restful hours I've had in a long time. I feel as though I could tackle the worst that the world could dish out today."

"That's great," Annie said, "but we never did finish that train tape."

"Aren't you even a little tired yet?"

"Not really. And I wanted to see that part about the Orient Express."

I had to get to work soon to take care of the business at hand, so I told Annie that we could watch the segment on European trains later that night. Suddenly I knew why Europeans were so fond of trains.

Annie asked me if I had ever seen the movie *Murder on the Orient Express*, and I said it had been a very long time. "It's a great movie, though."

"I think so too," she said. "Maybe we should watch it together, after we finish the documentary."

More trains, more fun, I thought. "Great idea. Do you have it in your collection?"

"No, but I'll stop at the movie store in Burlington before I come home, and see if I can pick it up. They have a good selection of old movies. I'll put it on my errand list so I won't forget."

Annie walked to her dining room and scribled on a notepad atop her buffet. Then she turned and headed toward her bathroom. "My shower is tiny," she called, "but you can soap my back if you want. Just give me a couple minutes first."

I heard the water start running in the shower. I am a nosy fool, so I walked over to the notepad and read the list. Under "To Do," she had jotted several errands and items she needed to pick up, including toothpaste and coffee. When I read the last entry, it was if Chandra Harper had sneaked up behind me and whacked me over the head with the truth.

Chapter Forty-Two

I've often wondered what passes through a person's mind in the moments before they "slip the surly bonds of earth." On his deathbed, Charles Foster Kane used his dying exhalation to utter his famous final word: Rosebud. It's the opening scene of Orson Welles's *Citizen Kane*, which many critics consider the greatest American film of all time. It takes the entire movie and a retrospective of the character's entire life to reveal the meaning of the word.

It had taken me even longer to discover the meaning of Chandra Harper's dying clue. Like Kane, she had made a final declaration. She just hadn't said it out loud.

In her last moments, Chandra Harper had reached out and placed her bloody fingers upon the cover of a book, pointing to two letters: O and X. They were in the title of her bedtime reading, *The Ox-Bow Incident*. Detective Roger Tyrrell had believed it was a coincidence—that her hand had simply fallen on the book by chance as she reached toward her cell phone to call for help.

But I didn't believe that. The inn's phone was within reach. And everything I knew about Chandra Harper told me she would've found a way to have the last word.

I had scoured the pages of *The Ox-Bow Incident* for clues, gaining no insight into the murder. Chandra had recommended the book to me on the night I first met her. But she and I had also played a silly trivia game, in which I had stated the name of many characters from many novels, and each time, she had named the corresponding title and author. Chandra was much better at it than I was—in fact, she had "total recall" in literary matters, especially names.

Unfortunately, none of that had meant anything to me—until Annie had written her to-do list. The last note jotted was a reminder to pick up the movie *Murder on the Orient Express*. Annie had written it in shorthand: Murder on the O X. Suddenly I knew. In my head, Chandra starting laughing with glee, then she chided me for taking so long to figure things out: "O X" was Orient Express. And the killer was Greta Olsen.

Admittedly, I had been just as certain about the guilt of Drew Turkley only a few hours earlier—and all the evidence still pointed in that direction. I also knew that Tyrrell would think I was crazy for putting so much stock in such a wild theory. But during my bar game with Chandra, she had revealed an extra bit of trivia: Greta—or a character with her name—had been one of the killers on the Orient Express. The character's last name was even the same; it simply had a different spelling.

Minutiae were piling up in my head like scraps of wood collected for a bonfire, then the match was struck and I saw the light. Greta Olsen, with the full knowledge and support of the feckless soon-to-be widower Hector Harper, had murdered her wealthy "best friend" Chandra. Hector was caught under Greta's powerful spell, and his newfound wealth would soon be Greta's.

From the moment I had first placed my eyes upon the temptress Greta Olsen, I couldn't get her out of my mind; I mused, dreamed, obsessed, and fantasized about her. And yet, after having spent half the night with her enjoying incredible sex, I inexplicably wanted to avoid her. It's true that many men are all about the chase, losing interest once the prize is won, but that wasn't my usual style. On some level, I simply knew that I should stay away from Greta—and it was not because of the small-town gossip, or the complications of dating within the peer group of a murder victim.

One by one, the details became clearer. Greta had been chasing me, not the other way around. She'd been mesmerizing me so I'd never suspect her guilt. She'd asked me to stay with her that first night and watch her sleep. But she wasn't sleeping—and had I paid closer attention, I would've noticed that. Women deny it, but just like men, they coo, snore, and make other strange noises in their sleep. Greta had made no such noises—not the first night, and not the next, after we'd had sex. She hadn't even breathed like a sleeping person. The morning after, she had emphasized how guilty she'd felt, because she'd been having sex with me at the same time "poor Chandra" was being murdered. But her account of the timeline wasn't accurate. I had left Greta's room at roughly three a.m., and the murder had taken place a short time later.

Other details came to mind—things that made more sense to me in hindsight. The next morning, Greta had also offered me a cup of coffee that she had retrieved from town, announcing she'd bought it for Chandra, leading me to believe she knew nothing about the murder. Her performance was brilliant, but the coffee was black—not diluted with "extra cream" and sweetened with those little brown packets of raw sugar, the way Chandra took her coffee.

I knew this new "evidence" against Greta was circumstantial and far from compelling, but there had to be physical evidence we could find—such as dirt on Greta's shoes, from the tunnel. I had no doubt she'd discovered the tunnels during her research and later used them to her advantage. The diary pages we'd retrieved from Drew Turkley might also reveal something about Greta's connection with Hector. Perhaps Turkley was right—and the evidence he'd stolen from Chandra's room did point to another killer besides himself. We just had to look more closely.

I strode into Annie's bathroom and pulled open the shower door and kissed my astonished and gorgeous assisting officer very hard on the lips. "Sorry, gotta go," I said, "but I'll definitely see you tonight."

As I headed out the door, I punched a speed-dial button on my cell phone and woke up Detective Tyrrell.

Chapter Forty-Three

Tyrrell groaned when I called, but it wasn't because I woke him. He was already wide awake.

"Let me get this straight," he said. "You want me to get a search warrant on Greta Olsen's room because she gave you some black coffee? The judge will laugh in my face, especially when we've got another guy in custody already—with the murder weapon in his possession, I might add. What if Greta Olsen just meant for the victim to add her own damned cream and sugar?"

Tyrrell also didn't seem impressed by my epiphany about the letters O and X and the Orient Express, even after I explained why I knew Chandra was leaving me a clue because Greta's name was among the roster of fictional characters. "Forget about this writer's group—you should be writing fiction yourself," he said. Then he sighed. "Okay, wait a minute. Let me think this through . . ."

As it turned out, Tyrrell was just giving me a hard time. He'd been up for hours, poring over the handwritten pages of Chandra's diary—and what she'd written had raised a lot of doubts in his own mind about the murder. Chandra hadn't been suspicious of Greta Olsen or her husband, "but maybe she should've been," Tyrrell explained. "According to the diary, Chandra Harper was worth at least five million and some change, and she told Greta all about it. She also told Greta she was planning to change her will and give half of it to the Society for the Prevention of Cruelty to Animals, because PETA wouldn't have approved of her chinchilla coat."

As for Hector, Chandra was even thinking about cutting him loose financially. "And what do you know?" Tyrrell continued. "It was Greta who convinced Chandra to rethink her plan and hold off on changing the will." And shortly after that, Greta and Chandra had started sleeping together, just for fun.

"I tell you," Tyrrell said, "that diary made me blush, and I never blush. Chandra Harper slept with just about anything that moved. There's even a little note in there about you, Chief, right at the end, but apparently you were too busy to play with her."

It wasn't difficult for me to convince Tyrrell that Greta had also seduced Hector Harper—and persuaded him to go along with her plan to murder Chandra. After all, I had firsthand experience with Greta's considerable talents of persuasion—and I didn't have a multimillion-dollar signing bonus like Hector.

"When I interviewed John Ratz," I said, "he called Greta a Svengali. I think he was pretty close to the mark."

Tyrrell flipped through his notes as we talked, pointing out the pieces that fit this new theory. "We ran the phone records. There's a call from Hector Harper's Chicago apartment to his wife's cell phone at five a.m. on the day of the murder—unanswered, no message from Hector. We thought it supported his alibi and helped rule him out, but that was probably the whole point of the call. Hector never expected Chandra to answer."

"Either that, or he got nervous and he was checking to see if she was really dead," I said.

I could hear the countdown clock ticking inside my head. Greta and the other writers were set to check out of the French Country Inn in less than five hours. We needed stronger evidence against Greta—something that put her at the scene at the time of the murder. Unfortunately, there was so much stacked against Turkley now that she could use him as a viable defense. "It's not me—the other guy did it," she'd say. The icing on the cake: "The chief of police is just screwing me over . . . again."

Detective Tyrrell and I quickly worked out a strategy. Greta's prints were no doubt among those found in Chandra's room, but that wasn't conclusive on its own—they were friends and lovers. I'd seen Greta come out of room 303 myself, which, in retrospect, was probably by design. We needed to get a judge to issue an immediate search warrant on Greta's suite, her car, and all her personal belongings, so we could check them for traces of blood and dirt from the tunnel. We also needed to search Hector's room and his car. It wasn't going to be easy to convince the judge to act quickly on what we had, but Tyrrell thought he could swing it.

I suggested we ask Greta to come in for questioning just before the search took place. "We'll tell her we've got our guy, Chef Turkley, but we need her help to make the case. I think she'll buy it—after all, she's the one who set up Turkley. Once she's in custody, she'll be easier to handle. Otherwise, there's no predicting what she'll do."

We also intended to bring Hector in for questioning right away, and isolate the two suspects. From what I'd seen, Hector Harper would be very forthcoming if we gave him a choice between hard time in prison and ratting on Greta.

And so began Greta Olsen's downfall . . .

She must have thought she had the perfect alibi: "Why, it could not possibly have been me. At the time of the murder, I was sleeping with the chief of police."

It made me feel cheap, but it didn't clear her. She'd had plenty of time to sneak through the tunnels, steal the knife, kill her friend, then sneak back out again. But she hadn't had time to steal Chandra's diary, or she hadn't thought of it. It was probably her biggest mistake—besides trusting Hector Harper to keep his mouth shut.

After ten minutes of questioning at the stationhouse, Hector folded like a nervous poker player in a high-stakes card game. He told us the entire scheme. Greta had been the brains, of course, concocting a murder plot worthy of an Agatha Christie novel. And she had found the perfect fall guy in Drew Turkley. Even if the chef hadn't killed Cassandra Collins all those years ago, he had a strong motive to kill her sister Chandra. All Greta had to do was nudge us in his direction and the chef would look guilty. Then Turkley made himself look even guiltier by stealing the murder weapon. Greta must've been thrilled by that little development.

As soon as we were armed with Hector's confession, we moved in on Greta. Currently, she was growing agitated in an interview room, unappeased by her second cup of coffee. I put my hand on the handle, breathed deep, and prepared to go into battle.

I was glad Annie wasn't watching through the one-way glass, hearing what Greta had to say about me and our "relationship." What were the odds? I thought. I hadn't slept with a woman for more months than I could count, then in a span of five days, lightning had struck twice. Annie would hear every lurid detail about my liaison with Greta eventually, but she didn't need to hear it directly from the other woman's lips.

Tyrrell had agreed that I should do the initial interview, taking advantage of whatever edge I might have with Greta Olsen. Officer Burr accompanied me into the room.

Greta sat at the table with her usual air of sophistication. She was dressed impeccably in gray wool pants and a matching sweater, which gave her a businesslike appearance. She asked me to explain what was going on. "I've been waiting here for almost an hour," she complained. "I thought you needed my help with Andrew Turkley. You said you just needed to tie up a few loose ends."

Unfortunately Officer Burr was so excited that he couldn't contain himself. Before I could speak, he started to read Greta her Miranda rights. He probably imagined he was a New York cop making the arrest of a high-level Mafia boss.

Greta's eyes opened wide. "Chief, is this a joke?" She was pretty good at playing the "shocked and innocent" role.

"It's no joke, Greta," I said. "You are under arrest for the murder of Chandra Harper. Officer Burr here just happened to jump the gun a little."

Greta asked if she and I could speak alone, and I agreed. I told Bert to wait outside, knowing full well he'd take up a position on the other side of the one-way glass with Detective Tyrrell.

Greta must've sensed they were watching, too. She leaned in so close I could feel her warm breath, and she gave me a little smile, but I could see the fear in her eyes. "You can't be serious," she whispered. "This must be some kind of ploy, some terrible mistake. What's going on here, Chief?"

"Give it up, Greta," I said loudly. "Hector told us everything. The whole plan, how you were going to stick Chef Turkley with the murder, your plan to share the inheritance with Hector . . . everything. Except maybe your plan after that. How did that part go, Greta? You'd marry Hector, then one day soon, he'd have a little accident? So much for Hector being gay, by the way."

Greta showed no emotion except to bite her lower lip. "You cannot be serious. You have Alden Torrence in custody—or Andrew Turkley. Whatever his real name is, he killed Chandra. How could you possibly accuse me of killing my own dear friend? I was with you when Chandra died, you know that."

She reached across the table to put her hand on mine, but I avoided her touch.

"Stop it, Greta. We have all the proof we need." It was a little white lie—we were still waiting on the forensics from the room search, but I had no doubt it would support Hector's account and my own gut instincts.

There was total silence, then tears welled in Greta's eyes, and she started again. "Please, Chief. Don't even imagine that I could do something so terrible. It's not true. Hector is lying. I don't know how he's involved in the murder—maybe he put Andrew Turkley up to it. Did you ever think of that? You know me, you know you do, and you know I was with you that night. It hurts me that you could even think about me in this way . . . when I care so much about you."

I could hear Bogie's voice in my head: She was good, real good.

I thought Greta's next move would be to play the trump card, telling me it had been an incredible night filled with incredible sex and I was the greatest lover she had ever experienced. She might even have expected me to say it was all right if she had killed Chandra—the sex between us was so hot, I'd look the other way, as if murder were a parking violation.

"What about us, our future?" Greta pleaded.

"Your future is twenty years to life," I said. "But don't worry, babe. I'll remain celibate until you get out."

I couldn't help myself. I'm the king of inappropriate comments. Unfortunately, those comments often elicit bad behavior from the person on the receiving end of the barb. Greta acted accordingly. She flew at me like a hawk in a death-battle, talons flaying and scratching while she called me every name in her extensive vocabulary. If I had harbored any glimmer of doubt about her true nature, it was now gone.

Bert exploded through the door, coming to my rescue with his gun drawn as if he were arriving late to the OK Corral. I was afraid he might fire a warning shot into the ceiling and hit someone in the room overhead. We didn't need the paperwork.

Luckily, Bert holstered his side arm and managed to subdue Greta without any gunfire or bloodshed. He read her the Miranda rights a second time as he put on the cuffs. Instead of remaining silent, Greta screeched and swore up a blue streak as Bert led her down the hall to a cell.

"And 'she was dancing with an air of a depraved virgin,' " I said, to no one in particular. That's how an art critic had described Jean

Avril, a Moulin Rouge performer featured in a painting by Toulouse Lautrec. I'd watched a documentary on Lautrec at Christmastime, and the words were stuck in my head. I wasn't sure why Greta's behavior had brought the phrase to my lips. Greta Olsen was depraved, but she was definitely no virgin. And when it came to sex or murder, she was far from innocent.

Chapter Forty-Four

Once again, Duke Tedeski had been right: It was all about the money. Chandra had it, Greta wanted it, and Hector Harper was caught right in the middle. I felt a little sympathy for Hector—he was a dupe in Greta's plan. The hapless husband didn't even realize exactly how much money his dead wife was worth. He'd gone along with Greta's scheme, all the while believing he'd wind up with a million or so and get the girl of his dreams. He was oblivious to Greta's manipulative powers until we helped him see the light.

The district attorney had offered Hector a reduced sentence to secure his testimony against Greta. Other evidence mounted fast. As we'd expected, the county forensics team discovered traces of Chandra's blood on Greta's clothing. There was also dirt from "the Sewer" on Greta's shoes, with more of the same in Greta's room at the inn and at the crime scene.

We also found more damning prose on Chandra's laptop computer. She'd kept better records than a CPA with an IRS agent peering over his shoulder. It was all there: personal letters, daily planners, notes about who was sleeping with whom . . . and in this case, everyone was sleeping with everybody else: Chandra with the professor, the professor with his assistant, the assistant with John Ratz, and Ratz with Chandra. I had a strong suspicion that Alexandra Hale was not polishing her manuscript on the night of the murder—instead, she was polishing Ratz's knob. Being married, Hale simply hadn't wanted to say so. Evidently Chandra had missed that affair—it wasn't in her notes.

I had to wonder how these people ever found time to actually write. Only the Godfather fan and the two gay men sharing a suite seemed halfway normal to me. But those other liaisons were for enjoyment's sake. Greta had slept with Chandra—and Hector, and then me—all for the love of money.

Slowly but surely, all the remaining details of Greta's nefarious plot became clear. She began planning the murder the previous summer, during a visit to the inn—after she'd caught of glimpse of Andrew Turkley. He looked familiar because Chandra had shown her a photo of Cassandra's fiancé. A little sleuthing had confirmed Greta's speculation: Drew Turkley was indeed Alden Torrence. Researching the inn's history had provided a perfect cover; it allowed Greta to snoop around the buildings and discover the old tunnels. Greta was the driving force behind the murder plot, but Hector still went along for the ride. I must admit, the man cut quite a dashing figure when we arrested him in his powder-blue blazer and gold ascot.

* * *

A few days after the arrests, I walked into Kirsch's bar at the French Country Inn. I was a happy man. Everything was back to normal—the bar, like my township, was nice and quiet, just the way I liked it. A young couple was seated at a table near the fireplace, sipping cocktails and whispering in each other's ears. Otherwise the place was empty. I had considered going to Muddy's, but Gus's patter about the "crime spree" was already getting old.

I ordered a vodka rocks from Roy and rubbed the copper surface of the bar for good luck. I was hoping it would be a long time before I experienced another week like the one I'd just had. At least one good thing had come out of it: after fantasizing about a dalliance with Annie Madden for years, it had finally happened. That was a very good thing, in fact.

Moreover, I didn't have to worry about workplace complications arising from our relationship. Shortly before she seduced me, Annie had applied for a new job—and naturally, she got it. She had been offered a position as the assistant chief of police for the City of Burlington. The only formality left was their complete review of her references. I told her I'd give her a "well qualified" rating, provided she would sleep with me again. She agreed to my proposal.

Familiar chatter at the bar disturbed my thoughts. Kirsch and Frankel had arrived, swaggering into the room in their usual insouciant manner. They waved at me and complained how badly they needed a drink.

I laughed; they needed a drink about as much as Hugh Hefner needed a cottontail.

"Anyone get killed today?" Kirsch asked.

Before I could muster a comeback, Frankel settled onto his favorite barstool and replied, "No-sirree, not on the Chief's watch."

"Aren't you guys a little old to be carrying on this way?" I said.

"We may be old," answered Kirsch, "but we're immature."

Upon hearing that pearl of wisdom, I decided to steer the subject away from liquor and age. I apologized to Kirsch for having caused the arrest of his chef. At that moment, Alden Torrence, a.k.a. Andrew Turkley, was still in custody and facing a long list of charges, from trespassing and breaking-and-entering to theft, obstruction of justice, and tampering with a crime scene.

"I realize the lack of a chef must put you in a bind," I said.

"Nah, don't worry about it," Kirsch replied. "I was going to fire the bastard anyway. I don't mind a chef who drinks my liquor—I just can't stand one who only drinks my premium liquor. You saved me the expense of a severance check."

"Glad I could help."

"Besides," Kirsch continued, "I've already hired a replacement.

We're going to close for a month, and then we'll have a grand reopening with the new head chef. I'm bringing back de Bullion."

I knew de Bullion—and his cooking. Dante de Bullion was Kirsch's former head chef and ex-partner. He was also the only chef I liked. During de Bullion's tenure, the cuisine had been its best, and Kirsch's restaurant had enjoyed its greatest popularity—it was the place everyone wanted to be seen. The Chicago Tribune had raved, "When visiting the Geneva Lakes area, if you have time for just one meal, make sure you eat it at Kirsch's."

Unfortunately for Kirsch, de Bullion had big dreams outside the kitchen. He'd left Wisconsin to pursue his lifelong ambition of playing professional baseball for the Chicago Cubs. He gave it a year, but he never even made it to Double-A ball. It seems de Bullion was more talented with a spatula than he was with a bat.

I finished my drink and decided to head home. I had a big day planned for tomorrow: paperwork, a few errands, and a long-overdue visit to an old friend.

Epilogue

At the foot of a large hill at the edge of town, a giant oak tree stands bent and gnarled, guarding the gate of Oak Hill Cemetery. I come here often, and during all four seasons. In spring, lilacs fill the air with a fragrance that transports me back to my childhood in Chicago. Summertime brings the smell of fresh-cut grass and the memory of carefree nights, long and hot. The cemetery is filled with towering oaks, but also elms and maples and birch trees, and in fall, the sunlight varnishes their turning leaves and they become a portrait painted by God. But it's winter I love best, when the landscape is hushed, and a shroud of snow blankets the graves.

This sacred place, a mile north of Geneva Lake, holds many of the town's early men of prominence. Several are linked to Chicago's history, but for the most part, no one here is famous. Hobart Hermansen's grave lies next to the plot of his wife, Lucille Moran Hermansen, and a son named John. A few hundred yards to the east is the modest headstone of the son of Heavy Mullins. A tiny American flag rests atop his gravesite.

Near the crest of the hill, a weeping willow inexplicably holds a faint tinge of green even in winter. Beneath it lies the grave of my huckleberry friend, David Tedeski. A man as decent as Dave should not have died so early in life. His death robbed his family of a husband and father, and me of a dear friend. For me, Tedeski was someone who made the world a little easier to tolerate. There are many good ways to live, but no good way to die, and stomach cancer, with its gruesome wasting away of the body, is among the worst. During his protracted ordeal, Dave never complained, and he never lashed out; he simply accepted his fate as the will of God.

I head to Oak Hill whenever I need to talk to Dave or simply want to reminisce. Sometimes he even answers my questions—not directly, of course. But in the days after a visit, an answer will often come to me suddenly, and then I'll smile, because I know that Dave has helped me out with a problem.

This was the week following Chandra Harper's murder, and I made a long-overdue trip to the cemetery. As I cleared the snow off Dave's headstone, I knew I wouldn't be asking him for advice, though I undoubtedly needed it. Nor would I ask him to tell me the future—I prefer some things to remain a mystery. With the help of God and Dave Tedeski, I had solved my first murder case, but it had left me with many questions. For one thing, how had I allowed myself to be so mesmerized by Greta Olsen? And what was lacking in me, or in my life, that had made me so blind to her schemes? I sincerely hoped that Annie Madden would help to fill that void, but if Annie didn't stay in the picture, then perhaps . . . someday . . . another love would come along. I didn't ask Dave about any of this, because I didn't want to know the answers.

Instead, I simply thanked him for helping me yet again and apologized for not stopping by earlier. I also confessed the obvious—that I was still just as bad with women as I had always been—and I encouraged him to throw some luck my way whenever he could. And then I said goodbye, and, as always, I promised I'd come back soon.

As I walked down the hill from the gravesite, I recalled a poem that I had memorized for my sophomore English class at Saint Malachy Academy. It was a verse about Buffalo Bill Cody by E.E. Cummings. My teacher, Father Macklin, had liked my selection, but not the author's lack of capitalization or punctuation. The poem read:

Buffalo Bill's
defunct
        who used to
        ride a watersmooth-silver
                                        stallion
and break onetwothreefourfive pigeonsjustlikethat
                                                                Jesus
he was a handsome man
                                and what i want to know is
how do you like your blueeyed boy
Mister Death

—E.E. Cummings

I wasn't entirely sure how Cummings felt about Buffalo Bill, but I knew how I felt about Dave Tedeski. "How do you like your blue-eyed boy, Mister Death?" I asked. "Because you know, we miss him here."

Then I passed through the cemetery's iron gates and headed home, where Dawg and Annie were waiting.

Appendix

– Historical Notes –

All gangster photos from FBI.gov

Vintage hotel photos courtesy of Allen Hermansen, grandson of Christian Hermansen.

View of Lake Como Hotel, circa 1934

The Glorious and Notorious History of the French Country Inn

The historic French Country Inn is an actual place, located just outside the resort town of Lake Geneva in southeastern Wisconsin. Tucked on the quiet shore of Lake Como, the inn has the flavor of a secluded hideaway, a quality that has attracted many guests through the years, including gangsters.

In the early 1900s, the property was a hunting-and-fishing resort. An ice-storage business was also located on the property at one time. (Ice cut from the lake was used for refrigeration.) Early owners included C.N. Smith and the Notter family. In 1921, the Notters sold the property to Christian ("Christ") Hermansen, a Danish carpenter and businessman with three sons: Hobart, Inar, and Harry.

The Hermansen family's acquisition of the Como property began a legendary period of hotel ownership and management that spanned 50 years and three generations. Under the Hermansens, the resort now called the French Country Inn was the "Lake Como Hotel." In the 1930s, the Hermansens also purchased the Lake Geneva Hotel, a Frank Lloyd Wright masterpiece in downtown Lake Geneva. (Regrettably, Wright's design was razed in 1971. It was replaced by a mid-rise condominium with cement walls, dubbed "the seven-story basement" by its detractors.)

The most interesting of the Hermansen brothers was Hobart, who managed the Como resort. During the gangster era, he was on friendly terms with Baby Face Nelson and Dillinger gang-members Tommy Carroll and John Paul Chase. Hermansen also befriended Jimmy Murray, a bootlegger who, during Prohibition, supplied the Lake Como Hotel with beer from his New Glarus brewery. All these characters vacationed or "holed up" at the Como resort during the 1920s and '30s. Hobart was known for his gambling operations; he eventually earned the nickname "the Slot Machine King of Walworth County." During Prohibition, he ran a speakeasy and gambling den called "The Sewer" in the basement of the Lake Como Hotel.

Hobart's strongest "gangster connection" links him to George Moran—as well as to Moran's wife, Lucille. George "Bugs" Moran was Al Capone's rival in Chicago, and the intended target of the St. Valentine's Day Massacre. Mr. and Mrs. Moran were both frequent guests at the Como resort and at Hobart Hermansen's private home (a short stroll down the shore). The trio remained friends even after the Morans divorced following the St. Valentine's Massacre—and after Hobart married Lucille Moran in 1932.

A skilled poker player, Lucille, born Lucille Bilezikdijan, was a native of Turkey. She left her home in Constantinople for France, then moved to America with her young son, Louis Logan. With Lucille's marriage to Bugs, "Louis" was renamed John Moran. He became the stepson of Bugs—and later, the stepson of Hobart Hermansen. Hobart and John were also boss and employee. In fact, John Moran worked in various positions at all three of Hobart's properties: the Lake Como Hotel, the Lake Geneva Hotel, and the Atlantic Ocean House in Boca Raton, Florida.

In July of 1959, John Moran was found dead in a room at the Lake Geneva Hotel. The official cause of death was coronary thrombosis. Some claimed it was actually foul play. Today, it's said the ghost of John Moran still wanders the grounds and halls of the French Country Inn (his "favorite haunt"). The current owner of the inn, Anthony Navilio, says he never leaves his office or suite without a master key—because often when he exits a room, "John's ghost" playfully closes and locks the door behind him.

Hobart Hermansen, along with his brothers and a nephew, Allen Hermansen, managed the Lake Como Hotel until 1971, when it was sold to Fay and Gene Liechtey. The Liechteys named it The Red Chimney Inn, and ran the property for several years. The Sal Argento Family owned and operated the resort after that, returning the property to its old name, the Lake Como Hotel.

In the early 1980s, the resort was closed. It lay fallow until 1986, when it was purchased by Anthony Navilio and his wife, Kathleen Durnin Navilio. Inspired by European inns they had visited and admired, they renovated and resurrected the Como property as a boutique hotel, which they named the French Country Inn.

Navilio carefully preserved the inn's best original features. Two of his favorite elements are the lobby's oak staircase and exotic inlaid floor. The elaborate woodwork, and perhaps other portions of the inn, were originally on display at the Danish Pavilion during the 1893 Chicago World's Fair. Like several other structures from the fair, the Danish Pavilion was dismantled and sold, and eventually relocated to the Lake Geneva area.

A coaster and matchbook from the Hermansens' Lake Como Hotel, 1940s. The family also owned the Atlantic Ocean House in Boca Raton, FL.

The French Country Inn began as a hunting and fishing resort. These postcards above show early 1900s views. The train to Como Station and Williams Bay ran right past the inn, with regular service to Chicago.

The Notters ran the inn as the Lake Como Hotel. This view is circa 1920. Automobiles would soon replace the train as preferred transportation.

Another early view, circa 1920.

A 1940s postcard. The lake is to the left. A pretty side garden is to the right.

The lakeside "Annex," circa 1940.

The "Bungalow" was once a favorite gangster retreat. This view is circa 1940.

A shoreline cottage called the "Doll House" was also favored by gangsters and their molls, as well as other romantic couples seeking privacy. Circa 1940.

Vintage postcard circa 1940s: Pretty Garden at Hermansen's Lake Como Hotel, Lake Geneva, Wis.

White linens and grand views greeted guests at the dining hall, circa 1940.

Boating was a popular pastime at the Lake Como Hotel. The charming playhouse in this 1940s view still exists, though it has been relocated.

The 150-long sun pier and beach, circa 1940.

HISTORY OF THE DANISH PAVILION and The French Country Inn

Over the years, it has been repeated that the Lake Como Hotel, now known as the French Country Inn, has an architectural link to the 1893 Chicago World's Fair (officially the "World's Columbian Exposition"). The fair celebrated the 400-year anniversary of Columbus's discovery of the New World. One of the exhibits was the Danish Pavilion, celebrating Danish craftsmanship and fine woodwork. At least part of the Danes' exhibit eventually made its way to Wisconsin after the fair, to be reassembled at the Lake Como Hotel. The most obvious evidence appears in the lobby of the main building, which features an extraordinary oak staircase and an elaborate inlaid wood floor.

According to the current owner, Anthony Navilio, some armchair historians have said this "Danish Connection" cannot be true for two reasons: first, because there's supposedly no record of a Danish Pavilion at the fair, and second, because it was impossible to dismantle a building and ship it from Chicago to Wisconsin. Neither argument is correct.

Historical photographs of two Danish structures appear in *The Book of the Fair* by Hubert Howe Bancroft, Bancroft Company Publishers, 1893. (The entire book can be seen online at the Digital History Collection of the Paul V. Galvin Library, Illinois Institute of Technology.) The smaller structure has the name Denmark proudly displayed; the photo is captioned "The Danish Pavilion." The larger structure bears the Danish flag, the *Dannebrog*, which is red with a white cross. The vertical piece of the cross is shifted slightly toward the hoist side.

The pavilion is also mentioned in the 2003 bestselling book *The Devil in the White City* by Erik Larson. According to Larson, the Danish Pavilion was located in the Manufacturers and Liberal Arts Building, part of which was destroyed in a fire shortly before the opening of the World's Fair. The Danish and French pavilions, Larson writes, were undamaged by the fire.

For those who doubt that a large or elaborate structure could be transported by train to the Geneva Lake area from Chicago, one needs only to visit the Yerkes Observatory in Williams Bay, Wisconsin. Yerkes houses the largest refractor telescope ever built. The almost 20-ton gargantuan was first displayed in 1893 at the Columbian Exposition. After the fair, when the observatory building was completed, the telescope was transported to the shores of Geneva Lake. A special Chicago and Northwestern Railway train delivered the lens to the Williams Bay Railway Station (which was located on the current site of two restaurants, Café Calamari and Harpoon Willies).

The telescope and the French Country Inn are not the only exhibits from the fair that were relocated to this area. Ceylon Court, an exotic estate on Geneva Lake, provides another example. According to a July 10, 1904, article in the *New York Times*: "On Lake Geneva there is a unique cottage, formerly the Ceylon Building at the World's Fair held in Chicago. It was built by the Ceylon Government and was afterwards owned by Frank R. Chandler of Chicago."

The "cottage" resembled a Singhalese temple at the heart of Chandler's elaborate estate. It rested on a 40-foot bluff until its demolition in 1958. The exhibit for the fair was originally erected in Jackson Park by Singhalese craftsmen, who were brought from Ceylon to Chicago, along with 300 tons of native materials. After the fair, the estate's owner, Mr. Chandler, had the structure disassembled, transported by railroad from Chicago in 21 flatcars, and then reassembled on the shoreline of Geneva Lake.

Chandler's endeavor was a bit of an architectural folly, but in the case of the French Country Inn, the connection appears more personal. Christian Hermansen, one of the inn's early owners, was a Danish-born carpenter who worked in Chicago during the fair—and according to Douglas Steiner of the Steiner Agency (www.steinerag.com), Hermansen "most likely worked on the Danish Exhibition." Years later, Hermansen obtained part of the treasured Danish exhibit and moved it to Lake Como. A major rail delivery to the French Country Inn would have been even easier than delivery to

Chandler's estate, Navilio points out. Old postcards and photos from the inn's early days show its proximity to the Chicago and Northwestern Railway—the tracks ran directly alongside the resort.

The Danish Pavilion at the Columbian Exposition, 1893. Photos from Paul V. Galvin Library.

GEORGE "BUGS" MORAN
Born Adelard Cunin • Aug. 21, 1891 – Feb. 25, 1957

No other Roaring Twenties mobster was more of a nemesis to Al Capone than George "Bugs Moran, leader of the Chicago's North Side gang. In 1927, Moran attempted to murder south-side Chieftain Johnny Torrio—in retaliation for the assassination of Moran's former North Side boss, Dion O'Banion. Moran's hit failed, but it was the catalyst that elevated Scarface Capone to leadership of the South Side Gang. With O'Banion dead and Torrio wounded, civil war raged between the rival gangs.

After years of bloody strife, Capone attempted to deliver a final blow to Moran and his gang in an assault that became known as "The St. Valentine's Day Massacre" (perhaps the most notorious event in gangster warfare). On February 14, 1929, seven members of the Bugs Moran Gang were murdered at the SMC Cartage Company garage by Capone assassins dressed as Chicago police officers. The garage was located at 2122 North Clark Street (in Chicago's Lincoln Park neighborhood). Luckily for Moran, Capone's hitmen mistook another man at the scene for Moran—and Moran, late to arrive, was not among the dead or wounded.

Moran was never the same after the massacre. His gang was decimated, his power diminished, and his money was running low. Fearful for his safety, he was constantly moving from place to place, safe house to safe house, until he became irrelevant to the gangs in Chicago. His wife, Lucille, had to hide out as well. In 1930, the couple divorced. Moran's life continued to spiral downward. He jumped from counterfeiting to rum running to union racketeering and finally, in the 1940s, to bank robbery.

In 1956, after having served 10 years for a payroll robbery, Moran was paroled from the Ohio State Penitentiary. But freedom would be fleeting. As he left the penitentiary gate, he was arrested by federal marshals. Within two months, Moran was tried, convicted, and sentenced to five years in Leavenworth Federal Penitentiary for his part in a bank robbery that had been committed 11 years earlier.

Shortly after his arrival at Leavenworth, on February 25, 1957, George Bugs Moran—former big-time Chicago bootlegger, enemy of Al Capone, survivor of the St Valentine's Day Massacre—died of lung cancer. He was 65 years old.

Mr. Hermansen, owner of Lake Como Hotel.

Bugs Moran (Al Capone's arch enemy) and Lucille Hermansen, wife of Hobart Hermansen and ex-wife of Moran.

"BUGS", LUCILLE & HOBART
the Lake Como Connection

The gangster George "Bugs" Moran and his wife, Lucille, enjoyed the beauty and solitude of southeastern Wisconsin, and they intended to build a home near Lake Geneva or Lake Como. They were scoping properties in the area in the late 1920s when they met hotelier and restaurateur Hobart Hermansen, owner of the Lake Como Hotel (now the French Country Inn). According to Rose Keefe, author of the book *The Man Who Got Away*, Hermansen had "plenty of experience handling visiting gangsters. Al Capone had been a guest at the Lake Como property." However, few outlaws enjoyed more friendly hospitality and frequent visits than Bugs Moran and his wife Lucille.

The current owner of the inn, Anthony Navilio, has heard stories about Moran at the lake firsthand. He says a neighbor and longtime Como homeowner, the late Lou Heubner, recalled seeing Bugs Moran many times while the gangster vacationed at Lake Como. "Lou told me Moran always walked with a passel of bodyguards surrounding him," Navilio says. The property became a favorite spot for the entire Moran family, which included young John, Lucille's son from a previous marriage.

As Capone's enemy, Moran was the intended target of the infamous St. Valentine's Day Massacre, which claimed seven lives in 1929. Authors William J. Helmer and Arthur Bilek also describe the Moran-Hermansen connection. In their book *The St. Valentine's Day Massacre*, they write: "Moran remained out of sight and out of range for better than a year" after the massacre took place. And much of that time, they were "in southern Wisconsin on Lake Como."

After the massacre, the pressures of gangster life became too tiresome (or dangerous) for Lucille and John. In late 1930, Lucille and Bugs divorced. With John in tow, Lucille returned to the peace and quiet of the Lake Como Hotel. Lucille began to work for Hobart Hermansen as co-manager of the hotel. No doubt her ties to the Chicago syndicate helped draw clients looking for illicit activities.

On the premises were slot machines, high-stakes poker games, and free-flowing liquor at the speakeasy named The Sewer. Rumor has it that on one occasion, Hermansen was tipped off that federal agents were on their way to raid the hotel. As a precaution, he dumped all of his slot machines off the end of his 100-foot-long pier into Lake Como. (The illegal gambling continued into the 1940s, and it's unclear when the alleged raid occurred.)

After the Morans divorced, Bugs Moran continued to visit his ex-wife and his friend Hobart at Lake Como. The trio remained on good terms even after Hobart and Lucille married in 1932. According to author Rose Keefe, Moran remained an attentive father to his stepson, John. Keefe writes that Moran's help "was particularly welcome" after Lucille found some risqué "French postcards" tucked in John's schoolbag. Evidently, Lucille called Bugs and asked him to give John a little father-son chat at Lake Como.

"Moran and John spent an hour by the lake," Keefe writes, "having the 'talk' that all parents and teenagers anticipate with unease."

Compared to several of his gangster peers, Moran lived a long life. He died of lung cancer in Leavenworth prison on February 25, 1957. Lucille Moran Hermansen preceded him in death; she passed away in 1946. Her husband, Hobart Hermansen, died on February 25, 1984. Hermansen was buried in Lake Geneva's Oak Hill Cemetery, alongside Lucille and stepson John.

Hobart Hermansen, his wife (the ex Mrs. Moran), and stepson John were laid to rest in Lake Geneva's Oak Hill Cemetery.

GEORGE "BABY FACE" NELSON
Born Lester M. Gillis • Dec. 6, 1908 – Nov. 27, 1934

On July 22, 1934, federal agents gunned down John Dillinger outside Chicago's Biograph Theater. Afterward, FBI Director J. Edgar Hoover designated Baby Face Nelson "Public Enemy Number One." Federal agents had begun methodically eliminating every member of the Dillinger gang during the spring and summer of that year. Finally, only Baby Face Nelson and John Paul Chase remained. Nelson was considered by many to be a psychotic killer, responsible for killing more federal agents than any other gangster. Even John Dillinger had been appalled by the violence Nelson seemed to relish.

Like many gangsters, Nelson changed his name for "professional reasons." He was born Lester Gillis on December 6, 1908, in the shadows of the Chicago stockyard. The seventh child of Mary and Joseph Gillis, he was a frail boy, but his career in crime started early. In 1922, at the age of 14, Lester was arrested for grand theft auto and sentenced to a stretch in a boys' reformatory school.

Gillis stood just 5 feet 5 inches tall, but he wanted to be known as a tough guy, so he gave himself the name "Big George" Nelson. His fellow street toughs called him "Baby Face" instead. The moniker stuck, even after he joined Al Capone's gang and became an enforcer. After a short time, Nelson was dismissed from Capone's gang for excessive violence. Capone was unhappy because Nelson had killed the people he was sent to scare into paying protection money.

While still in his early 20s, Nelson was convicted of armed robbery. Enroute to the penitentiary, he escaped and fled west. In California, Nelson met bootlegger and smuggler John Paul Chase, who would become a lifelong friend and partner in crime.

Nelson and Dillinger merged their gangs in 1934. Although Baby Face Nelson never eclipsed Dillinger's fame, Baby Face did gain notoriety—especially after the infamous shootout at the Little Bohemia Lodge in northern Wisconsin in April of that same year. The combined gang was holed up in the isolated lodge when they were besieged by federal agents intending to eradicate the lawless bunch. Bedlam broke out as the gangsters ran from the battle in a hail of gunfire. Agents mistakenly shot bystanders. Nelson escaped out the back (like his companions), then stole a car, but was soon spotted. In the subsequent battle, he wounded two lawmen and killed Special Agent W. Carter Baum. Nelson escaped after commandeering the agents' vehicle.

Dillinger and Nelson were a hot commodity in '34, sought by local and federal authorities with their faces splashed on the cover of every newspaper and magazine. To escape pursuit, Dillinger tried to erase his fingerprints with acid; he also changed his face through plastic surgery. Meanwhile, Nelson hid out, mostly in southern Wisconsin at the Lake Como Hotel (now the French Country Inn).

Nelson and his young wife, Helen Gillis, intended to remain isolated on the shores of Lake Como for the winter—along with cohort John Paul Chase. Betrayed by Chase's girlfriend, Sally Bachman, Nelson and company drove directly into the jaws of an FBI trap. As luck would have it, Nelson managed to escape from the inn unharmed—but his luck was fleeting. As he sped back to Illinois, he encountered additional special agents. The daring chase and bloody gunfight, known as the Battle of Barrington, ended with demise of the 25-year-old "Public Enemy Number One."

Tommy Carroll

John Dillinger

Baby Face Nelson

John Paul Chase

THE JOHN DILLINGER GANG at the Lake Como Hotel

With his rugged features and matinee idol face, John Dillinger was more famous than most Hollywood movie stars. In the 1920s and 1930s the American public, suffering from the effects of the Great Depression, was searching for a hero. They found him in the likes of the notorious John Dillinger.

Bank robber, gangster, and murderer to the FBI, Dillinger was a Robin Hood and superstar to the masses. At the time of his death outside Chicago's Biograph Theatre in 1934, his notoriety had reached almost mythic proportion.

According to Rose Keefe, author of *The Man Who Got Away: The Bugs Moran Story,* the Lake Como Hotel was the "hideout of choice for Baby Face Nelson, John Dillinger, and Roger Touhy" and "Al Capone had been a guest." Little is known of Dillinger's and Capone's visits to Lake Como, but not so for fellow Dillinger gang members Baby Face Nelson, Tommy Carroll, and John Paul Chase.

The week of June 1, 1934, was an eventful time for The Lake Como Hotel (currently known as the French Country Inn.) It was on June 1 that Baby Face Nelson, his wife Helen Gillis, Tommy Carroll, his moll Jean Delaney Crompton, and Nelson's henchman, John Paul Chase, all arrived for a leisurely stay at the Lake Como property. According to their book, *Baby Face Nelson: Portrait of a Public Enemy*, authors Steven Nickel and William J. Helmer write that Nelson and his wife took up residence in the main building of the hotel "and mingled frequently with other guests, giving the impression they were young newlyweds." Later, Chase took a room nearby.

On June 5, 1934, Tommy Carroll and his wife Jean left the Lake Como Hotel for Minnesota to case out banks Carroll intended to rob. En route to St Paul, Tommy Carroll was shot dead by police officers in Waterloo, Iowa. The next day, news traveled to Nelson and company, who were still at the Lake Como Hotel.

Nelson, wife Helen, and Chase must have liked Hobart Hermansen and the out-of-the-way location of Lake Como Hotel, because the trio returned on Labor Day, September 3, 1934. During this two-day visit, Chase and Nelson met with Hobart and his assistant, Eddie Duffy, in order to make arrangements for an extended off-season stay at the hotel. The date was set for sometime between Halloween and Thanksgiving.

On the fateful day of November 27, 1934, the trio of Baby Face Nelson, his wife Helen Gillis, and fellow Dillinger gang member, John Paul Chase, once again arrived at the Lake Como Hotel for their intended off-season stay. But their time at the Lake Como property was short. Federal agents, tipped off by Chase's girlfriend, Sally Bachman, waited in ambush for Baby Face and company.

The Chicago Daily Tribune FINAL EDITION

TUESDAY, NOVEMBER 27TH 1934

SHOOTOUT IN BARRINGTON

BABY FACE NELSON DEAD!!!

GANGSTER, 2 FEDS DEAD IN SHOOTOUT!!

SURFACE 7 CTS., ELEVATED 8; EVANSTON 14

Oak Park Rate 9 Cents; Transfers to Be Free.

14 POINTS WENT INTO DISCARD IN PARIS; LANSING

Secretary Tells Senate He Never Protested About Shooting.

REPORT SAYS THEY CONTROL FOOD, PRICES

Criminal and Civil Actions Will Be Hastened.

5437

(1931) K5440

RUNNING GUN BATTLE KILLS 3

THE BATTLE OF BARRINGTON
The Death of Baby Face Nelson – November 27, 1934

© William J. Helmer

Editor's Note: William J. Helmer is a former senior editor for Playboy Magazine. He is the author of six books, including: **The Saint Valentine's Day Massacre** *co-written with Arthur Bilek;* **Baby Face Nelson: Portrait of a Public Enemy** *co-written with Steve Nickel. His most recent book is* **Al Capone and His American Boys** *(published by Indiana University Press, available fall 2011.)*

To learn more about the colorful William J. Helmer, visit: www.gangstersandoutlaws.com.

Of the many headline gun battles that marked the Public Enemy Era, the most bizarre and illogical was the machine-gun shootout near Barrington, Illinois, after Baby Face Nelson left the Lake Como Hotel. It cost two federal agents their lives but permitted Nelson to escape despite many gunshot wounds. He died a few hours later in the Chicago suburb of Wilmette, attended by a possible FBI informant whom the Bureau made no effort to prosecute.

Nelson, born Lester Joseph Gillis, had grown up in a neighborhood on Chicago's Near West Side known as the Patch, had graduated from stealing car parts to robbing banks in the early 1930s, knew several ascending members of the Chicago mob, and escaped from a guard en route to prison. But he had not attracted much attention until Dillinger, using a wooden pistol and bribe money advanced by Nelson's crew, escaped from the Crown Point jail and joined Nelson's fledgling gang. That Nelson, to his annoyance, suddenly found himself described as a member of the famous Dillinger gang, instead of the other way around. This bruised his ego, leaving Dillinger obliged to flatter "Jimmie Williams," Nelson's favorite alias, and defer to his sense of personal importance. More difficult was keeping peace among the members of this "second" Dillinger gang due to the irascible Nelson's willingness to shoot police and civilians unnecessarily; and he even had threatened to shoot crime partners who too-easily incurred his wrath. On the other hand, he was cool in a crisis, and utterly fearless in a gunfight.

Following Dillinger's death in Chicago in July 1934, Nelson and his wife Helen fled to California, leaving their young children, Ronald and Darlene, with relatives. That November the two returned to the Chicago area with a star-struck young bootlegger named John Paul Chase, intending to hole up at Wisconsin's Lake Como Hotel (now the French Country Inn), just north of the Illinois state line. The Lake Como Hotel was a pleasant, no-questions-asked waterfront resort owned by Hobart Hermansen (not Hermanson, as commonly spelled), a one-time bootlegger who also accommodated John Dillinger and other outlaws, and was then courting the estranged wife of

Bugs Moran, the intended victim of the St. Valentine's Day Massacre, who had his summer place also on Lake Como but farther down the same road.

Tipped off in late 1934 that the Nelsons intended to winter at the hotel, FBI agents scared Hermansen into loaning them his house, but were caught off guard a few days later when a Ford, which they mistook for Hermansen's, pulled up in front. Nelson, intending to hole up at a separate smaller part of the hotel called the Doll House, realized he'd driven into an unset trap. At the same time the agents recognized their visitor. A G-man on the porch exchanged a few pleasantries and Nelson, holding a pistol under a newspaper, sped off unhindered, for one agent had driven the FBI car to the nearby town of Lake Geneva to pick up groceries.

A frantic phone call to the Chicago office sent three carloads of federal agents rushing toward Wisconsin in hopes of intercepting Nelson on what still is called the Northwest Highway (then US 12, later US 14). The first team of G-men in a coupe driven by Agent Thomas McDade encountered Nelson's car near the village of Fox River Grove and turned around to give chase, only to discover that Nelson had done the same thing. As the two vehicles passed a second time, Nelson, instead of running, again spun his car around and began pursuing his pursuers.

The surprised agents floored their coupe and began firing out its back window as Nelson's new Ford sedan closed the gap. With his wife Helen crouching on the front floorboards, Chase, in the back seat, let go with a burst of fire from a .30-'06 Monitor, the commercial version of the military Browning Automatic Rifle. However, a lucky shot from the FBI car had punched through Nelson's radiator and disabled the fuel pump (not the water pump, as often reported), allowing the agents to escape. A mile or so down the road, the Bureau car skidded into a ditch and its two agents prepared an ambush.

Meanwhile, however, an FBI Hudson, carrying Inspector Sam Cowley and Agent Herman Hollis, had encountered the running gun battle, and wondered why McDade's car was heading back toward Chicago with

Nelson in pursuit. They turned around to catch Nelson from behind, but Nelson's Ford already was conking out. He managed to turn into the dirt road leading to Barrington's city park, and the agents' Hudson skidded to a stop nearby. A spectacular shootout followed and Hollis died with a bullet in his head when he ran for cover behind a telephone pole. Nelson, already hit by a Thompson slug, let out a curse and marched straight into the blasts from Cowley's shotgun, killing the second agent as well.

Though mortally wounded, Nelson managed to back the FBI Hudson up to his own disabled car, help load it with guns and ammunition, and with Chase driving made it into the Chicago suburb of Wilmette, where he was turned away by a trusted but now horrified "whiskey priest," Father Phillip Coughlan, spiritual advisor to the criminal community. Coughlan agreed to lead them to shelter, but (at least according to Coughlan) the Nelson car turned off and lost him, going instead to a cottage at 1627 Walnut Avenue—one of several suburban "safe houses" used by former mail-train robber James Murray, who was then running a "barbecue" restaurant that was also a hangout for bank-robbers and mobsters.

Nelson died at the house on Walnut Avenue about 7:30 that evening and was found the next morning, wrapped in a blanket next to St. Paul's cemetery in the neighboring town of Niles Center (now called Skokie). Helen surrendered herself on a downtown street the following day, but the FBI kept this matter secret long enough for newspapers to declare her a "public enemy" to be killed on sight. That was the lurid interpretation of a "show no mercy" order by the Justice Department, as the Bureau quickly tried to explain; but it would still insist that she had been "captured."

Few details of Nelson's death were reported by the usually inquisitive press, nor did the FBI reveal where he had died or charge those who had tried to save his life. Although agents placed the Wilmette house under close surveillance, Bureau files are strangely silent about the investigation, despite its prosecution of a dozen or more other people in other cities whose contact with Nelson was sometimes minimal or even innocent.

The only clue to this decision can be found in a document filed some four years later containing the statement of another Wilmette resident. He, with his wife, told the Bureau that a woman, Marie Henderson, still living in the house on Walnut, had dropped by for a visit one day and was telling him how surprised he would be if he knew where Baby Face Nelson had died. Without specifying that it was at her place, she said that the house belonged to someone connected with the FBI (probably as an informant) who also had been supplying Nelson with inside information concerning the Bureau. Nelson, she added, wanted to go where the G-men would never think to look for him. She also said that, as far as she knew, Nelson's guns were still somewhere in the city (or possibly in Chicago), awaiting a buyer.

Despite the limited information, this permits speculation that the Bureau, after discovering where Nelson died, decided to let the matter go rather than reveal that the most notorious public enemy of the day had spent his last hours in the care of someone the FBI had thought was a useful informant—even if Jimmy Murray had helped Helen move Nelson's body to a corner next to a cemetery, where police found it the next morning.

Photo Montage of participants of the Battle of Barrington from the files of FBI.gov.

TOMMY CARROLL'S CALLING CARD
Member of John Dillinger's Gang

Bank robber and member of the Dillinger Gang, Tommy Carroll, along with his wife Jean Delaney Crompton were frequent visitors to the Lake Como Hotel. Author Ellen Poulson, writes in her book *Don't Call Us Molls*: "Tommy Carroll would hold on to a Lake Como Hotel matchbook. An underworld calling card, it was one connection that hadn't dried up."

The Lake Como matchbook was Carroll's way of letting the criminal element know that he was connected to the "gang," the matchbook was his nefarious business card.

Tommy Carroll must have enjoyed pilfering items from Hobart Hermansen's Lake Como Hotel. According to author Bryan Burrough, Federal agents first became suspicious of the hotel as a hideout for mobsters and gangsters in 1933 after searching through Carroll's belongings. In his luggage they discovered a pillow case with the name "Lake Como Hotel" stamped on it.

Burrough is the author of *Public Enemies*, the book on which the Johnny Depp movie by the same name is based.

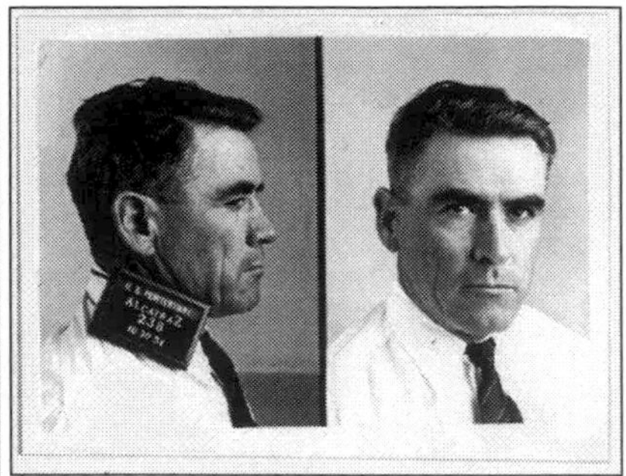

JOHN PAUL CHASE
Last Member of the "Second" Dillinger Gang

Born on December 26, 1901, Chase grew up in Marin County across the bridge from San Francisco. After dropping out of the 6th grade, he worked as a farmer, railroad clerk and later spent 5 years as a merchant marine.

John Paul Chase was a bootlegger, smuggler and small time crook until he met up with Baby Face Nelson and eventually became a member of the John Dillinger Gang. Chase first met Nelson at the Bridge Cigar Store in Sausalito in 1931. The two became instant companions and together would move on to a life of crime and infamy.

It is believed the duos first job together was the assassination of Roy Fritch who was to be a witness against two Reno, Nevada gamblers in a US Mail fraud case.

On June 30th, 1934 only days after an extended stay at Lake Como, Chase, Nelson, Dillinger and Pretty Boy Floyd robbed the Merchants National Bank in South Bend, Indiana. This is believed to be the only time that the high profile quartet of John Dillinger, Baby Face Nelson, John Paul Chase and Pretty Boy Floyd were involved in a crime together.

John Paul Chase visited The Lake Como Hotel on many occasions especially in 1934. He usually traveled with fellow Dillinger Gang members Baby Face Nelson and Tommy Carroll along with their molls: Helen Gillis and Jean

Delaney Crompton respectively. Often, Chase would bring his girlfriend Sally Bachman. It was a Labor Day visit to The Lake Como Hotel with Bachman that was the harbinger which later lead to the death of his best friend and the demise of the remnants of the John Dillinger Gang.

Sally Bachman, under pressure of deportation, informed federal authorities of Nelson's intended stay at The Lake Como Hotel during the winter off-season. Special Agents were waiting at the Hermansen property when on November 27, 1934 Baby Face Nelson, his wife Helen Gillis and John Paul Chase arrived for an extended stay.

Hours later, after the Battle of Barrington, Baby Face Nelson lay dead and John Paul Chase was on the lam. Three days later, Chase entered a police station to obtain a Chauffeur's License so that he could transport a car to Seattle. Since his only arrest was for public drunkenness, he received the license and traveled west eventually returning to his home state of California.

Chase's luck and freedom were fleeting, on December 27, the day after his 33rd birthday he was arrested at Mount Shasta, California. On March 18, 1935 John Paul Chase who in 3 short years went from small time crook to big time gangster, was sentenced under a new federal law to life imprisonment for the murder of a federal agent. According to the John Paul Chase website, www.johnpaulchase.com, after Chase was found guilty he was the "first man ever sent directly to Alcatraz after sentencing." His incarceration marked the end of the second Dillinger Gang, often referred to the Nelson-Dillinger Gang. All other members were now either dead or in jail.

While he was prisoner 238-AZ on Alcatraz Island, Chase became an accomplished, self taught artist. His 10-panel mural of the island can be seen on the Alcatraz Island home page web site. His paintings of the Alcatraz Warden James A. Johnston and a boat leaving the "Rock" shows the complexity of a second side of Chase. He was paroled from Leavenworth Prison on October 31, 1966 and worked as a janitor of St.

Joseph College for several years. On October 5, 1973, the last member of the second Dillinger Gang died of cancer in Palo Alto, California.

Chase on his way to Federal Court after the Battle of Barrington.

From the files of FBI.gov.

SPECIAL AGENT CHARLES WINSTEAD
The Man Who Shot Dillinger and Missed Baby Face Nelson

A rough-and-ready Texan, Special Agent Winstead was famous for killing John Dillinger outside Chicago's Biograph Theater on July 22, 1934. Other lawmen's bullets also struck Dillinger, but FBI director J. Edgar Hoover commended Winstead for making the fatal shots. In his memoir, Winstead referred to it as "a bad case of lead poisoning."

With Dillinger now dead, Baby Face Nelson was designated by J.Edgar Hoover as "Public Enemy Number One". Fresh from his victory over Dillinger, Chicago FBI Chief Melvin Purvis wanted Nelson and Chase apprehended.

In late November of 1934, FBI Special Agent Winstead and two other agents were lying in wait at Lake Como, hoping to nab the notorious gangster Baby Face Nelson and his associate John Paul Chase. Through an informant, the agents learned that Nelson was planning to hole up for winter at the Lake Como Hotel (now the French Country Inn). A stakeout was then set up by the FBI.

It was at Lake Como where Winstead missed his opportunity to kill Nelson.

When Nelson, his wife Helen Gillis, and Chase drove up in a Ford V-8 on November 27, Winstead and a fellow agent, James Metcalfe, initially failed to identify their target. By the time Winstead took aim, Nelson was driving away. The agents couldn't pursue—their stakeout partner, Colin McRae, had taken their car on a grocery run. Other agents soon encountered Nelson near Barrington, Illinois, delivering the fatal shots.

Born in Sherman, Texas, in 1891, Winstead was a cowboy, Army field clerk, and a sheriff's deputy in Brownsville before he joined the FBI in 1926. He stood 5 feet 7 inches and weighed 135 pounds. In 1942, Winstead made Patton-esque remarks to a reporter about communists and American sympathizers. Hoover demanded an apology and attempted to transfer him to Oklahoma. According to author/researcher Rick Mattix, Winstead told Hoover to "go to hell." Winstead's formal resignation was accepted without prejudice. He died in 1973 at age 82, and was buried in New Mexico.

Baby Face Nelson and wife Helen Gillis

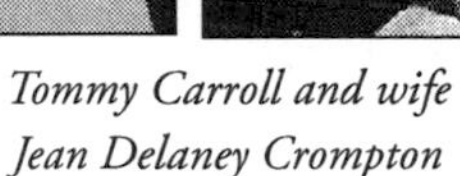

Tommy Carroll and wife Jean Delaney Crompton

John Paul Chase and girlfriend Sally Bachman

THE DILLINGER-NELSON GANG AT LAKE COMO – A 1934 Timeline –

May 28 — A man who identifies himself as "John Scott" inquires about reserving rooms for his friends at the Lake Como Hotel. *Note: Hotel owner Hobart Hermansen later describes this meeting with "John Scott" in sworn testimony to federal agents. Agents soon determine that Scott was actually John Paul Chase, a California bootlegger and cohort of Baby Face Nelson—and fellow member of the Dillinger Gang. (In 1934, Nelson and John Dillinger merged their gangs. Dillinger and Nelson seldom traveled together, however; both were wanted men.)*

June 1 — Baby Face Nelson (a.k.a. Lester Gillis) and wife Helen Gillis check into the Lake Como Hotel. Accompanying them are fellow Dillinger gang member Tommy Carroll and his wife, Jean Delaney Crompton. Also present is Nelson's henchman, John Paul Chase. Nelson and his wife decide to stay in the main building of the hotel—telling other guests they're on their honeymoon. (These events were also later confirmed by Hobart Hermansen in sworn testimony to federal agents.)

June 6	Tommy Carroll and wife Jean check out of the hotel. Carroll has plans to drive to St. Paul, Minnesota, to purchase weapons and case banks to rob.
June 7	Tommy Carroll is killed by the local police in Waterloo, Iowa.
June 8	Baby Face Nelson, wife Helen, and John Paul Chase are still vacationing at the Lake Como Hotel when they hear the news of Tommy Carroll's death. (Nelson called Carroll a "true friend"; Helen said Jean was "like a sister.") The trio checks out of the hotel.
July 22	John Dillinger is gunned down by federal agents in Chicago, outside the Biograph Theater.
September 3	Baby Face Nelson, wife Helen, John Paul Chase, and Sally Bachman arrive for another visit to the Lake Como Hotel. By now, Nelson has been designated Public Enemy Number One by FBI Director J.Edgar Hoover, so he needs a place to hole up for the winter. On the evening of September 3, Nelson and Chase meet with hotelier Hobart Hermansen in downtown Lake Geneva (at another hotel that Hermansen owns). Chase tells Hermansen the group wishes to return to Como and be Hermansen's winter guests, after the resort has officially closed for the season. Hermansen agrees. Nelson says he'll return between Halloween and Thanksgiving.
September 5	Nelson and his group leave the Lake Como Hotel.
October 22	Sally Bachman, girlfriend of John Paul Chase, informs federal agents that Nelson plans to return to the same inn on a small lake that she herself visited in September. Curiously, she cannot recall the name of the inn, the lake, or its exact location. Eventually she describes the property

well enough that the FBI agents believe it to be the Lake Como Hotel.

November 2 Federal agents question hotel owner Hobart Hermansen and his assistant, Eddie Duffy, who are both "shocked" to learn their guest was the notorious Baby Face Nelson. Within days, three federal agents move into the cottage at the Lake Como Hotel to lie in wait for Nelson.

November 27 Baby Face Nelson, his wife Helen, and John Paul Chase arrive once more at Hermansen's property. They pull up to the front porch in a black Ford sedan. Nelson is driving, Helen is seated next to him, and Chase is in the rear seat. Special Agent Metcalfe, who is standing on the porch, at first does not recognize Nelson, but soon realizes the car's driver is Public Enemy Number One. By then, a wary Nelson is already speeding away. Agent Charles Winstead, positioned by an upstairs window of the inn, is unable to get a clear shot at the escaping sedan. The two agents are stranded, unable to pursue—their partner, Agent McRae, has taken their only vehicle into town to buy groceries. The officers quickly alert fellow lawmen in Chicago and describe Nelson's car. Other agents intercept Nelson just south of the Illinois border; the famous "Battle of Barrington" ensues.

ACKNOWLEDGEMENTS

Thanks to Andria Hayday for developing and editing my original manuscript in order to make the novel more cohesive, readable, and certainly more enjoyable.

Thanks to Anthony Navilio for sharing his wonderful stories about the French Country Inn and its surroundings, and for allowing me unfettered access to the inn.

Special thanks to James Kirchschlager (the real "Kirsch") and Ron Frankel, for allowing me to fictionalize them in the book. I am privileged to call them friends—they are even finer men than the characters portrayed.

Thanks to Mary Haggermaker, Debbie Vanderstappen, Patti Bartz, Patti Goff, and the staff of the French Country Inn and Kirsch's restaurant for all their help and kind hospitality. They are an eclectic, eccentric, and extraordinary group; they make the inn a wonderful place.

Thanks to the professional chefs and cooks at Kirsch's for preparing the most appetizing food one could ever imagine. Apart from their culinary talent, they bear no resemblance to any of the chefs described in this novel; I am quite certain no one at Kirsch's has ever spit in my food or committed any crimes.

Special thanks to author and gangsterologist Bill Helmer for his *Battle of Barrington* article. Visit www.gangstersandoutlaws.com.

Special thanks to Allen Hermansen whose vintage photographs are a visual history of Lake Como and the Lake Como Hotel.

Thanks to Rose Keefe, author of *The Man Who Got Away: The Bugs Moran Story*, for her assistance with the history of the inn. Any errors in fact are mine alone.

Thanks also to William Michaels for his encouragement, and for suggesting I add more gangster stories.

Thanks to Jim Adams; visit www.babyfacenelson.com.

Thanks to Mario Gomes; visit www.myalcaponemuseum.com.

Thanks to Dori Hein for proofreading assistance on the novel.

For the record, the character of Chief is an amalgam, inspired mainly by a friend who wishes to remain anonymous. All the peace officers in this book are products of my imagination. The characters bear no resemblance whatsoever to the actual law enforcement personnel of Geneva Township or Walworth County, who are as dedicated, professional, and honorable as any I have ever encountered.

FURTHER READING

For those who wish to know more about the gangster history of Chicago and the Lake Geneva area, the author suggests the following resources:

The Man Who Got Away: The Bugs Moran Story, by Rose Keefe

Don't Call Us Molls: Women of the John Dillinger Gang, by Ellen Poulsen

Baby Face Nelson: Portrait of a Public Enemy, by Steven Nickel and William J. Helmer

The St. Valentine's Day Massacre: The Untold Story of the Gangland Bloodbath That Brought Down Al Capone, by William J. Helmer and Arthur J. Bilek

Dillinger: The Untold Story, by G. Russell Girardin and William J. Helmer with Rick Mattix

Public Enemies: America's Greatest Crime Wave and the Birth of the FBI, 1933-34, by Bryan Burrough

On the Web:

www.johnpaulchase.com

www.babyfacenelsonjournal.com

www.fbi.gov (search "famous cases & criminals")

http://historicalgmen.squarespace.com

http://gangstersandoutlaws.com

www.steinerag.com/flw (for Geneva Hotel, Lake Como Hotel)

www.myalcaponemuseum.com